THE SHERIFF

THE SHERIFF

A Novel

ROBERT DWYER AND AUSTIN WRIGHT

TWODOT®

Guilford, Connecticut
Helena, Montana

A · TWODOT® · BOOK

An imprint and registered trademark of The Rowman & Littlefield Publishing Group, Inc.
4501 Forbes Blvd., Ste. 200
Lanham, MD 20706
www.rowman.com

Distributed by NATIONAL BOOK NETWORK

British Library Cataloguing in Publication Information available

Library of Congress Cataloging-in-Publication Data

Names: Dwyer, Robert, 1987- author. | Wright, Austin, 1987- author.
Title: The sheriff : a novel / Robert Dwyer and Austin Wright.
Description: Guilford, Connecticut : TwoDot, [2021]
Identifiers: LCCN 2020052160 (print) | LCCN 2020052161 (ebook) | ISBN
    9781493058488 (paperback) | ISBN 9781493058495 (epub)
Subjects: GSAFD: Western stories.
Classification: LCC PS3604.W96 S54 2021 (print) | LCC PS3604.W96 (ebook)
    | DDC 813/.6--dc23
LC record available at https://lccn.loc.gov/2020052160
LC ebook record available at https://lccn.loc.gov/2020052161

For our parents

CONTENTS

PROLOGUE

SAL

Horse hooves sounded thunder on the hard-packed earth.

Queenie ran lathered beneath him, her body stretching and lengthening in rhythm with the beating of his own heart, his sweat dripping to mingle with hers.

A gunshot sounded, and Sal heard a whistle over his shoulder. It had missed, but not by much.

"Ya!" he cried, smiling so broad he could feel the wind cold against his teeth.

He shifted in his stirrups, turning to look behind him, careful not to upset Queenie's stride.

Jack and Tom were close behind, their mounts lathered, too, working harder than Queenie yet moving slower, falling behind by lengths every minute or so.

The edge of the wood was only a mile off now, Sal was sure, though distances could be misleading where the land flattened out this way, where the foothills of the Rockies gave way to that unending sea of grass. The flatness played tricks on the eye, especially after so many days spent in the narrow, winding trails of the mountains.

The next bullet whizzed over Sal's head. The Rangers were a long way back—half a mile, maybe. They had dismounted for better aim and had the high ground, their shots alarmingly accurate.

How did they find us?

Another shot sounded—*crack!*

Careful and fluid—always fluid—Sal turned again in the stirrups, readying a second exuberant cry, but another preempted his own, a primal scream that could have come from man or beast.

He watched Tom's horse falter and stumble and go down, dragging Tom with him.

"Ho!" Sal cried, reining Queenie abruptly, turning her in a wide arc.

"Leave the horses here," Jack said, dismounting with an economical leap. He still held the cigarette between his lips.

"But Queenie—" Sal protested. She had been his constant companion in the West, had made him an outlaw even, though he had not realized then the price he put on his own neck in freeing her from Spicer—an unrepentant abuser of horseflesh. It had been an easy initiation into that life outside the law. It had been right.

Jack did not bother to repeat himself.

Cursing, Sal dismounted and looped Queenie's reins around a branch so she would not follow. He looked her in the eye a moment—it was as long as he could stand—then gave her a pat on the neck and put her out of his mind with the rest.

Jack shouldered two gunnysacks and Sal did the same. There were four in all—packed with bills and even some bullion.

Wordlessly, Sal followed Jack into the woods at a trot, followed those unflagging legs until his lungs burned and followed them after.

An hour later they reached a stream where Jack slowed mercifully and stopped.

Sal dropped his load and doubled over, hands on his knees, sucking air.

Jack seemed unfazed by the exertion. He pointed down the bank to the streambed. "Follow the stream. Run in the water to cover your prints. You'll have all four sacks, so it'll be slow going, but you got to get far enough. Go a half mile at least and find a hollow and hide out 'til night."

All four? Sal adjusted his hat and swallowed hard. "Aren't you coming with me?"

Jack shook his head. "I got to lead 'em off."

Sal nodded as if he understood, as if his nerves were not vibrating with fear.

"Then, in the dark, you make your way south all the way to New Mexico," Jack instructed. "Then you walk it to Texline."

"That's fifty miles!"

"You walk it all night every night for a week if you have to. Then in Texline, you get yourself a horse. And don't steal it, neither."

"Queenie!" Sal began, but the protest died on his lips.

"You buy a good horse and then you ride another hundred miles 'til you find a sleepy town and you lay low. You wait a month and you send me a letter—in code like always. Send it to . . ."

Jack trailed off, indecision warping his voice.

For a moment Sal became aware of the depths of fear that would take him if anything happened to Jack. Even that brief, flickering uncertainty was a leak sprung in the hull of Sal's confidence. With Jack —*with Queenie?*—Sal had survived a hail of gunfire. Without?

"Send it to Graves Point, Texas," Jack said, the old confidence upon him again.

"Okay," Sal said, giving Jack his most earnest expression. "Graves Point."

"Then you keep quiet, 'til the boys and I come for you."

"Okay," Sal repeated.

"Good," Jack said. "Now git."

Sal sprang to action as if awakened from a trance. He shouldered the sacks and scrambled down the embankment, dropping one along the way in his haste.

He stooped to pick it up, now soaking, the meltwater climbing cold-fingered up his dungarees.

"Sal, one more thing," Jack called.

Sal hefted his load and looked up at Jack, who stood atop the embankment like a monolith. He was only five feet tall, but he looked bigger from this angle, casting a long shadow in the early morning light.

"For Christ's sake, don't go back for that goddamn horse!"

Sal stared a moment, thinking, his pale blue eyes shining silver in the light. Then he nodded and headed south, just as Jack had told him.

Behold the Caprocks of the Texas Panhandle—a thousand feet of abrupt, vertical rock, propelled upward by some unimaginable force, a brushstroke across the landscape, a new horizon. Yet for all their drama, the Caprocks are but an interval, a palisade beyond which spreads the real impossibility—that endless sea of grass, the Llano Estacado, sloping gently, almost imperceptibly, upward toward the distant Rockies.

This is where the Comanche and the Kiowa once made their homes, mingled their horses with the buffalo, watered them in fleeting playa lakes.

This is where Nash Warrick died.

This is where the railroad now runs, a steel river, bringing life to the land like a vein opened upon the earth, a gout of modernity, of spurs, of barbed wire, of towns, laws, circuit judges, and courthouses.

This is where John Donovan staked his fortune, where he sought the nascent town of Three Chop. This is where he chose to set his will against the indomitable vastness, to create from it a monument to civilization, one that would outlive him. He did this to prove—to whom? himself?—that he needed no birthright, that with nothing but his own clenched fists he could batter the landscape into submission.

This is where Jack Holloway, the enigmatic outlaw, would descend with his gang, following the trail of Sal, that steel-eyed boy. It is where they would seek to wrest their hoarded riches, a legacy of another kind, where a battle would be fought—not the final battle, for the war would drag on much as the war with the Comanche dragged on after Adobe Walls—but a turning point of sorts, a signpost in the struggle for the soul of the West.

And this is where, in the streets of Three Chop, fate would finally catch up with Pete Rayder, his one eye glimpsing truth at last, where with him would die, too, the dream of Nash Warrick, of unfettered primalism, of wilderness.

PART I:
HOT-BLOODED MEN

"Reckon we'll have more rain this year?"

Donovan shrugged. "God willing."

"So says the Reverend." The man frowned. "Only the Almanac don't agree."

Donovan smiled back but said nothing, slowing his gait so the man would outpace him. He was in no mood for pleasantries. Already his back ached terribly, and he had only just risen.

"You worried about the election?" the man asked over his shoulder.

Donovan quickened his step. "Worried?"

"About Jacob?"

"What about him?"

"Ain't you heard?" the man asked, grinning now, pleased to know something the Sheriff did not. "Jacob is going to run against the mayor next month."

Donovan stopped in his tracks, his own dust cloud catching up with him.

The farmer looked back, waiting for Donovan to say something, then shrugged and plodded on.

Donovan clenched and opened his fist to feel the old calluses pull taut.

It took him a minute to realize he was standing still in the middle of the street. He ran his hand down his beard and started forward, sifting through the sediment of his preoccupation.

A man with a fruit cart waved to Donovan as he passed Marvin Stepshaw's boot shop and haberdashery and tossed him a red apple. He was one of the Reverend's congregants—*the* Reverend now that there was only one—friendly but sallow faced, though his name escaped Donovan. It was mostly the farmfolk who had fled to Reverend Aaron's congregation, but there were townfolk, too—enough to be counted.

"They came just yesterday," the man said. "On the express."

"Thanks," Donovan replied, touching the brim of his careworn hat. He polished the apple on his vest and ate as he walked, juice running down his chin and into his beard.

He ate mindlessly, the muscles of his jaw working like a cow's chewing cud. *Jacob for mayor?* He had known the bothersome saloonkeep's discontents—they were perennial, as old as the town itself—and yet somehow Donovan had never expected a challenge to his mayor. Perhaps he had become complacent. *Distracted?*

Mayor Cordell was a dependable man, if prone to occasional missteps. But folk knew who really ran the town, and a challenge to Cordell was a challenge to Donovan himself.

Three times Donovan had saved the town—four if you counted clearing the plains of the Comanche and Kiowa in the first place. First, in the 1870s, he had faced down Nash Warrick and One-Eyed Pete Rayder in the street, freeing the town of an existential violence. Then, in the '80s, he had restored order in the heyday of the cowpunchers, taming their energy and their silver as a watermill tames a river. And again at the end of the decade as the cattle boom faded and the cowpuncher silver dried up, he and Congressman Atwood had convinced the Fort Worth and Denver City Railroad to build Three Chop a feeder line, a coveted link to that great steel vasculature.

A legacy.

Still walking, Donovan passed beneath the shadow of the saloon, Jacob's saloon, the *Lady May*. He threw his half-eaten apple to the dogs and cursed the man beneath his breath.

He nodded curtly to the women on the porch, dressed in shambles of silk. They fanned themselves lazily, their legs and arms looped luridly around railings, their red lips parted, tittering.

"Hi, Mr. Sheriff." A blithe chorus.

Donovan felt his cheeks redden.

Even at this early hour, there were men around them—the eager, the constitutively amorous—although the girls would not ply their trade until after sundown. That had been one of Donovan's earliest reforms and his first real rift with Jacob.

Even in the disarray of the early days, the *Lady May* had flourished, rising from one story to three, an all-in-one bar, gambling hall, whorehouse, and inn. It stood higher now than any other building in town, a monstrosity casting a dark shadow in the late morning sun. And when it could not grow higher, it had sprawled outward, overtaking the surrounding buildings, an agglomeration of additions and renovations.

Donovan shook his head to think of the silver in Jacob's till. *How he has thrived thanks to the sweat of my own labor! And now!*

Suddenly a sharp pain bloomed in Donovan's spine and knocked the wind from his gut.

He staggered off Front Street into the alley between the saloon and Sallie Winthrop's dry goods store. Out of the view of passersby, Donovan hunched forward behind a water barrel and struggled for air, his heart pounding. He retched up black coffee and bits of apple, spilling his guts in the dirt. It took half a minute for the pain to ease and even then it left him feeling empty, a turned-out gunnysack.

Donovan stood straight and grimaced, wiping the sweat from his forehead. It was too early to go home. He had yet to make his rounds, and a lawman who did not make his rounds was as good as retired. *As good as dead.*

When he had recovered, Donovan hurried from the alley, lest he find himself confronted by the widow Winthrop. Twice this week she had accosted him over the drys, whom she accused of sabotaging her liquor shipments and of throwing rocks at Haddock, Jacob's half-brother, a crippled black piano man.

Donovan waved to a group of traders haggling over horses, hoping none had seen him doubled over in the alley.

They touched their hats, uttering the usual pleasantries. They, like most of Three Chop's residents, were grateful.

No one seemed upset by the drys except the usual malcontents: Sallie and Jacob, both of whom sold the stuff, and the blacksmith Todd Waiverly, whom Donovan could only surmise was overly fond of drinking it.

A trio of young girls in twill skirts passed with parasols, waving and giggling. Donovan smiled, suddenly overcome with nostalgia, remembering the days when he had been Three Chop's most eligible bachelor. It made his present circumstance seem altogether impossible, and a pleasant feeling of unreality settled upon him.

Sick? Beset by an election challenger? What were these beside the image of that younger man who had carved a path for civilization on the plain of the Llano Estacado? Death and defeat could not be his destiny. Surely Doc Marshall was wrong. Surely Jacob's latest ploy would fail just as every other challenge to Donovan's supremacy had failed over the years. A new century dawned, but he was still the same man.

I am John Donovan!

He quickened his step, turning his boots toward the offices of the *Three Chop Star*, driven by a new urgency, buoyed by a new optimism.

He spit, trying to rid his tongue of a lingering taste of bile.

CHAPTER 2

Chasby

"NEVER SEEN THE HILL COUNTRY SO DESOLATE," ROD SAID, WIPING bacon grease on his chaps. His mount ambled beneath him. "We'll have better luck here on the plain. It'll be good to see Three Chop, too. I got a girl or two must miss me."

Maze Chasby listened to Rod prattle as he finished his own bacon. It was burned near black owing to Ike's neglect, but even Ike couldn't burn off the taste of salt. Chasby tried to savor it, even if it was the same meal he had eaten every day for two weeks.

The boiled coffee was starting to take effect, too, reinvigorating his stiff limbs. They were off to a late start, having cleared their camp several hours after sunup. Then again, they probably would not be bandits if they had any measure of ambition.

"I'm not going back to Three Chop," Chasby said, mumbling into the mouth of a tin cup.

Ike rolled his eyes and looked at Rod. "Why're you so afraid of that old preacher anyhow?"

"He isn't that old," Chasby responded.

"Preaching ages a man," Rod offered. "Makes him soft. Gives him gravy-toss."

Chasby laughed. "*Gravitas*," he said. It was the first time he remembered laughing in weeks, and it surprised his companions.

"What's so funny?" Ike asked, twisting his wiry body in the saddle to look back at Chasby.

"Oh, nothing," Chasby said. "Only I never thought of the Reverend being soft. He beat me near every day growing up."

I am the Lord thy God, which have brought thee out of the land of Egypt . . .

"My daddy only beat me when he was drunk," Ike said, sounding impressed.

Chasby shrugged. "He held me to a high standard, I guess. Tried to, anyway."

Thou shalt have no other gods before me . . .

Somehow the Reverend had commandeered his own head, turned a part of Chasby against himself. He tried to shut out the voice.

"Explains why yer scared of him," Rod said, emptying the dregs of his coffee on the ground. "But I reckon you could take him now."

"Not scared exactly. Just . . ."

Chasby trailed off as his mind emptied. It started with a buzzing, and then, suddenly, he was floating outside his own head—disorienting but not unpleasant—though it usually presaged a bout of panic. He struggled to confine himself.

"It's just," Chasby said, his voice sounding like the echo of another man's. "I'm not sure I don't deserve it."

Thou shalt not take the name of the Lord thy God in vain . . .

He emptied his own dregs and dropped the mug in his saddlebag. Then he removed a flask from his jacket pocket and took a long swallow to settle his nerves.

"Ain't surprising you cain't follow the Reverend's rules," Rod mused. "You ain't got a reverend's blood. It's cold blood a man like that needs. Hot-blooded men like us—we ain't got a chance in hell of resisting certain temptations."

Chasby considered this as his belly absorbed the familiar warmth of whiskey. He thought of Hattie then abruptly forced her out of his mind, her memory equal parts joy and shame. He took another pull from his flask. "I reckon we all have a chance, but maybe the hot-blooded are too stubborn to take it. Or maybe the cold-blooded men are hot-blooded, too, and they've just figured out how to corral it."

"Chasby, how long we been together?" Rod asked, rhetorically, adjusting himself in his saddle. "Two months? And I cain't tell whether you got too much *corral* or y'ain't got enough. But yer always in yer own head, and what I'm sure of is t'ain't good for business."

"Business," Chasby scoffed.

Ike shook his head, packing his cheek with a plug of chew.

"See, that's it right there," Rod said. "You didn't have to join our little gang if you didn't want to. But you did join, knowing full well our proposition. T'ain't like we tricked you into nothin'. Y'brought yer own horse and yer own goddamn gun."

"Look, I didn't mean anything," Chasby said, squeezing his eyes closed, commanding himself to relax. "I'm glad to be here. It's just new to me—a new path."

"T'ain't a path, neither," Rod said, exasperated. "It's just doing something. Everybody's got to do *something*, and this is what we do. It don't lead nowhere." Rod sighed and rubbed his temples. "When Sid and Ambrose left to wrangle cattle at that old Mexican ranch, it left Ike and me a duo, and a duo don't cut it out here. So we looked around town for someone who could cut it. And we picked you, because we knew you could ride 'n shoot, and because yer an outsider like us. You didn't belong in town, and you definitely didn't belong in no church, and y'knew it, too, and I think that's why you came with us. But if we come to find you don't belong here, neither, then you got to start to wonder where it is you *do* belong."

Don't belong in church? Chasby wondered.

The three men rode in silence. Between the alcohol and the swaying of the horse beneath him, Chasby calmed. He reached in his jacket pocket again, this time to touch the dog-eared Bible he stowed opposite his flask. The worn pages had a reassuring softness.

"I have hot blood, too," Chasby said after a while.

"Hell yeah you do," Ike said, slapping his leg. "I've seen you piss drunk getting kicked out of the saloon enough to know you got hot blood!"

Even Rod smiled.

"Remember when the circus was in town and you were drunk, and you let them llamas loose and the whole circus was out trying to wrangle them llamas in the middle of the night?" Ike slapped his leg again and burst into a fit of laughter. "I'll never forget seeing that no-leg man running out of the saloon on his hands." Tears rolled down his cheeks.

Chasby shook his head, but he was smiling, too. He downed another slug of whiskey.

"Maybe yer real pa was a hell-raiser like us," Ike said when he was sufficiently recovered.

Chasby shrugged. "I don't know much about the man."

"The Reverend must've told you so," Rod said.

"Wasn't anything to tell."

"But you know why he left you—there's proof enough of hot blood in that story."

Chasby's mind took leave of his head again. He squeezed his eyes shut.

"The Reverend only told me he found me one morning in a basket on the church doorstep," Chasby said distractedly.

"The Reverend must be cold-blooded not to tell you a thing about yer pa in all that time," Ike said, spitting a jet of tobacco juice and wiping his mouth on his shirt sleeve.

"Maybe there ain't much to tell, like you say, except what brought yer pa to Three Chop in the first place," Rod said, taking a chaw of his own.

Chasby reined in his horse abruptly. He sat speechless, blinking. *What brought my father?*

Rod and Ike stopped their mounts, too, and turned their horses sideways so they could look at Chasby.

"You look like you seen a ghost," Ike said, scratching his head.

Chasby's hands had turned white where they gripped the reins. "What brought him to Three Chop?" he asked, his mouth dry as fresh sawdust on a saloon floor.

"Maybe this ain't a good time," Rod said. "We got a job to do, and I don't want you distracted."

"Tell it," Chasby demanded.

Ike and Rod exchanged glances.

"Alright," Rod said finally, crossing his arms. "What I know I seen mostly myself. I was probably fourteen or fifteen then. Yer pa was a homesteader, taking his family west like all the rest. It was your pa and ma and you and some kids—I don't remember how many."

"You met them?" Chasby asked, dumbfounded. *Kids?*

"Naw I never met 'em," Rod said. "Don't know how many or whether they was boys or girls. But don't get yer hopes up. They died with yer ma."

Chasby's stomach curdled, and he thought for a moment he might throw up the morning's drink. "Died? How? When?" Instinctively, he reached into his coat as he spoke, feeling the weight of the flask. *Half empty. How far again to Three Chop?*

"They was dead when yer pa showed up in town with you," Rod said solemnly.

Ike looked away.

"He said they was ambushed and killed by Injuns. He begged the Sheriff to raise a posse to go after 'em. Now Donovan—you know how he is about what goes on outside the county so long as it stays there—he didn't much care to chase a bunch of Comanche round the plains, and the mayor came out against it anyhow. Said the Injuns had been licked long before and it was probably highwaymen. So yer pa snuck off at night with an armful of stolen guns and never came back. Left you at the church. But he left hot-blooded sure enough! He left looking for revenge!"

"Hell," Chasby said, his mouth hanging open. He spat dust, closed it.

"I always figured you knew," Rod said.

"Hot-blooded," Ike added.

"I guess it don't change much anyhow," Rod continued. "Except you oughtta know yer one of us."

"What," Chasby swallowed. "What was he like?"

Rod looked up, ran his tongue across his teeth, remembering. "Well, he looked a lot like you. Or I guess you look a lot like him—same green eyes, dark hair. And he always had a book with him."

"A book?" Chasby's hand strayed to the pocket with his Bible.

"Yeah, always a book, always different. That's what folks said. Said he was a learned man."

This struck Chasby as a revelation.

"A Bible?"

"No, no," Rod said. "A book, like a . . . well, something you'd read. Not something you'd preach."

Chasby's thoughts jostled against one another in an effort to be heard, attended. *I look like him? The same hot blood? Books? Did he have the same fear? Or was it the Reverend who put that in me?* He vowed to ease up on the liquor, to consider this information in a clearer light.

"Thank you," Chasby whispered.

"Sure," Rod shrugged. "And there's somethin' else, too."

"Oh?"

"You wasn't delivered in no basket," Rod said, scratching at his beard, half black, half gray. "Your pa delivered you to the Reverend. They talked. The Reverend would know him better than any man."

A strange pressure was building behind Chasby's eyes.

"He was only in town a few days, mind, but the Reverend—"

"Hold it!" Ike interrupted, suddenly craning his neck northward, toward Three Chop, the direction they had been traveling. He stood in his stirrups and peered intently at the horizon. "I seen somethin'."

Chasby squinted into the distance, grateful for the distraction. He held up his right hand to block the sun, unable to find the right angle for his hat.

"Whaddya see?" Rod asked, scanning the horizon himself.

"Over yonder," Ike said, pointing north-northwest.

Chasby followed the line of his arm and saw in the distance a thin skein of gray smoke stretching into the sky. He had to blink to be sure it was there.

Rod searched his saddlebag and pulled out a telescoping spyglass. "Definitely a camp," he said, focusing the instrument. "Small. Cain't be more than a few people."

"How do you know?" Ike asked, still watching the smoke in the distance.

"They've only got one wagon with 'em and t'ain't a big one at that."

"What's in the wagon?" Ike asked, rubbing his dirty hands together with villainous glee.

"It's a spyglass," Rod replied. "It don't see through things." He drew his horse alongside Chasby and handed him the spyglass. "Here, see if you can make anything out."

Chasby held it to his right eye and tried to focus. The horizon wavered and distorted in the grip of his unsteady hands. The column of smoke looked bigger, but he still could not make out much about the camp. He thought he saw the wagon, but that was all.

Not this morning. Not with so much on my mind. Somehow the thought of his father reading books gave Chasby a sudden sense of new possibilities, of futures he had never envisioned for himself, to know that reading might be in his blood, too.

Owing to their lack of success in the hill country, Chasby had only been part of two holdups, and those occurred late enough in the day that he had been sufficiently drunk. Even so, he had been able to hang back, not even drawing his gun. He was a deterrent, a third man, a silent partner, and his lack of participation was so far the only thing that made the work bearable.

Thou shalt not steal . . .

"Hard to make anything out," Chasby mumbled, handing the spyglass back to Rod. *If the Reverend saw me now.* Chasby took another swig from his flask.

"Cool it on the booze," Rod said. "This is yer opportunity to show us you belong. I want you to take the lead. You think you can handle that, Chaz?" He spit into the dust beside his mount.

"Sure," Chasby lied. "Not much to it."

Chasby heard himself speak, and he understood the words, but somehow it felt like someone else had said them. *Where am I?* He was outside his head again, looking down at himself astride the old mare he had taken from the Reverend's stable. He wondered if it might be better to float away for good. *But where would I go?* he wondered. *Where would I belong?*

He patted the flask in his jacket and tried to forget the book in the other pocket. He tried to forget the Reverend, too, and thoughts of his family lying butchered on the plains and of his dad riding to his death with a haul of stolen guns.

Honor thy father and mother . . .

"Follow me," he commanded, as if he had said it a thousand times.

He spurred his horse forward. After a minute he turned to see that Rod and Ike had fallen in behind him, their mounts kicking up clouds of dust as they flew north across the plains.

Hot-blooded, just like yer pa.

It was in that moment that Chasby made up his mind: When they got to Three Chop, he would confront the Reverend. He would know the truth.

CHAPTER 3

Donovan

DONOVAN FOUND RASCAL REMINGTON PERUSING THE *THREE CHOP STAR* at his desk. The *Star* was the pride of Three Chop thanks to Rascal's prolific pen, and the only weekly newspaper on the whole of the North Texas plain.

Donovan listened from the doorway as the man whispered to himself, reading every word of a draft edition aloud, his eyes following his right index finger, his left hand engaging a crystal tumbler filled with Kentucky bourbon.

"Well!" Rascal exclaimed upon noticing Donovan in the doorway. He gave the Sheriff a heartfelt salute. "If it isn't our legendary Sheriff, father of this paradise!"

Donovan crossed the room, calibrating his ear to Rascal's prattle. "A paradise except for the damn paper."

"I'll drink to that!" Rascal said, raising his tumbler.

Donovan grunted as he took a seat at the desk opposite Rascal. The desk was piled high with ink-stained newsprint and half a hundred old notebooks. "I've found your newspaper works well for kindling, and that's about it."

"You have wit, Mr. Sheriff," Rascal chortled, slapping his belly and swilling a mouthful of whiskey. "Should have been a newspaperman yourself. In fact—"

"I never could sit still long enough even to read the paper, Rascal, much less write it," Donovan cut in. "Why do you think I have you give me the headlines?"

"You're too early for that today, Mr. Sheriff. Hours too early, I'm afraid. I'm still on my early drafts."

Donovan pulled a tin from his coat pocket and set it on Rascal's desk. He opened it, letting the scent of tobacco steal into the room.

"Is that Lone Jack?" Rascal asked, suddenly attentive.

"Sure," Donovan replied. "Came in just yesterday."

Rascal wet his lips with the pink slug of his tongue. "I've been out of Lone Jack going on a week."

"Oh?"

"Left the month's wages on the card table, you know." Rascal smiled sheepishly, eyes large as eggs and blinking behind his glasses. "A run of bad luck."

"A man's luck can be a fickle thing," Donovan allowed.

Donovan rolled a cigarette, sealing it with a protracted lick. He struck a match against the grain of Rascal's desk.

"A fine quirly," Rascal said admiringly. "Though I'm more partial to the pipe myself."

"Why don't you take a pinch?" Donovan said, motioning to the tin.

Rascal already had his meerschaum pipe in hand. He looked demented the way he concentrated, packing his favorite Virginia tobacco like it was flaked gold.

At one time imported tobacco might have been as precious as Rascal made it seem—before Three Chop had sway, before the railroad brought California produce and eastern manufactures twice weekly. Rascal was in fact Three Chop's first and longest resident. What had drawn the little epicure in those early days, Donovan could only guess. And why had he stayed?

Like so many towns in the West, Three Chop had been founded by speculators—eastern men with oiled hair, men who had never set foot on the plain, men who had long since been forgotten like distant ancestors. Greedily they had snapped up land under the Homestead Acts to stoke demand and sell it for twenty times profit.

Rascal had been the instrument of that frenzy, paid to distribute the *Three Chop Star* to the furthest reaches of the country to lure settlers with tales of fertile land and unimaginable wealth and nubile Indian princesses.

Donovan had found his own copy of Rascal's newspaper in a restaurant in Austin, though it was not the pursuit of wealth that had brought him exactly. It was something else—a sense of destiny, perhaps.

Rascal had the bowl of his pipe smoking. He sniffed the tobacco box between puffs, baring his incisors.

"Reminds me of my father, you know," he said, the pipestem clenched between his teeth. "A real bastard of a man, but he did a few things right, and tobacco was one of them."

"The headlines?" Donovan asked.

"Oh, Mr. Sheriff," Rascal lamented as he struck another match. "Can it really be true? Are headlines all anyone reads anymore?"

Donovan's laconic eyebrow said *they're all anyone ever did*.

"Very well," Rascal muttered, clearing his throat and resetting his glasses. "We begin, Mr. Sheriff, with a three-column head, 'Mayor Cordell Tumbles Down the Well.'"

Donovan smiled emptily. "The first sentence, Rascal."

"Yes, err, the first sentence," Rascal said quickly, and he began:

"Early Thursday morning, approximately two hours past midnight, none other than Three Chop Mayor Clarence P. Cordell emerged from the second-story kitchen of the *Lady May*, where, according to multiple witnesses, he was pestering Madame Fuselli for a second complimentary steak—free dinners wrought by the masterful hand of chef Mr. Sam, of course, being one of many perks that come with the almighty mayorship of this fine town—and then, witnesses say, clutching an empty bottle of bourbon in his right hand, an empty bottle of Scotch in his left, the bumbling Mr. Cordell stumbled, fumbled, and then tumbled, rolling like a sack of potatoes down the stairs and crashing into chairs and tables and onlookers below, not one of whom extended a helping hand to their poor, innocent mayor, whose fall from grace began like so many, with a belly full of drink and a series of unfortunate steps."

"All that was one sentence?" Donovan asked.

Rascal nodded gravely, puffing his pipe. "You asked. I delivered."

Donovan sighed. Ordinarily the mayor's antics did not concern him—after all, it was good to remind the town now and again who really held power in Three Chop. But with Jacob in the running . . .

Donovan clenched and flexed his fist. "What's next, Rascal?"

"To our delight, we have a second story about our sure-footed mayor, a two-column head that reads, 'Moreau to Chalenge Cordell.'"

"Challenge him to what?" Donovan asked, feigning ignorance.

"I'll be damned!" Rascal said. "C-H-A-L-E. I'm short an L!" He made a mark on his copy with a thick pencil.

"Challenge him to what, Rascal?"

"I'm two-for-two on piquing your interest," Rascal said, grinning. He licked his lips, adjusted his glasses, and began again:

"Mr. Jacob S. Moreau, the fifty-four-year-old owner and founder of this town's one and only drinking establishment, the beloved *Lady May*, pledged in the early hours of Thursday morning—in a fiery speech for which he cast aside his apron and stood atop his bar—to challenge our longtime mayor, Clarence P. Cordell, in next month's town election, pledging to restore dignity to an office that, just minutes before and in that very location, had plummeted to new depths of embarrassment—literally!—with a fallen Mr. Cordell writhing on the floor, squealing like a stuck pig for the assistance of his late Aunt Bess Parker, bless her soul, and complaining about the pain in his rheumatic knee—"

"That's enough," Donovan commanded, smoldering.

"Hadn't you heard?" Rascal asked, suddenly shy.

"I had heard a *rumor*," Donovan said. "I had hoped the rumor was false. And barring that, I had hoped Jacob's boast was something off-handed—not Sam Adams declaiming from a bar top."

Rascal cleared his throat and took a moment to polish his glasses on his lapel.

"I want you to strike the article," Donovan said after a minute. His tone made it an order.

"Mr. Sheriff!"

"Strike it, Remington."

"But I witnessed it with my own eyes!"

Donovan did not reply, only fixed the man with a stare.

Rascal took a series of quick puffs on his pipe, frowning at the smoke and fidgeting in his chair.

"Sir," he said after a minute. "Regarding tomorrow's newspaper—"

"Yes?"

"What I read aloud, as I said, was a first draft—very rough, very rough indeed—and in need of a rewrite, full and complete."

Donovan nodded.

"Perhaps I should *delay* publication until I can review the article again. Maybe find another source."

"That sounds reasonable," Donovan said, standing up and donning his hat. "You're a hell of a journalist, you know. The integrity of the *Star* is unimpeachable."

"Yes," Rascal agreed, his eyes losing focus.

"Any other troublesome headlines you want to run by me?"

Rascal pursed his lips in thought. "Not a headline exactly, but I do have an interview with Haddock about the violent incident—"

"Boys throwing stones," Donovan said, waving his hand. "Lamentable but nothing more."

"On the record?"

"On the record," Donovan agreed. He walked to the door, leaving the tin of Lone Jack on Rascal's desk. "Remington," he called from the doorway.

"Yes, Mr. Sheriff?"

"Cut the poor mayor some slack. It's not easy running this town."

"You would know it, sir."

CHAPTER 4

Chasby

FROM THE MOMENT CHASBY MADE OUT THE MAN'S SILHOUETTE, HE felt sick.

They had ridden a hard ten minutes to the camp, the telltale column of smoke growing larger until they could smell charred meat and burnt coffee.

What bothered Chasby first was the man's posture. He stood with hunched shoulders like a man trying to withstand the onslaught of a gale.

Chasby's discomfort only grew as they approached. When they were close enough to see the man's features, Chasby realized he was older than expected. His face was tanned and leathered and hatched with deep lines. He squinted at the riders beneath the brim of a worn riding hat. He held a shotgun in the crook of his arm, the gunmetal glinting in the sunlight.

A smarter man would have shot us already.

But the worst shock came when Chasby saw the man's companions and the state of their meager encampment. A woman stood behind the wagon clutching an infant to her breast. She seemed too young to be the man's wife—probably no more than seventeen—thin and red faced. A daughter, perhaps. Or a niece. Anxiety and exhaustion battled for control of her countenance.

Chasby thought immediately of Hattie, who was not much younger, with blonde hair and a heart-shaped face, and he prayed that she met no men like him in Wyoming.

Thou shalt not commit adultery . . .

The wagon was small and mostly empty, except for blankets and a smattering of supplies—a few days' worth at best. Their only other possession appeared to be a tired old horse with showing ribs.

Chasby looked pleadingly at Rod as they reined in their own mounts. *Let's just leave them alone.* He willed the thought at Rod.

But Rod jerked his head and mouthed, "Go on!"

Chasby grimaced. He patted the flask in his jacket and cleared his throat. *You've seen them do it. Just say the same words and try not to shit yourself.*

"Howdy," he managed. His throat was dry and the words came out a croak.

The old man gave the slightest nod, his gray eyes darting from one rider to the next. They had fanned out into a semicircle, half surrounding the small encampment. The man might kill one of them with his shotgun, but he would not kill two. Chasby watched him take a slow step backward toward the girl and her baby.

"Where're you headed?" Chasby asked. The day was noiseless, and in the silence that followed his question, he heard only the strain of leather straps and the jingle of spurs as the horses shifted and stamped.

"He said where're you headed," Rod spoke up impatiently.

"West," the old man said. "Far as we can git." He spoke with an accent that reminded Chasby of the Reverend. An Alabaman?

"Don't look like you'll get much further," Chasby said, nodding to the empty wagon. His tone was almost sympathetic.

The old man grunted.

"Some people ain't cut out for going west," Rod said.

Chasby looked at Rod again. He thought he would retch, but Rod urged him on.

"Well you know there's a toll through these parts," Chasby said weakly. If Rod and Ike did not want him, who would?

When the old man did not respond, Rod said, "We're lawmen, see? We provide a service. These plains're lawless. There's Indians who'd scalp you, bandits who'd murder you and do worse to yer girl and her babe. We keep 'em and their kind at bay for the safety of travelers like you. But there's a cost to it, y'know? Horses, guns, ammo, victuals. We sure ain't tryin' to get rich, but we gotta feed ourselves all the same."

"I reckon there's some good-for-nothin' lowlifes roaming these parts indeed," the old man said, pretending to survey the land. "Outlaws an' robbers. The kind of cowards that'd take advantage of an old man an' his daughter an' her sick babe." He spat on the ground, "Too bad for those men we ain't got nothin' left to steal."

"You got a horse," Ike cut in. "A horse'll pay the tax as well as anything, and so will bullets."

The scorn in the old man's face melted into fear. "It's a murderer who takes that horse," he said, stiffening. "That babe needs a doctor, and we're on our way to town to find him one. Without that horse, we'll die out here."

"You won't die," Rod said. "There's a town thirty miles west—Blue Spring. You can walk there in a day or two."

The old man shook his head. "Not tired as we are an' with a sick babe. We wouldn't make it, no. Not all of us. Y'kill him if you take that horse."

"What else you got?" Chasby asked, praying they had something, anything that would please Rod and Ike enough to leave them alone—a necklace or some family heirloom.

"I told you we ain't got nothin'."

"You got a horse!" Ike screamed, drawing his gun. "A horse'll do just fine!"

Ike's threat was interrupted by the crack of a gunshot.

Chasby heard the bullet sigh in his ear as it passed. Startled, he looked around. The old man still held his shotgun loosely in the crook of his arm. He looked as surprised as anyone. Then Chasby saw the girl. She was gripping the baby in one hand and a six-shooter in the other, its barrel pointed right at him. Her hand was shaking. Instinctively, Chasby reached for his gun.

Ike returned fire first, having already drawn his weapon. Rod was close behind, and before gun smoke clouded his vision, Chasby saw the old man raise his shotgun too, bewildered.

Chasby raised his pistol and fired six shots, emptying the chamber without aiming anywhere in particular. The gun kicked in his hand, jarring the bones of his arm up to his shoulder.

The sound of gunfire faded into a dull thudding as Chasby felt his mind leaving his body. This time he had no desire to wrangle it. His head buzzed pleasantly, but there was a wave of panic growing inside him. He was only vaguely aware of the horse beneath him whirling and bucking, agitated by the gunfire. He felt himself slide sideways and hit the ground as his mind still looked down from above. He watched as he scurried away from the stamping hooves on hands and knees. *Old Mary isn't used to gunfire, I guess.* She was a farm horse after all.

Chasby came to himself as the last gunshots rang out. He staggered to his feet, heart pounding. He was covered in sweat. As the gun smoke cleared, he saw Rod and Ike had dismounted and were milling about, apparently unharmed.

Rod's horse lay on the ground, kicking weakly, its chest a mass of blood and hair. Chasby watched as Rod loaded his six-shooter, spun the chamber, and fired a bullet into the animal's brain. It kicked once more and lay still.

The old man was lying still, too, beyond the horse. Chasby watched as Ike walked over to the man and kicked him roughly in the side. The man did not react.

"Dead," Ike called, the satisfaction evident in his voice. "The old bastard's dead."

Horror gripped Chasby as he looked to the wagon where the girl had been standing. Her body lay inert, her tattered white blouse blotted red with blood.

Chasby ran toward her and was kneeling beside the girl before he realized what he was doing. Her chest was still. Hot tears filled his eyes, and he choked back a sob. All the guilt he had felt over Hattie—the way he had used her, ignored her, gotten her sent away all for the sake of his own pleasure, his own weakness—came spilling out of his eyes then, loosed by the sight of another girl, innocent like Hattie, now dead before him.

And by whose hand? a voice screamed in his head. The Reverend's voice or his own? *By whose hand?*

His ears were still ringing from the gunfire, but he heard a new sound now, a sound out of place in this vast, desolate prairie where gun smoke hung blue and hazy in the air. It was the baby crying on the ground, spilled out of its mother's arms.

Rod heard it, too. "Shame," he said, walking over and pointing his gun at the baby the same way he had done with the horse.

"No!" Chasby cried, scrambling to his feet. He scooped up the child awkwardly, one hand on its head and one hand on its back—mimicking what he had seen Madame Fuselli do with one of the girls' babies at the *Lady May*. "You can't just kill it like that—like it's an animal!"

The baby cried harder in his arms.

"You want to leave it to starve? Or worse?" Rod asked, confused. Already there were buzzards circling overhead.

"No," Chasby said, although he had not thought through the alternatives. *We can't let it die!* Of this at least he was sure. "We'll take it with us."

Rod snorted. "You wouldn't know what t'do with a goddamn baby."

"We can take it to town and leave it with someone." *Like I was left.*

Rod shook his head. "Don't you think people will wonder how we got mixed up with a baby? Don't you think they'll start asking questions we cain't answer straight? We cain't draw attention to ourselves, especially if we're trying to sell any of this stuff." He motioned to the cart, which Ike had climbed into and begun inspecting.

"I ain't listening to that thing scream for the next three days, neither," Ike said. He was rummaging through the supplies. "This ain't no place for a baby."

Chasby thought Ike meant the prairie, but he might as well have meant the world.

"Besides," Rod said, walking toward Chasby. "His granddaddy said he was sick—sick near dyin', and we sure as hell cain't take him to a doctor." Rod reached out and put his hand on the baby's head. "He's hotter'n hell! Feel him!"

Chasby had already felt the baby's fever through the back of his head. Rod was right. He was burning up. As if on cue, the baby began to cough, a wet, sickly sound.

"He won't make it to Three Chop, will he?" Chasby asked, his chin trembling with emotion. "He won't make it without his ma."

By whose hand!

For some time he stood there, cradling the babe, wondering how it had come to this. Only yesterday they had been ambling carefree across the plains. *He'll never make it.* He turned his head away and held the baby out to Rod. "Take him," he said, closing his eyes.

The shot came only a few seconds later. Apparently Rod wanted it over quickly, too.

"Ike, git me a blanket," Rod called.

Chasby kept his eyes shut. The silence was overwhelming.

"It's alright," Rod said, putting a hand on Chasby's shoulder. "It's over."

Chasby turned around slowly. He saw a brown blanket spread on the ground a few yards away, covering a pathetic lump.

Rod looked appraisingly at him. "I'm still not sure you're cut out for this job, Chaz," he said, rubbing the stubble on his cheek. "It's a hard thing scratching a living from this here dry earth. But I like you. I think you got potential. Maybe you remind me of me someway. Besides, you saved my life."

"Saved your life?" Chasby asked, confused in his grief.

"Sure. You hit the old man just when he pulled the trigger. He would've got me instead of the horse."

The color drained from Chasby's face. *Thou shalt not commit murder . . .*

"We were all firing," he said, his voice quavering.

"Ike and I were firing at the girl," Rod said, shaking his head. "You got the old man. You saved my life."

"But I wasn't even aiming."

"Look what I got!" Ike yelled, interrupting. He held up a gold-plated pocket watch on a long gold chain. "Found it in the bottom of a flour sack! Lyin' old man was hiding it from us. I knew they had something!"

The old fool, Chasby thought. Suddenly he was angry—angry at the old man and his daughter for making him pull the trigger, for putting that black mark on his soul. *Was a watch worth dying for?*

Rod grinned. "Forget the cart then, boys," he said, clapping his hands. "I'll take the horse on account of mine being dead, and we'll head for Three Chop. I'm sure ole Stu Lassiter will know someone who wants to buy that watch if he don't want to buy it himself, and then we'll have money enough for a good time at the *Lady!*"

CHAPTER 5

Donovan

"LET HIM IN," THE REVEREND AARON CALLED. HIS SOUTHERN ACCENT was musical but viscous. It oozed around the doorway and into the hall.

A man stood between Donovan and the door. He had a narrow, pox-scarred face and greasy gray hair. His face held no expression, but there was a certain sadism reflected in his eyes, a timeless cruelty.

Donovan pushed roughly past the man, Loeb was his name, a recent convert to the Reverend's sect, though he had the fervor of a born believer. Donovan had heard stories about Loeb, Haddock's tale of rock-throwing only one among many. His origin was unknown. He was like the Reverend in this way, even his stringy gray hair a poor imitation of the brilliant blackness of the Reverend's. No one knew how he had climbed so quickly in the Reverend's esteem, either, though Donovan had his own opinions, which he kept to himself.

Upon the Reverend's command, Loeb let the Sheriff pass. He left no doubt as to who he thought held the higher power in the town. Donovan would have to disabuse him of that one day. When he was feeling better, when he had beaten back his illness.

Donovan entered the Reverend's office, shutting the door behind him, though he was sure Loeb would stay behind, ear pressed to the grain of the wood. Donovan was breathing heavily, mostly in anger. He tried to collect himself. The Reverend would not be strong-armed like Rascal.

"Morning, Reverend," Donovan said brusquely, taking his seat uninvited. His eyes darted around the room, searching for the Reverend's diamond-striped, gray-green snake, a boa as thick around as a man's arm. He saw no sign of it, a fact that brought him little comfort.

The Reverend leaned forward, studying Donovan with his dark eyes, as if sensing his fear, his frustration, as if feeding off it. "Afternoon, I think."

"Right," Donovan agreed, unimpressed.

The waxing gold of afternoon light streamed through a window behind the Reverend's desk. Otherwise the room was plain—austere despite the fullness of his collection plate on Sundays.

Donovan wondered absently where all that money went . . .

He looked a while at the Reverend, whose dress was as black as his eyes, waiting for him to speak. When he did not, Donovan asked, "What's wrong with your new man?"

"Loeb?"

Donovan nodded. "He acts like he knows something I don't. He nearly roughed me up in the hall when I tried to go by him."

The Reverend smiled enigmatically. "Loeb is faithful. Maybe overly diligent. He has trouble sometimes restraining his enthusiasm. But he is a godly man."

Donovan grunted. "He could do with a little reminding of who's sheriff in this town."

"I'll speak with him."

Donovan nodded. "I suppose he's the one who vandalized Jacob and Sallie's liquor?"

The Reverend shrugged.

"Threw rocks at Jacob's man, Haddock?"

"Why not ask him yourself?"

Donovan grunted but did not argue. He had not come to talk about Loeb, though he would have to do so, eventually. Corralling zealots was a tricky business, prone to making martyrs.

"Jacob is planning to run after all," Donovan said, getting to the heart of it. "Rascal says he made a speech last night in the saloon."

"I had heard," Aaron mused, steepling his fingers below his pale chin.

"I thought your people stayed clear of the place?"

"Oh, most do," the Reverend agreed, "but not all. When Pastor Bonham died, God rest his soul, many of his flock came to the Church of the Holy Light, and some have not yet embraced the doctrine entire."

Donovan shifted uncomfortably, thinking again of the snake and its place in the Reverend's doctrine. "It will complicate things if Jacob goes through with it. Cordell will have to run a campaign, and we'll need the support of your congregation."

"You have my support, John," the Reverend said. "I don't think Jacob will be a problem, especially when we make the closing of the saloon the primary issue of our campaign."

For a moment Donovan thought he had misheard. "We talked about this already, Aaron." Donovan was gratified to see the man bristle at this exchange of familiarity. "The town isn't ready. But after the election . . ."

"The town, perhaps," the Reverend cut in, a light flashing in his dark eyes. He ran his fingers through his long, black hair, pushing it out of his face. Then he reached into the drawer of his plain wooden desk and produced a trifold paper, which he slid to Donovan.

Donovan took the paper in hand and, removing glasses from his pocket, began to read. He frowned, setting his whiskers at odds. He looked from the paper to the Reverend. "It will never work," he began.

"It will," the Reverend said, interrupting again. "I think you should present it to the council at tomorrow's meeting."

"I'm telling you it's pointless, worse than pointless."

"You'd be surprised, John. I have spoken to some of the council members myself. Besides, they don't have to adopt it right away. Just present it. But they will adopt it in time—I'm sure of it."

Hesitantly, Donovan tucked the letter into his vest. He eyed the pale Reverend warily, half expecting the snake to slither up the man's arm.

"I'll see what I can do," he said.

The Reverend nodded, satisfied.

He spoke to council members already? Donovan wondered. *To whom? And when? This morning? And none came to me?* It was as if there had been a coup in the night.

Aaron's power had grown markedly in the last year after a long period of plateau, and Donovan was beginning to realize what a formidable rival he could become.

Had become?

The Reverend's burgeoning power derived from a series of seemingly fortuitous events. First, the influx of farmers that came with the arrival of the rail had swelled his congregation. Soon after, temperance had swept westward, energizing the farmfolk and splitting the townfolk, many of whom profited directly or indirectly from liquor sales. Aaron had embraced the gospel of temperance as quickly as a piano man embraces a popular tune, weaving it into his dark theology.

Then, as the religious divide between farmers and townfolk was at its starkest, Pastor Bonham had inexplicably died in his sleep at the relatively young age of fifty, easing the tension and bringing some reluctant townfolk into the Reverend's fold, even if they remained divided in politics. More than once Donovan had wondered if Aaron had played some part in Bonham's demise, but he dared not think on it long. The Reverend had a way of looking past a man's eyes as if reading his thoughts.

Then there was the business of Donovan's own illness—blinding bouts of back pain and persistent aches, exhaustion, weight loss. That pain—*that fear*, he admitted ashamedly—had eventually driven him into the Reverend's arms to seek a cure the doctor said he could not provide.

He was not finding the arms as accommodating as he had hoped.

As if reading his mind, Aaron asked, "How is the pain, John?"

Donovan thought he detected a hint of irony in the man's voice. "I have some pain," he said circumspectly. "I've been praying. Every morning and night, as you instructed."

"Prayer is good," the Reverend mused. "But you must be patient. God does not bargain with man, but he does reward the righteous. Prayer is not a transaction. It is an offering. You must let him work in his own time."

"I haven't got time," Donovan rejoined. He had sacrificed his pride to be here, and he intended to see results, not endure a Sunday school lesson. "Doc Marshall said I might only have *weeks*."

"Since when do you heed Doc Marshall? You came to me because he admitted he could not help you."

Donovan looked down at the floor. He had seen men die. Some went bravely with clear eyes and grim faces. Others went crying and begging and calling to God or their mothers. Which would he be?

It occurred again to Donovan what power he had given the Reverend in sharing his secret—not just the secret of his diagnosis, but of his fear.

"When I see a horse with a broken leg," Donovan said, "I can diagnose it. But I still have to shoot the damn thing."

The Reverend was silent for a moment, studying Donovan, his pale fingers tapping. Then he leaned forward. "Do you know how I got here, John?"

Donovan sighed. The Reverend often spoke in parables, an affectation. "You came from Alabama by way of Arkansas," he said. "A traveling preacher." *A traveling salesman?*

"That's one version of it," the Reverend said. "A newspaperman's version. But why would I leave the rolling hills of Alabama to come to a place like this? A town choked in dust in the middle of the plains of a great continent forsaken? A town littered with cow dung and steeped in sin three stories high? Of all the great cities in God's wide world, how did I end up *here?*"

Donovan watched a light growing in the Reverend's dark, deep-set eyes, and for a while he forgot the troubling business about his own mortality.

"I came to Three Chop as part of an odyssey, John," the Reverend began. "First, I was captured, a prisoner of war. I, like Jonah, came to my destiny in the belly of a whale. My whale was iron gray with a wood-burning engine and a boxcar for a belly. And it was *crowded* in there, John. And it was *hot.* And it smelled worse than Three Chop in the early days when the cowpunchers still drove their cattle down Front. Men died from the smell, John. Did you know a man could die from a smell alone?

"They suffocated in it as they soiled themselves and sweated. They were good Confederate men from Alabama and North Carolina. And they were beside me in the belly of that whale, dying."

Donovan frowned, knowing how much better the Reverend and his kind fared than the Union soldiers at Andersonville. But he did not interrupt the Reverend, dared not, so charmed was he by the spell of the man's lilting tongue.

"Three days and three nights we were in that boxcar," the Reverend went on. "Men went crazy. They gnashed their teeth and clawed their eyes and stripped naked and prayed to and cursed God in the same breath. But not I, John, because I *knew* something. I knew that my place in that train was not some accidental fortune of war. I knew the law of cause and effect. I knew the mercy and the wrath of God.

"See, I suffered because I had grown accustomed to pleasure, even in the midst of war. For all men it is the gratification of pleasure that brings misery. Don't you see that Heaven and Hell are one place, John—the belly of a whale? That one man's paradise is another man's nightmare? That the path of the righteous is the path of self-denial, of simplicity, of asceticism?"

The Reverend's eyes blazed. His thin, bony fingers twitched. "Don't you see that Three Chop, too, could be Heaven, John, with its parched earth, its bedraggled farmers, its humble church? Now it is a way station on the track from the glittering, self-absorbed East to the greedy, debaucherous West. But it could be the moral center of the continent, a haven, a paradise!

"Except," the Reverend said, now lowering his voice. "Except Three Chop has a cancer like your own."

Donovan shuddered. Hearing the diagnosis out loud filled him with a fear that penetrated to the very seat, the essence, of his soul. He was a rapt parishioner, hypnotized. He strained to hear the Reverend's every word, afraid he might miss the pronouncement of his cure.

"The saloon," the Reverend resumed, almost whispering, "is a blight that could undermine God's will in Three Chop. And yet it flourishes. The townspeople grow rich from the passing hordes, and the richer they get, the harder it becomes to excise the tumor. And the richer they get," he added, "the more powerful Jacob and his fugitive Negro will become. We must save the town."

"And to save myself?" Donovan asked, swallowing, his heart in his throat.

"Only God can save you," the Reverend said. "But the story of Jonah also teaches us that a man who is the instrument of God shall not perish even when he is cast into the ocean in the midst of a storm and swallowed by a fish."

Donovan stared at his boots. "The townfolk won't allow it, I tell you—closing the saloon."

The Reverend sighed. "Temperance is a movement bigger than Three Chop, John. It's bigger than you or me. And it's about more than liquor. It's about uniting the laws of the land with the word of God, of making this a godly country once more, for its people have been led astray.

"Jacob would remake Three Chop after Sodom. He cannot be allowed to win nor even prosper lest we invite God's wrath, lest we desire his *Negro*—" the Reverend pronounced the word with disdain "—become First Lady of our fair town."

"That might be so." Donovan shrugged, surprised by the heat of the Reverend's hate. Had he always been so fixated? "It doesn't make it possible."

"My boy—" the Reverend said, trailing off. He looked down. "Chasby. He was a victim of that pestilence. He was a good and godly boy. But once he started hanging around that place, the saloon, he was led astray. Drinking, gambling, whoring . . ."

The Reverend expelled a frame-shaking sigh. His voice was tremulous, torn between anger and lament, and Donovan wondered briefly if Aaron would cry.

"He'll return," the Reverend continued. "Like the prodigal son. And when he does, I'll show him the path of righteousness."

The Reverend locked eyes with Donovan.

"It's not just politics, John. It's right and wrong. It's a crusade. You're the Sheriff. Do you think you're only meant to protect the town from gunslingers?"

Donovan lowered his head, breaking eye contact.

In the quiet that followed, he heard the oily hiss of the unseen snake.

CHAPTER 6

Kat

KAT SAT ON A PILLOWY DUVET WEARING ONLY A NIGHTDRESS AND black stockings. Spread beside her was the most beautiful dress she had seen since she left San Francisco those two years past—yellow silk with lace trim and inlaid pearls, cut exactly to her size. The fabric was butter between her fingers.

She frowned a moment, caught in a remembrance—surrounded by Señora Alvarez's silk dresses, a hundred of them crowded around her on hangers, limp and grasping where she hid. But the silk was real, and for the first time in her life she could call it hers.

And haven't I earned it?

The bedroom was fine to match the dress—spacious with gilded mirrors and a marble-topped vanity. Every other surface that skin might touch was made soft and plush—feather bed, overstuffed sitting chairs, oriental rugs, and silk curtains. Like the dress, it was a room fine enough for Señor Alvarez's house, except for the overwhelming red.

Kat smiled, forgetting those spoiling remembrances in the grandeur of her new room. Already the move to Three Chop seemed worthwhile. It was for the *Lady May* that she had made the trip from San Pablo, or rather for this parlor house, which was said to be the best in two hundred miles. There were rumors congressmen sometimes stayed the night, and the madam was said to be honest and kind and to treat the girls well.

Kat shivered, and the fine hairs of her arms stood on end.

As if sensing her change in mood, a white cat stirred upon the vanity, blinking its yellow eyes, which were turned up like her own. Earlier that morning she had fallen asleep under the cat's watchful stare and awoken

34

to it just the same. She had panicked then until she remembered where she was. She had been dreaming of Reggie, and in those first waking moments she had not been able to tell whether it was the dream or the room that was real.

Kat shook her head and ran her hands across the yellow dress once more to reassure herself.

A moment later Kat heard footfalls in the hallway—the sharp crack of a woman's heel and the softer tread of a man's boot.

A man?

Kat's mouth went dry. She scanned the room for a ready weapon—a paperweight or a candelabra—but found nothing. She made fists with her hands, leaving the thumb out like Vern had taught her, taught her before he had abandoned her to Reggie.

"Eer I 'ave 'er, Jacob, a precious zeeng!" cooed the woman as she opened the door to the bedroom.

Madame Fuselli was squat with strong arms and a waddle of skin that swayed beneath her chin as she talked. She wore a purple velvet dress adorned with fake gems and a high, pink collar. Her hair was dyed burgundy, and she spoke with the whisper of an accent that Kat had heard before somewhere in the cosmopolitan milieu of San Francisco but could not place.

"Oh, she's gorgeous," her placid companion remarked. He had a waxed moustache that curled up at either end. He was dressed fastidiously in white boots and a white coat with a striped silk kerchief. His accent was southern, genteel, as sophisticated as the woman's in its own way. Even in the perpetual dust of North Texas, his ensemble retained its virgin whiteness. "What's your name, darling?"

Kat said nothing—only forced a smile and kept her fists clenched and ready in her lap.

"Her name's Katarina," Madame Fuselli answered for her. "She's ze one whose debt we paid to bring here."

We paid? It was one thing to be indebted to a madam and another altogether to be indebted to a pimp. Another pimp. *Reggie.*

"She's proficient according to ze madam at her old brothel," Fuselli continued, addressing the man while he studied Kat. "She brought a letter of reference, see?" The madam pulled a letter from under her arm and waved it before them. "Beautiful but a lot of trouble to hear her tell it, ze madam."

The man grunted and turned back to Kat, holding out a ruddy palm. "Katarina, I'm Jacob. It's a pleasure to make your acquaintance." The blond hair of his wrist showed thickly beneath the white sleeve of his coat.

Kat grasped the hand reluctantly. The man's palm was soft, although she thought he could break the bones of her hand if he wanted to, and he held it long enough to make her uncomfortable.

His eyes met hers only for a moment, and she saw an aloofness there, which she thought might be the look of a man admiring his property. *A procurer?* His stare moved quickly to her breasts and her stomach and thighs.

"What kind of trouble was she in?" Jacob asked, still looking at Kat, though the question was not addressed to her.

"Apparently more zen a few in ze company favored her. It made ze other girls angry, and she egged ze men on, too, made zem jealous, made zem act rashly—a girl's vanity."

Jacob nodded as Madame Fuselli spoke, as if he had expected as much. "She's exquisite, though." He looked thoughtful. "Stand up and give us a twirl," he said after a minute, rubbing his red palms together.

Kat stood to turn.

"And do it slowly," Jacob added. "Don't be shy, now."

Kat thought of her mother, and prayed a silent prayer for the woman to watch over her, to protect her even now when she had strayed so far, the woman who had once dressed her in dowdy clothes and hurried her through the streets of San Francisco lest she be noticed for the wrong reason.

She turned a slow circle before the bed, feeling like a goose strung up in the window of a shop.

Jacob stared approvingly at her long legs while she pranced, his fingers toying with the end of his moustache, touching his purple lips. Kat noticed gold rings on the fingers of his other hand, the one she had not grasped. There was enough to buy her freedom and then some. She thought of chopping those fingers off to get to the rings, thought of them wriggling on the red floor, a bouquet of worms. Did she have it in her to be so hard? She did not think so, and that was the problem.

When she finished turning, she did not sit down. Her heart began to beat fast then, preparing for whatever came next.

"Bravo," Jacob muttered. He clapped his hands together softly.

The white cat purred in agreement.

Kat smelled perfume rising with the heat of her body. *Roses.*

Jacob stepped toward her. His boots were soundless on the carpet, moustache bristling.

Kat saw the sheen of oil and sweat in his hair. *Just like Reggie.* She remembered Reggie's pockmarked face and the feel of his rough red whiskers on her neck. The memory made her mouth turn sour, sick.

A pimp like Reggie, she lamented. *Will the woman watch?*

The madam wore a sickly sweet smile on her face.

The thought of Reggie overwhelmed her then, filled her with an irresistible fear—Reggie who had first chained her, Reggie who had taken his due, Reggie who had pocketed ninety-five cents of every dollar she made. She steeled herself to lunge, to tear, to gouge. Jacob was so close now she could smell the sweetness of his breath. She realized the rose smell was his own cologne, radiating in sickening waves.

But before she could move, Jacob put a gentle hand on her shoulder and said, "Katarina, do not be afraid." His voice was soft, almost friendly, but like his handshake still somehow powerful, masculine. "I think you'll fit in well here." He gave her half a wink.

Kat looked from Jacob to Madame Fuselli and back, nonplussed.

But he only smiled and added, "You might be the prettiest girl in all of Texas. I think we'll do well together."

Softly, he squeezed her shoulder then turned to leave.

"Do you want to have her undress first?" Madame Fuselli asked, fanning herself with Kat's letter.

Jacob waved his hand dismissively. "I trust your eye, Madame. Just make sure Doc Marshall has a look at her."

Kat let out a breath she had not realized she was holding as she watched the door close behind him. Her heart still beat a frantic rhythm.

The madam had her strip naked then. "No scars," she said approvingly.

When the madam had finished and Kat had dressed, a feeling of debasement and loneliness crept upon her—the familiar black mood—and she began a restless pacing.

"Settle down pretty girl," the madam said soothingly, motioning for Kat to sit on the bed beside her, beside the yellow dress. She looked somehow matronly patting the duvet.

When Kat ignored her, the madam continued, "You know Jacob does not lie with any of ze girls. Ze girls do not lie with anyone who does not pay, and neither Jacob nor I will stand for even ze slightest abuse. Ze men of our house—Jacob and his brother, our piano man, Haddock—look out for ze girls.

"Meanwhile, you will be paid well—ten dollars a guest and half to keep for yourself, and you will find ze merchants in town will provide you with good credit in my name." She motioned to the dress beside her, which she had ordered be brought for Kat the moment she arrived. "Wine and dresses and hats and perfume as fine as any lady's on Front."

Kat stopped pacing. She glanced at the yellow dress again, wondering for the first time since she arrived whether its sheen was not so fine after all. But where else could she go? What else could she do? She studied the paleness of her bare feet against the pattern of the red-hued carpet. For weeks she had thought only of getting here, and now that she had made it, she saw the long road before her, and she found the blackness had followed like a loyal dog.

"Some of ze girls learn to read from a lady in town, Annabel Meacham. And some save enough to leave and start zer own parlors or find husbands—you know men still far outnumber women in the West, even in a town as big as zees."

Kat was not listening. She thought of San Francisco and the old daydream—a mansion on the cliffs like the one Señor and Señora Alvarez owned. *Only it would be mine, and someone else would clean it—a man.* She thought of Vern, too, with the quick smile and strong arms and the way he wore his six-shooter slung across his hip. But California was a long way off.

"You will learn to be happy here," the madam said, rising. She fingered the pearls of her necklace, drawing it idly from the depths of her trussed bosom. On the end of the necklace hung an iron skeleton key.

The madam did not even look at it, but the message was clear enough.

The cat hopped down from the dresser to rub itself against the madam's leg. The pair departed together, leaving Kat alone—ostensibly free but with nowhere to go.

When she was abed with a man, Kat told herself he was a fool—they were all fools—paying for this thing that for her was free. *And Señor Alvarez used you the same, mother. Only he didn't pay you for it, did he? And you still had to clean the floors!* These thoughts helped ease the shame in the moment, to pack it in a box in the attic of her heart to be forgotten until the next time.

The world was for men. It had always been so, and it would always be so, and Kat knew that to buy a piece of it for herself, she would have to buy it *from* them the same way she had bought her way out of Reggie's, out of San Pablo, out of the debt that Vern had pinned on her—Vern who had tossed her aside, abandoned her alone in a strange place with no way to fend for herself.

He must have known what Reggie would do, that he would exact his payment one way or another, whether from Vern or from me. What did it matter to him?

She mouthed a silent prayer then, wishing Vern was dead, a pile of bones bleaching in the desert.

Yet even so a part of her missed him. After all, she was only seventeen.

CHAPTER 7

Donovan

THE TOWN COUNCILORS SAT AROUND THREE SIDES OF A GREAT WOODEN table, the fourth side left open to petitioners. Mayor Cordell presided, resplendent in top hat and tails, the gold double chain of his pocket watch climbing up his paunch to anchor in the buttonhole of a striped vest.

The councilors were arrayed in space as they were in politics—Stuart Lassiter of the Loan and Trust and Marvin Stepshaw of the haberdashery, the allies, to Cordell's right. On his far left sat Jacob and his faction, the dour Doc Marshall and the alcoholic blacksmith Todd Waiverly. And, of course, between the factions sat Ms. Annabel Meacham, the only independent vote on the council, its center and fulcrum.

It was for Annabel that Donovan had come—to make a personal appeal. That was what the Reverend's petition—*the farmers' petition*—would take, an appeal to all her remaining affection.

That Annabel, a woman, was on the council at all had been something of a controversy. There had been others waiting in the wings, expecting to take their turns when Lem died—agreeable, dependable, competent men. But Annabel had claimed her husband's place on the council just as she had claimed his appointment at the post office—quietly, astutely—and there was a certain stubborn rectitude in it, and when it came down to it, men would grumble but none would confront her outright. Besides, possession being nine-tenths the law, the plaintiffs would have had to lift her bodily from the chair.

The meeting was already underway when Donovan approached the council room on the second story of the municipal building. By the sound of it, debate had commenced on the topic that all but those with special knowledge—himself and Cordell—assumed would be the most fraught of the day: an advertisement for a new pastor.

Donovan stopped just short of the doorway, feeling half an interloper. The Reverend's trifold paper burned hot in his pocket like a brand—Aaron's brand, marking Donovan for his own. It was an irrevocable step presenting this to the council, and Donovan found himself hesitant. *Afraid?* He recoiled at the thought, rebelled at his servitude, yet he did not turn and leave.

Instead, he listened from the doorway, caught between impulses as debate roiled the room beyond.

"My feeling, personally, is that we shouldn't be hasty," Cordell was saying. "As you know, many of the late Pastor Bonham's congregants have gone over to Reverend Aaron's Church of the Holy Light, and more are going by the day, and it may be that we don't need to replace Bonham after all—it would be a shame to bring some poor man all the way out here to find his congregation couldn't support him, some young buck straight from seminary with romantic visions of the West."

"Well said, man," Stuart Lassiter concurred, scratching at the sparse side whiskers that scattered his cheek. "Bonham was a good man but staid by comparison."

"Doing the Reverend's bidding, are we?" Jacob asked. His voice had an edge to it that Donovan did not recognize. There was an air of change about the man . . .

"The Reverend?" Cordell repeated dumbly.

"He wants a spiritual monopoly, I suppose," Jacob continued, musing. "No one to challenge his edicts: Thou shalt be dry, thou shalt cast stones, thou shalt sabotage thy liquor, thy spirits shall be torn asunder . . ."

"Blasphemy," Lassiter mumbled.

"This has nothing to do with the Reverend," Cordell said. "If the Reverend had his say he would probably want *more* men of God in the town, not fewer. And yet would he—would any of us—want a man to come all this way for nothing?"

"Yes, but whose God?" Jacob asked. "Confound it. It's been an hour already, and we've yet to talk about the drys!"

From Donovan's vantage outside the doorway, Jacob was only a disembodied voice, but he could imagine the splotches of color appearing red and purple on the man's face where his powder was thinnest.

"They attacked my brother and sabotaged our liquor," Jacob said, his temper flaring. "By comparison, this business about a pastor is nonsense!"

"There's nothing more to say about the liquor!" Cordell rejoined, exasperated. "I told you the Sheriff has spoken with the Reverend. The Sheriff and his deputy will escort your liquor from now on."

"And what of Haddock?" Jacob demanded.

"What of him? A bruise will heal. We don't know who threw those stones. If we did, I warrant the boys would be locked up—"

"Boys! It was no boy, Mayor. It was a man—the Reverend's man, Loeb."

"I saw Haddock," Annabel put in. "It was no mere bruise, either—there were many—great lumps the size of fists. They were purple, and across his back a gash, and his nose bloodied. The doctor can attest."

"Ecchymosis, yes," the doctor said quite seriously. "A severe case indeed."

"Ekky-what?" Stepshaw asked.

"Bruise—a bruise," the doctor clarified. "And epistaxis—bloody nose, et cetera."

"Be that as it may, be that as it may," Cordell said, waving off the doctor's expertise. "He will recover, yes?"

The doctor nodded gravely.

Donovan chose that moment to stride into the room, and a hush fell over the council.

Mayor Cordell was first to break it. "Ah, Mr. Sheriff, please, take a seat. I was just telling them—telling Jacob—that you already spoke to the Reverend, that you'll escort the liquor, that there's nothing to fear."

"And what of my brother?" Jacob repeated.

Donovan took his time in taking his seat, in part for the drama of it, in part because it hurt his back.

He doffed his hat and set it on his knee. He ran his hand through his hair, which was still thick as a mane despite its going gray. Only then did he turn to fix Jacob with his stare.

"Did your brother see who attacked him?"

"He saw who smashed the liquor, who overturned our cart—it was Loeb and his men! I've told you."

"Did he see who threw the stones?"

"Who else!"

"I've spoken with the Reverend. He will not pay a restitution that will go to buying more liquor, but he said he would pay toward something else. As for your brother, without a witness—"

Jacob scoffed.

"—without a witness," Donovan repeated, "I can only go so far as to talk to the man, which I've done, and I've told the deputy to keep an eye on him. What, would you have me hang him?"

Jacob pulled at the curled end of his moustache, then folded his arms peevishly and looked away. "We'll see," he muttered. "We'll see how far your admonitions go."

Donovan took that for retreat. He had known he would have to endure Jacob's scorn when he came to council. He had bigger concerns.

"We were just talking about the advertisement for a pastor," Annabel said, turning her dark eyes to Donovan.

Her look, at once familiar, intimate, and alien, made Donovan swell with a kind of anxious remorse. *Foolish*, he chided himself, a boy's imaginings. He savored her attention a moment then replied, "It's already taken care of. I saw Rascal this morning and told him to place the ad."

Annabel raised an eyebrow.

"That's council business," Jacob protested. "Unless you plan to pay out of your own pocket?"

Donovan did not deign to look at the man. He chose the ceiling instead. "Oh, I thought this was one issue on which the council could agree."

Jacob grunted, but, as Donovan had taken his side on the matter, he shut up.

"Ah," Cordell said, shuffling some papers in front of him. "If the Sheriff believes there's interest enough . . ."

"I think enough for an advertisement, Mayor," Donovan said.

"Ah, right then, ah, let it be resolved."

43

And easy as that, Donovan had taken the venom out of Jacob's stinger, had mollified the room, had put the contrarians on a backward footing.

"To what do we owe the pleasure, then, Mr. Sheriff?" Annabel asked. "Did you come just to weigh in on our religious life?"

"The mayor called me here," Donovan said. "To present a petition." He looked to Cordell and braced himself for the onslaught of the mayor's wind—a speech the man had been rehearsing for days.

"Ah, yes, and, well," Cordell said, taking his cue. He pulled reflexively at his collar. "There come certain times in the life of any democratic organization—be it polis, county, state, country—certain times wherein mother Democracy chooses to bring a new constituency to her breast— when . . . when . . ."

Here Cordell seemed to lose himself in the labyrinth of his own rhetoric, but a gentle cough from Lassiter reset him, and he continued, ". . . when it comes time to bestow that God-given right of participation . . ."

As Cordell spoke, approaching obliquely the matter at hand, the trifold petition continued to smolder in Donovan's pocket. Twice he looked up to see Annabel's eyes upon him, but her countenance probed and measured more than it admired. A sense came over Donovan suddenly that perhaps she knew what he was about, and he wondered again which councilors the Reverend had already beseeched. Surely Aaron did not have Annabel's ear?

Jacob fidgeted and sighed and rolled his eyes in turns as the mayor droned on, the wax and wane of his ire read plainly in the color of the splotches on his face like leopard's spots.

Todd Waiverly let the lids of his eyes fall by degrees until he peered at the world through half slits. His breathing fell to a lower register.

For his part Doc Marshall watched with his usual inexhaustible attention, occasionally muttering to himself the same way he did when treating a patient.

Donovan knew the doctor's bedside habits well. Even after so many years, he still had vague memories, nearly formless, of the doctor's head— snowy even then—hovering over him like the visage of God, probing painfully at the wound Nash Warrick's bullet had bore in his gut. For weeks Donovan had languished, convalescing in an upstairs room of the doctor's house, tended by the doctor's beautiful young niece Missy . . .

Annabel had been there, too, of course—she had been his fiancé all those years ago, before he spurned her. Why had he done it? What madness had come over him?

He could not say, so hazy was his recollection. Missy had overcome him somehow, so much so that his memories of that time were still imbued with a light—Missy's light—that persisted despite the changes that had occurred later in her, despite the mirthless woman she had become.

Yes, he owed more than his reputation to Nash Warrick, Donovan reflected. He owed him his choice of wife, his children—even if they were dead. In a twisted way, he owed him his life, owed him the man he had become.

Donovan's reverie was interrupted by the grate of the blacksmith's graveled voice.

"Mayor," Todd said, his voice catching as it does upon waking suddenly. "Mayor, what in God's good name are you blathering about?"

Cordell paused his declamation, mouth agape, the index finger of his right hand, which had been held up in emphasis, wilting into his fist. "Err, you see, of . . . of . . ."

"Of the Pantheon of Lady Liberty, I believe," Doc Marshall prompted.

"Yes," the mayor agreed. "Yes, of course—of the Pantheon of Lady Liberty, surely, and of the Platonic ideal of—" Cordell stopped. "Well," he muttered. "I suppose you understand—understand where it is I'm *headed*, after all. Point being that we have received something . . . a document . . . a request . . . a *petition*."

Donovan removed the document from his pocket and set it on the table before him. He was relieved to have it off his person, to have it now before the council. The thing was all but done.

"First, I need the council to reaffirm its discretion," he said, looking at each councilor in turn.

"Discretion?" Annabel asked.

"I believe the councilors can only consider the petition fairly if they consider it wholly, dispassionately, privately, and present a united front."

"What is this?" Jacob asked, leaning forward, waking from the stupor Cordell had cast upon the room.

"Discretion," Donovan repeated.

"We never divulge council business before it's decided," Jacob said.

"If it's discretion you're after, you have it, man," Lassiter said. "Discretion is the byword of this council."

Donovan nodded.

"The farmfolk have made a petition," he said. "They want to vote in the town election." Sometimes directness was best.

"But it's not a county position!" Jacob said, disbelieving.

"Why would the farmfolk vote in a town election?" Annabel asked, her voice measured.

"It's their position that decisions in the town affect them, since the town is where they buy their clothes and supplies, borrow their money, send their children to school, go to church. Most of the farmfolk make it to town once a week at least."

As Donovan made his point, he was gratified to see Jacob's color rise. When he finished, the man stood so abruptly that he knocked his chair backward with a clatter.

"You'd propose this weeks before the election! You're stuffing the ballot box for your mayor and for that infernal Reverend!"

"Stuffing the ballot box?" Donovan asked coolly. "As far as I know there's only one candidate running."

Jacob emitted a strangled, incredulous laugh. "You must know by now that I've challenged the mayor!"

"Maybe I had heard a rumor," Donovan allowed.

For his part, the mayor only looked at his hands in his lap. He was sensitive and could not help but feel Jacob's candidacy as a personal betrayal.

"Still," Donovan said, "it makes no difference to the purpose of the petition."

"It's just a prelude to forcing temperance down our throats. It's . . . it's . . ." Jacob seemed too agitated to finish his thought. "No, no. It doesn't matter—it will never pass."

"Is that all you think about?" Lassiter asked. "Swilling liquor? This is democracy we speak of—"

"Democracy!" Jacob bellowed. "Is the moneylender going to lecture me about democracy?" Spit flew from his mouth and landed in glistening beads upon the table.

The council descended into chaos—all but Annabel, who kept her big, dark eyes fixed on Donovan, probing.

He held her gaze as long as he could bear.

Donovan ignored the debate himself. He knew nothing would be solved that day. That was not his purpose. His purpose was to bring the petition forward. It would be decided by personal appeal, and Annabel would be the one to decide it. He would try to get it put to a vote in next week's council meeting.

Donovan wondered if Annabel thought of him still when she was alone. He wondered why she had spurned every one of his advances since Lem had died. Two years past!

And he wondered how his life would be different if he had not broken his engagement to her all those years ago.

It was as if all along Donovan had really led two lives: the one that was, and the one that might have been. Maybe he lived more, even—one for every choice he came to regret, and of those he had plenty.

CHAPTER 8

Annabel

ANNABEL WAS SORTING MAIL IN THE POST OFFICE WHEN JOHN ENTERED. Wreathed in the dryness of the sun-warmed street, he exuded a mineral aroma.

"Afternoon, John," she said without looking up. She finished sorting the letters in her hand, careful not to break her concentration. To a man like John, even the smallest interaction could be elevated to a contest of wills.

When she did look up, Annabel was taken aback by the sight of his graying hair, sagging cheeks, heaving chest—*heaving from the climb to the porch?*—which had not been quite so evident in the low light of the council room the day before. His age seemed to be accelerating, outpacing her own.

Or was she inured? Did he notice the same changes in her in the fullness of the post office light? Unconsciously, she pressed her fingers to the skin beneath her chin.

"Is it afternoon already?" John asked, leaning familiarly on the counter as was his custom. He crossed his wrists, holding his hat over the side in a lazy grip.

Annabel checked her watch—gold with a finger-thin leather band, a memento of her father—as much to look away from that ghostly face as to find the time.

"Sure as twelve o'clock is still noon," she said, conjuring a plaster smile, wondering if it looked as thin as his.

"You keeping Saturday hours again?"

"Not exactly. I was next door working on a stationary order, so I thought I might as well open up. Mostly I've been talking with councilors though—Todd and Sallie were just here. You've really kicked a hornet's nest, you know."

"I guess I shouldn't be surprised that everyone's first instinct is to lobby Miss Annabel Meacham," John said, emphasizing the *Miss*.

"I was married to Lem fifteen years, John," Annabel reminded him dryly. In truth Lem's death had been the greatest relief of her life, but she would not give John the satisfaction. She still thought of herself as a widow, if only because of Hattie.

"Mrs. Meacham," John corrected himself. "How could I forget?" He drummed his fingers on the counter, a nervous suitor warding against the silence. "Life is funny after all, isn't it?" he said after a minute, pulling shyly at his ear.

"Oh?"

"I mean, would you have ever guessed it would be the two of us standing together in the end?"

"Are we together?" she asked, sounding harsher than she intended. It had been a long morning spent listening to the needs of others. *And now this presumption?* She felt the two men, Lem and John, divvying her up, apportioning her memories—the one dead, the other dying. *Aren't we all?*

"You don't still harbor that old grudge, do you Annabel?"

Annabel gritted her teeth. "You give yourself too much credit, John. Marriage, children, time: These things have a way of erasing old memories. You know that as well as I."

Despite her frustration, she felt sorry for him. John was probably as lonely as she was—his wife and boys dead. But she could not love him now, not after all that had happened between them and apart from them, and she had more important business than love before her. That was a younger woman's conceit.

"I guess some things do get erased," John agreed, although he did not sound sincere.

"I suppose you've come with some scheme to win my support for the farmers' petition?" Annabel asked, eager to get on with it. "Something besides an appeal to my affection?"

John nodded thoughtfully. "I reckon I did, but standing here with you . . . well, I can see you've already made up your mind."

"Say what you came to say, John. I'm not so opinionated that I can't stand to listen."

John chewed his lip. "Well, it's nothing you don't already know—demographics and such, the ascendance of the farmer as the lynchpin of Three Chop's trade, the importance of inclusiveness, and on and on." He flipped his hand in a circular motion, signifying the unending struggle between rich and poor, urban and rural, there in the rotation.

"What I already know, John, is that the petition is Aaron's—not yours."

"What does it matter?" John scoffed. "The Reverend or not, it's good sense—the only sense, really. And if it happens to align with a religious movement in our little town, call it an expedient."

Annabel shook her head. Maybe it was just John's usual pragmatism, but in the last few months he had seemed increasingly taken with the dark, beguiling Reverend.

Annabel had attended Aaron's service once, a year ago, in the midst of her struggle with Hattie, which in the end turned entirely on her daughter's love affair with the Reverend's delinquent boy, Chasby. She had gone to see what it was that had possessed the girl with such intractable sectarian devotion.

The Reverend's service had left her shaken—all hellscapes and admonitions and the trading of eyes—no talk of forbearance, forgiveness, or humility. Compared to Bonham, he might as well have preached a different religion.

She missed the old pastor and his smiling eyes. She felt bereft when he died as she had not when Lem passed. But then Pastor Bonham had never struck her. She wondered if he had been the same man in private as he was in public, or whether all men, like Lem, had two faces.

John looked at her a long while, his hat half raised, then the frustration left him like a departing spirit.

"I won't pretend I like Jacob. I won't even pretend a part of me doesn't take pleasure in his misfortune. But I wouldn't have brought the petition to the council if I didn't think it was the right course for the town—the only course. Could you really believe otherwise? Believe I'd let a man like Aaron—any man at all—sway me?"

"I wouldn't have thought so," Annabel admitted, feeling the bulwark of her own conviction weaken before his sincerity. "But how else can I explain it? Letting the drys agitate in the streets, giving farmers a vote in the town?"

Annabel wanted to believe him, wanted to believe he was the same man she had known, the man who had built the town with vision, strength, and forbearance. But she could not be sure. How deep did the cynicism of experience go? How many layers were there to the man?

In the end, she decided it did not matter what motivated John. It was true—she had made up her mind before he had come to her, before any of them had come to her. Only it was for her own reasons.

"I'll support the petition," Annabel said, though she half swallowed the words, shrinking from their irrevocable, unknowable effects. She felt a sensation of the Earth tipping, realigning, charting a new course through time and space—not forced by her but nudged.

"There is one condition, though," she said, feeling stronger now that the decision had been made.

John nodded, wary but unmistakably pleased.

CHAPTER 9

Jacob

"IF IT ISN'T THE THREE MUSKETEERS!" JACOB EXCLAIMED, SLAPPING the bar top with a lusty palm. Every good barman was half an actor. "I thought maybe I'd seen the last of y'all boys. What brings you to town?"

"We found work down south," Rod Turner said, sauntering to the bar. His shirt collar was yellow with grease, and he looked like he had been living rough for weeks. He smelled like it, too.

Rod was followed by Ike Ludlow and Maze Chasby, the Reverend's boy, who took a seat at a round table near the door.

Jacob watched Chasby with special wariness—him, a likely saboteur. Jacob saw the Reverend's work everywhere now, a black mold spreading with the help of John Donovan's admiration. The boy looked pale and sick like his father, though they were of no blood relation.

"And work means we got spending money," Rod added, eyeing Jacob with that sideways look that was uniquely his, half a threat and half a jest. "And with spending money in our pockets, well, we started to miss you, Jake old boy."

Jacob smiled even though he hated when people called him Jake— much less "Jake old boy"—especially scoundrels like Rod. It was the kind of usurpation John would make.

Ike took an enormous bite off a plug of chew. Jacob turned to him and reminded him of the location of the nearest cuspidor. Ike grumbled but fetched it to the table. They were like children, these boys.

"I'm glad you thought of me," Jacob said, turning back to Rod. It took the better part of his acting ability to keep his grin from curdling. "Now what can I do you for?"

"We'll take yer finest Kentucky bourbon," Rod said. He removed his hat and smiled, oily as a grease slick.

Jacob lifted his brows in surprise. "You *have* come into a little money then, haven't you? Well, I'm sorry to say we're clean out of the good stuff on account of the drys. They sabotaged the last shipment on its way from the station, the scoundrels."

Rod looked aghast. "Sinful to waste spirits, especially good spirits." He shook his head. "Drys y'say?"

"That's right," Jacob mused. "I've seen a lot of things in Three Chop over the years, but nothing like these so-called Prohibitionists. They'll put us all out of business if they have their way. Like they don't know where the money comes from in this town."

"An' the Sheriff didn't have nothin' to say about them smashing yer liquor up?" Rod asked.

"He's one of them, by God!" Jacob said. "Hasn't been around here in months, and he's made fast friends with that Reverend. I've seen their like before, as a boy when they came for my daddy. We had no sheriff on the river—Mississippi was the West then—but he showed them how a Moreau responds to a threat with a threat of his own in the form of a shotgun." Jacob raised his shotgun from behind the bar, as much a warning to Rod and company as a prop in his reminiscence.

Rod whistled flatly.

Chasby fidgeted in his chair.

"Well, Chaz," Rod said, looking at the boy. "You can raise that issue, too, with the Reverend hisself, when you see him."

Rod turned back to Jacob, his grin mocking. "Chaz here has it in mind to confront his daddy about his daddy. His blood daddy."

"Oh?"

"Say, you know anything about Chaz's daddy?" Rod asked.

Jacob thought about it. He had a hazy memory of the man, but then again, he had hazy memories of a good ten thousand men who had passed through town. He remembered that the man had looked a lot like Chasby did now, though he had been older, and he had worn wire-frame glasses. He said so.

Chasby listened greedily.

"Glasses, huh?" Ike said. "Guess you can count on goin' blind, then." He laughed.

"He came around the saloon one day," Jacob said, ignoring Ike. "He pleaded at first, then got angry, stomped around the room, harangued folk to join his posse. No one did. Those were peaceful times. The start of them, anyway, and folk didn't want a part of it."

Chasby looked at his lap.

Jacob waited for him to say something, but it was Rod who broke the silence.

"Well you know we ain't picky, Jake," he prompted, giving Jacob a significant look as he dropped two bits on the bar top. "We'll take whatever you got."

"Hell," he added, jingling his pockets. "Keep 'em coming. We're celebratin'."

"What's the occasion?" Jacob asked, pulling gently at his cuffs.

"Chasby here is three days sober!" Ike called from the table, slapping Chasby on the back. "Had a fit an' poured his liquor out and regretted it the whole way here."

Jacob took a second look at the boy's paleness and at the trembling of his hands. "And here I thought his hands only shook when he played cards," he said.

Everyone laughed but Chasby.

Jacob poured three generous shots from a cloudy jar—River Water, the old family recipe. He always made the first pour generous.

"We got just the thing fer the shakes, don't we?" Rod said, winking at Jacob and picking up the glasses. "Time fer a shot of what ails ya."

"Say," Ike called from the table after he sat down. "Did them drys chase off all yer customers, too? This place is dead as an old boot."

"Girls don't come down 'til evening," Jacob reminded him. "'Til then Haddock and I'll have to do."

Hearing his name, Haddock stuck his head up from the piano where he was fixing a broken key. He gave Jacob an inscrutable look. Haddock detested Rod and Ike. Chasby was no good either on account of his association with the unreconstructed Reverend.

Jacob had nearly committed murder when, just last week, Haddock had come home bruised and bloody to tell him he had been attacked in the street by drys. Jacob had been on his way to the door—not with a shotgun but with his father's old dueling pistols—when Haddock put a restraining hand on his shoulder. Jacob could have easily pushed past the man, lame as he was, but that was part of their understanding, that Jacob treated him as a man whole, that he would not have his way by bowling him over. Haddock had counseled him to channel his rage into a campaign for mayor.

Haddock took his seat at the piano and played a few tentative scales, testing his handiwork. He had filled the *Lady May* with music every night for two decades, playing the sun to sleep and coaxing it to rise.

It was music that had first brought Haddock into his life, when Jacob was a much younger man at work on his father's riverboat. Haddock had appeared at the door between two hard-faced men—foremen from the Dunheep plantation—who had carried as much as escorted him there. Haddock's foot had been heavily bandaged then and could not bear weight. Jacob would learn later it had been brutally amputated, punishment for a third-time runaway. Haddock might have died of neglect, a broken farming implement left to molder, if his master had not discovered his talent for the piano. Jacob's father paid the master a good wage for Haddock's services. How could he have known his own son would fall in love? How could a man like his father comprehend such a possibility?

The pair had fled together as soon as Haddock's foot had healed enough to stand in a cinched stirrup, fled west to the freedom of that limitless frontier. For twenty years Three Chop had been a refuge, though they maintained the flimsy pretext of being half brothers. But now? For all his bluster, Jacob's lip trembled as he thought of the stone that had torn Haddock's shirt and bloodied his back. No one knew who had thrown it, and yet everyone did.

Jacob was still deep in thought when the stranger entered.

For a moment he was struck dumb by the man's appearance. He was young, a boy almost, and tall with one of the most handsome faces Jacob had ever seen—strong and angular like it was cut from stone. But the most striking feature of all was the color of his eyes—pale blue like the silver of the moon. The man's presence so overwhelmed Jacob that he barely noticed the six-shooters hanging at his hips.

The stranger looked around the saloon, ignoring the eyes of the men at the table by the door with easy unconcern. He nodded at no one in particular then sauntered toward Jacob.

"Howdy," Jacob greeted, twisting one end of his waxed mustache.

The stranger touched the brim of his brown slouch hat as he sat and ordered a bourbon.

"Haven't got bourbon," Jacob said ruefully.

The man shrugged. "Whatever you got then."

Jacob commenced pouring a slug of the ubiquitous family recipe. "What's your name, friend?" he asked as he set the glass before the stranger. "I'm Jacob."

The man took the shot and laid down a silver dollar, ignoring the question. "You got a cigar?"

"Sure." Jacob produced a five-cent Stinko and handed over a book of matches.

Jacob judged the man no more than twenty. *A cowpuncher?* He certainly dressed the part in dungarees and chaps and a brown vest. It was not unusual for one of the few cowpunchers on the remaining ranches to come to town on occasion, except they were usually paid at the end of the month.

"Welcome to the *Lady May*," Jacob said. "She's the best saloon in two hundred miles. That liquor's my own recipe, and the girls—they'll be down later—they're chosen by none but my own eye." He tapped his temple knowingly. "The prettiest in Texas."

"Best saloon?" the man said lazily. "Only saloon." He looked down the bar. "Keep 'em coming."

"Why, others have tried—they just can't seem to stay in business if they're within two days' ride of the *Lady*," Jacob boasted, pouring the man another shot.

The stranger lit his cigar.

The trio at the table by the door could not disguise their interest. They had seen the flash of silver.

"Most towns I seen this size have a dozen saloons." The man pulled deeply on the cigar so the coal burned orange.

Jacob nodded sagely. "You've got a sharp eye, friend. There were a few others here not five years back—but times are changing, and it turns out some folks don't appreciate this particular line of business. Politics, you know. Sin tax and the like. The better the sin, the higher the tax."

The man closed himself off then, but Jacob kept talking.

"You got a place to stay?" he asked. "I only ask because I've got rooms to let. That hotel by Peabody's restaurant is mine, too."

"I got a room already," the stranger said, looking back at Jacob. "Is that Peabody's any good?"

"Good enough. Of course, I have food here, and folks say it's better. If you stay long enough, there's a good time to be had at the dance hall Friday night. That's mine, too—"

"I'm just passing through," the stranger said peremptorily.

"Sure, sure," Jacob nodded. "Most people are."

The man tapped the rim of his glass for another slug.

Jacob could see from his eyes that the liquor was starting to loosen him. The narrowness had gone, the suspicion.

"This is some queer whiskey you got," the stranger remarked. "What'd you say the name of it was?"

"My daddy called it River Water. He had a saloon himself—where I was born and raised—a riverboat on the Mississippi near Vicksburg."

The man nodded knowingly like he had figured as much. "The *Lady May*, I reckon?"

Jacob grinned. "Indeed it was."

The man nodded again and was silent. After a few sips of River Water, he said, "Say, when's it get busy in here?"

"Busy enough for a game of cards?" Jacob asked, following his gaze, which had lit upon the felt-topped tables in the back of the bar.

The man shrugged, but his interest was clear enough.

"It'll be crowded by seven," Jacob answered.

Across the room a chair scraped.

"No need to wait if it's cards yer interested in," Rod interjected, standing. He ambled to the bar, proffering his hand. "Rod Turner," he said, "and sitting over there is Ike and Chasby."

The stranger took the hand warily, eyeing the men openly for the first time, but he said nothing

"What'd you say your name was?" Rod asked, flashing a candid smile. "I didn't."

Rod's smile guttered briefly. "Well we cain't play cards with a man if we don't know his name."

Ike was walking to the bar now, too.

Jacob watched the stranger's eyes flick from one man's face to the other, then to the guns at their hips.

"You can trust us," Ike put in. "Chasby here is a preacher's boy—honest as can be."

"Sal," the stranger said finally.

"Sal? You I-talian?" Ike asked.

"No," Sal said. "Sal for Salamander."

"Like the lizard?"

Sal nodded.

"That's a funny name," Ike said, scratching his chin thoughtfully.

"Oh, I've heard stranger," Jacob put in, trying to soften Ike's rudeness. "Haddock over there is named for a fish."

Sal looked at the pianist but made no reply. "Stud?" he asked.

"Sure," Rod said, accommodating.

Jacob handed Rod a card press, which he took to one of the green-felted tables.

"Don't forget the spittoon," Jacob called after Ike.

CHAPTER 10

Donovan

DONOVAN SAT ON THE PORCH OUTSIDE THE JAILHOUSE, HIS HEADQUARTERS, smoking a loosely rolled cigarette.

At two hours past sunset, Front Street lay quiet and mostly dark.

The only light shone in pools on the street, cast from the homes that dotted Front, old homes, the homes of Three Chop's first residents—and of course from the saloon, festooned, a ball of light like a Christmas tree reaching three stories into the night sky.

A group of children hurtled out of an alley and onto Front, squealing as they chased one another in the darkness. Someone knocked over a pail with a clatter, and, seeing Donovan on the jailhouse porch, shrieked and ducked into the shadow of the alley.

Donovan smiled as he drew on his cigarette, thinking of his own boys, who had been fast and strong. It was a cruel God who would fell those boys, no matter what Aaron might say about a plan or about paradise in death—his rant about Heaven and Hell being one place notwithstanding. Cruel for no other reason than it robbed their mother. Donovan was sure it was grief that had killed Missy.

Missy was many women in Donovan's mind now, many women at once. She was the young Missy he had met in Doc Marshall's infirmary, the nurse who had brought him from the threshold of death in slow increments after Nash Warrick's bullet tore through his side to lodge in his back.

When the pain in his back had first begun, Donvoan thought it was the old ache of that bullet wound—they had not been able to remove all the fragments. Maybe he still did think it, despite Doc Marshall's

59

diagnosis. Or maybe it was both, and those fragments like seeds had blossomed into something else: Nash Warrick's slow revenge.

The young Missy was beautiful with blonde hair and delicate features, lithe and somehow fragile, alluring. What madness had overtaken him, that he would break his engagement to Annabel? Was it captivity? The gentleness of Missy's touch as she changed his dressings? Her easy laugh? It was effervescent, that laugh, which like effervescence would dissipate with time, though he could not have known it then.

Missy was an older, more angular woman in his mind, too, the one who wasted away after the boys died, the boys whose names Donovan still had trouble mentioning, even in his thoughts, though sometimes they came to him in his dreams. She had withered before his eyes, and he had felt bitterness grow in him, because he knew then what he had long suspected—that without the boys they meant nothing to one another, that Missy would as well have died as stayed with him, and die she did.

"I oughtta put a bullet between Doc Marshall's eyes," Donovan mumbled between cigarette puffs, wondering for a moment if the good doctor should not have let him bleed out in his bed twenty years ago. Yet still Donovan clung to life, and he had begged the same doctor to save him all over again. He was desperate to stave off the same death Missy had embraced, even if that meant throwing in his lot with the Reverend. *Maybe she was stronger than I am after all?*

He watched the smoke drift and swirl in the lantern light, slave to the slightest current of air, wondering if he would see Missy again when he died, wondering if that was not half the reason he was trying to put it off.

Just then Donovan's deputy, Mance Richardson, stepped out of the jailhouse and onto the porch. He was a thin man but strong as if the fat of his body had been rendered away and left behind nothing but bone and knotted sinew.

"Mance," Donovan said, nodding, his mind only half retreated from remembrance.

Mance touched the brim of his hat. "Mr. Sheriff. How're you keepin'?"

"Oh, I'm alright," Donovan murmured, removing the cigarette from his mouth.

Mance had once been a Texas Ranger of some renown. He had been forced to retire after receiving a wound in a shoot-out with Samuel Moose, the infamous bank robber and kidnapper. The wound had festered, and Mance had lost his left leg below the knee.

A shame to survive the war intact only to lose a limb to a man like Moose. Mance was a Tennessean, so he spoke like a Southerner, but he had left his state to fight for the Union, which was a strong sign of character in Donovan's estimation.

Now he wore a wooden peg in place of his shin but fared little worse for it. It was a badge of honor for him. He had the left leg of his jeans cut short and hemmed so the peg showed neatly, and he still wore Samuel Moose's own gun, Dewlap, slung around his hip, a heavy 0.44 caliber Remington.

"You get the envelope I laid out for you?" Donovan asked.

"Yes sir," Mance said, patting his pocket. "No day like payday," He began rolling a cigarette of his own, tapping a fine dust of tobacco from his pouch.

"On your way to see Minnie, then?" Donovan asked.

Mance grinned. "Might be. Then again I hear Jacob's got himself a new girl, an exotic one with blonde hair."

"Careful you don't make Minnie jealous."

"I reckon in her line of work, that's somethin' she's got to learn to live with." Mance grinned again. "Did you see the new wanted poster?" he asked, striking a match on his wooden leg to light his cigarette. "It came in on the three o'clock. On account of that train robbery in Colorado. Bloody business—half a dozen dead—outlaws and Rangers alike."

Donovan grunted. "I've never seen two pictures of Jack Holloway that look alike."

"Dark eyes at least," Mance put in.

"Yeah. Dark eyes, broad face. Could be any working man in these United States as far as I can tell."

"Well, I don't reckon it'll fall to us to spot him," Mance said, a little regretfully. "Papers speculatin' he's probably in Mexico by now." Unconsciously, Mance touched Dewlap's grip like it was some great talisman.

"Imagine that? Mexico with half a million dollars in yer pocket. By God, you could buy yerself the whole Yucker-tan."

Donovan spit, grinned. "Mines are like railroads and whorehouses: You can't hardly build one without bribing someone to license the shovel and someone else to inspect the dirt. No doubt there was a lot of money on that train."

Mance stubbed his cigarette out on the doorframe. "Well, business is business, I guess. Never had a head for it myself."

Donovan grunted. He did not feel talkative.

Mance sensed his boss's mood and said, "Well, I reckon I'll head out unless you need me, Sheriff."

Donovan nodded, crushing his own spent cigarette beneath the heel of his boot, leaving a dark smear on the porch. "Try not to spend all your money in one place."

Mance grinned and started to hop-step toward the saloon.

"Hey, peg leg!" one of the kids called from the safety of an alley.

Laughter pealed and echoed off stores and houses.

Donovan watched Mance recede wraithlike into the darkness, appearing briefly again in the warm embrace of the saloon light like a swimmer come up for air. And just like that Donovan found himself alone again with his thoughts, contemplating the solitude of the street without even the company of a cigarette. Loneliness pressed upon him. Or was it impotence?

The ghost of Missy sat beside him. Maybe she had always been there. But he would not look at her.

Donovan's skin prickled. He swore. He stood. Before he knew what he was doing, he was on his way to the church.

Chapter 11

Kat

Kat paused on the landing, the yellow silk of her dress settling around her, clinging, assuming her shape. Her heart fluttered.

The first night is always hardest, she told herself.

She willed herself down the back stair, following the thick red carpet as it cascaded into the yellow brightness of the saloon.

The roar of conversation was overwhelming, and what few spaces there were between words, the black piano man filled with a raucous, jangling tune.

So many people! I've come a long way from Reggie's! She put the man out of her mind as quickly as he had come, lest Vern follow. She banished him to the depths of the blackness, which she had folded into a corner of her mind.

Kat forced a smile as she moved into the crowd, walking with an easy grace assumed by long practice. It was the same way she had walked the streets of San Francisco, trailing her mother, wearing dignity around her like a cape even as she entered Señor Alvarez's house through the servants' gate.

The crowd parted before her, and she walked freely. She started to worry she would pass through it and out the other side, that for all the stares she would fail to catch someone's eye and hold it.

Then a man said admiringly, "Well look-y here."

Kat turned. The man sat in a chair at one of the tables. His visage was bland, unremarkable. But he wore a badge on his vest and a heavy gun on his hip. And, as she moved toward him, she noticed he had a peg for a leg.

Revulsion was her first instinct. But it fled quickly, replaced by sympathy for broken things and then by the firm resolve of her profession.

"Hello," she said when she stood before him, the yellow silk still clinging.

"Howdy," the lawman said. "You must be the new girl."

Kat nodded, her blonde curls bouncing. "Kat," she said softly. The men around her pressed closer, taking courage from the lawman.

"Mance," he said seriously. Then he looked at the men around them and smiled like they all shared a secret. He held out his hand to Kat.

Kat took it, feeling the bony, sinewed strength of it. Then suddenly he pulled her onto his lap, twirling her deftly as she fell so that she landed, sitting, on the thigh of his good leg.

The men around them whooped, and the women rolled their eyes, turned, used to the antics.

"Welcome to Three Chop, Kat!" Mance cried, raising his mug. Beer spilled down the sides, darkening the yellow of her dress.

Kat glanced again at his badge. "Why thank you, Mr. Sheriff," she said with feigned breathlessness. She straightened the lawman's hat for him. "It's a pleasure to meet you."

"He ain't sheriff yet!" said a man with a floating eye.

Mance nodded. "Deputy Mance, ma'am. As for sheriff, I'll take my time on that. Who could hope to fill Donovan's shoes?" Mance lifted his peg leg then, and the men around them shared a thigh-slapping laugh.

The man with the floating eye added, "And you'd not find Donovan in the saloon these days, besides."

Several men grumbled at this, like it was an abdication or betrayal.

"He sends his deputy to do the dirty work, then?" Kat asked, trailing a finger down the front of Mance's shirt.

His cheeks turned pink, and the men exchanged sly looks as if to say, "There's our boy."

Kat felt herself loosening. The men in Three Chop were not so different from the men in San Pablo or San Francisco. Maybe they were not so different the world over. Simple creatures all.

But before Kat could say another word, a quiet came upon the group, and Mance abruptly pushed her off his lap.

She gasped and stumbled, nearly falling over the hem of her dress. As she straightened, Kat found herself looking into the eyes of a taller woman. They were haughty eyes, appraising eyes, though maybe beneath it all there was something of mirth. Kat recognized the woman as another one of the madam's. She had long strawberry hair that fell below her shoulders.

"Minnie," Mance said, standing hastily. The other men averted their eyes to avoid being perceived as co-conspirators, though most still had an ear turned toward Mance and the woman.

"Mance," Minnie said icily, though her lip curled in the beginnings of a grin that was not quite a sneer. "I see you've met our newest girl." The woman's inflection made "newest" sound like a curse. Kat took it to mean youngest, prettiest.

"Kat, err, yes," Mance stammered. "Said hello is all. Formally welcomed her to Three Chop."

Minnie nodded, her eyes holding Kat's.

A heat rose in Kat's cheeks. In San Pablo she had learned how difficult the girls could make her life if she provoked their anger or jealousy. Worst of all they could shun her, close her out, make her into a thing apart, alien even in this fringe, a margin of margins, liminal.

It's too soon for this, she scolded herself, even as her pride made her hold Minnie's gaze.

"It is nice to make your acquaintance, deputy," she said, swallowing, making half a curtsy.

She felt Minnie's eyes on her back when she turned.

She walked sedate through the crowd, her earlier fears realized. Despite a few lingering looks, she reached the edge of the room without a word from anyone. Even in that crowded space, she was alone.

Kat pretended to look at one of the paintings on the wall, a riverboat as white and clean as new sheets. She studied it until she thought she had made a reasonable show of genuine interest. Then she turned and made her way back to the bar, passing unobstructed as a ghost.

CHAPTER 12

Donovan

DONOVAN GRIT HIS TEETH AND THREW OPEN THE SALOON DOOR. IT swung wide, hit the backstop with a thud, and juddered in place with brittle applause.

Clouds of cigar smoke billowed in greeting, and a wash of raucous voices swept over him. There must have been over a hundred bodies packed inside—sitting, standing, leaning, draping; eating, drinking, gambling. Most he recognized as townfolk, but there were many he did not— strangers arrived by wagon, horse, and rail to pour wealth into the saloon and the rest of the town.

Haddock Beauvoir, Jacob's supposed half brother, sat at the piano, deftly hammering the keys as he had every night since civilization had been birthed upon this patch of plain.

Behind Donovan, arrayed silent yet durable, stood twelve of Aaron's congregants, brought freshly from the church, hats in hands, respectful yet wary.

Donovan exchanged an uncompromising stare with Jacob, who stood behind the bar, his presence commanding the room like a ship captain's. All the splendor, the frivolous gaiety of the occasion, seemed to ebb in that stare, and for a moment Donovan wondered if here, now, the thing would be settled in blood.

But Jacob only nodded stiffly. It was no kind of welcome, nothing more than a gesture of allowance—*as if the choice was his to shut me out!*— before he returned to the business of depositing that steady stream of silver in his till.

The rest of the room did not return so easily to revelry. Though the noise resumed by degrees, Donovan and his followers suffered the pummeling of mistrustful glances, even from the whores, who lifted their chins and threw their festooned heads.

Donovan forced himself out of that twilit mindscape of reminiscence and worry—he had been living there near full-time the last few weeks—and put on a magnanimous grin. He grabbed a beer from a passing whore, flipped her a bit, and plowed into the crowd in search of friendly hands to shake. He was vaguely aware of the men behind him doing likewise, theirs the charm of the salt of the earth, which he had bade them spread about the room. What better way to strengthen his position than to show the town that the farmers were men just like them? What better way to get them the vote?

He had, of course, left Loeb behind—he was a committed dry besides.

As Donovan worked the room, he noticed the entire town council was in attendance—even Doc Marshall, who had left Three Chop earlier that morning on some doctor's errand. The man stood in a circle with Annabel, Sallie, Todd, and other like-minded townfolk.

Everyone is here. The whole town is here.

He knew then just how big a mistake he had made in foregoing regular visits to the saloon. No matter how tired he was, how much his back ached, he could not cede this territory to Jacob. *Not as long as it remains open, anyway*, a voice in his head whispered. *Aaron's?*

Donovan took another draught of beer.

Mayor Cordell sat at his usual table with the usual company—Stuart Lassiter, Marvin Stepshaw, and Rascal Remington, the ever-present notepad sticking out of the newspaperman's jacket pocket, a pencil tucked behind his ear.

"Mr. Sheriff!" Stepshaw bellowed, standing. He raised his glass and said, "A drink to your health!" Then he turned his mug to the ceiling and finished his beer in three monstrous gulps.

Rascal followed suit, spilling as much beer on his collar as he got in his mouth.

Donovan nodded and grinned but did not approach the table. He had not come to ingratiate his friends.

It took half an hour of hand shaking and pleasantries before Donovan worked his way to the back of the barroom where the gamblers played. Stud was the game of choice that night. Men had gathered around the card tables like spectators at a bear baiting. He pushed his way through three rows of rapt faces to find a familiar but unexpected trio playing cards. He tried to hide his surprise when he saw the money piled on the table—it must have been a thousand dollars.

"Fellas," Donovan said, meeting eyes with Rod and Ike before he let his gaze linger on Chasby. "It's been a while." He wondered if the Reverend knew his boy was back in town. Chasby's face was sallow, waxy, yet still darkly handsome.

The three men returned perfunctory greetings, but the cards had clearly soured their moods. Most of the money on the table was piled before a fourth man—a boy, nearly—whom Donovan did not recognize.

Donovan eyed the boy, the stranger. He had a roguish look with a broad chin and the palest blue eyes Donovan had ever seen.

A cardsharp? A shootist?

The boy looked up when he heard Chasby and the other Three Chop men greet Donovan as "Sheriff."

"What's your name, son?" Donovan asked, noting the six-shooters at the boy's hips. He did not relish seeing a stranger take money from his townspeople, especially from ones so volatile. *Should've forced that penny stakes law through council last year . . .*

"Name's Sal," the boy muttered.

Donovan touched his chin thoughtfully. "Sal," he repeated, like he was testing the weight of it. "That's a lot of silver, Sal."

"It is, and uneven, ain't it?" Rod cut in with a sneer. "Cards are runnin' lucky tonight—for some."

Sal said nothing. Donovan saw his right hand rested near his holster, though his eyes stayed on the table, on the silver.

"Where're you from, Sal?"

"From down the line."

"Down the line, huh?" Donovan mused. "Sal from down the line. I've known a few folk from down the line. They have a way of causing trouble. You aren't planning to cause trouble, are you, Sal?"

"No mind to. Just playing cards. Can't help if I'm winning."

Rod grunted.

Donovan nodded. "That's good. And don't mind these three." He winked at Rod, though the gesture held no mirth or conspiracy. "They're old friends of mine. They won't cause trouble. Now you boys enjoy your game. And remember, the Sheriff and his deputy are both here if you need us."

"Why don't you deal 'em again," Sal said to Rod as if he had not heard Donovan's warning, though Donovan saw the boy's eyes flick about the room in search of the unknown deputy.

In truth his whereabouts were equally unknown to Donovan, who had seen Mance sometime earlier with Minnie in his lap, though she had been in a state of undress that led Donovan to believe they might not have lasted long in the main room.

Rod looked at his cards, then at Ike, who shrugged. Chasby had already folded. "Alright," Rod said, throwing down his cards. "Didn't have a hand anyway."

"Gentlemen," Donovan said, touching the brim of his hat. He saved a parting look for Chasby.

Donovan had not come to bicker over cards. This night was about politics, about being seen, and it was time for the main event. He was not sure what he would say—so far the night had been wholly ad-libbed, the product of a stray thought on the jailhouse porch—but he was sure that whatever he said, his words would be overheard, shared, remembered.

It was a campaign.

"What's a man got to do to get a drink around here?" Donovan asked good-naturedly, as he came upon the bar.

"Evening, John," Jacob said. He was in the process of pouring a dozen liquor shots. "Gimme a minute here." He finished the pour, stoppering the bottle with nary a drop spilled. He handed the tray to the madam, saying, "To our friends at the card table."

Fuel to the fire, Donovan grimaced, but he let it go.

The madam glided out from behind the bar, passing Donovan with an overwhelming smell of perfume. *She still smells like a whore*, he thought, nearly coughing. In the old days, the madam had been Jacob's first girl.

Apparently her toilette had not changed with her station. She gave Donovan a smile that he could only interpret as a flirtation, though her age made the gesture grotesque. *And yet she's probably younger than I . . .*

"Beer," Donovan said, fishing in his pocket for the requisite silver.

"Beer?" Jacob said, wiping down the bar then coming to Donovan. He looked him in the eye. "Beer won't suffice. Not on a night like this—not when the Sheriff has come for the first time in . . . how long? Has it been a year?"

A crowd began to coalesce around the men, who stood only feet apart, separated by the width of the bar top, the barrier somehow drawing them into closer proximity than was customary.

Donovan could see the fissures of Jacob's skin, the age spots revealed where runnels of sweat had carved trails in his makeup. "You exaggerate, Jake," he said, his smile fixed. "Time gets away from old men like us, but not as fast as that."

Jacob shrugged and, by way of response, placed two tumblers on the bar top, followed by two generous pours of whiskey. He slid one toward Donovan and took the other in hand. "River Water. My daddy's recipe." He took a sip then ran his tongue along his teeth in reminiscence. "He was a political man, my daddy. But he always said politics should never come between friends."

"Your daddy sounds like a wiser man than mine," Donovan said. "When my daddy politicked back in New York, he had a saying, 'Don't hit a man if you can avoid it, but if you hit him, you hit him hard.' He made no allowances for friends—at least none he ever told me."

The men and women around Donovan laughed, and he heard a few cries of "hear, hear, Sheriff."

Jacob nodded, raising his glass and saying, "To Three Chop, then, old friend."

Donovan took his own glass in hand, hesitating. For a sheriff, everything was a statement of allegiances. He knew his companions, the Reverend's congregants, were watching him, though he had been careful to choose moderate men, if such could be said to exist. What would they report to the Reverend? How would the Reverend respond? And what of the townfolk surrounding him now?

Donovan's independence won out. *To hell with the Reverend.* He raised his glass beside Jacob's. He had done enough of the Reverend's bidding to satisfy the man, surely.

"To Three Chop," Donovan agreed. He knocked the shot back, feeling suddenly like a younger man. The whiskey burned his throat, and his eyes watered. The old family recipe was as Donovan remembered—caustic.

Jacob refilled the glasses.

The onlookers pressed closer, some even migrating from the card game to gather around Donovan and Jacob.

Jacob raised his glass again. "And to a fair and free election," he said, putting the glass to his lips and throwing his head back.

This time Donovan only nodded.

A dozen arms raised to drink with him as he took his second shot. The sting was not so bad this time.

Again Jacob filled the glasses. "And to the drys!"

Accustomed to the rhythm of the ritual, Donovan had raised his glass automatically, only to stop when he heard Jacob's words.

The onlookers muttered, some cursing, some snickering. Several jeered. Like Donovan, half still held their drinks before them, halted in the midst of a toast. The other half had already downed their liquor, swindled into toasting their own bad luck.

"What's the matter, Donovan? You won't toast the drys?" Jacob asked, his face a parody of confusion.

"Is this how you politic, Jacob? By ambush?" Donovan asked. He drank down his whiskey in one great gulp, offering a belated toast, "To a fair and *friendly* election!" Tears welled in his eyes, and his head began to swim. He tried to measure the impact of his words on the crowd, but the half who had refrained from toasting the drys had lowered their glasses, expectant. He drank alone.

"You won't toast the drys, then," Jacob said, as if working something out for himself. He stroked his weak chin, which gave the appearance of receding like his hair, of fleeing his preposterous moustache. "But you'll take their votes, sure enough." The barkeep refilled their glasses a fourth time.

It was a challenge—those words, the whiskey in those glasses. The lamplight reflected something sinister in Jacob's eyes. All pretense of friendship had fled.

"You forget, Jacob, that I'm not running for mayor."

"Ha!" Jacob raised his glass. "Would that you weren't!" He finished his shot and poured another.

It made Donovan look weak, he knew, but he dared not take another swig. His head already swam. Besides, was moderation not, after all, the onetime meaning of temperance?

"Have you told them about your petition, Sheriff?" Jacob asked, nodding to the crowd. "It may not be your name on the ballot, but we'll see who believes it's not you who's running after all."

Donovan froze. It took him a moment to understand fully what Jacob had said, what breech of conduct he had made in discussing openly the business of council. He tried to compose himself. "Not my petition, Jacob. The farmers' petition. You'd do well to recognize the difference."

A wry grin split Jacob's face, his moustache raised in a snarl. "You haven't told them, I take it? I suppose it falls to me then." Even as he spoke Jacob levered himself atop his bar, untying his apron and throwing it to the ground like a gauntlet.

How easily the faithless man broke his vow of discretion, trampling years of council precedent!

Donovan seethed, craning his neck to meet Jacob's eye. For a moment he considered climbing atop the bar himself, but he thought the effort might double him over. *Or worse, make me fall like Cordell. Stumble, fumble, tumble.*

"Only yesterday," Jacob began, wiping his forehead with a silk kerchief, "Donovan presented the council—no, *surprised* the council, *ambushed* the council—with a petition to give every man in the county a vote for mayor!"

Collectively, the crowd gasped, shocked at first, then angry.

Donovan dared not look behind him.

"He calls it the farmers' petition," Jacob continued. "But make no mistake—it's his petition! Who profits by letting the farmers vote in town elections? By letting the *drys* vote in town elections?"

Angry voices swirled. The crowd began to seethe and jostle.

Donovan wondered if some of the men around him were not putting elbows in his back on purpose.

Jacob whipsawed them into a frenzy. The piano could barely be heard above the rising din of voices—no, it had stopped entirely, Donovan realized.

"Outrageous!"

"A travesty!"

"A gift to the drys!"

Jacob's face was comically grim, filled with a self-righteous indignation.

Suddenly the Reverend's haste to close the saloon did not seem so ill-conceived after all. Who could afford to give this man a pulpit of his own?

Like a master actor, Jacob let the emotion of the crowd play out, let it froth to a peak, then raised his finger in the air to deliver his peroration. "And all the while he would have us believe that he's just a diligent lawman, unaware of the politics in town. Well I propose this to you, Mr. Sheriff." Jacob turned to Donovan, letting loose a sickening rictus. "We've got the council in attendance. We've got a *quorum*. There's no need to wait for the council meeting—I say we have the vote now, so the townfolk can see firsthand who bears their interests in mind!"

Donovan had not thought it possible, but the crowd grew louder still. Whistles and cheers split the air, spinning around Jacob like a dervish as if to bear him up to the rafters. And for his part Jacob looked triumphant, pink faced and gleeful, his moustache aquiver.

Of course, Donovan knew what Jacob did not—that the gambit would fail—for he had made an arrangement with Annabel. He knew she would vote in favor of the petition, as long as she kept her nerve amid the hectoring, the antagonism of the crowd. He set his jaw. *But at what cost? How will the churchmen react?*

"Todd Waiverly," Jacob intoned. "How do you vote on the Sheriff's petition?"

Todd's glower confirmed that Jacob's transgression, his lack of propriety, of decorum, was no conspiracy. The man shifted uncomfortably in the limelight, looking from his companions to Donovan to Jacob but avoiding the eyes of the crowd. He cleared his throat and said, "I vote nay, if a vote's to be had." His voice was slurred. He took a draught from his mug, a white froth of beer clinging to the black of his beard.

"Nay!" Jacob repeated, his finger thrust into the air. He wiped his brow with his kerchief, exaggerating his movements like a stage performer. The crowd shouted approbation, their confidence in the outcome of the vote beginning to mirror Jacob's own.

"Doc Marshall?" Jacob asked, turning to that white and wizened physician.

The doctor blinked unhappily behind his spectacles, but he answered all the same. "Nay, of course," he said quietly, refusing to shout.

"Another nay!" Jacob cried, tallying the votes on his hand. "And my own makes three."

Jacob turned to Cordell's table then, where the mayoral party was standing in spite of their usual lassitude. "And what of our illustrious Mayor Cordell? How does he vote?"

"I vote yes!" Cordell bellowed. "Yes, yes, yes!" The crowd hissed and jeered, but Cordell's still-strong voice carried above them. "The farmers are no less a part of this town than the rest, and their voices deserve to be heard!"

"Here, here!" Stuart cried, preempting Jacob's roll call. "For the good of the town!"

"Me three!" added Marvin Stepshaw.

"There you have it!" Jacob said, grabbing a handful of his receding hair in consternation. "Three for and three against. Now you see how precariously your rights hang in this town, how close you are to being overrun!"

Jacob turned to Annabel then, along with the rest of the crowd, turned to that even temperament, to that serene beauty. The crowd turned with confidence and anticipation.

Donovan watched Annabel return that confidence. Unlike the others, she looked to the crowd, met their eyes, and she did not flinch. In the quiet that followed, in the space of heartbeats, Donovan felt his power stretched as thin as it had ever been since he faced down Nash Warrick for the soul of Three Chop. A single word from Annabel would either spare it or sever it.

Annabel saved her last look for him. In that moment she might have been the only other person in the room, on the planet. But he could read nothing in her face. Donovan held his breath like the rest.

"I vote yes," she said finally, firmly. "I vote yes."

Jacob's color blanched, shock and disbelief extinguishing the fiery aura of his triumph. Maybe he thought he had misheard.

The crowd remained hushed, too, subsumed by shock—men and women muttering and shifting and looking to one another with uncertainty.

"What?"

"I don't understand."

"Why, Annabel?"

It was quiet enough that Donovan could make out the clink of silver at the card tables. Even Haddock sat agape.

For their part, the mayor and his coterie looked just as surprised as everyone else. Rascal's hand had frozen halfway to the pencil behind his ear, eyebrows climbing his forehead.

Only the farmfolk looked unruffled. The farmfolk and Annabel. Donovan found himself smiling. She had held firm.

Jacob was the first to recover his wits. "What womanly frailty has brought you to this calamity?" he cried, half a question and half a scream. To the crowd, "What has she done? She's ruined us!"

Annabel gasped, then put the insult aside like a grasping child, vaulting herself atop the bar beside Jacob. Her acrobatics shocked the crowd into silence.

Still she raised her voice until veins stood out upon her neck. "I vote yes, because it has been agreed that, in addition to extending the town vote to the rest of the county, the farmers' petition will be amended to extend the vote to the *women* of the town *and* county, beginning with this mayoral election!"

The room was turned on its head then, and everyone began to speak at once. Townswomen who had been aghast moments before now flushed with pride, confusing their menfolk who were not sure whether to rail or to congratulate or what the ramifications of either might be. Jacob's girls cheered, whistling and spilling beer, and that gave pause to the townswomen, who had not considered that it would be extended to all classes of women. The farmers who had been so satisfied before now looked doubly uncertain, and the council members, save Annabel, were unanimous for the first time in years in their disbelief.

"Bribery!" Jacob railed. "These two have conspired to steal an election! These councilors didn't even know what they were voting for! Look at them!" Jacob held out his arms to the council's two factions. "They are as confused as the rest of us! This is not democracy! This is not a free and fair election!"

Haddock rose ominously from the piano. He must have sensed the sudden danger as surely as Donovan did.

Where before it had been disorganized, inchoate, the men's anger began to coalesce. Suddenly Donovan felt unsafe, unsafe in his own town! He searched for Mance but saw no sign of his deputy or of Minnie. All the while the crowd grew more restless, their discontent fed by Jacob's harangue.

"Annabel was not even elected to her post!" Jacob cried. "She inherited it from her husband! And she calls this democracy!"

Donovan raised his hands for silence, for calm, but the gesture was ignored. He no longer wondered if the elbows buffeting him were intentional or not. He started to head to Annabel, but the crowd would not let him. No one man stood in his way, but somehow the many cooperated to block him with unnerving anonymity.

Women put restraining arms on their husbands, but men outnumbered them five to one in the saloon.

"Well that you could bear witness to the vote!" Jacob continued. Sweat poured down his neck and soaked his collar, but he did not bother with his kerchief anymore. "Imagine if it had happened behind closed doors! Too long Three Chop politics have been kept hidden!"

The crowd pressed tighter around Donovan—these men who had known him twenty years, who had tipped their hats to him in the street. They were unrecognizable now—each individually blameless yet part of an anonymous press that threatened to suffocate him. His back was being ground by increments into the bar behind him.

Donovan was near the point of giving up, of crying out, of begging mercy, when a gunshot sounded.

Indoors it was loud enough to deafen a man. The sound came from every direction at once. At first Donovan thought the worst had happened, that he had been shot by someone in the crowd. He touched his belly, but his hands came away clean. Besides, he had been shot before, and he knew he would have felt the impact.

Donovan saw Jacob turn for one wild-eyed moment to the card table before he threw himself to the bar and rolled off. In the same instant the press of the crowd around Donovan dissolved into panic, parting and piling without object or order like a wind-whipped sea, its fury turned upon itself in confusion.

Instinctively, Donovan spun and drew his weapon. It took him only a moment to orient.

Plaster dust showered from a black hole bored in the ceiling directly above the barrel of Rod Turner's upraised gun.

Screams sounded upstairs, lovers startled by the sudden intrusion of violence.

"Cheat!" Rod screamed. He was standing, his chair fallen behind him where it had been thrust back in haste.

The crowd around the card table had likewise fallen away—men and women scattered on the ground or pushed to the door, their clothing wet with spilled drinks, their boots crunching over broken glass.

Soft, Donovan thought even in the midst of the chaos. *They've grown soft. Every one of them.* Half the men in the saloon had guns at their hips— they would not think of leaving the house without their guns any more than they would their boots—and yet they huddled like the rest, only a few even with the presence of mind to fumble for their weapons, these men who had been so brave moments before as they threatened a coup.

There's been peace too long in Three Chop.

Donovan stood in that tumult and strode to the card table, his gun drawn and raised but not yet pointed at anyone in particular.

Rod still stood, rage in his eyes, and fear, too, as he seemed suddenly to realize his gun was pointed impotently at the ceiling while the cold-eyed cardsharp's gun sought the meat of his belly. Like most of the other players at the table, Ike had toppled over backward in his seat. Only Chasby remained upright with Rod and Sal, though he had not drawn his gun. The Reverend's boy only sat, his face painted in shock, his hat pushed back on his head as if lifted by the blowback from Rod's gun.

"I know you're cheating someway, and I won't let you leave 'til you hand that pile over!" Rod said, though the threat sounded unsteady.

Donovan acted quickly when he reached the table. "Put the gun down, son," he said, pressing the barrel of his own gun into the small of Sal's back. His voice was calm—almost fatherly—though his blood was hot.

Sal looked at Rod and Chasby in turn then slowly holstered his weapon.

"You too, Rod," Donovan said, though he did not point his gun at the Three Chop man.

Rod holstered his gun quickly, visibly relieved to be free of the entanglement.

"Now," Donovan said, aware that he commanded the room once more. "What the hell is going on?"

"This son of a bitch is cheating us at cards," Rod said angrily. His voice cracked when he spoke, and his hand trembled, whether with rage or fear Donovan was not sure.

"Cheating how?" Donovan asked, keeping Sal's right hand in his sight all the while.

Rod shrugged insolently. "I don't know. But he is."

"He is. I swear it," Ike chimed in, raising himself into a squat and straightening his hat like it was his dignity.

"Chasby," Donovan asked, "was he cheating?"

The Reverend's boy hesitated, adopting that characteristic look that was at once sullen and abashed. Rod caught his eyes momentarily. A warning passed between them, and Chasby finally said, "Sure. Yeah. He's a cheat."

Donovan felt those hundreds of eyes on him again, the eyes of the men, that might have killed him now rapt. The thrill sent a warm sensation spreading over his skin, raising hairs as it went. Now he thought he could not have planned this night better if he had been given a year.

Donovan tucked a thumb behind his belt buckle and spread his feet shoulder width. He stood tall, tall enough that his head might reach through the ceiling, might reach to the upper floors, to the roof, to the sky. He stood like the giant of Three Chop once more. "So," he turned to Sal, "you stand accused."

"I ain't cheating," the boy said. "They're just bad at cards."

"So you're calling these boys—these Three Chop boys—liars?" Donovan asked. Pointing at Chasby, he added, "You know this boy's daddy is a preacher?"

Chasby flushed and slumped further in his chair as if he would disappear.

Sal ground his teeth but said nothing.

Donovan stared at the cardsharp a long moment. The room was silent, every breath held, waiting for him.

Finally, Donovan said, "I think you'd better get some air."

Sal frowned, but he understood the command. He bent forward to gather his winnings.

"And leave the money on the table," Donovan added. "All of it. We'll call this one a draw, and consider yourself lucky for it."

Sal turned and looked Donovan in the eye, the pale blue sending shivers down his spine. There was an insolence in him, a danger that made Donovan want to shoot him on the spot, the kind of insolence only a young man could possess, a young man who thought his honor was the only thing of value in the world. Donovan had seen his like before, only it had been a while.

"You have something to say?" Donovan asked.

Sal shook his head slowly and said, "Only that men get their due." He said it as much to the men at the table as to the Sheriff so that all were offended but none had cause. Then he strode through the door, a cloud of malignancy swirling behind to stir the skirts and jackets of the disheveled townfolk as they parted to let him pass.

Donovan looked after him, committing everything about the boy— *no, the man, a killer*—to memory.

When Sal was gone, the room itself seemed to inflate as the crowd released its collective breath. The townfolk started to murmur, their voices growing louder as they regained some composure—standing, dusting shirtsleeves, retrieving glasses, fans, hats, and earrings from the floor.

Haddock returned to his seat at the piano and began to play a ragtime tune, as if he alone could dictate the mood of the room.

Jacob had picked himself up to lean with his hands on the bar top, scowling, his hair, jacket, and bowtie askew, his moustache pointing in aberrant directions. At some point he had grabbed his shotgun, as if he might have been prepared to use it, as if he had not been cowering the very moment it was needed.

Donovan caught Annabel's eye then, standing in the crowd beside the bar, her face barely showing above Todd's broad, interposing shoulders. She gave him a smile, albeit thin for all the fullness of her lips, and nodded approvingly like it was a concession.

He almost winked before he caught himself.

The rest of the town seemed to share her mood, even his staunchest detractors—thankful, begrudging, impressed.

They parted before him as he made for the door, some averting their eyes. He dared not linger long enough to see his fortune turn again. He did not even speak, and somehow that seemed right.

CHAPTER 13

Sal

SAL SAT ON A WATER BARREL BEHIND THE SALOON, SHIVERING OCCA-sionally in the coolness of the night. He listened to the muffled sound of the piano and the hum of a hundred voices now recovered from the gunfire. Salacious laughter drifted from windows open on the second floor, the empty mirth of the working women, reminding Sal of what he had lost.

Sal was drawn instinctively to the saloon like a moth, attracted by its light and its gaiety—a jewel half buried in the plain. It spilled joy into the night like the scent of a bakeshop or the slipping shoulder strap of a woman's dress. Even now, after he had just suffered the indignity of being cast out, he sat beside it, leaned against it—his shelter from the loneliness of the Western expanse—while he smoked and brooded and schemed.

Thrown out by a two-bit sheriff old enough to be my grandaddy.

Sal stood abruptly, the shame of the encounter making him restless. He imagined all the things he should have said, should have done.

Jack would have shot him dead.

He paced from the barrel to the other end of the building and back, casting a slouch-hat shadow across the yard whenever he passed beneath a bright-lit window.

At some point after he had churned the thing enough with his legs, Sal admitted that he was angry with himself as much as he was with the Sheriff and his "Three Chop boys."

I did the hard part—carried those heavy sacks all the way to Texline without stopping, walking day and night 'til my feet were blistered and bloody, and then bought the horse, rode her a hundred miles—two hundred miles!—to find this place, to bury that fortune nearby. And all I had to do was watch and wait!

81

But after all that, I got myself on the wrong side of a sheriff over a game of cards I shouldn't've played in the first place. And I did it in front of the whole goddamn town!

He stopped at the barrel and beat upon the top with closed fists, listening absentmindedly to the dull echo like a drum. He felt the barrel quiver as the water sloshed inside, a fire barrel. Sal thought he might as well climb in and seal himself up to wait for Jack.

The thought of being trapped that way made his breath hitch so that he could not tell if his lungs were empty or full. It was the same feeling he had gotten in his room, let from old Mrs. García, as he lay on the bed, staring at the ceiling, trying to nap through the day like a dog. He was never made to be shut up like that. On the third day the restlessness had overcome him, and he had ventured outside to roam the streets of his new town, the last way station to fortune.

Fortune if I can bring myself to mail that damned letter!

Sal knew that once he sent it, he would be tethered to the place.

The heart of the matter resolved suddenly before him like a mother's voice in his ear—that he must unearth the treasure and carry it to another town where he could start over, preferably a town without a saloon, if that was even possible. It was not a question of cowardice after all but a question of pride and of common sense. He was too proud to let a man beat him at the card table, and so he would find a place that had no table, and he would shut himself up in a fire barrel if he had to.

And this time I won't tell nobody my name! he thought belatedly.

And yet it was intolerable to think of letting stand the Sheriff's injustice. That oversight would mark his manhood, yellow his reputation so that every highwayman, cutpurse, and upstart shootist in the West would take him for an easy mark.

But after the Oregon *job, what do I need a reputation for?* Sal did not know how to live as a rich man, owing so much to someone else.

It was Jack who had rescued him from the course of violent, anonymous death he had made for himself when he fled Spicer's, a naive cardsharp, age fourteen, riding a fifty-dollar horse.

Queenie.

Until he saw him with his own eyes, Sal had assumed Jack Holloway was a myth. Half a hundred murders were attributed to his name, and twice as many robberies. It was said he was so quiet that even his gun was noiseless, that he could track the wind across the plain, that he slept with his eyes open, that he had been shot through the heart but could not be killed.

In the following years, Sal had learned there lay some truth in every rumor.

Sal had cheated Jack at cards without realizing who he was. One-Eyed Pete had wanted to kill him. But Jack had only smiled that half smile of his, which let you know he operated in a higher dimension, that he had already seen the way ahead for miles and for days.

Sal drummed his fists on the water barrel again, emotion lingering longer than memory.

"I'll leave. I'll leave tonight," he whispered to himself, stopping over a patch of light cast by the window. He said the words even before he had decided them, testing their effect, and when he heard them, he knew they were right.

I owe Jack that much at least.

He made to step from the rut he had tracked in the dirt where he paced, to go to his room, to gather his things and lead his horse into the night to where he had buried the loot and then to who knows where. He made the first step, but he stopped when he heard her voice.

"Boy," she said, the word sounding like music in the same key as the piano.

Sal had his back to the saloon then, but he turned his head sideways so he could hear her better.

"Boy," she said again.

There, in the lowest window at the back of the saloon, which hung halfway up the back stair, was the silhouette of a woman backlit in yellow-gold.

Instinctively, Sal turned fully and took off his hat and held it in his hands. He approached the window until he could see her clearly.

She was a face then, peering over the sill, her arms folded upon it, displaying her bosom to the coolness of the night. There was a sheen of sweat on her, and the ringlets of her hair near her temples were damp with it.

Her face was the most beautiful he had ever seen. It was sharp featured, even severe, until she smiled warm as the rising sun. Her eyes were velvet brown and her lips were swollen and red with the fullness of youth—a young woman, no older than himself.

"Boy?" Sal asked, turning a circle like he was searching. He put the hat back on. "He must've gone, the boy."

The girl smiled again like daybreak.

"It's hot in there, boy," she said, fanning herself with a white-gloved hand. "Better to be outside, I think."

Sal studied her, trying not to leer. "Why don't you come out here, then?"

"I was only trying to make you feel better, poor boy. The whole town is inside, except you."

"My name isn't boy."

"I know. Your name is the *Salamander*. I saw you playing cards."

Sal flushed. *She must have heard then—heard the whole thing.* His pride came upon him. "A fake name—anyone can see."

"I don't think so!" she said, laughing. "I think it's your name, boy!"

"What're you sticking your head out here for anyway?" he said angrily. "Get back inside, if it's so nice like you say."

The girl thought a moment then shrugged, disappearing.

"Wait!" Sal called before he realized what he was doing.

Interminable seconds passed. He wondered if she had even heard him.

Better if she didn't . . .

Then she reappeared, and Sal was shocked at his own relief. "Yes?" she asked as if she was busy, and maybe she was.

In his ecstasy Sal could think of nothing to say. After longer than he would have liked, he asked, "What's your name?"

The girl frowned pityingly. "I was just making conversation with the poor boy. Now he wants to know my name!" She shook her head at the sadness of it, and Sal felt the last of his dignity evaporate.

He shrugged, giving his most disinterested look. "Not a boy, nor poor, neither, so I reckon I'll survive without your sympathies."

The girl considered this. "A nice try, but I saw the money you left on that table." She looked over her shoulder. "Yes, it's still there. There's another game going, you know? Going with your money? It's how I know you're poor. A life savings for a poor cowpuncher mixed in with the rest on that table." She gave him another one of her sad looks and added, "At least your boots are new."

Sal grinned, then waved his hand dismissively. "That pot? They can have it. They need it more than I do."

Curiosity kindled in her eyes.

"Are there more cards in your future then, Sal?" she asked, using his name properly for the first time.

"Depends. Who wants to know?"

"Guess," she said, pulling absentmindedly on the ends of her hair. The sheen of sweat had evaporated in the coolness of the night air.

Sal took the command as an opportunity to study the girl. "Belinda," he offered when he had stared as long as he dared.

"An ugly name for an ugly woman!" she exclaimed, standing up. "The boy—" she started, but an aggrieved shout interrupted her.

"Katarina! What are you doing in ze window? I've been looking for you—zer is someone who wants to meet you."

Sal recognized the madam's accent.

The girl's—*Katarina's*—self-possession lapsed for the briefest moment, and Sal saw inevitability there, resignation, in the subtle blanching of her face.

The next town would have to wait. It was a decision made for him, by a part of himself that he could not hope to override or even to dissect.

Sal the cardsharp and shootist, the orphaned son of a railroad engineer, had found his next mark. Perhaps he had not left the saloon empty-handed after all.

CHAPTER 14

Annabel

ANNABEL DID NOT THINK SHE BREATHED UNTIL SHE REACHED HOME.

Her hands shook. The eyes of the town had been upon her, the barroom as quiet as she had ever known it, quiet as she had ever known Three Chop, quiet as the streets when she used to walk them in the depths of night, Hattie in her arms, trying to coax the babe to sleep. Yes, quiet as those times and as full of possibility, too. And into that quietness she had spoken her words, which, like a spell, had opened a new reality. As much as she had rehearsed them, the act of speaking had been terrifying, irrevocable. Yet she had spoken.

And who did she do these things for if not for Hattie?

"We have the vote," she said, said it quietly to herself as she closed her heavy wooden front door, said it smiling as wide as her wedding day.

With those eyes upon her, she had held a power she had but dreamed of possessing, not even when she had assumed Lem's place on the council. *Oh, the irony that this would be his legacy!* But that was the way of life. Even John had looked uneasy, uncertain in the hush before her pronouncement.

Of course, the vote only extended to local elections. But it was a start, and it was influence that might be peddled all the way to state conventions if she could find the right leverage with John and the rest—that unlikely bloc that had delivered her a God-given constitutional right.

There would be costs, though, yet unaccounted. She had lost Jacob, surely, when he turned on her like a maddened dog, mouth frothing, spitting bile, breaking a twenty-year friendship over the knee of politics. How many men like him would turn their backs on her? How many wives and daughters would follow? How many would use the voice she had given them to disavow her?

Annabel's thoughts were interrupted by a sound in the street, out of character with the silence. A thud. A grunt?

She was on the verge of dismissing it, when suddenly a window shattered, spewing glass across the room.

Annabel felt something warm on her ankle and looked down to see that a shard had sliced her calf. She fell back onto the sofa, full of dread and animal fear as her understanding caught up with reality.

At her feet lay the round egg of a river stone, as big as her palm.

How long she sat frozen, staring at that unlikely messenger, she could not say. Long enough for blood to pool in the heel of her shoe, a squelching, sickening wetness.

Then, slowly, she leaned forward and took the stone in her hand. It was heavy—deadly. She thought of Haddock.

It has begun already, the reprisal.

She thought of the press around Donovan, threatening to subsume even that pillar, the father of Three Chop, the press that had been her friends and neighbors.

Who? she wondered, head buzzing and empty. The possibilities were as endless as Three Chop's divisions—a man? A woman? Aligned with whom? Aaron and the Church of the Holy Light? Jacob and the saloon and the liquor interest? Any of the townsmen who saw in the petition a double dilution of their power?

Annabel stood. Her leg did not hurt. For all its weeping blood, the wound was superficial. She walked to the window, parted the curtains, peered past her lighted porch into the darkness of the street, but it was quiet and empty again.

Annabel found a roll of grease paper and tacked a sheet to the muntin, covering the broken windowpane to keep out the chill of night.

Then she went to the bedroom and removed Lem's old revolver from the cedar trunk at the foot of her bed where she stored it with the winter quilts in camphor. She cleaned and oiled it the way her father had taught her. What she would have given to have her father's gun instead! His sturdy spirit to guide her! But it was lost somewhere in the wilderness with his body, and Lem's gun would do just fine if she could find the courage in herself to use it.

That night Annabel went to bed with the revolver on her bedside table. A new reality, indeed.

CHAPTER 15

Sal

HE SAW HER NEXT IN THE DUST OF THE STREET ONE MORNING, WHEN there was heat in the sun and a chill in the shade. For two days he had been walking the streets around the saloon, hoping to run into her again.

He ducked behind the corner of the post office, where he had just deposited his letter to Jack. It was addressed to "Conway Mathers," Jack's alias. The momentousness of the letter and the impending reunion with his companions was superseded by the sight of her, and the rest fell from his mind. He would not hate being trapped in Three Chop a while longer.

She moved down Front Street in the direction of the saloon. She held a parcel under her arm and wore a white touring hat like a lady.

Sal noticed other men staring at her, too, forgetting their work, leaving crates unpacked, and letting horses lead their carts astray. Even the boys stopped playing to watch her pass.

Women looked, too, from porches and doorways with hard eyes and folded arms.

Sal ran to the end of the alley, hurrying to Second Street. He looked for her through the alleys between buildings as he passed. She was walking by the jail when he saw her, and thankfully she did not glimpse him.

He ran past the barbershop to the railroad tracks then cut up to Front, slowing so that he was ambling by the time he stepped onto the boardwalk, though his breath was labored. He found her walking toward him.

He nodded when she saw him and touched the brim of his hat like her appearance was some pleasant surprise.

She waved her free hand but did not change her gait. She stepped onto the porch of the saloon.

Sal walked as fast as he dared without giving away his haste.

She had just reached the door when he was near enough to speak.

"Mornin', Katarina," he said. He did not break stride either, giving the impression that he was on his way somewhere else.

She stopped and looked at him a long moment, then said, "Kat."

Sal slowed to a stop, still standing on the boardwalk a few yards off.

"Kat," he repeated thoughtfully, trying it on like a new jacket. Up close he saw rings of tiredness beneath her eyes, covered over imperfectly with a smear of flesh-toned makeup.

"Whaddya have there?" he asked, trying not to wonder how late she had been up or what she had been doing.

She looked at the parcel as if she had not known it was there, shifting it to her hip.

"I don't know. Just a package from Winthrop's. It's for Jacob. The madam sent me."

Sal looked at his boots.

He opened his mouth, hoping words would come like a reflex, but none did, and he only succeeded in standing dumbly, agape. She gave him a queer look and made to go inside.

"Wait," he stammered. "Why don't you walk with me?" He had meant to be subtler but was thankful he had said anything at all.

The question hung between them, circling.

Sal thought he might rather endure a holdup at gunpoint than bare his pride so.

Kat smiled, but it was the same pitying smile she had given him from the window of the saloon. "Not today, Salamander," she said, and turned to go inside, leaving the poor boy to watch and scratch his head.

CHAPTER 16

Annabel

ANNABEL STARED VACANTLY AT THE FAR END OF THE POST OFFICE AND into the adjoining stationary shop, a book open before her but mostly unread. It was an old copy of *Deerslayer*, her father's, yellowed and frayed with a dozen readings.

She was having trouble concentrating. Her nerves thrummed as bowstrings. Her mind kept returning to the stone that had flown through her window. She would not believe it existed if she did not keep it with her, tucked now in the pocket of her twill suit as a reminder, counterweight to Lem's revolver.

The door opened. Annabel looked up to see John enter.

"Morning, Annabel," he said. He grinned and removed his hat to twirl it about his finger.

The frivolity of that gesture confounded her. She could not see the world as it had been before.

He came and leaned against the counter in the usual way, still grinning. "Reveling in your victory?" he asked.

For a dozen heartbeats Annabel was silent, her mind torn between contemplation of the stone and the words of her visitor. She had to make an effort to refocus.

John seemed to take her silence as some sort of criticism. He grew still and stern.

"It's okay, John, I'm just . . . distracted."

"I thought I'd find you over the moon," Donovan said, looking concerned. "Three Chop must be a generation ahead of its time, maybe a lifetime."

Annabel nodded. "Yes. I'm proud. I'm thrilled, only—" She removed the stone from a pocket in her dress. It seemed heavier every time she hefted it. Could a man have thrown it so far? Out of some dark alley, across the street and into her home? Or had he crept closer? Onto her porch? Had he watched her through the window?

Annabel set the stone on the counter between them.

Donovan looked at it, his eyebrows climbing.

"That came through my window last night," Annabel said. "When I got home."

Donovan started as if slapped. He snatched the stone up and studied it as if it might hold some clue to who had thrown it, turned it over in his hands.

"Who?" Donovan demanded, looking up.

"I don't know. I was in the parlor when it happened. It must have been after midnight. After we left the saloon."

Cupping the stone in his hand, Donovan held it to his cheek as if to listen to it speak. He was thoughtful. After a moment he pocketed it.

"I'll post Mance on the porch," he said. "Have him lay his pallet across your very doorstep. And I'll make extra rounds, too."

"No," Annabel found herself protesting. "It's more than you would do for someone else." She did not invoke Haddock, but he was the silent presence beneath her words. "I won't be given special treatment, and I have my own assurance here." She took out Lem's revolver for John to see.

John took it in hand as he had done with the rock. He held the revolver before him, ran his hand along the frame, checked the cylinder, tested the hammer.

"I'll have Mance make extra rounds at least," he said. "If something were to happen to you after the vote, it would send a message of true lawlessness—that the law itself could be threatened. It's everything I've fought against." He looked at her in earnest. "To say nothing of what it would mean personally . . ."

Annabel averted her eyes. John's words had given her new confidence, but not in the way he intended. She wanted even less to rely on him, to rely on anyone but herself. She took Lem's gun—her gun—back from him and secured it in the folds of her dress as before. She was her father's daughter, that intrepid explorer—dead these many years in the wild, uncharted Rockies—and would comport herself as such.

Besides, John already had his share of work . . .

"John," she said, fully present now. "John, about last night—the crowd—there was a moment when they turned on you—our neighbors turned on you."

"It was nothing," John said dismissively. But he spoke too fast, put her off too easily. "It was a political debate, spirited, enlivened by spirits."

"It was more than debate, John. If Rod's gunshot had not sounded when it did—"

Annabel stopped. There was something in John's expression—a plea? She saw his discomfort. She would not press him, would not break the illusion. He was sheriff after all, and maybe he knew the truth of it.

"I'll have Mance make extra rounds," John said, as if that were the final word on everything. "And I'll speak to the Reverend—see if he knows any more of this rock." John patted his pocket.

Annabel only nodded.

"But if I had to wager, I'd put my money on that cardsharp," John continued. "He has an air about him, Annabel. And the coincidence is too much. He shows up in town after Jacob declares his candidacy, shows up in Jacob's saloon, and on the very night he ambushes the council with a public vote?"

"What are you saying?"

"That Jacob hired the man. That he knows 'Sal from down the line.'"

It was preposterous. "He saved your life in a way," Annabel wanted to say, for it was at the very moment she thought the crowd would turn on John that the gunshot had rung out, and who else but Sal, the blue-eyed boy, could be said to have engendered it?

But Annabel held her tongue. She would not break the Sheriff's illusion now. He needed it, she saw. Maybe all great men needed it—the illusion of control.

Hattie had disabused Annabel's own illusion. Annabel cringed as she always did when she thought of Hattie and Chasby together, the way she had found them in the darkness of the post office one night—fumbling, the smell of liquor on their breath. *My own flesh and blood—rebelled, sent away . . .*

And yet she harkened back to Jacob's words, pronounced with such scorn, "What womanly frailty . . ." They echoed in her mind as surely as Rod's gunshot, as surely as the sound of shattered glass. Could Jacob be so conniving, so reckless to hire a gun? Surely not. But who could know men's hearts these days?

"I saw him this morning," John said. "The cardsharp. He came here to mail a letter, didn't he?"

Annabel froze. Yes, the boy had come. She had been preoccupied with the night's events, and her memory of it was imperfect. He had put the letter in her hand and asked her how long it would take to deliver. He had said it was important . . .

But it was not the memory of the boy that set her on edge. It was John—it was knowing his mind.

"Maybe," she said "I've been scattered today. I don't recall."

"I saw him come in with a letter and leave without it," John pressed. "Mail doesn't go out until the three o'clock." His eyes wandered to the canvas mail bag that hung from a hook on the wall behind the counter. "In these uncertain times . . ." He looked at her, insinuating.

"John, we've been through this . . ."

"A little favor could go a long way to helping law and order," he said, unrelenting. "Think of the terror of last night, of that stone crashing through your window!"

"Even if I were inclined to let you see the letter, it would mean breaking the law."

"Annabel, the circumstances!"

Annabel shook her head. "You're blinded, John, blinded by your mistrust of Jacob. We already know who's throwing stones in this town. Haddock will tell you. You needn't read the mail to find out."

"Blinded!" John exclaimed, clenching and stretching his hand. "The cardsharp nearly started a gunfight before our own eyes." He leaned over the counter, leaned until she could smell his breath like coffee and tobacco yet somehow pleasant—a man's breath like she remembered her father's.

He lowered his voice conspiratorially. "Has he mailed anything before? Or received anything?"

Annabel shut her mouth, pressed her lips together until they turned white and bloodless.

"Annabel, I wouldn't ask if it weren't important. You're as responsible as I am for the upheaval in town. Now we must shepherd Three Chop through the tumult."

His words had an echo of the Reverend. There was a look in his eyes that Annabel recognized from long ago, a look she had once admired— determination, obstinance. Now it revolted her. What kind of ally had she made?

"I don't think we should talk about this anymore," she said, a final effort to forestall him. "And maybe you should leave."

John inhaled long and slow, straightening himself.

Annabel steeled herself for whatever was to come. *He will do whatever he wants. He will take what he wants and leave when he wants, and what can I do?* Her throat felt tight.

"I'm sorry, Bel," he said, using the old name, the one he had called her when they were young.

For a moment she thought he had relented. She saw his age again, his haggard weariness, and she felt pity.

But he had never intended retreat, for he said softly, "Perhaps it's time I had Cordell write the congressman."

Annabel was dumbstruck. Did it make a difference that it looked like the words pained him, too? She could not speak.

Donovan averted his eyes, angled his gaze toward the window, toward the rising heat of the sunbaked street, toward that procession of slow-moving carts.

That threat had always been there between them, Annabel realized, unspoken. Ever since Lem had died, his estranged protection vanished. She served only at the Sheriff's pleasure.

"It's been nagging me, you know," John said, after an interval. He turned to her, meeting her eye. His face was stone now. He was another man. "I held out as long as I could, on account of our friendship. But Congressman Atwood is a great benefactor to our town, and it would be a betrayal to let his patronage appointment languish like this without any return."

"You'll ruin me," she whispered. She thought of Atwood's aquiline face—not unkind but unfailingly pragmatic. He would have no problem replacing her, no matter her service.

She searched John's face for some trace of the man she fell in love with all those years ago, the man she could love enough to break her heart. But he was gone. Too much had changed in him. *Or has it? Has he always been like this? Ruthless? Self-absorbed?*

She felt a tear trail hot on her cheek and turned away so John would not see it.

"We don't have to do it this way," John said, still stone. "Just let me see the letter. You don't even know the man."

"It's wrong!" she snapped. "You haven't got the right!"

"He's an outlaw! I'm asking for the town. I'm asking for *you.* Not for myself."

"Do you know the difference?" Annabel spat, even as she stood and retrieved the sack of mail. She heaved it on the counter and shoved it roughly into his gut.

"If you would bully an honest woman, make her choose between her livelihood and her honor, I can't stop you. But I won't give you a damn thing. You can *steal* the letter yourself, if you must, Sheriff."

John looked hard at her and at the mail bag then glanced over his shoulder to make sure they were alone. He reached into the bag, removing fistfuls of letters, shuffling through them until he found the cardsharp's.

Annabel caught a glimpse of the unpracticed lettering before John tucked it into his vest. He shoved the rest of the letters back in the sack.

"Got what you came for?" she asked acidly.

"Yes," Donovan grunted. He turned to leave, then stopped. "It's a thankless job, you know, protecting the town. People see whatever impositions you have to make to keep them safe, but they never see what would have happened otherwise."

Annabel did not give him the dignity of a response.

John shook his head. "You should be happy, Bel. You got what you wanted. The women have the vote. This is a small price to pay."

"I thought siding with you and the Reverend was payment enough," she said bitterly.

Donovan gave a mirthless laugh. "If it makes you feel better, the Reverend is livid about our little bargain. But he'll come around when he gets what he wants."

"And what's that?"

"The saloon of course."

Annabel bowed her head. That would surely divide the women, to say nothing of what it would do to Jacob, to Haddock, or to the women of the saloon—so many of whom were Annabel's pupils—who would lose their livelihoods. Aaron must have known it. John probably knew it, too.

And what of Sallie who sold liquor in her own shop? How long before they came for her? Sallie who had so often sheltered Annabel from Lem . . .

Maybe Annabel had been a fool.

"The election isn't decided," she said—said it as much to herself as she said it to John, a final defiance.

"Isn't it though?" John asked, taking his leave, and Annabel feared he might be right.

CHAPTER 17

Sal

TWICE MORE HE FOUND HER IN THE STREET, ENTREATED HER. TWICE more she demurred.

The fourth time he found her—morning again, in front of the saloon, another package tucked beneath her arm—he brought her a gift, a drawing he had made of a flower, and made it an offering.

Kat bit her lip when she looked at the drawing, her face inscrutable.

Again Sal felt exposed. His face flushed red, and he vowed this would be the last time he embarrassed himself this way. Suddenly it seemed like everyone in the street was looking at him.

"The madam bid me come straight back," she said.

Sal crumpled the paper and made to put it in his pocket.

"Oh!" Kat exclaimed, as if hurt. Uncertain, she looked at the door. "But I suppose I have . . . come straight back." She smiled wanly. "Okay, Salamander," she said finally. "Let me just drop this inside first." Then she held out her hand.

It took him a moment to understand, then he handed her the drawing, smoothing it hastily against his vest.

She reappeared a few minutes later, dressed as before but looking somehow different, refreshed.

Sal stood up where he had been leaning against the porch post, his heart beating fast. He had not planned past asking her to walk. He smelled her perfume for the first time, and it reminded him of the wisteria that grew purple outside his window as a boy.

"Where are we walking?" Kat asked.

Sal shrugged. "To the edge of town? Where else?"

"Okay, Salamander."

She fell in beside him, and they walked like this for a few minutes in silence, his mind overwhelmed by the novelty of this exotic and unfathomable creature.

When they passed the bank, Kat asked, "Where do you come from?"

Sal thought about this, because there was no easy answer. "Virginia, I guess. It's where I was born."

"I've heard of it, I think."

Sal laughed. "I take it you aren't from the East?"

"No," she shook her head, and Sal could see she was remembering. "I'm from Russia."

"Russia!" Sal adjusted his hat, a habit of his when he encountered something unexpected. "They speak English there?"

"No!" She looked at him and smiled, and he saw her teeth were big and white like the kitchen tiles had been in the big house at Saddle Creek Ranch, where he had first met Queenie.

"Well you speak it fine," he said.

"I came to California when I was a girl—when I was young enough to learn to speak it right."

"Do you still speak—"

"No. I have not spoken it since I left there—or near enough."

"Not even to your parents?"

Kat made no reply, but her face grew somber.

"Sorry—" Sal stammered, feeling ungainly. "I only—I don't have any, either," he added, trying to make amends.

They passed the livery stable, and Sal stopped to show her his horse.

"Does she have a name?"

"No," Sal said wistfully. "I couldn't bring myself to name her yet. I had a good horse, Queenie, and I lost her."

"I didn't know a boy like you would ride a mare."

"Some don't, but if you knew Queenie—sometimes a horse can be good enough so's it makes no difference. Now I've grown accustomed. They're gentler, you know."

Kat nodded. She cupped the horse's nose in her hands and marveled at the heat of her breath.

"I've ridden," she said. "But I've never owned a horse."

Sal could not believe this. "California is the land of horses! The old Spanish stock. Everyone owns one there, and if they don't, they wander wild for the taking. You can buy one for two dollars they say!"

"Not in San Francisco," she said. "Not everyone owns a horse in San Francisco."

"San Francisco," he said, trying out the word, which felt as exotic as Russia. "I always wanted to go."

"Oh?"

"Sure. Who wouldn't want to see El Dorado?" He walked a few breaths, imagining the place. "I hear the card tables are the best in the world."

"Maybe once," she said, "but now it's just a city like Denver or anywhere else."

"Never been to Denver."

"I've only been once." She grew quiet again. "On my way to Texas. It's another mining town, you know. Silver."

When they reached the edge of town, they stopped and stood like driftwood clung together in the sea.

"It's lonely here," she said, considering the vaulted emptiness of the sky. "There is nothing but space."

"Oh, but it's everything!" Sal disagreed. "We could ride to the Badlands or to Mexico or to California to the coast. It's all before us, here, spread out like a map!"

Kat chewed her lip, and it made her more beautiful somehow to see the life in her lips and the thoughtfulness at work behind her eyes, a spark of consciousness apart from his own, one that he wanted somehow to possess. Now she was more than the image he had kept of her as a painting framed in the window of the saloon. She was alive as the grass that whipped and sawed before them in the breeze.

"I knew that freedom once," she said. "Only it wasn't my own."

Sal did not understand her words, but he nodded all the same, the way his father would nod sometimes and look at the sky or at the sheer face of a mountain.

"What do you do for work, boy?" she asked. "Cards?"

It was Sal's turn to grin, remembering the secret of his superlative wealth.

"Cards, among other things," he said enigmatically, unconsciously brushing his right arm against his revolver.

"I see," she said, still regarding the horizon as much as him.

She turned to him. "Would you ride to California?"

"Sure," he said, the need to reassure and protect rising inside him.

"I have always wanted—" she started. "When I was a girl, we worked in a house, my mother and I—we worked for a rich man in a big house on the bluffs of the bay. I remember watching the ships come into the harbor—that was the freedom I knew—to be able to take those ships anywhere. From Russia to California. From California to—who knows? Just like the man did—Señor Alvarez.

"And all I wanted in the world was to have a house like that and to watch the ships and to know that if I wanted to I could take one somewhere else, and live another life, and still have the house watching, waiting for me like a patient dog when I came home.

"One day I'll return for that house, when I can make it my own. Maybe I'll return on the back of a horse."

She was quiet a minute then exclaimed, "Oh, Salamander!" She laughed at herself, a sad smile parting her lips. "Why do I tell you these things? A strange boy?"

Sal grinned. "You'd make a good cowboy," he said. "It's the same feeling on the plain—being able to take your horse anywhere in the world—only you don't have to wait on no ships' captains. You just wake up and make your coffee and your bacon and roll your bed and ride."

She was looking at him again, and Sal could feel something between them that needed acknowledgment, only he did not know how. He put his hand on her arm, his heart beating the way it did when he was galloping with Queenie, and for a moment he was afraid the way he had been when she had disappeared from the window or when he had asked her to walk with him.

But she did not protest. Instead, she moved closer.

"I'll take you there if you want," he said. "We can go together. I'll buy you a horse, and we can go."

"Easy as that?"

"Sure. I have a little business yet in Three Chop, but I'll be ready to ride in a week or so."

She shook her head. "I won't be ready then. Not until I can buy that house."

Sal wrestled with himself then. *But why have the thing if I can't use it?* He thought of his father, who had not been much older than him when he met his mother.

"What if I bought it?" he asked.

She laughed, but there was a plea in her eyes, a hope.

"Why would you go and do a thing like that, Salamander?" she asked softly.

"Don't you know?" he said, the words coming easily now, and that seemed to be enough.

Before turning back, they watched the horizon a while longer, both aware they were looking west.

She has made up her mind, hasn't she? She understands?

"Meet me out back of the saloon tonight?" he asked.

She smiled. "Okay, Salamander," she said, and looped her arm in his.

CHAPTER 18

Kat

KAT AWOKE DAMP BROWED FROM A NIGHTMARE. IT WAS THE SAME nightmare she had been having for years, and yet each night it was somehow different, more grotesque. She was a girl again, hiding in the closet of Señor Alvarez's bedroom where her mother had sent her when she heard the front door open.

She knew what would happen—it always happened more or less the same—and yet she could not stop it.

"Marta?" Señor Alvarez would say, stepping into the room. Like every room in that mansion on the cliffs by the bay, there was a palpable, near audible glitter of gold and crystal.

Kat's mother, who had been changing the bed linens, stood rigid in shock, not daring to turn, her fears confirmed. Here Kat was often herself and her mother at once, watching Señor Alvarez from two sets of eyes, feeling two emotions.

"Señor Alvarez," her mother would say without turning. "What happened to Puerto Vallarta?"

"The crew fell ill," he would say, smiling, his mouth full of broad, white teeth, snapping—too many teeth for one mouth. "The ship is delayed until they can find replacements."

Here he would set his attache case down just inside the doorway, and after a moment it would fall over, spilling its contents, which were different from one night to the next—sometimes papers, other times gold, and once a crying baby. But by that time the señor was across the room at her mother's side, and Kat had no time to contemplate the attache case.

He would put his arms around her mother, hugging her from behind and whispering in her ear. Kat always felt the same emotion, the original emotion—confusion and something else—hope. *Will mother marry Señor Alvarez?* She laughed at herself in the dream, at her own stupidity.

In the dream she could hear what Señor Alvarez said in her mother's ear. It was only after she had run away—after her mother had sent her away—that she heard it, that she understood why she had been turned out alone and abandoned this way.

"Where is Katarina?" Señor Alvarez would ask, his breath hot and sending shivers down her mother's spine, her spine.

"She is sick," her mother would say, her accent thick as the day they left Russia, thick as kavardak stew. And though her back was turned, Kat could see her face somehow and knew that it was a mask of plaster.

"Everyone seems to be sick today," Señor Alvarez would say, clucking as he began to unbutton the back of her dress.

Kat wiped her brow and blinked until the nightmare subsided. It was dawn, and a gray light filtered in through a grimy glass window. She was in a room—Sal's room, she recalled, the night coming back to her in snatches like pictures lit briefly by the explosion of a flashbulb.

It was bare except for the bed where they lay—she on her back and he on his side facing the wall—and a chair and a small bureau. It did not look like the kind of room a rich man would let, a man who could buy a horse or a house for that matter.

At night and in the urgency of passion it had been filled with possibility—the dark corners hiding chests in their shadows like Sal was the Count of Monte Cristo.

Kat knew she had made a mistake.

Her father had introduced her to such disappointment on a morning much like this one. She remembered in stark relief the image of him in that moment when he thrust upon her that first understanding of the cruelty of the world—his visage unrelenting, his hair full of grease, his chair half turned from the table, the bottle before him. She remembered the look on her mother's face when she saw their income had been squandered again, and she remembered the black bruise that made her face into a half-moon and was his repayment to her.

That was her awakening, that unrelenting face, and Señor Alvarez and Vern and Reggie had confirmed her disappointment and the inevitability of it.

Yet here she was in the Salamander's room, watching dawn color the walls, succumbed to her weakness all over again.

Why?

It was Madame Fuselli's skeleton key, she decided, on its pearl chain, which had made her desperate. It was the fear she had lost control of her own destiny and the blackness that made her feel a girl again, as scared and alone as she was the morning she woke to find Vern gone. *Sal's probably just another highwayman who stole a purse.*

Quietly, she rose naked from the straw mattress and found her discarded clothes, her mind already at work dreaming up excuses to tell the madam.

After a minute the cardsharp must have sensed that she had left his side, for he began to stir. She watched warily as he opened his eyes. She was in the process of lacing her corset.

He stared openly at her half-clothed body and grinned his wide, toothy grin, which was not unlike the grin of Señor Alvarez in her dream.

Kat had the disconcerting feeling she had given away something of value for free.

"Where to, Kat?" he asked, arranging the blanket so it covered only his manhood. It was barely morning, but the room was already growing hot.

Kat noticed the hair on his legs did not grow much past his knees, and his tan chest was mostly smooth. She wondered how old he was. He looked much younger unclothed—without the aid of a holster and cartridge belt.

He really is just a boy.

"The madam will be expecting me," she said, stepping into her dress. "I really shouldn't have—" She stopped mid-sentence, seeing the pleasure on his face.

"I'll talk to her," Sal said authoritatively, dismissively. He lifted his leg and adjusted the blanket.

She shook her head, marveling at the spectacle of his confidence. Vern had been the same. *Are they all this way?*

"Talk to her?" she asked.

"Sure. In a language she understands."

"French?"

He laughed and laced his fingers behind his head. He seemed lost in his own thoughts.

She needed to ask him for money. It was the only excuse she could give the madam. But the thought of it made her sick.

When men came to her with a token to lay at her feet, it was an offering that made her powerful, a goddess to be worshipped. But this—asking for money in the daylight after the fact—it made her a beggar.

And there was something else, too, which she was loathe to admit, which was that this was not the normal transaction. There was a feeling mixed up in it that could not be sanitized with a common ledger entry. She felt a thrill when she thought of the handsome figure Sal cut at the card table or ambling down the street in his vest and hat. It was the old weakness—her mother's weakness, perhaps, for what else could explain her father?—alive again in her heart.

Sal whistled a few bars, still grinning.

She thought she recognized the tune from the piano in the saloon the night before. The memory overcame her like a flood—the rendezvous outdoors by the barrel where she had first seen him, the liquor, the excitement that came from stealing away from the saloon, the hope and the heat that had overcome her like a spell—and she blushed despite herself.

"You sure you gotta leave already?" he asked.

"I'll be in trouble as it is," she said, trailing off into an expectant silence, inviting him to intervene with his wallet.

Wouldn't that make it worse though? If he offered?

He only grinned wider.

"I thought I might have to send ze Sheriff after you," Madame Fuselli said, sitting on the side of the bed. Her face was freshly powdered, and the powder fell off her like dandruff, parched as the dust of the earth.

Abella, the white cat, had followed her into the room. She came around the bed and perched on the windowsill, her attention split between the humans and the birds that flit outside.

Kat, who had been nearly asleep, sat up alertly and smoothed her hair.

"I looked for you when I got in," Kat said reflexively, apologetically. "The other girls said you were out."

"Where were you last night?" Fuselli asked, ignoring Kat's fumbling penitence.

"I went with Sal—the cardsharp—remember him?"

"I remember wondering where you were. I remember looking for you all over ze building. I remember wondering if I would have to call ze Sheriff and have him bring out ze dogs."

"I wasn't!" Kat protested, imagining being hunted that way, like a runaway slave. "I wasn't running. Only I thought since Sal has money—"

"Sal, Sal, Sal," Fuselli aped, a hateful smile parting her garish red lips. "Why do you use his name like zees? Are you old friends? Is it possible ze girl is so naive?"

"It's an investment, see? To make him want—"

"An investment!" the madam scoffed. "Here I thought you were a whore and I a madam! But I learn now we are investors! Do you think he loves you zen? You silly girl!" The madam's sarcasm had turned malevolent, and it showed in the fleshless wrinkles of her upturned mouth.

Kat looked away.

"Ze men say you tease zem, put zem off. How long do you think Jacob will pay your way without return? *You* are ze investment, Kat, not ze boy, and it's you who must be profitable."

All this time I had dreamed of working for myself, she thought bitterly. *And still I am indebted to a man!*

"You told me I could go where I please!" Kat cried, growing frantic. "Mr. Moreau told me I could leave if I wanted! And you said some of the other girls leave and get married!"

"Oh," Fuselli cooed, shaking her head in a way that seemed motherly where before she had been harsh. "Not you, child. Not yet. You are new. You have been here a week. I don't know if I can trust you. In fact, I believe zat I cannot.

"Ze other girls are angry with you. Do you think zey behaved so when zey were new? Oh, you really are so naive! And I told you ze girls who leave must do so without debt. And you have debts, child, because we pay for you—your clothes and your board."

"I have money!" Kat cried. She shook as fear, anger, and hopelessness churned inside her, driven before that pitch-black cloud.

Fuselli shook her head again, her lips pressed in a hateful red line.

The animal instinct of flight possessed Kat then, and she rose, preparing to scramble out of bed, to race to the door, to Sal, to beg him to pay whatever was the price in money or in blood.

But the madam rose too, anticipating Kat's resistance, having known and mastered a hundred girls just like her. She slapped her in the face, wrenching her jaw and blurring the vision in one eye.

Kat fell backward, dazed, her head ringing, reverberating. Stars lived and died before her eyes.

Is that how it felt? she asked her mother.

The madam's words came to her as if from a great distance. "You will learn to obey and to work before you entertain any ideas of leaving us."

Kat turned her head to look at the madam. She watched her square form receding, the power of her arm and the seriousness of her threats now proved by the reddening mark upon Kat's cheek.

Kat closed her eyes. She heard the door click shut. Then a moment later she heard the scrape of the skeleton key as it turned in the lock.

CHAPTER 19

Donovan

"AIN'T SEEN A BIRD LIKE THAT IN SOME TIME," MANCE SAID, SCRATCHING his cheek, which was packed fat with a wad of chew. He sat with Mayor Cordell and Donovan on the jailhouse porch.

Donovan grunted without taking his eyes off the bird. It was the biggest bird he had ever seen, its head naked, red, its skin rumpled and drooping as though its feathers had been scalded off.

"Must be five foot," Mance said.

"Huh," Cordell said by way of agreement.

The bird stood in the middle of the empty street, hunched over and tearing something apart. The usual foot traffic was absent on account of it being Sunday. Most of the town was asleep or at church—one church, for the time being, until a new Methodist preacher could be found.

Donovan hoped the Reverend was doing his part in the pulpit. The election was only a few weeks away, and Donovan had the sense he was losing his grip somehow, even as he tightened it. He was having trouble anticipating the reactions of the council, Annabel chief among them. He had hoped that by throwing the stone through her window, he could scare her into a closer alignment, but it had done the opposite, made her intransigent. *She was always stubborn . . .*

"What do you figure he's eating?" Mance asked, narrowing his eyes to peer into the brightness.

Donovan craned his neck but could not say.

"It's one of those brown lizards—a fat one," Cordell said, lacing his thick, stubby fingers behind his balding head.

Donovan watched the vulture tear a long strip of gut from the dead reptile and choke it down, head turned skyward.

"Looks like a turkey if a turkey got syphilis," the mayor observed.

Mance smiled and spit a jet of brown tobacco juice over the edge of the porch.

"It's a turkey vulture," Donovan said, unamused. Increasingly, the mayor seemed unable to distinguish his professional and barroom personas. Even with the farmers' petition settled, Donovan wanted to take no chances, to risk no scandals.

Out of the corner of his eye, he saw Mance unholster his pistol, Dewlap, the magnificent gun with the gold-banded butt. The deputy drew it eye level, bracing his right arm with his left.

"What're you doing?" Donovan asked scornfully.

"I'm gonna scare the brute off. I'm only aiming at his feet."

"Let him be," Donovan said, fixated on the buzzard's revolting beauty. "He's nearly done."

Mance shrugged and holstered his weapon. He drummed his fingers on the arms of his chair and spit again.

A moment later the bird, having picked the carcass clean, took a few ungainly steps and lifted slowly into the air, wheeling overhead and turning south.

Donovan leaned forward to get a better view of the sky from beneath the overhang of the jailhouse porch. When the bird was gone, he lifted his coffee mug. He took a large swallow and felt the hot liquid all the way down his throat until it disappeared into the emptiness of his dyspeptic stomach. Lately, his appetite had been weak, and he had begun to notice his clothes fit loosely, too.

When he leaned forward again to set the mug down, a bolt of pain shot up Donovan's spine as if the bones were burning to ash. It took all his willpower to straighten himself, and he could not help but cry out as he did. He tried to cover the outburst with a fit of coughing.

"You okay, Mr. Sheriff?" Mance asked.

Donovan nodded, trying not to retch. "Coffee down the wrong pipe," he managed to say, wiping his mouth. As suddenly as it had come, the pain receded, teasing. Donovan despaired.

Still, there was comfort sitting with these men on the jailhouse porch, sanguine Clarence and affable Mance, the old hands, though neither they nor the spectacle of the bird were enough to distract him from his worry.

Even his concerns over the election paled beside the guilt he felt for blackmailing Annabel. He could not forget the mist in her eyes or the way she tried to hide it from him. Somehow that was the worst part, that she feared for her dignity so, feared for it before him, her greatest admirer. It had been like turning a knife in her side. He clenched his fist and stretched it taut.

"How I wish I could close it down," Donovan mumbled absentmindedly.

"You won't have an easy time of it," Cordell said, interrupting Donovan's daydream.

Donovan realized he was scowling and blew his cheeks out. He looked around, afraid someone might have overheard. But there was only the empty street and the faint sounds of worship from the church.

"Yes, but we've got to do it right," Donovan said. "Otherwise, before we know it, he'll have red, white, and blue bunting running down bar and bannister, and he'll be handing out free drinks and having the whores whisper campaign slogans into the men's ears in bed."

Cordell chuckled. "I believe that new girl, the gold-haired, foreign one—she might be able to convince me to cast a vote against myself!"

Donovan grunted. He had seen the girl skulking about with the card-sharp earlier in the week—walking with him, even returning to the saloon wearing yesterday's clothes. He had begun to worry—really worry—that Jacob was in some kind of cahoots with the boy, that the boy was a hired gun. And the girl? Two new faces just before the election?

Oh, how Donovan hated the boy. The boy had made him do evil things, had made him throw that rock through Annabel's window. What had possessed him? *Fear*, a part of him whispered. *Fear of the boy*, but Donovan could not accept that. John Donovan feared no man.

He shuddered and told himself it was the ache in his back.

Donovan had pored over the boy's letter a dozen times, searching out what he was sure must be a hidden meaning. It was short, and he had it memorized.

Dear Conway,

No work in Topeka, but I heard of some in Missouri, maybe Texas— heard a place called Three Chop is alright. Maybe I'll go. Maybe I'll just drift 'til fall. I'll write if I find something.

Yours,
Salamander Soot

Donovan clenched and stretched his hand, wondering what kind of scheme Jacob might be plotting, what forces he might be calling down on Three Chop. He was more determined than ever to campaign against the saloon. *But how?* He was running out of time.

"Maybe we could have Rascal write something about it in the paper," Donovan said.

"Hmm," Cordell commented sleepily, his words lazy, half formed.

"Like what?" Mance asked, pulling off another plug of chew. Soon the church folk would disperse, and the town would all but go to sleep.

Donovan slid his lower lip along the iron gray of his moustache and shrugged. "I don't know yet, but Jacob'll make a mistake, even if it's only a word. He'll slander Aaron or the drys, and we'll have Rascal publish it and spread it throughout the county."

Donovan turned to gauge the mayor's reaction.

He found the man had slid forward in his chair, his ass perched on the edge, buttressed only by the lip made by the cross brace. His trousers bunched around his groin and his pant legs lifted enough to show a band of pale, veiny skin. He was still except for the rise and fall of his belly, his eyes white and hooded. He was sleeping.

Donovan leaned over and grabbed the mayor's tie by the knot, shaking him awake.

"I'm here! I'm here!!" Cordell spluttered, eyes bulging.

"You heard what I said about Rascal?"

Cordell sat upright, busily adjusting his garments.

"Publish an article . . ." Mance prompted.

"Right, right," Cordell said, waving his hand dismissively, as if he had always known the answer, maybe originated the concept himself.

"Jacob is naive and inexperienced," Donovan said. "Unlike you and I. We will goad him."

Cordell nodded.

"He will stumble, and we'll have Rascal publish in full view of the town."

"Yes, yes. Of course." Cordell trilled his lips and blinked sleep from his eyes.

It was a start—something to sate the Reverend's lust for a time.

CHAPTER 20

Chasby

CHASBY, IKE, AND ROD WERE THE ONLY SOULS IN THE BARROOM BESIDES Jacob. It was early afternoon, and a Sunday besides. Nearly everyone was at church or gone home.

I should be at church, Chasby thought, shivering. *Not to worship but to see the Reverend.* He imagined the look on the Reverend's face when he caught sight of Chasby in the pews, imagined him pausing mid-sentence, hands gripping the lectern, finding his boy just another stranger in the crowd. Chasby would convey with nothing but the hardness of his glare that he knew the truth, that he knew what the Reverend had kept from him all these years, the knowledge of his origin, of his father—his blood father.

Chasby swallowed, blinked, came back to the room, and realized his own fists were clenched tight. He uncurled them, and his fingers trembled.

He ran his fingertips over the green felt of the card table. He half listened to Rod and Ike talk nonsense while they dealt cards. Here and there he played a hand, but mostly he folded. He could not focus.

When he was not thinking of the church and the Reverend, he was thinking of the old man he had killed. *Murdered? No!* Killing a man in the act of killing Rod was not murder. *Even if Rod is a murderer?* Chasby followed this logic around and around, a snake eating its own tail. All the while in his head he heard a series of sounds: a baby's cry, a gunshot, and silence, repeating. So passed the hours.

"Kings!" Rod exclaimed, triumphantly raking a pile of coins toward him. It was low stakes—pennies mostly. They did not play seriously unless there was an outsider to swindle. Otherwise, what was the point? They shared most everything as it was.

Ike threw his cards face down on the table and shook his head. "You're one lucky bastard, you know that?"

Rod only grinned.

How can he smile like that? Chasby felt like whatever mechanism it was in his head that let him smile had broken down—the strings had been cut—and maybe for good. *You shot a baby the other day, for Christ's sake*, he thought, studying Rod. Reflexively, he touched the Bible in his left breast pocket.

Thou shalt not take the name of the Lord thy God in vain . . .

He wondered what his blood father would say, whether he felt the same kind of guilt, or whether it was the Reverend in him again.

But could he face the Reverend like this? Filled to bursting with guilt? Drunk? He wanted to sober up, but the memory of that dead old man stopped him, hounded him in his waking hours, tormented him in his sleep. Chasby knew of only one relief.

Rod dealt another round of cards. "Ante there, Chaz, if you're playing."

Chasby threw a penny into the middle of the table, where it rolled and spun and settled.

That Rod and Ike seemed to have forgotten the triple murder was unfathomable to Chasby. He had gone almost three days without a drink before arriving in Three Chop, having poured his liquor on the plain, and it had been unbearable, his head a cacophony of guilt. Rod and Ike may have been in the saloon with him at that early hour, but Chasby was the only man drinking like his life depended on it.

"Go on and look at your cards," Rod said, prompting Chasby.

He picked up his cards. His hands shook and he had to blink his eyes a few times to focus. "I got nothing," he said, and threw the cards down. "Fold."

"No one's even raised you yet," Ike protested.

"Fold," Chasby repeated, flicking his hand over his cards in disgust.

Rod shrugged. "It's yer money."

"It's that man's money, really," Chasby said sullenly. He took the last remaining swallow of whiskey before him and raised his hand for Jacob to bring more.

"That man who?" Rod asked, taking the bait.

It was as easy with Rod as it was with the Reverend. "The old man with the watch," Chasby said. "Or the boy whose money we took the other night—Sal."

Rod looked hard at Chasby, searching his face, more calculating than angry.

"Y'know, y'did good out there last week," Rod said, his eyes still on Chasby's face. "I told you once I didn't know if yer cut out for this kind of life, and I didn't mean the outlaw's life, neither. I meant *this* life." A flick of Rod's hand indicated he meant the room, the town, the frontier, the West.

"Anyway, you been doin' good. You need to relax, though, to enjoy yerself and yer spoils, and not worry so goddamn much. It was yer first scuffle—I get that. It'll pass. You can trust me 'n Ike on that. In the meantime just hunker down and wait it out however you like. Cards, booze, and girls have always worked for Ike 'n me."

"I don't want the money," Chasby said firmly.

"What d'you mean?" Ike asked, unable to comprehend that particular construction of the English language.

"I mean I don't want it—any of it." Chasby pushed his chair back from the table minutely, a gesture only but unmistakable. This was something that had been coalescing in him, unconsciously at first, until he found it suddenly precipitated in the words now spewing from his mouth. He listened even as he spoke, and the words sounded righteous. "It's blood money. And it's not even our money anymore. It's the boy's. It's the card-sharp's blood money now, and good riddance." Chasby turned to Rod. "I know you say it'll get better, but—" Chasby couldn't finish his thought. His eyes grew wet and his lips trembled, his whole visage already swollen grotesquely with drink.

"Chaz," Rod said, "if you want out you can get out, but yer going to have to wait a goddamn week until we're sure we're in the clear before you join the clergy or the army or whatever the hell it is you plan on doing. One week. I don't want to hear a goddamn peep."

Chasby thought Rod's anger was meant to cover something else. *Guilt? Fear? Could Rod feel those things?*

"Just deal again," Rod said, sitting back in his chair in disgust. "I lost my place."

"But I had a hand," Ike protested, checking his cards again.

"I said *deal*."

As Ike shuffled the cards, Jacob came by to refill Chasby's glass.

"Getting an early start?" Jacob asked as he poured three more shots of cloudy River Water.

"Had a headache is all," Chasby replied. He kept his hands in his lap so Jacob would not see them tremble.

Jacob nodded, stoppering the bottle. "Have you seen your daddy?" he asked, looking at Chasby. "I heard he was asking around about you."

Chasby felt the color leave his face. It would not do for the Reverend to find him, he knew. He needed to be the one to find the Reverend, or else he would have no power, no spine to ask the questions that needed asking. He needed to be one among the many, a stranger with a piercing stare.

"No, I haven't," he said, then added, "yet."

"He's not likely to come around here," Jacob said. "But if he does, you tell him I'll kill him on the spot. You warn him if you see him so I don't have that on my conscience. But I won't hesitate." Jacob had turned red with anger as he spoke, his usual placid manner marred by a jaw clenched to breaking.

Before Chasby could answer—if his overwrought brain could have found one at all—the squeak of the front door intervened, and everyone turned to see a man enter.

It was Sal, newly shaven and wearing a clean set of clothes. His guns gleamed newly polished in their holsters beneath a lopsided cartridge belt, which carried enough bullets to stock the general store.

Rod cursed.

The cardsharp scowled in return, his jaw jutting forward. He let his eyes linger on the men around the card table, and Chasby saw murder there. Then, turning, Sal pushed his hat back and approached the bar, waiting for Jacob to come take his order.

"You oughtn't to be here, son," Jacob said, hastening to meet him. "There's been enough trouble this week without your influence."

"Huh," Sal grunted. "You'll take my dollar or not?"

Chasby saw the man thump a silver dollar on the bar top—his pockets must have been twin mines to produce silver after what was lost at cards the other night. How he was not weighed down by it, Chasby could not fathom.

Ike and Rod watched, too.

Jacob looked at the coin then at the cardsharp. He pulled a double barrel shotgun from beneath the bar and laid it where everyone could see.

"I don't want any trouble, you hear?" he said, his hands resting on gunmetal. "There'll be order in my saloon, whether the Sheriff is here or not."

"I don't aim to make trouble," Sal said. "I just want to know where Kat is."

"Girls don't work 'til four," Jacob said. "Sheriff's rule, not mine. Take it up with him if you—"

"I didn't ask when she worked," Sal interrupted, his pale blue eyes flashing deadly. "I asked where she's at."

The men at the card table made no pretension of restarting their game. Rod had the beginnings of a smile on his face.

"Where she is?" Jacob asked dumbly, looking more confused than afraid. "She's upstairs, the madam—"

"You got her locked up there? I haven't seen her in days."

"The madam—" Jacob paled, and that was answer enough. "Sometimes," he explained. "Sometimes the girls try to run away—early on, before they get to know this place, before they see how fair I am—"

"Fair!" Sal sneered. "Fair!" He practically choked on his own anger.

Chasby shrunk further into his chair.

The shotgun still lay untouched between Jacob and the pale eyed boy, a barrier between them, a challenge.

Suddenly Sal grabbed Jacob by his starched lapels and dragged him over the bar top, throwing him to the floor.

"Give me the key or I'll blow down the door!"

"The madam," Jacob said, supine and cowering. "She's got it. On a chain. Please."

Sal put his boot on the softness of Jacob's belly and stepped over him. He left a brown smear on the barkeep's bright white vest. He made to go upstairs.

Chasby was already breathing his sigh of relief when Rod did something entirely inexplicable, something so out of place that it seemed to make the whole world stop.

He laughed—long and loud and gay.

"My God!" he said, slapping his knee. "If this ain't the saddest son of a bitch I ever laid eyes on." His body quaked with laughter.

There he goes, Chasby thought. Whatever abominable plot Rod's twisted brain had engineered was about to be birthed into the world. Chasby could feel it coming like an aching joint before a storm.

"What're you on about?" Sal asked, eyes flashing beneath the brim of his hat as they moved between Rod and Jacob.

"Let me ask you a question, friend," Rod said when he had fully composed himself. "Is it that good that she's got you all twisted up over it?"

Sal's face darkened.

"I only ask," Rod continued, waving his left hand lazily, his elbow resting on the felted green tabletop, "because you come to a new town and got felled in love in four days' time, and here I'm thinking this must be one special gal with one special cu—"

Rod turned like the rest as the door opened again, and Haddock stepped in from the street. His shirt was covered in dust and sweat. He took in the scene with a flick of his eyes.

"Trouble?" Haddock asked, his deep voice a rumble of far-off thunder.

"Stranger's got himself worked up over one of the girls," Rod said, his hand relaxed beside his holster.

"Sure has," Ike added as if it were three of them now having a conversation.

Chasby wanted to scream. *Shut your goddamn mouth, Rod!* But he knew he would not say it any more than he would have said it to the Reverend.

"Fella's ready to risk his life on a whore's honor," Rod added.

Haddock limped slowly into the room, his crippled foot scraping out a rasping beat.

"T'ain't risking your life to walk through this room of cowards," Sal rejoined, spitting onto the floor.

Rod bristled, but the sneer never left his face.

"What're you after, anyway?" Sal asked. "Stealing my money weren't low enough for you? You got a big mouth, you know? It'd look better shut."

As the men jawed, Haddock was moving closer to Sal—incrementally, obliquely, his maimed foot making him nonthreatening, invisible. Then suddenly Haddock lunged at the man. He threw his arms wide, trying to tackle him, but he could never have hoped to close the distance.

Sal sidestepped him easily. It was as if the turn of his head made no difference, as if he could see the whole room at once. In a flash the snake head struck, the gun raised in the space of half a heartbeat—a tenth part, even—bristling an arm's length from the piano man's sprawled back.

"Haddock!" Jacob cried, but he dared not move lest the boy fire.

Then without pausing, the cardsharp drew from his other hip—the gun barrel raised to Rod, who had started to draw his own gun. The boy had read Rod's mind, beat him before Rod could get the gun out of his holster.

Chasby was overawed. Every move the cardsharp had made was economical, precise, and lightning fast like the whole thing had been planned—a dance choreographed and practiced—every word, every turn, every flick of his pale eyes. Somehow this one man had taken five men hostage and he seemed as calm as he had been ordering a drink at the bar.

Sal said nothing. He only looked each man in the eye.

When Chasby's turn came, he studied the floor.

Then Sal asked, "How much for the girl?"

It was so quiet then that Chasby could hear the ticking of the grandfather clock on the second floor—and of course the baby's cry, the shot, and the silence.

"A . . . a dollar. I don't know. Whatever you want," Jacob stammered. He was standing now, still afraid to reach for his shotgun.

"Not asking for a lay," Sal said. "I mean how much to take her out of here."

"She's yours," Jacob said breathlessly. "Take her. She's more trouble than she's worth. Just put the guns down. You have my word we'll let you leave in peace, right boys?"

Jacob turned his sweaty face slowly to Chasby and the others at the table. "We'll let him leave, right boys?" he repeated, putting the edge of command in his voice.

A new grin came slowly to Rod's face, one that Chasby did not recognize. It was something unhinged, demonic, a grin without a sense of self-preservation. Rod looked to Ike.

Jacob blanched, near ghost-white now, his ruddiness compressed to pin-prick spots like the pox. He put the weight of all his authority into the question: "RIGHT, BOYS?"

"You think you can kill five men at once?" Rod asked. Somehow Rod seemed as relaxed as the cardsharp now, like he had already travelled through that valley of shadow and glimpsed the place beyond fear.

"Rod, don't—" Jacob began, but Rod cut him off.

"You'll never leave alive unless you leave now. Without the girl. Leave. I have a mind to spend a token or two tonight. I already spent the one, see. But you're so worked up over her, well I figure maybe I missed something. Maybe she's worth another?"

Sal's eyes showed a hardness then in their pale depths like the cold fury of Death himself.

Chasby opened his mouth to say that he only wanted to leave, but no noise came out.

Slowly, goaded by Rod's stare, Ike moved his hand to the butt of the gun at his hip.

"Goddamnit, Ike!" Jacob growled. "You'll get us all killed you stupid bastard!"

Sweat ran down Ike's face, and his arm twitched like Chasby's did after a day without a drink. "Don't yell at me!" he said.

"Draw on him," Rod said, almost whispering, looking almost beatific.

"You move that gun an inch, and I'll shoot your cock off," the cardsharp said, still wrapped in that inscrutable calmness. "I'll shoot it off and leave you alive so every man knows you got no cock."

Rod urged Ike on with his eyes, but it was the cardsharp's eyes that seemed to have him now, the pale blue freezing him in place, his hand limp on the butt of his gun.

"Goddamnit, Ike," Jacob muttered. He turned to Sal then, to the back of the man's head. "Look, son, that boy Ike is no good. I can't condone him. Take your gun off Haddock and put it on Ike. You won't move a muscle, will you, Haddock? You'll go to the bedroom and shut the door and lay down like it's all a dream."

The crippled man nodded his head. He wanted peace. Even Chasby could see that. There was none of the hate in his eyes that showed in Rod's. He had only wanted to protect his own.

"Ike, I know yer not a coward," Rod said firmly. "Don't let 'em push you around like that—he's a yellow-bellied scalawag."

"I'm going to pick up my shotgun," Jacob continued as if Rod had not spoken. "I'm going to do it slow so you can watch. It's Sal, right? I'm going to lift it slow-like so you can see, Sal, and I'm going to point it at Ike so you don't have to worry about him drawing, and when it's balanced like that, we'll untangle it, okay? And nobody gets hurt."

Rod sneered. "You gonna let him do you like that, Ike?"

Ike licked his lips but did not budge.

Jacob moved with exaggerated slowness to lift the shotgun, making sure to keep the barrel pointed anywhere but toward the cardsharp, moving it in a slow arc until it was pointed at Ike. Sweat dripped off the man's ridiculous moustache.

"Don't you draw, Ike," Jacob said, a measure of confidence having returned to his voice. "I won't hesitate to kill you. I knew your daddy, and he was no good, and I always knew you were no good, either."

Ike grunted. "I guess he wasn't much good." But there was a look in his eyes, too, like Rod's, like he had lost himself. If the feeling was contagious, it did not spread to Chasby.

And so, the five men were frozen by the immutable logic of the standoff.

Chasby closed his eyes. His whole body trembled. The air in the room was so taut he could barely breathe. He imagined the trajectories of the bullets from every gun at once, filling the room with crisscrossing lines. He felt tears in his eyes.

The baby, the gunshot, and the silence echoed again, louder now than before. He thought of his own blood, his father going out into the desert to avenge his family, and wondered what such a noble man would think of what his son had become.

How has it come to this? How have I let it get this far? He opened his bleary eyes and saw before him his last shot of whiskey.

Chasby smiled a wry smile and reached for the glass.

Give the man his drink. He's weak and lower than a goddamn toad.

Chasby raised the glass to his lips, hands shaking. He would fight his own battles his own way and in his own time.

Don't spill, you fool. First you need your medicine.

He drank the liquor in a single gulp and savored the burn. Then he set the glass down.

Only, he did not set it down as he meant to.

Halfway to the table it slipped from his trembling hand. He watched it fall, his vision still blurred by tears. It seemed to fall forever. When it hit the floor, it made a crash like a gunshot and shattered into a thousand glittering pieces strewing and skittering across the room.

Then there were more crashes.

Has everyone dropped his glass? Chasby asked himself this question as he tipped backward in his chair.

Tipping?

He had felt the blow that sent him backward but did not know where it came from. It was like someone had punched him.

When he hit the floor, he felt suddenly tired and thought he might sleep.

Sleep? Here? How funny!

There were sounds all around him, but they came from very far away. They were shouts and footfalls and splintering wood.

He felt a warmth spreading beneath him, from his belly across his back and down his arms and around his hands.

For a moment Hattie's face appeared before him, smiling, lurid.

He lifted his hands. They came away from the floor slowly, and it took him a moment to focus. They were red and speckled with glittering shards of glass. *I have cut myself!*

He tried to sit up but could not. The heat was growing now. He let his arms fall back to the ground, his palms up. He managed to turn his head. Blood was everywhere around him, red and slick and *hot*.

Yes, he thought, slipping down into the darkness. *Yes, it's hot! It's hot! It's hot!*

Part II:
Conway Mathers

CHAPTER 21

Pete

THREE MEN FORMED A TRIANGLE IN THE STREET, GUNS HOLSTERED. IT was high noon.

Pete Rayder adjusted the patch over his eye. Sweat sloshed in the empty socket and dripped down his cheek, a faint trickle of glistening pink.

Nash Warrick spat, and Pete did likewise.

This was a hot and dirty business, but Pete did not mind a bit of honest work. Hell, he would set fire to these towns and kill these lawmen for free to keep alive that dying freedom, the freedom to live or die, to kill or be killed.

It was a bonus that speculators all over frontier Texas paid good bullion for Nash and his gang to scupper rival developments.

Like removing warts.

And a wart stood before them now, if a wart could be said to cower. A lone sheriff, a greenhorn, a shining, misplaced penny. He would fall easily. That he was standing there at all was a kind of miracle, though his shaking knees spoke loudly of his fear.

Nash wore an easy smile that gave Pete confidence. Nash had killed dozens of lawmen in his life. What was one more? And this, an upjumped Yankee?

Nash touched the brim of his hat, a brief gesture that another man might miss. But to Pete, who knew Nash better than he knew himself, who idolized him, to Pete it was an acknowledgment of virtue, that this sheriff, green as he was, at least had the stones to stand before them and die for his duty, a sinking ship's captain.

"Mr. Sheriff," Nash said. It was a greeting and a death sentence at once.

The Sheriff stood defeated, though stand he did.

Pete felt the bloodlust rising in his belly then, felt it in the tinny taste marshaling at the back of his throat. This would be an easy kill, another eye taken.

"I'm nobody's sheriff," Donovan said weakly. He trembled visibly, watching his boots. *Why didn't he flee with the rest?* Pete wondered. For all his standing, Donovan seemed not to have much fight.

"Ain't that the truth," Nash said. "The whole town up and left you here to die."

"The town left town!" Pete added, licking his lips.

Then Nash began his monologue.

There was little as satisfying as hearing Nash narrate his justice as he doled it.

When he was done, the bullets flew—three from the Sheriff in a quick succession that Pete could barely distinguish, much less comprehend.

Fire flared in his leg, but Pete would not fall. He had eyes only for Nash. He watched the man's easy smile turn to shock, then confusion, then disbelief.

Then Nash toppled over, pronate in the dust, this the last town he would ever terrorize.

What now? Pete thought. Where would he go? Who would he follow?

He ran down Front Street, which could not even be called a street but a void between buildings. He ran on his injured leg, trailing blood, incensed and insensible. He ran without turning to see the Sheriff, though he knew somehow the man still stood, shaking.

Pete woke irritably to the usual smell of burnt coffee and frozen air. He checked the eastern horizon for a sign of impending dawn. There was none. He figured it must be five in the morning.

He had dreamed of Nash again. The dream had been coming more often—almost every night, lately—an old friend visiting after so many years. *How long has it been? Two decades?*

He turned onto his side knowing his shoulder would start aching before he could fall back asleep. The aches came quicker now, and some days they never subsided.

After lying a few minutes on his side, Pete accepted that he would not sleep. He crawled grunting from his pallet, his fossilizing flesh straining. A breeze blew a night's worth of accumulated warmth out of his long johns in a single breath, but it did not hurry him as he dressed methodically in flannel and breeches. By noon he knew he would be bare chested and sweating beneath his Stetson in the heat of day. Such was the way of the desert.

Pete kicked his pallet into a rough heap then lit a cigarette. He inhaled deeply with lungs as leathered as the skin on his nut-brown face. Shivering, he walked toward the low light of a concealed cook fire on the perimeter of camp, affixing a black patch over his gaping eye socket as he went. It was his singular vanity, covering that maw.

"It's too goddamn early for this," Pete said as he approached.

Owl Winston, with his oversized ears, had inevitably heard Pete's footsteps even before he spoke, but the man did not turn. He sat apart from the fire, attuned to the darkness, keeping dutiful watch as he did every night.

Tim Ripper was the only one of the two men to respond. "Sorry, Pete. I couldn't sleep. Decided to go on and start my day."

"Well you started mine, too," Pete grumbled, joining Tim by the fire.

It was a low fire—mostly embers—burning at the bottom of a three-foot hole. Tim sat on the edge with his legs dangling, his feet bare to better absorb the heat radiating from the coals. It was an old Indian trick—all the warmth but none of the light. It was good for a camp in the flatness of the desert.

Jack had shown them how to build the fire, of course, the way he had shown them all the old Indian tricks. It was rumored Jack himself was part Comanche—after all, he was dark skinned and hairless with a round face to match. It explained a good deal about what Pete mistrusted in the man. He seemed to have a delicate strangeness about him, which Pete thought made him weak.

Still, he would have preferred Jack to Arch. *Anyone's better than Arch.* Arch was dumb as he was strong with a temper that set him apart even here among outlaws. But none were better than Nash had been. Nash Warrick had understood the West, been born to it like a desert shrub.

Pete peeled off his socks and dangled his feet in the hole near the heat of the embers. He saw the pale reflection of a tin coffee pot set among the coals.

"That coffee ready?" he asked Tim.

"Shortly."

Pete cursed, realizing his cup was still in his saddle bag. He hustled barefoot to his place in camp and rummaged through the bag, careful not to wake the others. He wanted to talk with Owl and Tim alone while he had the chance. Bill would have done, too, but he was not an early riser. Neither would Pete be if he could have helped it.

He found the cup at the bottom of the bag, tin like the coffee pot and caked with a residue of dust and coffee grounds. There was dust in everything out here in the desert.

Pete pondered the mug as he walked back to the fire pit. It had been with him since the war, when he took it off a Union soldier, a blue-eyed boy who was his first kill. How many times had the Yank died since? Every time Pete had coffee at least. He saw the man crumpling to the ground a hundred yards away, folded in half as if by some invisible force issued from the barrel of Pete's rifle. That was the power and the freedom of the West, felt first on the battlefield, the power and the freedom that Nash had exalted.

"Alright then," Pete said expectantly, holding out his mug as he reclaimed his seat on the edge of the pit.

Tim pulled a rag from his pocket and carefully lifted the pot from the embers. He poured Pete the first cup out of respect for his age and wisdom and temper.

The coffee steamed in Pete's hand. He removed his cigarette and took a gulp. It was black and bitter like drinking molten metal—the way he expected it. He scrubbed his teeth with a finger then spit into the embers with a sizzle.

Pete caught Tim's eye and nodded at Owl, who still faced away from camp, listening.

"Owl," Pete said, straining another swig of coffee through the gaps in his teeth.

Owl turned his head to the side so Pete could see his profile. The man's features were a caricature of ugly— big ears, wide eyes, and a nose like a beak. Only his mouth was not oversized, drawn straight and pencil thin.

"Whaddya make of the last few weeks?" Pete asked.

Owl shrugged. "Been quiet."

"You getting tired of keeping the watch?"

Owl shook his head. "Nah."

"Owl, how long I known you?" Pete asked, changing tack.

"Longer'n anyone else in camp."

"Right, so we built up some trust, you and I?"

"Sure," Owl said, scanning the darkness once more.

"So you can tell me the truth, then? Seeing as you know I owe you for rescuing me from jail. Could've hanged there in Rolling Springs after all."

Owl nodded. "We got trust, Pete."

"Alright, then you can tell me the truth about it. What do you think about the last few weeks? What we been doing here?"

Owl was quiet, thoughtful. "I guess we ain't been doing much of nothing."

Pete whistled softly. "Ain't that the truth, Owl. Goddamn! We been sitting on our asses doing nothing for over three weeks, while Jack and Tommy and that kid Sal are out there doing God knows what. We're just waiting around like old maids for 'em to come back. Thing is, do you think they're even coming back?"

"Sure," Owl said. "Jack ain't the type to walk."

Pete frowned. It was true—Jack was not the type. But then Jack was no Nash, and even Nash had gone in the end.

"I'm not saying he's swindling us," Pete said. "Only maybe he's run into trouble. Hell, maybe Sal turned on him. I don't know. All I'm saying is we ain't doing ourselves any favors sitting idle this way."

"You gonna talk to Arch, then?" Owl asked.

Pete spit into the coals again then jammed the cigarette back in his mouth. "That bastard hasn't got a lick of sense. No, I ain't gonna talk to him."

"Then what?"

Pete looked at Tim.

Tim looked away, though Pete knew he was as eager as any of them to leave. It was practically all he talked about when they were alone. Tim stood, restless.

"I'm wondering what you think about getting rid of him?" Pete said, not that it really should have needed saying by that point.

Owl was quiet. "How?" he asked after a minute.

"The usual way," Pete replied, folding his arms. He was finally starting to get warm. "I'll tell him how it is, and we'll see what comes. It'll be his choice how he wants to go."

"Arch is good with fists and knives," Owl mused.

Pete did not respond.

"And you want me to back you?" Owl asked after a while. There was a grayness on the horizon now, the kind that makes a man wonder if he's imagining the dawn.

"Sure do."

"What about you?" Owl asked, turning fully for the first time to look at Tim.

"I'm with Pete," Tim affirmed. "I can't stand to stay here anymore—knowing my fortune is God knows where."

"Who'll take over after Arch? You, Pete?" Owl asked.

"Who else?" Pete answered.

"I don't know. What if Monty backs Arch or steps up himself? Most of the boys look to Monty with Jack gone, even if Arch is the one thinks he's calling the shots."

"Well that's the other thing, ain't it?" Pete said venomously, spitting again. "I ain't taking orders from Jack's Negro sidekick."

"Monty ain't even black," Owl said.

"Sure as hell he is. I whipped enough slaves to know one when I see one, light as he is."

"He's got red hair," Owl protested.

"I ain't had time to research his family tree, for Christ sake. The point is if we're gonna get off our asses and do something, we need a change in leadership, and I'm the one to do it."

"I suppose," Owl said, nodding.

Pete grinned, gnarled and gap-toothed. "Alright then. We got ourselves a threesome. I know the other boys are restless, too. Even if they're partial to Arch, I think they'll side with us when we promise to pack up camp."

Suddenly Owl put his index finger to his lips and cocked his head sideways, listening to something far off.

Pete and Tim locked eyes, a look of significance passing between them, and strained their own ears.

Just as Pete was about to say, "I don't hear a goddamn thing," a shot rang out in the twilight.

Tim cried out in pain, clutching his knee, which had been obliterated by a rifle shot. He fell and rolled onto his back, his bone showing white through the wound.

Owl and Pete drew their guns reflexively and stood in a crouch. The sound had come from somewhere outside camp, vaguely east.

"Guns!" Owl cried.

The rest of the camp was making noise now, too. Startled men kicked off blankets and fumbled at their weapons.

Pete followed Owl's gaze with his working eye. A hundred yards out, he saw something begin to move, a shape, a blacker darkness unfurling itself in the low light where before there had been nothing but dirt and grass.

It was a man, and there was no mistaking his easy walk. It was Jack Holloway making his way to camp, rifle slung over his shoulder.

CHAPTER 22

Jack

JACK'S MEN STOOD IN A LOOSE BUNCH, HANDS RAISED TO SHADE THEIR eyes from the dawn, guns half returned to their holsters.

Arch was first to speak. "The hell, Jack!" He was tall and muscled like a heavyweight prizefighter, his neck nearly as thick around as Jack's waist.

It was an ambivalent group arrayed behind Arch. Only One-Eyed Pete, Jack's constant detractor, seemed as resolute as Arch, his scowl half a grin—probably at the thought of killing Jack. But that was why Jack kept him around. The day an old bastard like Pete managed to kill him was the day Jack wanted to die.

Then there was Eagle-Eye Monty, his wiry red hair aglow in the sunlight, Monty who was as reliable as Sal in his own way. Jack had found good fortune with orphans. He would have just as well sent Monty off with the loot if he had been as natural a killer as the steel-eyed boy.

The rest of the men seemed more alarmed than angry—Owl Winston with his head cocked, eyes wide and blinking; Bill Snyder pulling shyly at his ear lobe and rubbing sleep from his eyes; Johnny Baldwin shifting nervously, unable to meet his eyes; and on and on. Most were half dressed and half asleep. Even Arch wore his gun belt around yellowed long johns, though he had managed to don his black Stetson.

Then there was Tim, groaning and thrashing in the dirt. He writhed halfway between Jack and Arch like some prize to be won, like the body of Patroclus.

Jack stood square, silent, his face schooled to incomprehensible stillness, an expression he had honed as a child—sheet-white, all emotions and none—inscrutable.

"You shot Tim," Pete spoke up. Of all the men, Pete's hand looked the most dangerous. It hung easy by his side, yet Jack knew the old sinews were pulled taut, ready to draw.

The rest of them had fists to loosen, belts to clear, hands to drop from ears and faces.

"I hope I did more than shoot him," Jack replied, starting forward again, daring the men—*his* men—to react. He knelt beside Tim, peering at the man's wound, though he kept Arch and Pete always in view. "Looks like I crippled him pretty good."

Arch scoffed, incredulous. "Hear that boys? I say we hang him from the nearest tree!"

The men murmured, though there were no trees in sight. But no one supported Arch outright. Arch scowled when he realized no one would. "Go on," he said, half turning to the men. "Tell him."

The men shuffled their feet, but all kept quiet. Pete grinned beneath his wire-gray beard.

"Tell me what?" Jack asked naively, though he figured he already knew. Men did crazy things when left to their own devices.

"Well if they're too shy to tell you, I ain't. It's why I'm standing here, after all," Arch said. He spoke with a big man's self-possession. "We had a lot of time to think while you were gone. And as we got to realizing you weren't coming back, we voted, and the men chose me to lead."

Jack nodded thoughtfully, watching the men, none of whom would meet his eyes except Monty, Arch, and Pete—Pete still wearing his own private smile.

Still squatting, Jack shifted his feet to peer around himself—to the sides and behind—as if trying to remember where he was.

"Not coming back?" Jack asked, his brow furrowed.

"Well of course I see you're back now!" Arch snapped. "Back for God knows what—to shoot Tim, I guess. Another betrayal!"

Then Jack saw Arch loosen his fist—the barest movement—and in the same moment Jack had his hand resting almost lazily on the grip of his own gun.

Jack watched realization pass behind the brute man's eyes, realization that he would be two beats too slow, that if he drew that gun then his last act on this earth would be firing it into the dirt.

Arch grunted but kept on running his mouth, his fists balling tight again.

"I don't see any loot with you, neither," Arch added, piling on the accusations. "No loot after all that effort, after all them months. After all them *dead*. So tell me again, why shouldn't I have these men here string you up for dead yourself?"

Jack stood slowly to keep the men from spooking. He pulled his hat low so the brim nearly covered his eyes, letting the silence draw wide until it must have felt unbridgeable to them.

None looked willing to lay hands on him—not even Pete—and yet you could never really know what men like these would do, especially in a moment of panic. Yes, he had left them far too long.

With his left hand, Jack pulled a loose-rolled cigarette from the pocket of his shirt. The hem was still damp from the Pecos, which he had forded in the night. "Anyone got a match?" he asked.

No one moved.

Jack shrugged and pulled a match from his own pocket. He struck it on the leather of his gun belt, struck it so his hand brushed the butt of his gun. When the cigarette was lit, Jack dropped the match into the dirt and crushed it with the heel of his boot. He did all this silently, and no one else said a word. He could hear the skitter of sand blowing across the desert.

"You got nothing to say for yourself, Jack?" Arch finally asked, his voice reaching a register too high for such a big man.

Jack only looked at him, blowing as much steam as smoke into the coldness of the morning air. "Who are you to hold me to account, Arch Parker?"

"It's eleven to one, Jack," Arch said, glancing at Jack's gun hand. "I reckon we'll make you tell what happened to our shares one way or another."

Jack looked behind the men then, looked far off, almost expectant.

It took Arch a minute to understand. "You got Sal and Tom crawling around out there like a pair of goddamn snakes?" he bellowed, whirling sideways, trying to see in two directions at once.

The men had turned variously, too, scanning the horizon uneasily as if Jack might have an army hidden behind him with some old Indian trick.

Jack drew on his cigarette. He nearly smiled seeing the big man so nervous. What did bigness matter anymore in a world of guns?

The men had stepped inward now, falling in on themselves like a herd beset by wolves. All but Monty who stood apart, as sure of himself as Jack.

"Tom's dead," Jack said like Arch should have known already. "Rangers got him."

"Another!" Arch said, slack-jawed but not speechless, never speechless. He threw up his hands, his gun truly forgotten. "Add him to the list then! Curse this goddamn train job! And what about Sal? Is he dead too?"

"No, Sal's hiding out safe and sound with the loot."

"Oh, I bet he is!" Arch scoffed, his face red with fury. "I bet he's got it all piled up on the floor like hay, and I bet he fucks you on it, too, that pretty boy. I bet you've made quite a life for yourselves with our goddamn loot, you goddamn Injun, goddamn half-breed!"

Pete's grin was gibbous.

The men shifted, on edge as if blood had been spilt, which surely it would be now.

Jack shook his head. For an instant he was that kid trekking along the Mississippi, turned out from his father's house, turned out from the army. But he let his younger self go—did not fight him, only let him go, and like that he was gone again.

"Pete," Jack called, forcing down the anger that made his gun hand itch. "What do you reckon got in and spoilt Arch while I was away?"

"Ain't no reason to talk to anyone but me," Arch growled. "I'm the leader of the Jack Holloway gang now."

Jack shook his head. "Ain't come up with a new name yet, huh?"

"He's sick is all," Pete chimed in, ignoring Arch. "We all are. That raid on the *Oregon*—most of us didn't even want to do it in the first place. We ain't as greedy as that. We're all of us rich men—richer than we ever hoped or had a right to be."

Jack knew Pete did not speak for the gang in this. Pete might be rich enough for his own taste, but for most men, there was no such thing. Half the men had squandered their earlier takes besides. There were as many ways to spend money in the West as to make it.

"Harry and Jean killed dead," Pete went on. "Now Tom and maybe Tim. And the rest of us near to being hanged. And what've we got to show for it? And you run off—what'd you think we'd do?"

"That's right, Pete," Arch said, cutting him off before he could campaign any further. "We got nothing at all except scattered. Scattered in ten directions and chased for days. Took us a week to find our way back here. We spent all that time planning the *Oregon* just to get harried near dead. We knowed you was slipping, Jack. But by God we didn't realize by how much!"

"Huh," Jack mused. "All this fuss like you ain't made men now."

"Made on promises!" Arch rejoined. "Made if you hadn't doublecrossed us. Made if you hadn't planned it all along, called the Rangers down, too, I reckon."

"You're not all the way wrong," Jack said, stamping out the stub of his cigarette and spitting on the ground.

The men cursed at that, hawed, kicked the ground. "Not all the way?" they asked one another. "What does he mean?"

Jack let them grumble and spit. He let Arch savor it. Then he said, "But you ain't all the way right, neither. No, not in some important ways. Tell me why'd I come back if I'd just had a double-cross in mind?"

"I don't know why you came back," Arch spat. "Maybe Sal doublecrossed your own double cross and you're so crisscrossed you ain't got nowhere else to go. Maybe you were afraid if you left us knowing the truth, we'd hunt you down. Or maybe," he paused for dramatic effect, "maybe you're just plain dumb."

"It was Tim who tipped the Rangers," Jack said matter-of-factly, like Arch should have known that, too.

There was a hush and rustle as all eyes turned to Tim, who lay whimpering in the dirt, oblivious.

"You know he's got a cousin in Limon, Colorado?" Jack continued. "A cousin with a big mouth. Must be a family trait. Sal overheard him in the saloon playing cards. Same way we found out about the *Oregon* in the first place. He was trying to round up a posse. I guess Tim thought he could get rich off a reward with none of the risk."

Even Arch looked dumbstruck.

137

"I couldn't call off the job." Jack spoke quietly, drawing the men forward on their toes. "The *Oregon* was once in a lifetime. And every man here knows stick-up jobs make just as dangerous work. We came ready for a fight. And we had surprise on our side, because I never told nobody the time or place, not exact, and I knew they knew."

"If that's true, you shoulda warned us," Pete said angrily, "We rode out with that bastard, and he might've turned on any of us!"

By the sound of their murmuring, the men agreed.

"Too much fuss," Jack said, dismissing the thought with a slow shake of his head. "Would you still've gone if you'd known?"

"I guess that's my business," Pete said, gritting his teeth.

"No it ain't, either," Jack replied.

"Even if your story's true," Arch broke in, "it don't make up for the fact that you let Sal take off with our loot. You're either a double-crosser or a fool, and either way you ain't fit to lead this gang."

"I reckon I don't need to explain myself to you," Jack said.

Arch sneered, stuck out his barrel chest, and raised the veins from beneath the meat of his neck. "You really are that dumb, ain't you, Jack? We voted, and we voted you out. Now the only thing left is to kill you."

"We need him to tell us where Sal is," Pete pointed out.

"Course we do, Pete," Arch said, glaring at the man. "I was getting to that bit." To Jack, he said, "Now how 'bout you make it easy—"

But he did not finish the thought.

Jack fired a hole through Arch's gun hand, affecting a bloody stigmata. Two more shots tore into Arch's belly, doubling the big man over in agony.

All this occurred in the space of a single heartbeat. Only Pete had found the wherewithal to reach for his own weapon, but he did not attempt to use it—only let his hand brush it as if by accident. He folded his arms in submission, if a bull steer could be called submissive.

There was no doubt who held charge now, if ever there had been.

"This ain't a democracy," Jack said quietly, pushing his wide-brimmed hat to the back of his head.

The men looked at each other and kicked at the dirt. They looked to Arch, too, but he had been transported to some far-off place, shock and pain contorting his face as he bled out in the dirt not far from Tim.

Eagle-Eye Monty walked round to stand behind Jack's right shoulder, his rifle now aimed at the men, his coarse red hair akimbo.

"Well. What do you boys have to say for yourselves?" Jack asked, eyeing what was left of his gang.

Now they all spoke at once.

"We just didn't know what to do, Jack!"

"You was gone so damn long! And Arch—he got to talking—"

"What were we supposed t'do?"

The men nodded and looked to one another for support.

"And we ain't been paid, neither," Bill Snyder said, still with his hand at his ear. He was a short, fat man with a thick brown beard that stretched to his belly. "It ain't much of an excuse, I know. But when a man's up at night, his troubles weigh on him. And nothing weighs heavier than empty pockets."

Jack spit and adjusted his hat and said, "Now, the way I see it, you all forfeited your shares when you raised your hands to vote me out."

The men grumbled and sulked but did not protest openly in the face of Jack's quick draw.

"But I know you men are like a weathervane. And I should've known better than to leave you unattended so long, especially with a sweet talker like Arch around. So I'll let you all keep half your shares.

"That's still a lot of money, especially when you consider Tim and Arch are counted out, as are those who fell. Your shares will still be worth ten bank jobs." Jack folded his arms high on his chest. "And it's voluntary. Any of you who don't believe Sal's waiting with the loot are free to leave. More for the rest of us."

"Where is he, Jack?" Owl asked, finding his voice for the first time. "Where's Sal?"

"Somewhere in Texas is all I'm prepared to tell you."

The men scratched their heads in contemplation, weighing the odds that Jack was telling the truth, that Sal had not run off on his own, that they could make the trip to Texas without being found by the law.

"If you choose to take your shares, you're under my command 'til we lay our hands on the loot," Jack added. "That's the deal."

The men nodded, and Jack nodded back, and that was enough.

Jack turned to Arch, squatting again.

Arch had curled up on his side, cradling his belly like a baby. He looked up at Jack, whimpering, his eyes wide with fear. He was panting and bathed in cold sweat.

"Arch, I know you got a big head," Jack cooed, stroking the man's hair. "Problem is you ain't got the brains to fill it." He rapped his knuckles softly on the man's skull to demonstrate its emptiness.

A tear brimmed in Arch's eye then slid down his cheek into the orange dirt below. He opened his mouth, ropes of spit clinging to his parted lips. A guttural cry escaped, unintelligible.

Jack leaned forward and whispered into Arch's ear so only he could hear.

The man's eyes went wide. He tried to speak, but by then he could only gurgle blood.

"What about Tim?" asked fat Bill Snyder when Jack stood.

Jack nodded, forgetting Arch like the rest. "Tim's coming with us," he said to the evident surprise of his men. "He'll be an ever-present reminder to all: what's the cost of crossing Jack Holloway."

The men did not like it, for it seemed cruel, but they understood. Even Bill acquiesced, who was as close to Tim as any. No punishment could be too harsh for betrayal.

To demonstrate this fact, Jack walked up to Tim and ground the heel of his boot into the man's wound. Jack felt the grit of sand scouring the man's flesh.

Sprung from his stupor, Tim cried out in renewed anguish.

"Later, when you think your leg hurts bound and tied on the back of a horse, remember this," Jack said, twisting his heel. "Remember this and maybe you'll be thankful at least that the you then ain't the you right now."

Shortly the pain became too great, and Tim passed out.

Jack lifted his boot, breathing heavily. He turned to the men. "Bygones is bygones. Let's break camp. We've got a man to see by the name of Conway Mathers."

CHAPTER 23

Jacob

SOMETHING MOVED BEHIND HIM WITH A CLATTER LIKE A GUNSHOT.

Jacob whirled to see Haddock staring at him, chest heaving like his own, having stumbled over a chair.

Haddock!

Somehow he had forgotten the man in the moments after the gunfight as surely as he had forgotten himself. A quick look around the room told him they were alone. Of course, he had known that. He had seen Rod and Ike flee, had seen the gunslinger—*surely he was a gunslinger!*—stagger out, clutching his side. All three had left bloody boot prints behind, tracking a path as wide as the boardwalk outside. All these things he had seen, and yet he could not shake the feeling of danger and of death that filled him to bursting, as if they were still standing in the room, guns drawn, life and death in fragile equipoise. He felt a disconnect in himself like a chain had come loose in the machinery of his brain, his thoughts whirring without purpose or effect.

Ordinarily Jacob would have been comforted by Haddock's presence, yet the unflappable man looked as afraid as he felt, his fear compounding Jacob's own.

Haddock's eyes yawned wide, swallowing light, staring at something on the floor.

Jacob's wits came upon him suddenly, the old apparatus lurching. "Haddock!" he cried, his voice sounding strange, foreign. "Are you hurt?"

Haddock shook but did not move, still fixated on something Jacob could not see beyond an upturned table where the men had been playing cards.

Jacob left the bar and ran to Haddock's side, reaching for the man's hand. He brought it to his face, feeling the smoothness of it against his cheek, clutching it like a doll. Then he gasped.

The preacher's boy, Chasby, lay on his back, broken like a vase fallen off its stand.

Dead? Jacob did not realize he had asked out loud until Haddock replied. Or maybe he had read his mind.

"Dead," Haddock answered, his deep voice pronouncing it like the will of God.

Haddock did not need to check Chasby's pulse to know the boy's fate. Surely he had seen enough death in his life—on the plantation, in the war, in the West. Nor did Jacob need to check himself once he really looked at the boy—strewn on the floor, his face pale against a halo of blood, eyes wide and staring.

The force of the bullet that killed him must have knocked him off his chair.

Dead!

Suddenly Jacob realized the front door of the saloon stood ajar. He cursed and ran to slam it shut.

Haddock followed, dragging a stout oak chair behind him, which he used to bar the door.

Hastily, Jacob loosed the tiebacks that held the curtains. When they had fallen in place, he parted each to peer into the street, repeating the action at every window until he was sure no one lurked there, no steel blue eyes. It was Sunday, thankfully, and the street stood deserted as far as he could see on either side.

Haddock had already moved to bar the back door.

Madame Fuselli appeared on the stair then, calm but expectant. It could not have been more than a minute since the shoot-out. She took in the scene with poise, pausing only a moment when she saw the boy. It was a practiced eye, one used to violence, though her experience must have dated from a time before Three Chop.

Where, then? Jacob wondered, realizing how little he must know of the woman, even after so many years. As long as she had worked for him, with him, nothing like this had ever happened at the saloon—plenty of gunshots, plenty of broken plaster, but the murders always happened in the street.

Jacob wiped his hands.

"I'll keep ze girls quiet," the madam said, nodding her head curtly. "But you must prepare for trouble."

Jacob heard the nervous patter of feet above. He wondered if the girl, Kat, had heard Sal's remonstrations, if she had gone berserk in her room. It was a wonder more of the girls had not come down. Maybe the gunfire was just a wrinkle in the velvet of their opium dreams.

The madam pulled a revolver from her voluminous skirts and trundled back up the stairs without waiting for Jacob's acknowledgment. She would set a watch at the window and let them know if anyone came to call.

Only when the sound of her footsteps had receded, when the doors and windows had been shut, when the room had been checked and rechecked so he was sure they were alone, only then did Jacob let himself feel the weight of the calamity before him.

He felt it in the mind-blanking horror of that pool of blood, in its copper smell, in its slickness, tracked inadvertently over boards and carpets. The preacher's boy, Chasby, lay dead in his saloon, killed by a gunslinger, killed in a dispute over one of his girls, *killed by the sound of a liquor drink shattered!* Everything the Reverend preached against had conspired to kill his one and only son. It was everything Donovan had repeated, everything the drys of the county had feared, come to pass. Right before the election.

And Haddock! The implication! After all that had happened, what would the Reverend do when he discovered Haddock had been in the room where his boy had been killed? Stones in the street would not be enough unless it was a biblical stoning. They would hang him, surely, and the Reverend would tie the knot himself. How Jacob wished he had followed his first instinct and killed the man the minute he had seen Haddock's bruised and bloodied back.

Suddenly the coincidences seemed too exact, too convenient. The horror of realization stole over him. *They must have planned it!* He gasped.

The cardsharp, Rod, Ike, Chasby—any or all could have been the Reverend's agent, John's agent, the whole scene a clever piece of theater.

And yet the blood was real. Chasby's corpse was real, at least as real as these things could seem which were so out of place.

Haddock came up beside him then, placing the flat of his palm on Jacob's shoulder, Haddock, a black man of uncertain status even here at the end of the earth, Haddock with blood slicking his boots. By God, Jacob had seen less blood on a slaughterhouse floor.

"You've got to leave," Jacob said suddenly, looking up at the man, at the even, unlined face, at the unblemished color of his dark skin. There were the beginnings of a beard on Haddock's jaw, though he shaved clean every morning. Jacob could almost tell the hour by it. "Leave before they come—the Sheriff, the Reverend, the rest. They will come."

Haddock squeezed Jacob's shoulder and looked at him a long time without speaking.

Jacob feared in those moments that he would refuse to run again after so long, refuse to allow himself to be chased, to be prey.

"And you?" Haddock asked finally.

Jacob shook his head. "I've got to stay behind and try to salvage this." *This*, meaning the saloon, the town, their life.

Haddock nodded and embraced him, grabbing a handful of the hair that grew white on the back of Jacob's head, pulling him close, kissing his mouth, which still tasted of the copper of fear.

Jacob felt the hardness of his body beneath the loose weave of his cotton shirt. "Brother," he said wryly, before pushing him away. "You must go. Now." It felt like tearing out a vital part of himself.

Haddock took a last look at the preacher's boy, shaking his head, then disappeared through the back door.

A lifetime of struggle weighed on Jacob then. He felt like a sagging shelf holding all those memories. He thought he could feel the fibers cracking, finally cracking, ready to spill his pulp even as he began to straighten up the room, preparing for the inevitable onslaught of the aggrieved.

"What happened here?" the Sheriff demanded as he burst into the barroom.

Jacob had known by the madam's signal, a certain staccato beat on the floorboards above, that he was coming.

Donovan stopped short when he saw Chasby, the boy's dead face already contorted by rigor mortis. "Hell," he said, jaw going slack. "What have you done?" He said it almost to himself, the way a man looks at some natural disaster—the aftermath of a tornado or a flood—sober, overawed, beyond anger.

Mance and Cordell filed in behind him, registering shock and nausea in turn.

For Jacob, the effect of the gore had worn off. It had been an hour nearly since Haddock had left, and he had already made good progress in tidying the room, though it would take a remodel to restore it—shattered lamps, dented brass, torn damask, and the stain, a sea.

Jacob wondered why it had taken the Sheriff so long to arrive. Rod and Ike must have skipped town without saying a word, or maybe they had died in some untrod alley.

For his part the cardsharp—*the shootist!* must have been halfway to—*to where?* Jacob shuddered to think of Haddock crossing paths with the steel-eyed boy out there on the plains, ambushed by his flashing hands, fast as whip falls, whistling in the air as they flayed. Still the odds were better for him than remaining here.

"I said what happened!" Donovan demanded again, stalking the perimeter of the violence like a shoreline.

"Happened?" Jacob repeated, still wrapped in his own thoughts. *Will the blood soak through the floor?* For the first time in a long while, he wished he had put down sawdust.

Jacob caught Donovan's murderous look and wiped his brow reflexively, trying to focus. His silk kerchief was already soaked through. He wished he had thought to have Madame Fuselli fetch another from his armoire.

"It was that cardsharp, Sal, with Ike and Rod."

"You let that man back in after I banished him?" Donovan asked, incredulous, as if the saloon was his property to do with as he pleased.

"Not to gamble—he wanted a girl," Jacob said, trying to keep his emotion in check.

Donovan looked at his watch. "You're not supposed to work those girls before—"

"He wasn't looking for a tumble," Jacob interrupted.

Donovan held Jacob's eyes until Jacob had to look away, wiping his brow once more. The kerchief added more sweat than it took away. He hated to give John the satisfaction, but the terror of the last hours threatened to unman him. His moustache drooped prodigiously.

"So the outlaw came down and then what?" Donovan asked. He had stopped across the room from Jacob, the crime scene a gulf between them.

"He had words," Jacob said, leaving out the words and their object, letting the Sheriff draw his own conclusions. "Rod started to needle him. Next thing I knew, the guns came out. It happened so fast, I don't even know who drew first—Rod, maybe? Or the boy?"

A cough reminded Jacob that there were others in the room. Cordell sat at a table in the far corner, putting as much distance between himself and the dead boy as possible. He cleared his throat again and wiped his hands on his suit pants.

Mance had turned a fallen chair upright—*Ike's chair*—and sat in it, chewing his lip thoughtfully, the boot of his good leg on the card table, his hat pushed back on his head, looking unruffled now as a barnyard cock.

"Who shot him?" Donovan asked, motioning to Chasby.

Jacob shrugged.

"Is that yours?" Donovan asked, pointing to the shotgun on the bar top.

The sweat on Jacob's brow turned cold. He had never stopped to wonder if it was shot or a bullet that killed the preacher's boy. Everything had happened so fast, just like he had said. He thought he had hit Ike and maybe Sal, but who could say for sure? Who could say which gun had killed the preacher's boy in that maelstrom?

The room swam before Jacob's eyes as Donovan took his first steps into that pool of blood, crossing the shoreline of that violence to crouch gingerly by the body. He probed the stilled chest with an unflinching index finger.

Something gave the man pause.

Donovan rose slowly as if it pained him, regarding Jacob coolly before he spoke. "It isn't shot, if you're wondering," he said, though his look said it may as well have been. "You know where they went?"

Jacob shook his head, feeling sick again. "No." At least the room had stopped swimming. *At least the Reverend's boy did not die by my hand!*

Donovan nodded as if he had expected as much then turned to Mance. "Run get the Reverend. And tell him what happened on the way so the shock doesn't kill him."

"You sure he should see, boss?" Mance asked as he rose, knocking his chair over with a *crack* that made Jacob jump. "He ain't gonna like seeing his boy dead in the *Lady*."

"Aaron will want to see," Donovan replied, and that was that.

Mance shrugged and crossed the room to the door, tracking blood with both boots along the way.

When the Reverend Aaron entered, night was falling, and the deepening shadow made the barroom seem even more macabre than it had by day. Chasby's corpse took on the yellow glow of lamplight.

Aaron stood at first by the doorway, staring at Chasby from across the room as if coming too close might make the thing real, irreversible.

Jacob could see Mance through the doorway peering over the Reverend's shoulder, his cheek fat with chew.

For some minutes Aaron did not say a word, nor did he move perceptibly.

Jacob had come to hate even the sight of the man, his wire frame, black eyes, long dark hair. He felt a schadenfreude that revolted and pleased him at once, like probing a loose tooth.

"How?" the Reverend finally asked, moving into the room, eyes flicking from Jacob to Donovan.

Mance followed him in and perched on a table by the door, his peg leg swinging free in the air. He seemed unconsciously to stroke the butt of his famed pistol.

Somehow Jacob knew the question was not meant for him, though he was the only witness.

"Outlaw—calls himself the Salamander," Donovan said. "Came in this afternoon to visit some of the girls. Got to talking with Chasby and the boys, who he said owed him money. There was a misunderstanding, guns were drawn. The outlaw killed your boy."

The Reverend turned his dark gaze to Jacob then. His eyes glittered with an unnatural light, their hatred palpable even in the depths of their blackness.

But the Reverend said nothing, only moved to Chasby and knelt by the boy's side. He placed his hand on the boy's chest as Donovan had done. Chasby's shirt was covered with blood so the hand came away dark red.

Jacob watched the Reverend start at the sight of his palm, his eyes wide, but his hand remained steady, and his body did not tremble.

The Reverend probed Chasby's chest with his pale, spidery fingers, a kind of grotesque imitation of a hand at the keys of a piano. After a minute he discovered the wound that had killed his boy, a dark hole bored through Chasby's shirt pocket. From the pocket the Reverend removed a book.

Jacob saw that it was a Bible—bound in leather, its pages worn and stained with use and now with blood.

Slowly, the Reverend stuck a long, pale finger through a hole in the center of the book. It came cleanly through the other side, just as the bullet must have done.

Through the Bible and into Chasby's heart! Jacob shuddered.

Wordlessly, emotionlessly, the Reverend tucked the Bible into his own black shirt. He looked at Chasby a minute more then stood as if searching for something.

Aaron cast his eyes about the floor, about the halo of blood with its glass shards like winking stars. He turned a circle, his feet sure even in the slickness, spinning like a dancer, the arc of his gaze spiraling wider and wider until suddenly he stopped, his eyes fixed on a point on the edge of the scene.

Like everyone else in the room, Jacob followed the man's gaze, and he felt color drain from his face.

There, on the edge of that frozen chaos of broken furniture and blood spatter, was a single truncated boot print, faint but unmistakable, as if the man who left it had been walking on his heel, as if he had no foot.

Haddock.

Jacob cursed.

A sneer cracked Aaron's thin lips, and that unnatural light danced like fire in his eyes when he turned them on Jacob. "Where is your brother?" he asked, his voice calmly sinister.

"He—I sent him away," Jacob stammered, his belly numb. "On an errand."

Donovan frowned and began to hoist himself out of his chair.

"Do you lie in the face of such clear evidence?" the Reverend pressed. He savored the accusation, like the snap of a trap, the confirmation of some long-held suspicion.

Without thinking, Jacob strode from behind the bar. He saw a flash of confusion and maybe something else—*fear?*—cross the Reverend's features, as if he thought Jacob might throttle him on the spot.

But Jacob stopped a foot away from the man, thinking only to tread on the boot print, to smear it over with his own shifting feet, though, in such proximity, his fingers did itch to feel the brittle cartilage of the demagogue's throat. "What evidence?" he asked.

The Reverend looked from Jacob to the now obscured print and back. He said nothing, but then the sneer did not leave his face, either, as if to say the evidence did not really matter anyway.

Donovan studied the floor, saw nothing, for there was nothing left to see. He looked quizzically at the Reverend.

"Donovan, a word alone?" Aaron asked—*commanded?*—his eyes never leaving Jacob's.

Donovan nodded. "Cordell," he said, but the mayor was already on his way out, probably relieved to be excused to dinner.

Mance followed him without a word, ever the loyal deputy.

"And you?" Donovan said, turning to Jacob in dismissal. *Dismissal from my own property no less!* He seethed, yet there was something in John's face that gave him pause, something unexpected—pity, perhaps. Could it be? Jacob sought the words to make his case, but none came to him, and in the end he left. In truth he wanted to be gone, if only to rid himself of the stench of that room, to rid himself of the shadow—*the light?*—of the Reverend's black and glittering eyes.

Jacob left through the front door to walk down Front Street, wondering if he should not hire a horse from the stable and follow Haddock, wondering if they should not flee and start over after all.

CHAPTER 24

Donovan

DONOVAN SAW GRIEF STAMPED UPON THE REVEREND IN A DISPLAY OF emotion he had never before witnessed in the man. There had always been something of incandescence about him, but nothing earthly until now, nothing of weakness, nothing to show that as he impacted the world so too was he changeable. Chasby's death had penetrated his shell and touched his soul.

"It is a sign," Aaron said, placing his hand over his shirt where he had tucked Chasby's Bible. The hand left a red-brown smear, iridescent against his black vestments. "Our sin is too great, undeserving of mercy. God will not protect us now."

Donovan gritted his teeth, seeing the logic of it, remembering the image of the Reverend's finger probing that fatal hole, a wormy apple, a promise broken. But what did it mean for him, for his salvation? What did it mean for his prayers, his demonstrations of faith?

The Reverend came so close to Donovan that he could smell the man's breath—hot and sweet and cloying like anise. "It is not enough to campaign," the Reverend said. "It is not enough to plan for some far-off reconciliation between Three Chop and the Word of God. We have been slothful, cowardly."

Donovan found himself stepping back, fleeing the paleness of the Reverend's gaunt face, the light of his eyes.

"We cannot leave our obligations open-ended. It is not enough to campaign on closing the saloon."

Pain throbbed in Donovan's back.

"Look, you, at this scene!" The Reverend cast his arm over the floor and the body that lay supine upon it. "We are in the very belly of the beast, and we see the carnage on which it feeds!"

The Reverend began to pace, tracking still more blood across the barroom.

"So what do you propose?" Donovan asked, apprehensive.

"We use this," the Reverend replied, motioning to Chasby's body, though he would not look at the boy directly anymore. "We close the saloon tonight. We call it temporary. No one will question the logic when they learn what's happened. We'll call a town meeting to explain ourselves and make sure the multitudes of the faithful attend."

"And that'll put us back in God's good graces?"

The Reverend ceased his pacing then and regarded Donovan as if for the first time that night. "It is a start," he said after a few slow, thoughtful breaths. But his face had changed, the anger replaced by something else—a mix of pity and revulsion that Donovan understood was reserved for the sick and the dying.

"Surely your stunt with the Meacham woman has set us back with God as much as with the faithful, yet closing the saloon would be a start."

Donovan clenched and stretched his fist. Doc Marshall had failed him, but surely God would not. *And what did Annabel have to do with anything? Did God really care how men governed themselves on Earth?*

"Then you'll ride for the outlaw," Aaron continued, resuming his pacing, said it like it was nothing. "By the time you're back, by the time they see the man hanged, they'll be used to the saloon being closed, and they'll hail you as a hero for doing it."

Donovan's pulse quickened. He had forgotten the outlaw. He had seen murder in the man's eyes, yet he had let him walk freely out of the *Lady May* the night he banished him from the card table. Why? Had he been afraid then, too?

Well, he was certainly afraid now, contemplating a chase across the plain, wounded though the outlaw was. Donovan did not know if he could even rise from a pallet in camp without help, much less sit his horse. Already he had suffered two attacks of blinding pain that day. They were coming more frequently now. Another sign of God's displeasure?

Perhaps. God had taken two sons from him and a wife, and who was left now but for him?

"I'll send Mance with a posse," Donovan said, but the Reverend dismissed the idea.

"It must be you. You will find him and hang him, and we'll dress Chasby up in his Sunday finest so the town can see what kind of man he really was."

The Reverend stopped at the feet of his boy then, his shyness suddenly gone, and drank him in. His long black hair shrouded his face so Donovan could not see the emotion there, but his shoulders were as rigid as the cross. After a minute he said, "And when enough time has passed and Jacob's Negro brother-wife hears the outlaw is hanged and returns thinking himself safe, you will arrest him and hang him too."

"Haddock?" Donovan asked, confused.

"You saw the half-print as well as I, Sheriff. Two men have fled the scene of their crime. Surely both are guilty. I'd have Jacob, too, if I could prove it—the husband and the wife."

"Aaron," Donovan began, but the man silenced him with a look, his eyes coal black and burning. Donovan swallowed his protest.

He nodded.

He would deal with Haddock when the time came. Aaron would come around when his blood had cooled, when his own boy's blood had been scrubbed and bleached from the floor. He just hoped Haddock did not return too soon, if ever, for his own good.

CHAPTER 25

Pete

PETE HAD SUSPECTED JACK DID NOT KNOW SAL'S WHEREABOUTS EVER since the wispy man had shown up in camp, guns barking. Now he knew it. Not because he had learned anything new but because he could read a man, and Jack read wrong. Pete let his opinion be known in a quiet way that Arch had never had the sense for.

He spit into the deepening twilight, aiming into the narrow space between horses.

They were riding close, Pete and his companions. Bill's leg brushed Pete's, and Pete grunted. Bill steered his mount away, putting a half step between them again.

The gang was strung out in knots along a quarter mile. Jack rode at the fore, his mood so foul that even Eagle-Eye Monty kept a few horse lengths behind the man. Pete and his contingent brought up the rear, riding slow as they pleased. A number of the younger men rode with them, too. Young men appreciated strength, and Pete felt himself waxing radiant.

"I wonder why I ever complained about being bivouacked," Bill Snyder said, looking to the light as it died along the horizon, vanquished by the bulk of the Earth. "I thought I'd wanted a bed. Now I only wish I had sleep. He's gotta call a stop soon."

Jack had kept them riding three days straight. His only consideration in that time had been for the horses.

Bill frowned and tugged at his waist-length beard.

"I thought I needed a woman," Owl put in. "Thought I'd go stir crazy in that camp. And now I reckon I couldn't get it up for Bathsheba herself."

Listening to their prattle, Pete seethed. Griping was what soldiers did. There was always griping. Where the griping stopped, mutiny began. He had thought the men were nearly there this morning, riding silent and sullen through the frozen air. They had been dragged on a fruitless chase through grueling desert, over endless plains. He had thought the time not far off when they would turn on Jack with finality. But they were accustomed to following orders, to following Jack.

"I dunno, boys," Johnny Baldwin said. Johnny had big eyes that were oddly shaped like tilted half-moons, sunken deep in bruised sockets. "It feels like we're riding into a hangman's noose to me. They got Jack's picture on all the wires and in all the papers. Who knows if they got us in there, too?"

"How do you know?" Bill asked. Johnny, like most of them, could not read.

"Tim read the papers while we was bivouacked," Pete answered. "I seen 'em myself."

"It don't feel right is all," Johnny said. "There're eyes out here in the dark."

Even Pete shivered a little, grizzled old man though he was. It struck him that a good ghost story might be just the thing to keep these men on edge. When Jack slipped up, he would have them ready.

"Yer just worryin' like always," said Bill.

"I was right about the *Oregon*, wasn't I?" Johnny rejoined. "I said I had a feeling, and look where it got us."

"You always have a feelin'," Bill said. "Ain't nothing to worry about we can't handle, right, Pete?"

Pete grunted. "I reckon it ain't a risk worse than most we've taken. Then again, you all know I been fated to hang since I was a young man."

"Fated?" Johnny asked, squinting as if his eyes were not already deep enough in shadow.

"Sure," Pete said, lighting a cigarette and settling into his saddle. "I ain't told you it before?" He looked sideways at the men and bared his crooked teeth in a grin.

The men around him shook their heads, already awed before the tale had begun.

"Well it was one of Nash's favorite stories," Pete said. "Another man might have called it bad luck, but Nash loved it. That's the kind of man he was.

"See, when I was a younger man, I got work managing plantations. Before I was overseer at White Oak Grove in Missoura, I took appointments all around the Southern states, including one in Louisiana.

"Now this plantation was a small affair with a handful of slaves only, and it was so near the bayou we was practically raising cane in the swamp, but by God, I kept 'em working and earned my keep doing it.

"And it happens one of the slave girls falls pregnant. She was one of her master's favorites, see, so I had to keep my good eye on her." Pete thumped the bone of his socket for effect. "And I had two back then, mind you.

"On the day she gives birth, she disappears from the fields early, and I go looking for her, and I cain't find her nowhere. I searched all over that goddamn plantation. Then as night's falling, I set out into the swamp, expecting to find her half eaten by a gator, hoping not to get 'et myself.

"But no, I find her long after the sun is set in the home of this old Creole woman, the girl with the babe in her arms, and she's sleeping on a cot peaceful as can be.

"The home ain't like a one you've ever seen—it's raised above the bayou on stilts with a kind of knotted rope ladder hanging down. It was surrounded on all sides for miles by nothing but cypress and tupelo, the Spanish moss hanging thick as curtains around the whole place like it's some kind of four-post bed, hanging so you'd never find the place unless you knew to look or came upon it just right like I did.

"I'd heard tell of an old woman alive in the swamps. Said you could hear her at night speaking in tongues, but I had never believed it 'til I saw it myself.

"It was just the one room, but it was full of all manner of strange candles and symbols and jars of the unknowable.

"The old woman is blind as death and yet she burns candles! Maybe the spirits need still to see for her to work her chants. And draped around her neck are enough beads and necklaces and bones to weigh a man down, and woven in her wiry hair are feathers and bones and beads, too, wove so tight it ain't clear where the feathers end and the woman begins. And she looks at me, with her dead, pale eyes like mother of pearl, like she knowed me my whole life when I come to get the slave girl and her babe.

"She walked up to me and laid a hand upon my face! And ordinarily I would have had her whipped for that kind of insolence, only she was blind, and I could tell—I ain't done the place justice nor her in telling it—but I could *tell* that this woman had that voodoo spirit in her for real, come in from them godforsaken islands. She looked me in the eyes when she was done feeling my face, when she was done feeling my hands, and she told me I would die in the noose but die an old man, and I knowed it was true, by God. I just knew it."

When Pete had finished, only the horses dared make a sound. The men were caught up, each pondering the impossible clairvoyance of that old Creole woman, each wondering at the magic of the world.

"What'd you do?" Owl spoke up, asking for them all.

"I roused the girl and took her back and I set that upraised voodoo hut afire. I tell you I have no idea how that old blind woman climbed up that ladder, but she sure never climbed down, not while I was watching. But I never heard her cry, neither, only smelled the strangest smells you ever smelt in the smoke and saw the strangest colors you ever seen in the flames.

"I watched the fire 'til it subsided into the bog, and I never heard and never saw a thing save the cicadas and the swallows and the crackle of kindling."

"Maybe she knowed you was coming," Bill said, "seeing how she knew how you would die."

"Must've," said Owl, raising a hand as if to cross himself.

"Maybe," Pete allowed, drawing deeply on his cigarette so the coal burned bright in the settled darkness. "But that's the thing about fate, ain't it? You can know it, but that don't mean you can change it. Old woman like that would've knowed as much."

The men nodded at the simple truth of this. They rode on in silence. Rode, Pete thought, toward a revelation unknown even to Jack.

CHAPTER 26

Kat

A FAINT SOBBING CREPT ALONG THE HALL AND INTO KAT'S ROOM AS SHE tried to sleep.

She had cried enough tears of her own to feel immune. She had entered a world of restless sleep, of sleepless rest.

She rolled onto her side to search the trees outside the window for that inevitable tinge of pre-dawn light. But the leaves rustled darkly still, and Kat closed her eyes once more, begging to be swept from consciousness. Her own internment and Sal's shoot-out—*death?*—had blurred into one interminable waking nightmare, a calamity of loneliness and despair. He had come to save her. He might have died for it. She thought of him alone astride his mare, bleeding upon that great prairie, adrift.

She had heard the shouting and the gunfire. She had felt the thing go wrong, had known it, had watched the boy lope into the gathering dusk through her window, his gait unmistakably altered, his arm pressed against his side. A thousand times he had run like that in her mind, and she had watched each time until she could not tell when she was awake and when she was asleep. Each time she saw it with the same horror, and the emptiness grew inside her, like her heart had swelled and pushed everything out of her then burst to leave nothing but a space for the blackness to take hold.

Madame Fuselli had come to her then. Had unlocked the door and left it so, taunting Kat with a useless freedom.

Kat was nearly asleep when the faint sound of sobbing pulled her back again. Angry, she rose and padded barefoot through the hall to locate its source, pausing, arms folded, to listen outside each girl's door. At the fourth door, she found her mark.

Minnie?

Kat had expected it to be one of the younger, weaker girls, one of the sops or opium eaters who would sometimes bawl with a pitiful senselessness that sickened her. But Minnie, Mance's Minnie, was older—probably thirty—beautiful and confident as a stage actress.

Kat turned the knob and pushed the woman's door open.

She found Minnie on her side, looking out her own window. Kat saw the same trees outside her own, here from a new angle, and again she thought she saw a glint of dawn in the leaves.

She closed the door behind her, and the sound of the latch made Minnie turn suddenly.

"Who is it?" she asked, sitting up and wiping her eyes.

"Kat," Kat said softly, uncertainly. She had stopped just inside the room, shivering in her nightdress.

"What are you doing?" Minnie asked. She sounded more embarrassed than angry, her voice hoarse in a swollen throat.

"I heard you," Kat said. "I couldn't sleep."

Minnie looked at her a long while, and Kat heard the first call of the waking songbird, that unmistakable harbinger of day, which could not play tricks on the ear the way light did on the eye. Minnie groaned and slumped beneath the blankets.

Then she began to cry anew. When she was able, she turned to Kat and said, "Aren't you cold?" She patted the bed beside her.

Loneliness drove Kat beneath the covers, the loneliness of her prison room, of her wounded lover, for that was somehow what he had become in trying to save her, a sacrificial death being, to her young heart, the greatest gesture of a lover, unmistakable and pure.

Minnie whimpered and dried her eyes once more with the corner of her duvet.

Kat waited patiently for the woman to unburden herself. It was something instinctual, the waiting. In the meantime she enjoyed the warmth.

"How do you like Three Chop?" Minnie asked eventually, when the birds had begun to sing in earnest and early dawn mottled the room. Soon

Madame Fuselli would stir, and the old cook, Sam, would start frying bacon in the kitchen.

Kat answered honestly. "It's not what I expected."

"What did you expect?"

"I don't know."

Minnie smiled wanly. "How old are you?"

"Seventeen."

Minnie nodded. "You miss your mother."

Kat thought this was probably true, and she would have cried herself if the emptiness and the blackness had not already conspired to make her numb.

"Is this your first job?" Minnie asked.

"No, I worked in San Pablo."

"For a dance hall or a saloon or a wagon?" Minnie turned around to face Kat. She pulled a sheaf of hair forward over her shoulder and began to play with the ends. It made her seem almost a girl.

"A saloon."

Minnie considered this. "I bet the saloonkeep's wife didn't like having you around."

"He wasn't married."

Minnie nodded. "That's worse." She stayed quiet a while, averting her gaze and staring at the wall beyond Kat, her fingers still teasing the ends of her hair. Then she said, "It's kind of you to come here."

Kat shrugged. "I don't aim to be here long. At the *Lady*, I mean."

To Kat's surprise and consternation, Minnie smiled. "Oh, I thought that too when I started!" she said knowingly. "I thought I would come to Three Chop and work a few years and take my purse full of silver somewhere else, where I could make myself into a respectable lady. You know there are so many men in the West and so few respectable women! Not Three Chop, of course—Three Chop has the soul of an old town, but in newer towns, boom towns, the men always outnumber the women ten to one, and I thought I would take my purse and buy a house and have my pick of all the men in the mine or on the ranch—find me a strong man who did not drink and was kind." She laughed, then, seeing Kat's crestfallen face, grew serious. "I'm sorry. I didn't mean to laugh at you, but it's better to know. You do this to survive, not to prosper."

Only the numbing embrace of the blackness kept Kat from weeping. She pressed on stubbornly. "But in a town this big—five dollars for time with a man, fifteen for the night—I'll make a cowpuncher's wage ten times over in a year! A lifetime's wage in three!"

Minnie clucked. "But the saloon takes a share and so does the madam, and you'll have to pay for your room and board besides, and you'll fall ill and get tired and there'll be days you can't get out of bed, not to mention days you're on the rag. And there'll be expenses, too, for the doctor, if you contract a disease or if you find yourself with child."

Minnie grew bitter as she spoke, and by the end tears wetted her cheeks once more.

Kat had known a girl in San Pablo whose teeth fell out from mercury treatment for her bad blood. Her gums were always bloody, and still men paid a quarter. Truly men were a species apart.

"What about the madam? She has bought herself out, and I heard of a woman in San Pablo—"

"No," Minnie interrupted, serious now. "There will always be a girl who makes it that way, the way there will always be a man at the mine who strikes a seam and makes a lifetime's fortune in a week on his claim, and it is their stories that pull the rest of us in, pull the rest of the men to the mountain to sweat into the rock, but for most of them—nearly all of them, of *us*—there will be nothing but the pain of labor."

"Minnie, I didn't know," Kat stammered, but she could think of nothing to say to this woman who had invited her into her bed.

She made to rise then, but Minnie grabbed her arm, bitterness turning to fear. "No! Wait. I just—" she paused, drying her eyes. "Please stay."

Kat settled uncomfortably back into the mattress to stare at the ceiling. She wondered how long before the clock in the hall would strike, giving her an excuse to leave for breakfast.

"I'm pregnant," Minnie said after a while. She had stopped crying. She sounded empty now like Kat, her voice an echo in her chest.

Kat turned to her then, not understanding exactly, because she had never been with child, only she thought a part of her knew what it would be like since she had seen the way her own mother had looked at her. Again she felt the doubleness of her dreams, seeing herself through her mother's eyes. Her mother thought she was watching her child, but truly it was Kat watching her mother watching her, observing her tenderness with a kind of sympathetic detachment.

She reached out and put her hand on Minnie's arm beneath the blankets.

Minnie moved toward her, laying herself against Kat, and Kat draped her arm around her.

"Have you been pregnant yet?" Minnie asked a few ragged breaths later.

"No."

"You're lucky. You'll be luckier still if you can't."

Kat thought what a curse that would be. She had always imagined herself with a daughter, now faceless as her husband, but she had never questioned her destiny.

"This is my fourth time," Minnie continued. "I use all the powders and the pills that the other girls swear by. But still it happens. There is only one sure way, and the doctor does it, and it is torture."

Kat stayed silent, though her heart beat full and fast.

"Most girls stop getting pregnant after two or three. But not me. It would be a blessing if you can't."

The clock in the hall struck, and Kat could hear some of the other girls moving and talking in the hall, but she did not stir. She wondered how she had not thought more about the risk. It was something that happened to women, not to girls like her who were not ready, and yet she bled.

It must have been the sense of destiny that did it—the vividness of the dream—the house on the bluffs by the bay, the faceless daughter, the husband who would protect her. There was no history of false starts in that dream, no barrenness, until now at least. Minnie had cast a pallor over the dream in a way even Kat's own blackness could not.

But there is a face to the man after all, isn't there? Sal's face. And he is already rich, and he will protect me. He killed a man already, didn't he? Just downstairs?

Her heart went out to him, watching over him as he rode. She closed her eyes and groped toward him. *Surely I would know if he had died?*

If they did not bring him in, she vowed to find him and nurse him to health. And if they did bring him in, she vowed to save him. Either way they would be even—she would not owe him anything for his protection, because she would have given him his life.

"Do you know whose it is?" Kat asked. It was a foolish question, but somehow it was important to her.

"Yes," Minnie said. "A mother knows. It is the deputy's, Mance's, and it is a girl."

Kat did not question the logic of this, because she was not a mother. She believed it could be so.

"Will you tell him?" Kat asked.

"I had not thought to," Minnie said, but Kat could tell by the way she was breathing that she was thinking of it now. She met Kat's eyes.

"Mance isn't so bad," she said. "And what's the worst that could happen?"

She touched her belly then, and Kat did too, instinctively.

It felt no different, and yet it was different somehow. There was life there, and a certain reverence stole upon her.

CHAPTER 27

Jack

JACK RODE EFFORTLESSLY, AND HIS MOUNT RAN THE SAME. IT WAS THE old Comanche blood, passed down by his father, the lifeblood of generations of horsemen. The gang trailed miles behind him now. Only Sal might have kept pace, if he was there, if he had his black mare beneath him.

A white-framed farmhouse resolved on the horizon, a point just on the verge of seeing, and Jack spurred the horse—not *his* horse, who had been left by the wood next to Sal's, but another—Janus, a fleet-footed stallion. Jack rode him hard until the house loomed clear on the plain, and Janus was slick with lather.

Jack could make out the porch now, and in the yard he saw a figure in canvas pants and a white work shirt scrabbling at the ground.

Jack swallowed. Here he would learn his fate, whatever it was, by the presence or absence of a letter from Sal to Conway Mathers.

The figure stopped his work to follow Jack's steady approach.

Michael was handsome as ever, with a square jaw and a shadow of black stubble on his chin and cheeks. His eyes were dark, his lashes full as raven's wings. There was more of their mother in Michael—*taibo!*—in his features if not his complexion, ironically. Michael had always been his father's son, loyal to the tribe and to the land, though he bore a white man's name.

Michael was muscular with strong arms and rough hands. How Jack had envied him as a child, had wondered what it must feel like to live in such a body and with such height!

"Michael," he said, touching the brim of his hat. His heart beat hard, but he stilled his face.

Michael rested his hands atop a long-handled hoe. He stood astride the furrows of a garden plot, where he had been turning the soil before the freeze, the last in a line of fierce nomads, born a generation too late, turned reluctantly to tilling the old reservation soil—first given, then taken away, then earned again in defiance.

To Jack, who had been away so long, who had found his own frontier to carry on the fight, the figure his brother cut seemed more parochial than his memory allowed. Then again there was defiance in the straightness of those furrows, in the honest labor of those folded hands.

"Jackie," Michael replied.

Jack wanted to embrace his brother, but he had forfeited that right long ago. He saw Michael's eyes move to the horizon. Jack turned to see a column of dust rising in the distance—his faithless gang, following dutifully now.

He did not have much time alone. His stomach turned as much from regret for what he had lost as from fear for what he had come to ask. "Michael, have you got a letter for me? For Conway Mathers?"

Conway Mathers had been the name of their white grandfather, who had been killed by their father in the taking of their mother. Even this she had forgiven as she assimilated into the tribe, though she had not forgotten nor let him be forgotten to her boys.

Jack held his breath. He had not allowed himself to question Sal's fidelity or his ability until now, when he sat confronted with the thing, waiting for words to form on his brother's lips, unfamiliar yet not forgotten. He had the uneasy feeling that his plan was unraveling, its pieces so delicately crafted now strewn across the country from Colorado to Texas to God knows where. And all because of Tim's treachery.

Michael looked at him a long while then said, "No," as firmly as his feet were planted astride those straight-line furrows.

Jack set his jaw even as his vision momentarily swam, his brother's shape bleeding into the background like some monolith of stone. He doubted that he would ever know the truth of what happened to his treasure. His eye twitched. His belly twisted and bit like a nest of rattlesnakes, as if it would break free. He exhaled. He let it go. What could be done? He would search.

"When'd you last check Graves Point?" he asked coolly, composure cosseting him once more.

"Wednesday," Michael said, still looking beyond Jack at the rising column of dust.

Six days. There was hope, then, that Sal's letter had arrived in Graves Point since.

Jack nodded. "Is Pareiya inside?" He dipped the brim of his hat in the direction of the farmhouse.

Michael looked from Jack to the house and back.

"Yes, but I wouldn't." Michael made it a suggestion, not a command.

Would I have obeyed?

Jack leapt from Janus and led the horse to the porch where he tied the lariat to the rail. He did not look back at Michael, though he heard the scratch of the hoe begin again as he climbed the stoop.

It was not the homecoming he envisioned, not without the letter, but it would have to do.

Automatically, Jack removed his hat as he entered. He made a warning of heavy footfalls, yet no man came to greet him. Nothing stirred save the fingers of a small fire in the stone fireplace, incongruous with the hot, dry day.

Sunlight filtered weakly through a small window set high in the wall near the door. The house felt stale compared to the openness of the field. The house itself was a kind of surrender, like the farm, permanent.

He recognized a few items—rugs and skins and cookware—yet all seemed duller than they had when he was young, camped in the canyons of the Caprocks. It was as if everything had begun to decay when Jack left, and there was none of his mother's skill to make it new.

Jack found his father sitting in a crudely built chair before the fire, his thin frame overwhelmed in buckskin and quilts, a pillow at his back. He was frail with great bunches of loose skin about his neck and arms. His eyes were cloudy when they fell upon Jack, cloudy and gray where once they had been dark.

No wonder this wraith had not risen to meet him.

"*Ahpu*," Jack said, making his face harder than he felt.

Pareiya craned his neck on tremulous tendons, but he seemed not to see Jack or to know for sure if someone had spoken.

Jack moved closer until he could see the lines of that puckered mouth folding in upon themselves, until he could see the fragile network of blue veins beneath the paper skin, until the gray, iridescent eyes that had once been dark as pitch night met his own, and Jack saw recognition there.

Silence lay upon the room, stifling, punctuated only by the chatter of burning logs.

"You were gone a long time," Pareiya said, his voice the barest echo of what it had been once, yet unmistakably his—the voice that had chastised, denigrated, banished.

"Did you make it to Wyoming?" Pareiya asked, not waiting for a response. "I hear it's beautiful country there, with the river. Imagine that, a house by the river."

Then Pareiya laughed! It was half a cough, yet it was the only time Jack could remember hearing the man laugh in all his life. That famous stone face— now more like crushed gravel—cracked along the thin line of his mouth, showing what teeth remained to him, showing the blackness of his gullet.

Jack could not fathom the man before him. He stood paralyzed, breathing the sour smell of decay, a feeling of unreality coming over him, as if the scene were not real, or perhaps it was his memories that were not, or both.

"I tell you I wouldn't mind. I wouldn't mind at all," the old man said, his laughter subsiding. He smacked his puckered lips. "Of course it's a far ways from the Llano. What a drive! You'll have to tell me all about it. Through the ancestral lands?"

Wyoming?

"But there's things to do here, Ollie," Pareiya said, his face growing hard again. "*Pia* is ill, and we got work to get done yet."

Suddenly Jack understood. His father had confused him with Ollie, his sickly brother, Ollie who had been killed on a cattle drive.

It was a kind of victory.

"It ain't Ollie," Jack said, finally finding his voice. "It's me, Jack."

Confusion passed over Pareiya's face.

"No, *nami*'s gone outside," he said, shaking his fragile head. "She left when we wouldn't let her come to Adobe Walls! She left to join the *taibo* then and disappeared! Disobedient child!"

The man fixed his gray eyes on Jack, and the old rabid look was in them. "Why do you talk nonsense, Ollie?" he growled. "You would leave us, too, to join *taibo* on a cattle drive? We used to kill the cowboys and take their longhorns! Don't you remember? No, you were always too weak. You children, you grew up soft and empty-headed. Only Michael among you stayed! Only Michael!"

Pareiya chewed his lips and snarled, lost in convoluted remembrance. Then he cried out, "Jane! Jane!" The sound was not loud, but Jack knew it was a cry by the way it grated in the old man's throat.

Jack studied his father as the man yelled the name of Jack's mother, long dead, and the anger that had lived in him so long ceased, for he knew his father was well and truly dead, dead like her. He knew there were none left to deny him now but Michael, and Michael had forgiven him in his own way.

Jack stepped forward and grabbed his father's face by the jaw, turning it to his own, peering into it, vowing to remember him this way—as a husk.

To his credit Pareiya did not look afraid. That would have been too much to ask. He only sneered—what was left of him at least.

When Jack released the face, dark bruises showed where his fingers had torn the paper flesh, as pale now as *taibo*'s, hidden as it was from sunlight.

Pareiya stared absentmindedly into the hearth as if he had already forgotten the encounter. "Jackie's run off, you know," he said quietly, almost to himself. "Your mother will be devastated to lose her. Maybe you shouldn't go after all." Pareiya mumbled something else then laughed.

Jack turned and left the old man by the fire in a house he had barely known and would not know again.

The smell of manure and fresh-turned earth was overwhelming after the staleness of the farmhouse. Jack spit and donned his hat.

Michael stood with his hands folded over the handle of his hoe once more, his feet planted astride those furrows, eyeing the line of bandits sitting their horses in his yard. Jack saw them through Michael's eyes—hard-bitten men with grizzled faces, slouch hats, and glinting gunmetal. They looked a proper gang of outlaws. Even Tim played his part, trussed to the back of a trailing horse, delirious but grave.

"Mathers ain't at home, boys," Jack said, unhitching Janus and climbing onto his back. "Time to see if he's left word in town."

CHAPTER 28

Donovan

THE CROWD OUTSIDE THE GENERAL STORE WAS AS BIG AS DONOVAN HAD ever seen in Three Chop, and it was restless, too—as many as a hundred townfolk and farmers, all milling and stamping and waiting for news to fill in the spaces left by rumor. All morning they had been waiting for him, their Sheriff.

And yet it was Mayor Cordell who spoke first, just as they had rehearsed.

"Ahem," Cordell said, standing to address the crowd, clearing his throat and wiping the sweat from his palms on the pleats of his pants. "As most of you have probably heard, there was a murder yesterday inside the *Lady May*." Cordell removed his hat and held it before him, condolent. "Maze Chasby was killed in cold blood."

The crowd gasped.

"By whose hand?" someone yelled, and the rest of the townfolk piled on in their impatience for truth.

"By whose hand," the mayor began, already ad-libbing, to Donovan's annoyance. "Why, by the hand of an outsider! A man by the name of Salamander Soot, who had been skulking around our fair town for some days, causing trouble at every turn!

"You may remember him from the *Lady May*, where he nearly swindled his way to a gunfight just three nights past! And again last night, it appears he came to finish that work!"

The emulsion of townfolk and farmfolk churned, stirring the men to cross their arms and grasp their guns, the women to hitch their babes higher and clutch their apron strings. A tempest was forming, the town lifting from its foundations for Donovan to realign.

"However, as far as we can tell," the mayor said, raising his hands as if to quell a panic, "the Salamander acted alone."

It was an answer to a question no one was asking, but it had been one of Donovan's demands of the Reverend—to announce Sal acted alone, to leave Haddock's name unspoken. The Reverend had agreed too quickly by half, no doubt satisfied to take vengeance in his own time.

A problem for another day.

"Indeed, these are the facts of the case," Cordell continued, reciting admirably now from the script Donovan had written him. "First, the Salamander arrived in Three Chop one week ago. Second, he began a campaign of gambling, whoring, and drinking—that unholy trifecta. Third, he lied, cheated, and stole, defrauding his victims at the card table. Fourth, he murdered a man in cold blood and attempted the killing of two more over a whore as much as a game of cards."

Donovan looked toward Jacob as Cordell forged that unspoken yet unmistakable link between the saloon and the murderer. Jacob stood on the edge of the crowd, set apart, his face darkened in shadow. Donovan wondered again whether Jacob had hired the outlaw, called this destruction down upon his own head. It would be fitting. It would be just.

"Where's the outlaw now?" someone yelled.

"Eyewitnesses saw the Salamander fleeing the saloon between five and five thirty in the afternoon," Cordell answered. "He left on his horse, which a farmer's boy, James Weston, son of Bobby Weston, saw some time later headed due north on the plain." Cordell ostentatiously removed a gold pocket watch from his vest to note the time. "That was some fourteen hours past."

"And who will bring him to justice?" came another voice from the crowd, clear and carrying yet somehow quiet, self-contained.

Every head swiveled toward the source, toward the black-haired Reverend. Aaron stood ten feet tall then, soaking up sunlight as if the clouds had parted to bare a ray of sunshine for him alone.

This was Donovan's cue—more pageantry. He took his place beside Cordell, his gun polished and gleaming at his side.

"It's a tragedy, what's befallen our town," Donovan said. The expectation of the crowd invigorated his lungs so he felt like he could be heard for miles. He looked at the Reverend. "Who will bring justice, you ask? My horse is saddled. Mance's horse is saddled. We leave forthwith to bring the outlaw back to Three Chop to answer for his crimes!"

The crowd cheered those simple words, and the men began a call to arms.

Donovan tried to hide his haste as he raised his hand for silence. This would be the trick. "The man is wounded," Donovan said sternly, "and I'll not have him treated any way but lawfully. The deputy and I will ride out alone. We'll ride dispassionate." In other words, Mance would be the only witness to Donovan's frailty.

"We want to see him brought in!" yelled a red-bearded farmer, one of the Reverend's.

A hundred voices echoed in agreement.

"No telling what tricks he's got, Sheriff," said another, Florence Peabody's club-footed boy, Noah. "You may need us men—all of us!"

"I've been Sheriff of this town near on twenty years," Donovan said, setting his jaw. "I reckon I know what I need. I understand you men want blood, and it's blood I'll give you, but this is sober work. I'll bring the outlaw back; this I promise. We'll try him fair, and when he's found guilty, every last one of you can add a turn to the noose about his neck."

"Now," Cordell said, picking up the thread of the show. "While the Sheriff is off bringing the outlaw to justice—not justice to the outlaw, mind you—I have determined that the *Lady May* shall be closed for investigation and for repair."

On cue, Tom Brandywine circled around the front of the *Lady May* from the alley where he had been waiting with his sons and grandson, three generations and all of them carpenters, to board up the front of the saloon.

Donovan turned his eye to Jacob along with the rest of the crowd.

It took Jacob a moment to understand.

Methodically, Tom nailed the first board across the door.

"Get away from there Tom Brandywine!" Jacob cried, moving toward the man in a run-walk that was neither effective nor dignified. "That's my saloon you scoundrels! You've no right!"

Tom's sons and grandson intercepted Jacob, not laying hands on him—they were good, honest boys—but neither letting him pass.

The longer Jacob struggled, the purpler he became, the more impotent he looked, and he soon realized it and backed off, straightening his suit, adjusting his cravat, twisting the ends of his moustache into form.

All the while Tom nailed board after board.

It was symbolic, of course, the nailing of the doorframe. The back door was left accessible—there were a dozen women living in that saloon after all, though most of them numbered among the crowd at the moment, painted and redolent. But as long as the boards stayed up, they were a scarlet letter, and to take them down would be to defy Donovan at the very time he was risking his life for the town.

A fitting campaign event, Donovan gloated, winking at Cordell, who looked every bit the part of mayor in his fine suit even in the heat. It was a good plan—well crafted—and Donovan flattered himself that the particulars were his own.

Across the crowd, Donovan met Jacob's eyes and held them. They were too far, too deep in shadow to be read, but he fancied that beneath the bluster there was real fear.

CHAPTER 29

Pete

PETE AND HIS FELLOW RIDERS CAME UPON THE REST OF THE GANG ON the outskirts of Graves Point. Pete reined in his mount. The other men followed, forming a semicircle around Jack, who sat his horse smoking a loose-rolled cigarette.

"You're a quiet lot," Jack said, looking from one man to the next but looking longest at Pete. "I reckon you'll remember yourselves once you find the bar." He handed money to each man from his own pocket.

Pete looked at the bill Jack pressed into his hand—twenty dollars. It would go a long way in a small-town saloon. He sensed the men's spirits lifting. All but Tim, who lay splayed and semiconscious on his trailing horse, and Bill, who felt a certain responsibility for the boy.

"What about him?" Bill asked, grabbing the lead of Tim's mount protectively.

The men regarded the traitor with distaste. Most had already consigned him to the realm of the dead.

"I'll drop him with the sheriff," Jack said like it should have been obvious.

The men grunted, and Johnny's eyes went wide.

"Don't worry," Jack said, his eyes wrinkling in amusement. "The sheriff and I have terms. Still, don't cause more trouble than you're worth tonight."

Pete rode with the rest of the men to the saloon. From across the street he watched Jack and Monty tie Tim's mount to a hitch in front of what must have been the jailhouse.

The wildflower and his Negro sidekick. Pete shook his head and pushed through the door to the bar.

The *Mansion* was like any other in the new wave of Western saloons with upjumped pretenses—crystal and china dishes, cuspidors, carved trim work, patterned wallpaper, and a floor filled with cloth-covered tables that made it as much dining room as bar. Only the sound of billiards in a nearby room and the whir and clack of roulette wheels made it something more than a hotel. That twenty dollars might not go as far as Pete had thought.

"Mezcal," Pete grumbled as he approached the bar. He felt the eyes of a well-dressed citizenry upon him, eyes shining bright as their silver watches. He was suddenly aware of the grease in his unwashed hair, of the mud caked on his boots and dungarees.

He took the mezcal from the bartender—served in a crystal tumbler—and savored its bite as he thought of the hotels of the early days, the hotels of mining camps and cow towns, where the floors might be dirt and the beds might be unwashed blankets stuffed with straw and broken china, where men could be themselves.

He caught himself just as he was about to spit on the floor. No sawdust here—only burnished wood and oriental rugs. Where were the nude paintings on the walls? Where were the whores? Where were the jugs of moonshine, the canvas cots, the workmen?

Feeling worse than when he entered, Pete ordered another mezcal and made his way to a pair of tables commandeered by the rest of the men.

They seemed happy enough—oblivious to the incongruity of their surroundings.

Owl hooted as a piano man started a song at the bench.

Three times Pete got up from his seat for more drink. Three times he felt the eyes on him, three times he was disappointed by the smoothness of the liquor. His mood darkened by degrees until he could take it no longer and retired to the street. It would only be a matter of time before a hotel like that got its hydraulic lift, its electric light, until it became just like any other hotel in St. Louis or San Antonio or San Francisco.

Pete pulled a rolled cigarette from his pocket and lit it with a match he struck on his boot. Outside the air even smelled wrong—no dirt or horse shit or the sweetness of old straw.

He pondered the brick houses. He pondered the orderly flow of traffic on the sidewalks, which were limestone in places, limestone instead of wood! Everyone was polite and dressed up—ladies and gentlemen—the whores and johns must have been relegated to another part of town altogether. Pete thought he could probably find them if he only followed his nose, but somehow he did not feel like having a whore tonight.

Spitting on the paved walk, he crossed the street to the jailhouse.

"He's making an awful goddamn racket," the sheriff said when Pete entered, as if carrying on an earlier conversation.

A quick look around told him Jack and Monty were gone. *Probably gone to bugger each other.* There was only Tim, whimpering on the floor of an iron-wrought cell.

The sheriff was a stocky man with jet-black side whiskers and a squarish, upturned nose. The man leaned back in his leather chair, legs crossed on the table before him, reading the paper. Pete wondered if Jack was mentioned in that paper, or the *Oregon*, or even him. Not for the first time he wished he could read.

"Good of you to come," the sheriff said, putting down his paper and setting his boots on the floor. "I would've got Jack but I didn't know where to look."

Tim groaned like a dying animal.

"Oughtta put him out of his misery, maybe," Pete said thoughtfully. At least it would keep him from spilling his guts.

The man shook his head. "Not here you ain't. Too much mess."

Pete shrugged. The sheriff did seem an amenable sort.

The man rose and donned a tan Stetson. He lifted a heavy six-shooter off the desk and thrust it through his belt.

"Well I reckon I need a break from this varmint. How's about you look after him a while?"

Pete started to say no.

"Tell you what," the sheriff preempted. "I'll bring you back a bottle of liquor—any kind you like—if you give me an hour's peace."

Pete looked at Tim then back at the sheriff. "Fine," he said as if it made no difference to him. "A bottle of mezcal—and none of that watered-down shit they're pouring across the street. I oughtta have to hold my nose to drink it."

"I got just the thing," the sheriff said, grinning and fingering his side whiskers. "Be back in an hour, then, like I said. And don't you leave him alone, neither. Last thing either of us needs is to upset Jack."

Pete snorted.

The sheriff took one last look at him then nodded and left.

Poor judge of character, Pete thought. It was a good trait in a sheriff.

He walked to the cell, watching Tim as he lit another cigarette. He leaned against the coldness of the bars, close enough so he could smell the iron.

Tim looked worse than ever. His knee was swollen to the size of a melon and dripping overripe puss. Jack had done worse than kill him. It may have been the worst injury Pete had witnessed since the war, including the one that cost him his own eye. He could still remember the queer sucking feeling when he thought about it. He tried not to.

Tim was babbling nonsense between groans, calling for his mother, calling for God. Pete shook his head at the spectacle. In Tim's place, he would have killed himself already.

He walked to the sheriff's desk and picked up the paper. There were pictures in it, but none that looked like Jack, and none that looked like anyone else he knew. He did not see the word "Oregon" written anywhere, either, though he was not sure he could recognize it in all its possible forms, especially among that jumble of tiny marks on the page. Were all of them letters?

He went through the desk drawers. They were all unlocked save one. In the first he found a tin of chewing tobacco and a dull-nibbed pencil. In the second he found something worth his time—a bottle of whiskey that looked to have bite. A whiff of the unstopped bottle confirmed that it did.

Pete took a pull. He preferred the vegetal burn of mezcal to the corn sweetness of whiskey, but anything that stung would do, and this stung with a scorpion's fire. He saw no reason to wait an hour to begin enjoying himself.

"Tim," Pete called once he had finished licking the whiskey from his teeth.

"Tim," Pete said again, walking to the cell and tapping the bottle against the bars. "Tim, I got something for ya."

The sound of the bottle seemed to penetrate the fog of Tim's delirium. He hauled himself into a kind of sitting position, leaning against a cot in the far corner of the cell, whimpering as he did so. His eyes were puckered, suspicious, and there was intelligence in them, too. He licked cracked lips.

"That's right," Pete said, proffering the bottle. He took another sip himself and sighed with the pleasure of it. "Reckon this'll take the edge off?"

Tim's eyes darted around the room, suspecting a trap. Finding none, he scooted closer to Pete, dragging his bad leg behind him, leaving an organic smear like a slug's trail, grunting and moaning through gritted teeth. When he was near enough, Tim held out his hand to receive the bottle.

"No, no," Pete tsked. "One sip at a time." He held the neck of the bottle through the bars. When Tim tried to grab it, Pete pulled it away. "No touching," he admonished. "Just open yer mouth."

Tim glared at him a moment but complied, leaning back on one elbow and turning his mouth to the ceiling.

Pete poured a slug of whiskey into the man's upturned gob, spilling some on his yellowed shirt and more in his nose.

Tim swallowed quickly, thirstily, then coughed and snorted like he was dying, which surely he was. He got the whiskey down though.

"That's good, ain't it?" Pete asked. "I got more of it coming, too. Mezcal—my favorite. Strong enough to get yer bedbugs drunk."

Pete dandled the bottle before the bars so the liquid sloshed and gurgled. He watched Tim's eyes grow wet. He watched his tongue grow greedy.

"Tim," he said after a minute. "Tell me about the *Oregon*. I heard Jack's side. You got your own?"

Tim shied from the bars as if Pete might grab him, kill him, as if that would not be a blessing.

"Tim, you're already accused, convicted, and condemned. Don't make no difference what you tell me. Only, I'd like to know for my own sake— know how far I can trust Jack in all this. And I've got something to offer besides." He lifted the bottle and shook it for good measure.

"What's done is done," Tim said. His voice was hoarse. "It don't bear repeatin'."

Pete shrugged and took another sip of the whiskey.

Tim looked green with envy as much as with blood poisoning, but he kept his mouth shut. Pete had to give him that at least.

"Hm," Pete mused, tapping his chin. "Tell you what. There's something else I reckon you could do for me." He strode to the sheriff's desk, bottle in hand, and picked up the paper.

"You got your letters. I'll give you draughts from this bottle if you start reading from the paper. Good stuff, mind. Anything about the *Oregon* job or Jack or me or any of us or any of the Rangers or lawmen, or what have you." Pete dropped the paper and nudged it through the bars with the toe of his boot. "Just like old times."

Tim grimaced—whether from pain or predicament, Pete could not say. But he came back within reach of Pete and that stupefying liquor. He lay on his side, propped up by one elbow, paper spread before him, and he began to read.

"Special agents in Florida detained a steamship, the *Lagonda*, headed to Cuba with weapons for the rebels there," Tim said, raising his eyes to measure Pete's interest.

Pete grunted and poured the man a tipple, pining for Cuba as he did so, that onetime jewel of Southern expansionism. "Something relevant now, Tim."

"Looks like business is picking up," Tim responded. "Western furniture manufacturers, iron and steel dealers, they're all stocking up. And bank clearings are up. Easy money means easy bank jobs, I reckon."

Pete withheld the bottle.

"Fine," Tim muttered, scanning the page for a worthier tidbit.

Already Tim looked better. He had color in his cheeks again. "Here's something the sheriff might be interested in. From Mr. Byron Drew, legislator out of Kaufman County, a bill to fix sheriffs' salaries. 'Why should a county officer draw from six thousand to twelve thousand per year from the pockets of the taxpayers?' he asks."

"I don't pay tax," Pete said, though he gave Tim a drink to keep him going.

"Might be you don't need to read the paper then, neither," Tim grumbled.

He turned the page. "By God, here's one to get your blood boiling," he said, wiping his mouth. "'In Hunt and Collin counties for years past, there has been a crusade on the open saloon as an institution that civilization can dispense with. Many of the citizens of that section of the state declare that if the saloon was abolished the worst feature of intemperance would disappear. They argue that the social side of the case and the American custom of treating is responsible for a large percentage of the drunkards annually turned loose upon the country.'"

Pete scoffed. "Weren't nobody treating in the *Mansion* tonight."

"'Senator J. N. Sherill has prepared a radical measure, which he declares will abolish the saloon, but permit of the sale of vinous and spiritous liquors in quantities of one quart and upwards.'"

"Why buy a quantity less than a quart anyway?" Pete wondered, tipping the whiskey bottle generously. He imagined a West without whiskey. Well, that would be the final straw.

Tim took the payment happily, picked up the paper, and turned another page.

Pete watched the man's head as he scanned, marveling at the speed with which he read. Some minds were made for learning, he supposed.

Abruptly, Tim dropped the paper.

"What is it?" Pete asked, stepping nearer the bars, peering at the page as if all those little symbols might suddenly divulge their secrets after so long.

Tim raised his head to look at Pete, his whole face a grin. He looked like a boy and not the dying man he was. "When I tell you, you're gonna give me that whole bottle of mezcal," he said.

"What is it?" Pete demanded.

"Pete, I know where Sal's at."

CHAPTER 30

Annabel

THEY FOUND JACOB FACE DOWN ON THE FLOOR OF THE BARROOM, DEAD drunk.

"Good God," Doc Marshall muttered.

A blood stain covered the center of the barroom floor, three paces across. It was one thing to hear of murder and another to see it—and this only a shadow of what must have been before the body had been removed, before cleaning had begun.

Annabel thought of Chasby's brooding, tortured look, of his melancholy beauty. She dredged her soul for pity, but she could find none for him who had taken Hattie from her.

She mourned instead for her daughter, who would have seen her lover shot dead if she had not been banished. She pictured Hattie dressed in black, bereaved, standing beside the Reverend in the bosom of his congregation, irretrievably lost, mourning her martyr.

A martyr to cards and whiskey!

"He's got his goddamn cuff in it," Todd said, removing his hat and turning his head, wincing.

Jacob had passed out beside the blood stain, his arm swung out and resting upon it, his white cuff stained with a bloom of red.

Doc Marshall knelt beside the man to take his pulse, though Jacob's snoring belied a certain life force. A half-empty whiskey bottle stood beside him along with a bucket and a pile of rags.

Todd sniffed it and took a taste like he was collecting evidence.

"Jacob," Annabel said, poking his ribs with the tip of her shoe. "Wake yourself." It was not an easy poke. She had not forgiven the man his outburst. They had not spoken since the night in the saloon when he had decried her from his bar top, cursing her "womanly frailty."

Jacob groaned and reached reflexively for his kerchief, which was lost. He wiped crusted spittle from the corners of his mouth with stained fingers instead—all this without opening his eyes.

"Jacob," she said again.

Jacob rolled onto his side and opened one eye, squinting even against the dimness of that lamplit room. His disheveled moustache occluded his mouth.

"Nearly twenty years, Annabel," Jacob said thickly when he recognized her.

He must have tasted the blood that he had inadvertently wiped upon his lips. His eyes shot open, filled with horror. He scrabbled backward into a sitting position, leaning against the wall, aghast and panting. He looked at his hands and groaned.

"Ruined," he said. "Everything. *Ruined.*"

"What have you done, Jacob?" Annabel asked. "Got yourself drunk?"

"I thought I might have a taste before the drys got to it," he said, grinning to himself. The shock of lucidity ebbed, and his speech became ungainly once again.

Annabel walked to the window and threw open the curtains.

Jacob cowered in the morning light.

"I sent Haddock away at least," he said, shading his eyes with a trembling hand. "I thought of that much."

"Sent Haddock away?" Annabel said.

Jacob nodded. "The Reverend saw his boot print." Jacob motioned vaguely to the floor before his outstretched legs. He seemed unfazed now by the pinkness of his arms. "The Reverend will hang him."

"I thought it was the boy cardsharp who killed Chasby?" Annabel asked, her heart sinking.

"Yes. Lucky it was not Haddock or I," Jacob replied, hiccoughing and reaching again for his absent kerchief. He pushed the hair out of his mouth. "They all had their guns drawn, you know, and I had my shotgun, and I pulled the trigger, and Chasby died. But it was not my shot that killed him." Jacob reached up and ran his hand across the damask wall, feeling the bores his leaden shot had made.

"And Haddock had no gun," he continued. "Haddock killed no man, but the Reverend will have him hanged anyway, you know. And why not? He has always been detested."

"John would not allow it," Annabel said softly, but the words sounded empty.

Jacob looked at her then as if for the first time since she had entered. His lip trembled, streaks of pink emanating from his mouth where he had wiped it. "Annabel," he said. "After all he's done . . ." He slouched against the ruined wall, his shirt untucked, his hair askew, his arms splayed, palms up.

When she did not reply, Jacob sighed and said, "We've known each other too long. At least know that I forgive you."

"Insufferable!" Annabel gasped. "What have you to forgive me?"

"The petition. You gave him—" he hiccoughed, "gave them—the town."

If they agreed, Todd and Doc Marshall had the good sense to frown and look at their boots.

Before Annabel could think how to respond, Madame Fuselli appeared on the landing. She was dressed in silk as usual, her hair done up and pinned with a fascinator. She looked suspiciously at Annabel, her thin red lips pressed tight. She seemed otherwise unaffected by the scene before her.

"How long until he sobers up?" Annabel asked. She did not have a great deal of experience with drunkenness. Lem had spared her that trial at least.

The madam shook her head as she descended the stair. "He hasn't drunk like zees in a long time."

"Water would help," Doc Marshall put in, and Todd went to fetch some.

When they had forced a bit of water down his throat, Jacob seemed to relax.

"I came here as a friend to see that you were alright," Annabel said, folding her arms and regarding Jacob. "I was worried, but I find that your illness is mostly self-inflicted." She bit her tongue, relenting. "And as a friend, I appreciate your forgiveness, even if it's misplaced, and I forgive you, too."

Jacob nodded solemnly.

"I also came here as an ally," Annabel said, hesitating. "I'll be blunt. John is not fit to lead this town. He has let the worst of the Reverend's followers go unchecked. He has taken other liberties, too. He threatened to have Atwood replace me at the office."

"What for?" Todd demanded, pausing with the bottle halfway to his lips.

"He wants authority to read the town's mail."

Doc Marshall shook his head, staring.

"I fear the Reverend has a kind of grip on him," Annabel said. She still could not understand it. "But it's no excuse for what I did. I shouldn't have let him—only—" she lapsed into silence. There was nothing to say.

"Annabel—" Todd began, taking a step toward her.

She held up her hand, collecting herself. This was no time for self-pity. The blood stain on the floor was reminder enough of that. Besides, Jacob was wallowing in enough self-pity to drown them all.

"Jacob," she said, holding out her hand and speaking formally. "Would you accept my support and the support of the women of this town and county, as far as they'll follow me, in your campaign for mayor?"

"I've been waiting for you to ask," Jacob said. Then, his drunken eyes serious as wedding vows, he answered, "Yes, Annabel. Yes."

"And you'll support the farmers' petition—the *women's* petition —wholeheartedly?"

"I will." These words seemed harder, but he spoke them.

Annabel nodded, satisfied. Jacob would keep his word, even if he was still drunk.

"Now to business," Annabel said, addressing the group. She had spent the whole night thinking on it, and there seemed only one way forward. "Closing the saloon is another step down the path of tyranny for John. If temperance is to become the law in this town, it must come by democratic means. We cannot abide this use of force. We must reopen the saloon.

"We'll leave the front door boarded to avoid challenging John directly. But we should call a meeting with those townfolk and farmers we trust— bring them through the back door, show them a night they'll remember, show them the *Lady May* is still in business. It's high time we held a rally anyway, although our candidate leaves something to be desired in his present state."

Annabel gave Jacob an admonishing look, promising herself it would be the last.

"He will not be well enough zees day," the madam lamented. "He's too far gone."

For his part, Jacob did not defend himself but began quietly to snore.

"Open the saloon, the campaign, without Jacob?" Todd asked, skeptically. "But who will speak on his behalf?"

"I will," Annabel said with a finality that left no room for doubt. The rest had the good sense not to voice any opposition. "We'll need to get the mayor here, though, to surprise him, to get him on the record while John isn't here to supervise."

"How?" Todd asked. "You think he'll come after what John said? After he closed the place down?"

Annabel thought about it and nodded, turning to the madam. "I don't think the mayor can turn down a free dinner. What do you say?"

CHAPTER 31

Donovan

DONOVAN WATCHED THE DUSTY PLAINS SPREAD BEFORE HIM IN THEIR dizzying vastness. Despite the presence of Mance, who rode Blackjack a few yards behind, Donovan felt alone, because men die alone, and he was dying still.

It felt like he was floating in a dream—or maybe a memory. *Yes, a memory. Like the old days—a chase on the plains.*

His head filled with warm air, rising like a balloon at a fair.

Doc Marshall had given it to him—the laudanum—in a brown glass bottle the size of his fist. The first drop had been astringent, the second easier. By the third, he was afloat.

He patted the bottle tucked beneath his vest. *A gift. A blessing.*

Donovan wished he had not been so stubborn, had tried the opiate sooner. Then again it would have meant accepting the doctor's terms, his diagnosis, his prognosis, and that was inconceivable, because it would mean that Donovan would die, and soon. How could he be dying when a little taste of the doctor's medicine gave him such relief?

Donovan turned in his saddle to look for the speck that was Three Chop in the distance, but after a day and a half of riding, it had dwindled into something smaller than the spots that swam through the jelly of his eye.

"Been a long while since I was out here." Even though he said it aloud, he was startled when Mance answered. For a moment, he had forgotten everything but himself.

"Sure has, Sheriff," Mance said, pulling his horse beside Donovan's. His lip was packed with enough tobacco for three men. "I ain't been out here too recently myself. Not north noways."

"That right?"

Donovan could not remember the last time he sent Mance north, either. For that matter he could not remember the last time he sent Mance anywhere, and yet his deputy did go places, did do things—he kept the peace and visited the farmfolk and settled their disputes. Only he did these things of his own accord.

Without me?

Donovan looked hard at Mance for the first time on the ride, suspicions roused, delving him for some sign of ambition or deceit. But Mance wore the same benign look he always had, shallow as a puddle where men like himself and Aaron were lakes and seas.

Yes, Aaron. He would have to figure out what to do with that conniving Reverend.

But Mance, Mance was reliable. He was a follower. Donovan smiled. The world swayed, and men followed him. Everything appeared so *clear* today.

There was something familiar about this place. He had known they would find the boulder in the ground, half hidden by windblown caliche, its shape distinct like the shell of a great tortoise.

Memory came back to him then, memory he had set aside, perhaps hoped to have forgotten. No, he had not been north in a long while—not this far north—not since a time before Three Chop.

"You look like you seen a ghost," Mance said, spitting upon the turtle rock.

"The last time I was out here . . ." Donovan said, his mind drifting untethered into the past, ". . . well, it was a time I'd rather forget."

Mance nodded with a soldier's understanding. He did not press Donovan, but neither did Donovan hold back. Of all the weights that needed unburdening, why not begin at the beginning?

"I was with the cavalry when the war ended," Donovan said, lighting a cigarette and dampening the match head between spit-wetted fingers. "After the war near everyone mustered out, but I stayed, because I wanted adventure—an eastern boy, you know—and I didn't know what else to do.

"We were sent here to these very plains under Colonel Mackenzie. The buffalo were plentiful then, thick as the grass itself, and where the buffalo roamed so roamed the Indians." Donovan felt a bile in his stomach, but the feeling was apart from him, riding as he was in that cloud. A draw on his cigarette calmed him further. He was getting the hang of smoking again.

"The forts had been abandoned during the war, and the Indians had never kept to their reservations, either. We came back to find stories of another kind of war played out here, and the people looked at us sullenly, like we had abandoned them by choice, by cowardice.

"The men did not look it—many of them had fought or their sons had—but the women did. Besides, a man would believe that he could protect his family on his own, that it was no man's job to do it for him, but the women felt different, and we could see it in their eyes. Layers of duty."

"Aye," Mance agreed, spitting again—the thin jet of a man well versed in the art. "I spent time with the Rangers. And in Tennessee we had our fair share of trouble with the Injuns."

Donovan grunted. He had known these things about Mance as facts, but never had he pondered them. The town was not the only beginning, but for Donovan it was a beginning. What people had been before they came upon its stage—those were other people, other lives.

"I was with the 11th Cavalry when the Red River War began," Donovan continued, draping the reins over the pommel. "After Adobe Walls, Sheridan ordered us to the panhandle from Fort Griffin. Three days and nights we tracked those Indians until we reached the bluff face of the Caprocks near Palo Duro Canyon."

"They didn't give you the slip?" Mance asked, surprised.

Donovan shrugged. "Maybe they could have. But they didn't. Maybe they had decided on one last stand. Maybe not. But there in the canyon we found the entire tribe—women and children, too, preparing to overwinter. They were thin as reeds. Maybe it was hunger that drove them to be so reckless. With the buffalo gone, what was left to eat?

"We came down those steep bluffs tasting copper in our mouths. Their warriors fought fiercely, but there was as much fear as valor in that canyon, for they fought to cover the retreat of their women and children. You could see it on their faces. It was an end.

"I was used to the firing and the killing after five years in the war, but this felt different. The guns thundered, and the thunder redoubled in that canyon, and the Indians fell all around." Donovan coughed then to hide the emotion that had crept into his voice. "But it wasn't the guns that did the killing, really. It was the burning. We burned everything they needed to overwinter. We burned their food, and the smoke choked us in the slot of the canyon and we had to tie our handkerchiefs around our faces.

"There was no valor then. Only anguish and lament. I had my gun raised like the rest, but I had not fired." Donovan hung his head, hoping Mance couldn't tell the wetness of his fallen tears from the horse's sweat.

"They'd have done you likewise," Mance said, reassuring. He had the sense to look away.

Donovan took the opportunity to wipe his eyes on the sleeve of his shirt.

"Probably," Donovan agreed. "But what bothered me, what still bothers me, is I never fired."

Mance nodded, but he did not seem to understand.

"A man who believed what he was doing was right would have fired and told himself what you told me—that the tribe would have done him the same. But a man who didn't fire? Why was he there? Why did he march all that way? Why did he clear the plains of all those buffalo? What did *that* man *think* he was doing?"

Mance shrugged halfheartedly, maybe afraid.

Donovan shook his head. He knew he would not get the catharsis he wanted, not from Mance. Might as well confess to his horse.

Donovan clenched and flexed his hand, regretful as much for the telling as the doing.

Maybe Annabel would understand, if he ever got the courage to tell her, if she would still speak with him. With difficulty he put her out of mind.

They rode a long while in silence. Oil and water, the old memories separated again in his mind.

CHAPTER 32

Jack

"WHAT WAS THE NAME AGAIN?" THE BESPECTACLED POSTMASTER ASKED, blinking rheumy eyes. His lip quivered. He was a sorry sight in his night-gown. Jack had not given him time to change.

"Mathers," Jack said. "Conway Mathers."

"Mathers," the man repeated. He took a last, doubtful look at Jack before disappearing through a curtained doorway.

Jack drummed his fingers on the marble countertop. He was impatient. He dared not leave his men to their own devices long, and he had in mind to spend a little money at the bar himself. It had been a while since he let loose, though he would never let himself lose control like some of the other men did. He envied them that.

No, Graves Point was no longer a roughneck town. Sheriff Everett was amenable, but the town still paid his salary, and they would brook no disturbance.

Jack could remember when Graves Point was a lone dry goods store—selling more bullets than anything—a place where buffalo hunters would stop before riding north and west up the canyons that led like highways through the Caprocks and onto the plains of the Llano Estacado.

It had not taken Jack's father long to understand that this would be their true destruction—the market for buffalo hides in New York and Philadelphia—nor had it taken General Sherman long, either, though he pursued it on an existential level that outstripped the needs of any market.

Pareiya had fought a long war over the buffalo, then the cow, then the dirt.

Jack himself had known it was over when he had seen his first hunting party—an iron locomotive stopped in that sea of grass, its windows opened so men and women dressed in felt derby hats and frock coats, hoop skirts and lace gloves, could fire their rifles into the herd from the comfort of their conveyance—a slaughter to feed the tribe for weeks heaped like midden by the time the train rolled on to the next sighting. He had known it then and accepted it like anything else over which one had no control. He let it go.

The postmaster reappeared in the doorway a moment, but, apparently thinking better of something, retreated to the back room.

The man had not appreciated being rousted from bed at such an hour, but Jack had assured him Sheriff Everett was fully supportive and that his own gun was, besides. The collaboration had been convincing.

Again the postmaster appeared in the doorframe, and this time it stuck. He walked to the counter, his stride purposeful now, conditioned to be businesslike in this place. He had an envelope in hand.

Jack felt his heart flutter and cursed his own weakness. What should it matter if the letter was there or not? Who did he have to prove himself to anymore? He could pull another job like the *Oregon* if it came to it. He could pull a hundred of them, a hundred hundreds, and if his gang would no longer follow him, he would find others who would.

Still, Jack's hands trembled as he took the letter.

He turned it over twice before he read the address.

"Now that letter's addressed to Pareiya, but I know Mathers's mail gets delivered there, too," the postmaster said, proud of his ingenuity.

Jack ripped the letter open. Sal could not have known his father's name, and yet he had to be certain.

It was like any of a thousand letters his father received amidst the diaspora—a man who claimed to have known Pareiya or his father or his father's father, a man who needed help paying the mortgage on a tenant farm or securing train fare from California. Jack knew his father sometimes responded to such letters, or at least he had once. He would not respond to this one. Jack crumpled the parchment and threw it over the counter.

For all his professional hauteur, the postmaster paled at Jack's displeasure.

But Jack did not have the energy—nor the need, in truth—to accost the man. He turned. He left.

And Sal? He could be anywhere—dead or alive, faithless or loyal, wealthy or poor. Of course, Jack had known when he sent the boy off that he might never see him again, yet there was something about Sal that had made him believe.

But Jack would not indulge self-pity. He would enjoy the night, let his men enjoy the night, then give them the option in the morning to muster in or muster out, whatever they preferred.

He would not apologize. He would not tell them the truth, either—that it did not matter to him if the money was gone. What mattered was that the mining consortium did not have it, that the bank did not have it, nor the railroad, nor any firm in New York or Philadelphia. What mattered was that it was gone, like the buffalo, disappeared.

He would be the last warrior standing though no one knew the name of his cause, not even his own family who thought him a traitor.

Still walking, Jack came upon a contingent of his gang in the street, Pete's contingent, half drunk and hurriedly readying their horses.

"What's this?" Jack asked, stopping short of the men.

Their look told Jack this was a betrayal. They stank with fear at having been found out.

Pete was among them, of course, the perennial thorn.

The men deferred to Pete, an unofficial leader, subtler than Arch and more dangerous for it.

Pete studied Jack a long while, his chin jutted sideways, considering. Finally, he spat and said, "We're just getting the horses ready, boss." Then, kicking Bill Snyder, Pete said, "Well what're you waiting for, get the rest!"

Bill squinted a moment, trying to work out the meaning of Pete's command, then hurried off to round up the rest of the gang.

"We're getting the horses ready," Pete said, turning to Jack again, "because we figured where Sal is."

"Oh?" Jack said as if it was no concern of his.

Pete held Jack's eye a long moment, and Jack understood that he was deciding whether to test him. But for Jack, there was only one test that mattered. Pete knew this, and he relented.

"He's in Three Chop—or was. Wanted for murder."

Three Chop. Another small town on the plain, but this with some history, this the town where the implacable sheriff—*what was his name again?*—had killed Nash Warrick. Jack had to smile at that. It was the kind of coincidence that made you wonder if there was meaning behind it all, behind life.

"How'd you reckon it?" Jack asked as if it was a secret he had known all along.

"It's in the papers, Jack!" Owl said excitedly. "Tim found it in the papers. He's in Three Chop alright, but he killed a man and the Sheriff's after him!"

Jack nodded. "I'm surprised you're so keen to quit your revelry."

"What's another midnight ride with a fortune on the other side?" Owl said.

The men grinned and slapped one another and climbed atop their horses, relieved the danger was passed, thinking themselves clever to have hidden their deceit.

"Took an awful strange route to Three Chop, boss," Pete said when he had mounted his own horse.

Bill was returning with the rest of the gang.

"You don't just ride into Three Chop, Pete," Jack replied. "I reckon Nash Warrick learned that the hard way." That was all the excuse Jack would give. Pete could think what he wanted, as the hare thinks of the fox.

Chapter 33

Donovan

Donovan was caught in the beak of a great bird. It was folding him in half the wrong way.

Somehow he could see the bird's eye, bent as he was, and it was a black maw, the iris a thin gold band that shone and pulsed with the beating of the beast's heart.

Or is it my own heart?

Donovan did not struggle, fearing that the slightest movement would upset the delicate equilibrium that kept him whole. The sun rose and set with every heartbeat, reflected in the glassy wetness of the great black eye. He closed his own eyes, but the light shone through the lids like they were parchment. There was heat on his neck now, too.

Donovan did not know when he woke up, so seamlessly did the dream overlap reality. Only at some point he realized the sun before him was not reflected at all. He had been staring at it.

He blinked his eyes, the afterimage lingering green and purple, coloring the clear sky. But he dared not move.

The idea of pain he had known in the dream was replaced by the corporeal, and it was more terrible than any beast could inflict. It would be a blessing to be consumed by some great bird, to dissolve in its belly, to end.

Donovan panted and sweat where he lay. Carefully, he turned his head toward the guttered fire. Mance lay on his back, too, his arm thrown across his eyes to shield them from the rising sun.

Asleep still, thank God.

Donovan spied the rucksack where he knew the bottle lay. It was four feet away—just out of arm's reach—but it may as well have been a mile.

Beyond the bag, beyond Mance, Donovan saw the horses grazing peacefully, their heads bowed. He despaired of ever riding one again.

How then will I catch the outlaw?

He could not return to Three Chop empty-handed. It would be his final disgrace.

No—not final. That would be watching Jacob climb the steps to the mayor's office.

Donovan braced himself. Stomach tight, he stretched his right arm toward the bag. It was disorientingly foreshortened, an alien appendage.

He gave up, chest heaving. He thought he had grunted, but it must have been a cry, for Mance woke with a start, scrambling to a crouch, obscuring the horses, his hand reflexively clutching Dewlap.

Donovan groaned. He watched Mance's eyes dart over the plain.

"What is it, Sheriff?" Mance asked, wound tight. When Donovan did not answer, Mance came cautiously toward him.

Donovan felt the vibration of every step as if it were a clapper and he a bell. "Goddamnit," he cried, gasping. He dug his fingers into the dirt.

"What is it?" Mance repeated, alarmed. He knelt beside the Sheriff. "Did you get bit?"

"I told them," Donovan said—half a gag and half a whisper. He was not sure whether he was speaking out loud or not. He was past the point of caring. "I told them just yesterday. Said I'd shut it. Did you not believe me? The Reverend said—"

Donovan's thoughts were interrupted by a fresh wave of pain as Mance touched his shoulder. It was a gentle touch, he knew, but still excruciating.

"What is it!" Mance shouted, the unflappable man beginning to panic before an invisible foe.

"I told them! I told them!" Donovan yelled, and somehow it eased the pain. He beat his fists on the ground. "I told them! I'll keep my word! I'll close it!" Again he pounded the earth.

The gnashing of teeth. The Reverend's words sounded clearly in his mind. *The wailing and gnashing of teeth.*

Then there was a new pain. It emanated from his cheek. He heard it before he felt it, the sound of flesh hitting flesh. His head had been turned by some force. Donovan spied the shaded underside of Mance's palm. It rose and fell again, the obverse bringing a reciprocal pain to his other cheek, knocking his head back where it had been a moment before—the view of the bag and the horses and now Mance's single boot.

Donovan struggled to rise but could not. Feebly, he raised his arm and pointed. "The bag," he said quietly. *Or did I only think it?* He called again, "The bag!"

Mance grabbed the bag and pulled it to him, emptying it on the ground.

"The bottle," Donovan gasped. He felt himself slipping again. "I told them I'd close it."

"The bottle, the bottle, the bottle," Mance muttered, picking it up, its brown glass glowing angelic in the sunlight.

Mance unscrewed the cap and held the bottle to Donovan's lips, tilting it precipitously.

Donovan pursed his lips and shook his head, feeling the liquid spill down his cheeks. "No!" he sputtered.

Mance hesitated, righting the bottle.

"The dropper!" Donovan said. The wasted elixir brought him new anguish. "The dropper."

Mance went back to the bag. He found the dropper and sucked a few drops into it. With a shaking hand, he brought it to Donovan's lips.

Donovan held the sweet liquid on his tongue until it evaporated. "Another."

Again Mance brought the dropper to his mouth, and Donovan licked greedily until there was nothing left.

"Yes," Donovan sighed, relaxing his taut body. "It will take some time. Leave me. Leave me." By the time the words passed his lips, Donovan had fallen asleep once more, and this time it was not a bird awaiting him but Missy and the boys, beckoning.

When Donovan woke again, the sun was high in the sky. He smelled the acrid stench of burnt campfire coffee. His stomach rumbled, and he was suddenly aware of a great hunger. Gingerly, he raised himself into a sitting position. His back felt like—nothing. *Nothing.* He grinned.

Donovan met Mance's uncertain gaze.

"What is that stuff?" the deputy asked. He sat with his arms around his knees, a tin coffee cup held in his right hand. The brim of his hat cast his eyes in shade.

"It's medicine from Doc Marshall—for pain," Donovan said. Then, spying a second cup of coffee set in the coals of the low-burning fire, he snatched it up.

"What kind of pain?" Mance asked.

"Back pain. I wrenched my back a few weeks ago trying to lift a dresser." It was a half-truth.

Mance sipped his coffee, swishing it thoughtfully in his mouth. He strained the coffee through his teeth then spit out the grounds.

"I threw my back out once as a Ranger," he said, still sucking at his teeth with his tongue. "I was flat out near six weeks. Had something like you did, too." Mance motioned to the tincture of opium sitting beside Donovan's bag. "Harder to stop than it is to start."

"You're worried I'll turn into an opium eater?"

Mance laughed. "I reckon you're not the type. Still—do you think you should be out here with your back like that? I could—"

"I'm fine," Donovan interrupted. "Another time I would have let you go alone, but these are careful days. The townspeople need to know their Sheriff can still keep them safe."

Mance nodded—the soldier's understanding again.

Donovan started to say something else, but his thoughts were dashed by a movement on the plain. He held his hand to his brow to shade his eyes. For a moment he thought he had imagined it. Then he spied it again—a brown speck, fixed.

"A rider," Mance said, holding the brim of his hat.

"Just one?"

Mance crawled forward on hands and knees, rigid as a pointer. "One, maybe two." After a minute he said, "Yes, two."

By the time the riders reached camp, Donovan had holstered his weapon. First, he had realized that one of the riders was not a rider at all, but a captive lashed to the back of a horse. Then he had noticed a badge glinting on the free rider's breast. As the horses came closer, the unmistakable posture of Kip Mason resolved atop the lead—slumped shoulders broad as railroad gauge.

Kip was the biggest man in North Texas, big enough to make a man wonder if he should be the one to carry the horse and not the other way around. Donovan knew him well. He was the sheriff of neighboring Grigsby, a stern but honest and discerning lawman.

Donovan licked his lips, tasting the sweat that had beaded there.

Four men had fled the saloon—Sal, Ike, Rod, and Haddock. One man was bound on Kip's trailing horse. Sal would bring salvation. Haddock would bring more trouble than Donovan thought he could deal with just then. *Yes, him I'd have to cut loose.* The others? Well, they probably meant nothing but a distraction.

Kip reined his mount, and the trailing horse stopped a few paces behind.

The lawman's mouth was unemotive beneath his red beard, but Donovan saw the twinkle of recognition in his eyes. Donovan donned his hat to look up at the man.

"Kip Mason," Donovan said amicably, hiding his excitement.

Kip nodded. "Donovan. Mance." He touched the brim of his hat, white with a leather band.

"A gift for the wife?" Donovan asked, nodding to Kip's captive.

The man's hands were bound, his feet tied in his stirrups. A burlap sack had been pulled over his head, which lolled forward as if the unknown rider was half-conscious.

"For you, mayhaps," Kip said, swinging a long leg over his horse and dismounting.

Donovan feared to hope.

"Mayhaps," Kip repeated, walking to the rider. He reached up and pulled the sack from the captive's head.

The man's dark hair was mussed and greasy, made stiff by sweat. His face turned dazedly to Donovan.

"I'll be," Mance muttered.

"You know him?" Kip asked.

Donovan could not find the words. He knew him, alright.

The captive started with recognition when his eyes lit upon the Sheriff—blue eyes pale as steel.

PART III:
FATE DON'T MEAN A THING . . .

CHAPTER 34

Sal

SAL FELT HIS HEART SKIPPING BEATS. HE COUGHED REFLEXIVELY. IT WAS like Death himself had reached out and filled his chest with a triumphant fist.

When the feeling passed, he was left with a familiar, nauseating pain that burned down his right flank. It hurt more after the doctor had probed inside him to remove the half-dozen hard and angry pellets of shot that had lodged there.

Now the muscles around the wounds were knotted and inflamed, made more unbearable by the fact that he could not move or stretch them while his hands were bound to the saddle.

"I'll be damned," muttered a reedy man beside the Three Chop Sheriff. He had turned the cuff of his jeans to show off a missing leg. Sal guessed he had barely a stump below the knee. Otherwise he had the stamp of a lawman—mostly unremarkable except for the leg and the gun that hung at his hip. It was one of the biggest guns Sal had ever seen. He thought it must shake the Earth itself when it fired.

What I wouldn't give to have hold of it, Sal thought, wondering what Jack would say when he got to Three Chop and found him captured. Sal did not fear death exactly. But he feared Jack, and he feared being tortured by the Sheriff into giving up his secret before Jack could save him.

"Looks like the hard work's done for us," the deputy said when no one spoke. He almost looked disappointed to have caught his quarry so easily.

Sal struggled briefly against his bonds. He did not put much effort into it, for he did not have much effort to give, but pride would not let him surrender so easily.

"Quit it, boy," Kip growled. "I ain't gonna right you again." He grasped Sal by the collar.

Sal felt a piercing, nauseating pain as Kip grabbed him, wrenched him, turned his face to the men from Three Chop.

"Is this your man, Donovan?" Kip asked, turning to the Three Chop Sheriff.

Donovan. The Sheriff who took his poker winnings, who threw him out of the saloon in front of the town, who had severed him from Kat.

Hers was a memory that hurt worse than his wounds.

Sal's lament was cut short as Donovan stepped forward to study him. There was no mistaking the man. He wore the same hat and trousers he had that night at the saloon. He smelled the same, too, of stale tobacco and a staler wind like the draft from an old crypt.

Sal tried to put the hardness of steel into his eyes as he met Donovan's gaze, but he felt himself growing weaker by the second. His vision blurred.

"Where'd you find him?" Donovan asked, grinning like he could not help himself. "Mance and I've been tracking him all over creation."

"He broke into Doc Arkin's house looking for bandages," Kip said. His voice started to sound strange, like it was underwater. "He's wounded pretty bad. Still a little feverish. Doc fixed him up once I got there. Gave him fresh clothes. I'd seen the wires and had a hunch this might be your man. Was headed to Three Chop when I saw your fire. I suppose you can save me the trip?"

"I reckon we can," Donovan answered, positively beaming. "The town'll be thrilled to have the bastard back. He's got a date with a rope, and they were starting to worry he wouldn't show."

That was the last Sal heard before he slipped into a buzzing, fuzzing blackness.

Sal woke after an indeterminate time. He had been dreaming he was a spirit, a cloud, weightless and free. He supposed that might be because he couldn't feel any of his extremities. He knew they would hurt like hell when his blood started flowing again. For now he contented himself with being alive and mostly unbroken.

Sal felt a wetness on his neck and collar and figured one of the lawmen must have poured water on him. It did not smell like piss anyway.

By the angle of the sun, he decided they must have been riding for an hour at least, maybe two. Riding south toward Three Chop.

Sal judged they were still far from Three Chop when the shadows of their mounts began to lengthen, and despite their slow pace, Donovan stopped and called a halt while the sun had an hour's taper yet to burn. A surprising mercy.

It was not until the horses had been hobbled and watered and the men were seated around the fire, the creamy scent of black beans wafting from their plates, that the silence was broken.

It was Sal himself who broke it.

"You can't hang me," he said without looking up from the fire. He sat cross-legged, his hands still tied, though Mance had bound them in front this time and loosened the knots so he could move his fingers enough to feed himself.

He was clutching a fork. The painful ache of recirculating blood was almost passed.

Whatever fear Sal had felt had turned to anger. A draught of water and a belly full of beans could do that to a man, stiffen his back, waken his deadened resolve.

"Why's that?" Donovan asked, looking at Sal over his spoon.

"'Cause you'll die if you do."

"A man dies either way," said Donovan. Grease dripped from his beard onto the dirt. He lay contorted oddly on his side, propped up by an elbow.

Mance grunted, shoveling a spoonful of beans into his mouth with a slurp. "Want me to shut him up?"

"Let's hear him out," Donovan said, nodding to Sal. "Tell me, boy, who's going to kill me when you hang?"

"I'm an outlaw," Sal said.

Mance laughed, choking and spitting beans on the ground.

"That's why we're here, isn't it?" Donovan asked.

The firelight pushed only weakly at the night, and the faces of the lawmen were still cast half in shadow.

"I mean a real outlaw," Sal said, gritting his teeth. He hoped his own face was lit up like a goddamn jack-o'-lantern. "I've got a gang, and they're coming for me. They'll be in Three Chop any day now. And if they find I've been hanged—well I'd rather be hanged than die the way you'll die."

Sal saw the mirth had gone from Mance's face. He chewed dumbly at his food, the hair on his temples twitching with each bite. Sal guessed chewing was the only work the man's head had seen in a while.

Unexpectedly, Donovan gave a sly smile. "How'll they even know?"

"I sent a letter," Sal said, watching the Sheriff through narrowed lids. "There are a dozen of us—maybe more by now. Men are always joining up. Hard men. We've all of us killed before." He spit into the fire but did not take his eyes off the Sheriff.

"The letter," Donovan said thoughtfully. "I wonder . . ." He reached into his vest pocket and pulled out a sheet of creased paper. It was stained with sweat.

The hairs of Sal's arm stood on end.

Donovan cleared his throat and began to read, still propped lazily upon one elbow.

"'Dear Conway,'" the Sheriff began, "'No work in Topeka . . .'" He continued reading into the stillness of the night air, reading it like a death sentence.

When he had finished, Donovan looked up at Sal, suddenly sharp where he had been aloof. He must have seen the truth, even in the low light. He crumpled the letter and threw it in the fire where it caught and burned and disappeared inside the ravenous flame.

"No one's coming for you, boy," Donovan said when the last of the letter had blackened and fallen apart.

Mance began to chuckle again, his peg leg etching circles in the dirt. "Gotta get up pretty early to pull one over on the Sheriff," he said.

Sal closed his eyes, thinking Kat would be there at least—a chance to say goodbye.

CHAPTER 35

Jack

"What's on your mind, Johnny?" Jack asked, stubbing the butt end of his cigarette on the leg of his dungarees.

Jack had slowed the horses to a walk as dawn broke, giving the beasts a rest after a hard night's ride under the full moon. He felt Janus beneath him, only now beginning to catch his breath.

Johnny Baldwin looked around nervously at the other men as if expecting them to come to his aid. When none did, he turned his horse in beside Jack's.

Johnny was a younger man—most of Jack's gang were younger now. Jack had better luck with such men—they were amenable, eager. Johnny rode well for *taibo*, but he spooked easily.

Jack had sensed a nervous energy rattling his gang, even as their reunion with Sal and the loot was at hand. Of course, the newspaper tip was no resolution. Would they reach Sal in time? Would they find he had betrayed them? But compared to the torpor of the past weeks, the despair of ever finding him at all, they should have been joyous.

He hoped the rising sun would burn off that fear like dew. They had a job ahead of them.

"I haven't got a good feeling," Johnny said, avoiding Jack's eyes. "I told some of the boys earlier—it's like we're riding into a noose."

Jack nodded, thoughtful. "And you never felt that way about any of the bank jobs or about the *Oregon?*"

"Not like this. There's something certain about this."

Johnny fell silent like the rest of the men. The only sounds came from the mounts—labored breathing and the stub of hooves on the prairie grass.

Jack let Johnny ride like that a while. He was probably exhausted. They had only spent a few hours in Graves Point and none of them sleeping. Some of the men were still drunk. The rest maybe wished they were.

"There're just too many signs," Johnny said eventually, having ruminated on the thing. "The *Oregon* betrayal, you gone so long, us losing Sal, Sal getting in trouble, and in Three Chop! Even Nash Warrick himself couldn't stand against Three Chop and its Sheriff, and those were the early days. It feels cursed."

Nash Warrick again, Jack thought. Would he ever escape the man?

Jack eyed Pete. Pete rode a little ahead—too far to eavesdrop—flanked by the usual culprits, Bill and Owl. And there were a few of the younger men, too, walking their mounts near enough to hear whatever tales Pete was telling.

Jack guessed the source of this burgeoning paranoia.

Pete glanced over his shoulder then. He had to turn farther than an ordinary man on account of his missing eye. He made like he was scanning the horizon, but Jack could see his gaze flick past Johnny.

Jack decided then he would have to do something about Pete, and he would have to do it soon.

"Signs," Jack said, speaking to Johnny but letting his eyes rove, watching the ebb and flow of association in his gang, measuring their loyalties. "I always thought signs were an excuse for men to do what they wanted but knew they shouldn't." Jack's father had believed strongly in signs. They had kept him at war longer than he should have been, and then they had made him give up on living.

Yes, Jack realized, *the Pareiya I knew truly died a long time ago.*

"A hoof print—that's a sign when you're tracking," Jack said. "Or broken grass or upturned stones. But symbols? Legends? It takes a wise man to sift truth from these. Legends are what men want to believe—or what they want others to believe—but rarely are they truth. Nash Warrick is only a legend."

"You knew him?"

"No. I was still young when he died. But I met him once in a trapping town. Watched him kill a man. He had a dumb man's meanness. It weren't that he had a fast draw, only he always had the first draw, would kill before a man had time to realize that killing was afoot, would kill over small things."

Johnny winced to hear such blasphemy. "That Three Chop Sheriff must be a killer, too, then."

Jack shrugged. "Killers get killed every day by everyday men. Life has always been a gamble, and anyone can die when his luck runs out. The Sheriff is old now, besides. That gunfight happened twenty years ago, and I bet he hasn't seen one since. Nash was the last of his breed."

Almost.

Johnny did not look entirely convinced. "Then there's the business about Pete's ill luck," he said, lowering his voice.

"Oh?"

"Yeah, says he's fated to die by hanging. Another sign atop the rest. An old Creole woman told him so with that ancient island magic—said so himself. And Pete ain't getting any younger. Fate don't have long to catch up with him."

Jack frowned, considering. Then he drew his six-shooter. He kept it down by his thigh so only Johnny could see it. Jack pointed the barrel at Pete's back, at the base of the man's spine.

Johnny took in a sharp breath.

"What's the old Creole woman got to say about this, Johnny?" Jack asked, pulling back the hammer. "Whatever she foretold, what's to stop me from killing Pete right now with a gun in place of a rope?"

Johnny seemed unable to speak.

"Will you stop me, Johnny?"

Johnny blinked once, wide eyed, then shook his head.

Jack eased the hammer off and holstered his gun. He lit another cigarette. The morning was turning warm. It was shaping up to be another Indian summer. Jack undid the collar of his shirt.

"See," he said when he had taken another drag, "fate don't mean a thing to a man with a gun."

Johnny nodded vigorously even as he moved his horse away from Jack, putting space between them.

Jack dismissed him with a wave of his hand. He smiled to himself. At least that would give the boy something new to think about.

Jack let the gang ride all the way to the base of the Caprocks before he called a halt to water the horses by the Prairie Dog Town Fork of the Red River. They stood in the lengthening shadow of that great wall of striated orange rock, Palo Duro Canyon before them, a gateway to the sky.

Grass and shrubs dotted the steep face of the mesa cliffs as if cascading off the plains. The vegetation was too brown by half. The Prairie Dog Town Fork ran a meager trickle. The world was a bowl of dust.

Jack thought of Michael tilling the parched earth. The farmers would be up in arms if the drought kept on. They would be foreclosed, forsaken. The haze of dirt suddenly breathed like revolution, and Jack wondered if God had made up his mind about these plains, had put his finger on the scale against the small folk. Their subsistence dreams would have to perish before they learned to want better.

"We'll need to make time," Jack said, dismounting to stretch his legs with the rest of the men. Even the old Comanche blood grew sluggish when forced to sit a horse that long.

He caught Pete's eye. "Pete, pick your men and go on ahead. Take our freshest mounts and remounts, too. You're the only one of us who's seen Three Chop and its Sheriff. Discover what you can about Sal—whether they've got him, whether he's spilled his guts. But don't do violence unless you're forced."

Pete regarded Jack through narrowed eyelids, scratching at his mangy gray beard.

"Won't he be recognized?" Eagle-Eye Monty asked, though he made it more of a protest. Monty did not trust Pete, nor should he.

"There was only one man in town that day," Jack said. "Right, Pete?"

Pete nodded, though the insult had not escaped him.

"And that was some twenty years back. I reckon Pete looks a fair bit different now."

"Still only got the one eye," Pete said with a humorless grin.

Jack was calm, yet he sensed the gun at Pete's hip. He did not expect Pete to make his stand here, but who knew what foul ideas fermented in that grizzled head? Jack could see the man's old lump of brain at work as he bantered.

"Alright," Pete said finally. "I'll take Bill and Owl then."

That was no surprise.

"Tell you what," Jack added. "Take Tim along, too. I'm tired of his racket."

"I thought we needed to move fast?" Pete asked, suspicious.

"You do."

Pete sucked his teeth. He nodded, understanding.

"The rest camp here tonight," Jack said. "We'll follow fresh at first light."

The tired men jetted sighs of relief and set about making camp. Twilight was already upon them.

Pete chose mounts and remounts for his men, though he left Janus to Jack—perhaps out of respect. When the horses were well watered and had eaten oats from his hand, Pete mounted up beside his companions, and the foursome set off into the darkness of the canyon.

Jack wondered how much Pete understood. He would have to kill Pete one day, or Pete would kill him. Jack sometimes got a feeling about a man he would have to kill. He killed some without the feeling, and he let many more live. But he always killed a man who gave him that feeling, like Death himself had put the scythe in his hands.

Maybe the Sheriff of Three Chop would take care of Pete for him. But that would be a waste. A man should put down his own dog.

CHAPTER 36

Donovan

"Mayor! Come have a look at your villain!" Donovan called, wheeling his horse in the street, spraying dirt.

The usual contingent of dogs had come first to greet him, circling his horse and baying proudly.

Donovan fired his gun skyward, half a summons, half an irrepressible expression of joy. He had left town in political straits and returned against the odds, a hero with Sal in tow. Now it was time for the people to acknowledge his victory. It was time for the Reverend, for *God*, to acknowledge it.

Mayor Cordell threw open the window to his second-story office and leaned his head out, craning into the street, one hand raised against the mid-morning sun. It took him a moment to focus. He looked befuddled.

"I got your villain here, mayor," Donovan said, motioning to a pitiful figure lashed to the back of his trailing horse. Kip's chestnut whinnied, his eyes darting nervously, spooked by the gunshot.

"The Salamander!" Cordell exclaimed, coming to. He looked from Donovan to Sal to Mance, who sat his own horse stoically, his cheek packed with chew. "By God, how was it done?"

Then, before Donovan could answer, Cordell bade him wait with fluttering hands. The mayor shut the window and barreled down the stairs and into the street. By then a few dozen townspeople had come outside as well to investigate the tumult.

The Reverend was among them, having come from his church, a host of the faithful trailing. He had the appearance of a man who had not seen the sun in some time.

"How'd you do it?" Cordell asked, straightening his top hat, breathless.

Donovan smiled as if basking in memory. He would like to have waited for more people—*for Rascal at least! And Annabel?*—but he judged there were enough to begin. With luck the story would spread on its own legs.

"We spied him on the plain," Donovan began. He traced the horizon with his palm, his eyes following as if tracking something distant.

The crowd pressed closer to hear the tale.

"It was twilight. We had ridden for days. Mance skylighted him. It took us an hour to catch up with him—we were afraid at one point we'd lose him for the dark—but he wasn't far off from where we saw him in the first place on account of his wound."

Cordell and the gathering crowd studied Sal then. He looked ashen, the grit plainly having left him. He swayed like sackcloth in the wind, his body twisted at an odd angle to relieve the pressure on his injured side.

The Reverend pushed through the crowd to get a closer look.

Briefly, the Reverend's eyes found Donovan, and Donovan saw in them that eternal fire stoked hot now by the inevitability of his vengeance. Yet the orbs of his irises remained black against the wanness of his skin.

"We circled, coming at him from north and west," Donovan continued. "It was almost dark when we approached, but I could see the glint of a gun barrel. 'Hold it, partner,' I told him when I spied it, 'My deputy and I have each got a shot at you. There's no way out of this alive.'"

Donovan paused to let the drama of the moment percolate in the minds of the gathered electorate. "He looked at me, then at Mance, who had his rifle leveled steady at the man's breast. Then he lowered his gun—dropped it, in fact—and passed out. Tough son of a gun." Donovan shook his head as if in admiration. There was no point in making the taking sound easy. "But we got him in the end.

"Now, mark my words," Donovan bade, feeling as if he might explode with his own ballooning triumph. "The man will hang for his crime—at noon—the day the scaffold is built!"

"Justice is served!" Cordell exclaimed, clapping his hands.

The crowd nodded and gave their approbation, overawed by the ruthless efficiency of their Sheriff.

Mance sat motionless astride his horse, wearing an unreadable half smile.

Then, in the very center of that triumphant moment, a noiseless woman pushed her way through the inner ring of the crowd and approached the outlaw, brushing by the Reverend as she went. She held up a glass of water, which the outlaw bent toward, and he began to drink.

Greedily he gulped, water running down his cheeks, carving rivulets in the dirt that caked his face and chest.

And while he drank the crowd was speechless.

"Wait a minute," Donovan said, the first to recover. He recognized the woman as Jacob's newest girl, the one who had walked with the outlaw before his murdering spree. "There'll be time enough for the man to drink under the shade of the jailhouse roof."

The woman ignored him. All her concentration on Sal, she whispered something to him, though the outlaw seemed too dazed to understand.

Donovan frowned. With a single gesture this woman, this whore, had spoiled his homecoming. He felt the mood of the crowd shifting, turning ambivalent. Who was this outlaw before them, looking so weak, so young? Was he a murderer or a charity case? Could he be both?

Then rough hands grabbed the woman from behind. *Loeb.*

Donovan held up a cautioning hand. *Not like this!*

But Loeb ignored the gesture. He grappled with the girl, who began to struggle.

Suddenly Loeb cried out. The girl had bitten his hand, drawing blood. It showed bright red even through the haze. Loeb sucked the wound. Blood smeared his lip when he took his hand away, but he was grinning.

He smacked the girl with the full force of an open palm. The sound split the air, harsh as thunder.

The girl stumbled and fell to the dust but did not cry out.

A white-hot rage awoke in Donovan. "Enough!" he cried, urging his horse into the knot of acolytes who had gathered around Loeb, dispersing them, not caring whether any were trampled underfoot. He grabbed Loeb by the collar, hoisting him onto his toes. He saw no shame in those eyes, only a smoldering hatred, a distorted reflection of the Reverend's own internal light.

"I oughtta lock you up with the outlaw for a night," Donovan said through gritted teeth. "That's the outlaw's woman, you know. I'd like to see how long you lasted against the man, how long you lasted without an alley to cower in, without the anonymity of a stone in your cowardly hand."

The crowd swirled around them, agitated, confused, angry.

My homecoming, ruined!

Donovan struggled to keep his anger in check. He had seen a great deal of violence in his time, but he had never seen a man hit a woman that way, had never thought to see it. Even when he once had to hang a woman, he had done it with a certain gentleness, a certain deference.

Loeb stared at him, silent, insolent, and there was no fear in him.

Disgusted, Donovan shoved the man to the ground. It wrenched his back, but the pain was nothing before the heat of his own fury. Yes, it felt good to unleash it. There was an anger in him, buried deep, a festering corpuscle—anger at this indecency, anger at the town that was trying to wriggle free of his leadership, anger at his own body and at God—and he would bring it out for the town to see, for all of them to see. He would coddle them no longer, for they had forgotten too much about the truth of the world, the violence of it.

He caught sight of the Reverend then, a strange look on the man's face. *Disappointment? In whom?* Aaron turned, his black mourning cape flaring behind him, and stalked back toward the church.

You'll have your revenge soon enough, preacher, Donovan thought as he adjusted his hat.

"Are these the men you'd give our town to, Sheriff?" a voice called.

Donovan froze. The sound grated his nerves and sent a shudder of revulsion through him. Truly, he was beset on all sides. He whirled atop his steed.

Jacob stood on the saloon porch, making use of every one of his five and a half feet. His usual white resplendence had been supplanted by black. He was in mourning now as much as the Reverend, draped from head to toe, from derby hat to bowtie to boots. Even his kerchief was black. His moustache was waxed to perfect immobility. His eyes bore down on Donovan like he was God on the day of judgment.

"I give no one the town!" Donovan cried, the rage still coursing through him.

"That's not what your mayor says," Jacob replied coolly.

Donovan felt a moment of uncertainty. Something unalterable, something precipitous, had happened in his absence, he realized. It was not just Jacob's dress, nor his assertiveness. He noticed something in the expressions of the townfolk now, too, as they helped the girl to her feet, as if he had been the one to strike her. They closed protectively around her, Mance's Minnie among them.

"The mayor?" Donovan asked himself, looking for the man. Cordell was nowhere to be seen. Perhaps he had left with the Reverend and his acolytes?

Suddenly Donovan realized he had no allies there but Mance.

"Pray tell, Jacob," Donovan said, putting all the condescension he could into the name, "what did the mayor say?"

"That he had orders to close the saloon."

"Temporarily," Donovan corrected.

Jacob held his eye. "There was a debate last night," he said. "In the saloon."

Donovan felt a cold fear creep up his spine. "Tracking your boots through that poor boy's blood?"

"There was no blood. And no liquor sales, either. I did share a few bottles among my friends, though. And we got to talking, and well you wouldn't believe it, John, but Annabel and the mayor got to the subject of politics."

Donovan clenched and flexed his hand. No wonder Cordell had disappeared. *At the saloon so soon after I closed it? I'll kill the man . . . I'll . . .* Donovan set his jaw, took hold of himself. "Whatever the mayor said—"

"What the mayor *said*," Jacob interrupted, speaking over Donovan. "What he *said* was, when pressed, 'The saloon is closed now, closed forever, closed until Donovan says otherwise, because it's bigger than some preacher's boy—it's about Prohibition, about God, and about the Sheriff's goddamn *will*.'"

The townfolk grumbled at those words, and he could not help but remember the press of angry elbows that had nearly overwhelmed him in the saloon some days before. "The mayor got ahead of himself," Donovan said. His head was buzzing. It must have been the opium. He could not pick his thoughts out fast enough. "He—"

"No use denying it, John," Jacob said, interrupting him again. He pulled a newspaper from beneath his arm and threw it over the rail. "The truth is out. If you want to know the particulars, ask Rascal."

The paper landed at the foot of Donovan's horse. Even from that vantage he could make out the headline—boldface, all caps. "MAYOR CORDELL ALLUDES TO VICTORY FOR THE DRYS."

Donovan's head was swimming. *The paper doesn't go out for a few days*, he thought to himself.

But he must have said it aloud because Jacob laughed. "Special edition," he said. "That was Annabel's idea, too."

Rascal's office was messier than usual, the remnants of a frantic night's work strewn about as if dispersed by a whirlwind. A sheaf of blank newspaper spilled across the floor, mingling with misprinted pages. Typeset drawers stood ajar, their letters upset. Rags dripped with ink and grease, littering every raised surface along with bits of wire, twine, and ribbon.

Donovan picked his way through the mess toward Rascal, who was asleep at his desk—maybe passed out—even though it was early afternoon. Apparently the gunfire and the yelling of the crowd had not been enough to wake him.

"Damned drunk," Donovan muttered, shaking his head. He picked up one of a stack of identical notebooks from a workbench and began to leaf through it. Rascal's handwriting was too poor to bother reading.

Suddenly, a pain, crushing, overwhelming, seared through Donovan's back.

He dropped the notebook to the floor.

The pain of four days' riding had broken through the barrier of that brown-bottled tincture. He could feel his vertebrae grinding, the pain made all the worse for having been pent up and ignored. It was a jealous pain, a vindictive pain, come now with a vengeance.

Reeling, Donovan blinked back stars.

He took a deep breath and bore down, as if pressurized lungs could lend support to his withered spine. He retched on the ground, his yellow vomit spattering over newsprint and notebooks.

Donovan leaned forward, hands on his knees. His forehead dripped sweat into ink-like splotches on the blank papers at his feet. For some minutes he stood half bent like this until the pain receded. Then the cloud enveloped him in its warm glow once more, welcoming, comforting, like it was his mother—distracted for a moment by something on the stove, turned to find him hurt, scooping him up in her arms.

Breathing heavily, Donovan straightened up, smoothed the front of his vest over his belly, and decided that he did not have time to waste.

"Rascal!" he screamed, hammering his fist so hard on Rascal's desk that it rattled the drawers.

Rascal woke with a start, blinking. He fumbled for his glasses, his pupils struggling to find a suitable aperture.

"M-Mr. Sheriff," Rascal said once he managed to put on his glasses. He cast his eyes about the room, running his hands along the desk as if to ground himself. "W-what can I do?"

"You know where I've been?" Donovan asked.

"On patrol, err, posse, a mission—the outlaw."

"Are you drunk?"

"No, Mr. Sheriff," Rascal replied, hiccoughing. "Or rather, not any-more." He gave a strained laugh. The skin of his face was red and raw where it had rested on the desk.

"You know you missed quite a show this morning."

"Oh?" Rascal asked, instinctively looking to his notepad. "You caught the outlaw?"

"Indeed," Donovan said. "Caught him two days' ride due north after a near shoot-out. He's in the jailhouse now being tended by Doc Marshall. It seems a pity to fix a man up before a hanging, though."

Donovan wiped his brow, still wet with sweat from that bout of pain. "Was it a late night?" he asked pointedly.

Rascal averted his eyes and rearranged the papers on his desk. "Late? Err, yes. There was a bit of, mm, news that occurred. At the saloon, to be precise—there was a kind of debate. No, an exchange."

"An exchange?"

"Annabel and the mayor."

"Why was the mayor at the saloon after I closed it?"

"Err," Rascal muttered. He wiped the back of his hand across his mouth where a frothy white spittle had accumulated, the product of nervousness and dehydration. "He was there to keep an eye on things. Annabel reopened the saloon, you see. She left the front door boarded up, but she had people come through the back. She had word spread around the town. It was a statement, I think."

"The headlines, Rascal. Read me the headlines." It felt good to turn the screws on this wriggling slug, this bloviating idiot. Donovan clenched his jaw with relish.

Rascal nodded at nothing and patted his belly nervously. "I only—it seemed worth printing with the election looming." He began to shuffle the papers about his desk like a boy who did not want to eat the food on his plate.

"The headlines, Rascal." Donovan handed him one of the drafts of the *Star* that littered the floor.

"The headlines. Of course, John, err, Mr. Sheriff." Rascal re-situated his spectacles and began to read.

"We begin with a three-column head: 'Mayor Cordell alludes to victory for drys.'" Rascal read it as if for the first time, like he was surprised by the words on the page.

"The first line, Rascal, read me the first line."

Reluctant, Rascal cleared his throat and began:

"Just last night over tipples of whiskey in the recently reopened *Lady May*, our esteemed mayor, Clarence P. Cordell, gave the strongest indication yet of his administration's support for the cause of the Prohibitionists, when, speaking to a crowd of townspeople led by councilwoman Annabel W. Meacham, who was serving most unexpectedly in the capacity of bartender for the evening, the mayor admitted after much pressure that, regarding the nature of the saloon closure, quote, 'It is temporary as long as we say so, temporary until it's permanent,' the 'we' being understood in context to refer to the opinion of the mayor and his Sheriff, John Donovan, though—"

"Enough," Donovan interrupted, seething. "You saw it happen?"

"Err, yes, I was at the saloon myself, seated next to Cordell, in fact."

Donovan gripped the desk to stop his hands from lashing out. "Were any of the others there?"

"Others?"

"Lassiter? Stepshaw?"

"Err, no. They were invited of course but thought better of it."

Donovan could be thankful for that at least.

And Annabel leading the resistance. He should have known. Probably he had known. It felt like a betrayal, but what right did he have after what he had done?

Still, he felt the pent-up frustration of Jacob's coup, part of that infection in his soul. He felt it hard and round as a rock there in the pit of his stomach, and he decided he would let it out, just as he had done in the street with Loeb. If God wanted a man of action, he would supply one.

Wordless, Donovan smashed his fists into the desk, splintering pine.

With a yelp, Rascal lurched backward in his chair. Only a last second kick of his legs saved him from tumbling backward.

Just like Chasby did—backward into a pool of his own blood.

"I don't know why I let this paper run," Donovan cried.

"Let it run?" Rascal sputtered, incredulous. "Let it run? This paper put Three Chop on the map! It was here before you, Mr. Sheriff! It's the only reason people stop here at all! By God, you can read the *Star* in St. Louis!"

Donovan said nothing. He let his hands speak for him. They ripped typeset trays from their drawers so their contents scattered across the floor like so many coins. They spilled ink until it ran thick as oil on the floor. They upended tables, scattered rolls of newsprint, smashed the glass shades of the lamps that lined the walls.

Rascal cried out, lifting himself bodily on the arms of his chair in his anguish, scrabbling for purchase in the wreckage of that room. "You've lost it, John! You'll never outlive this ignominy! You'll never outlive the paper!"

Breathing heavy, his destruction complete, his rage sated, Donovan put on his hat. It was still covered in dust from the expedition. He looked at Rascal, stared him down until the man sank back in his chair, until he wilted, until he cowered.

Outside, he found the dogs waiting.

CHAPTER 37

Annabel

AM I WEAK? ANNABEL WONDERED AS SHE WATCHED MARY, ONE OF HER students and one of the madam's girls, gather her things and leave the post office. Annabel knew she could not survive the life those girls led, yet there was a certain parallelism in their lives. Like Mary and like many of the *Lady May* women, Annabel had lost her mother and father at a young age. How close had she come to that servitude? It was marriage that had saved her, though "saved" did not feel like the right word.

How long had she submitted to Lem's violence? Annabel shuddered to think whether Hattie had understood. Could that explain the girl's recklessness, her fascination with Chasby?

How many times had Annabel wished she could change the course of her life? And yet at what cost? Without Lem, Annabel would never have known her daughter, and so Hattie's birth locked in place all that preceded it, made it imperative, immutable, the unknowable logic of a fate that brought her to her greatest—*joy?*—everything from her father's death to the broken engagement with John to her marriage.

But when Hattie was born—healthy, squalling, pink—she could have regrets again, and she stored them up like comforts, which she brought out now.

In her weakness Annabel had indulged that other man in her life, John, turning her eye—blinded as it was by that residue of feeling or by the struggle against it—lending her decisive support to the farmers' petition, which, though rightful in its aim, she could admit had been poorly timed. She had thought she got the better of him. Who could—

A voice interrupted that stream of self-loathing.

"Ms. Annabel?" it called from the door, a woman's voice, tentative.

At first Annabel thought Mary had returned, had forgotten something after her lesson.

How long was I sitting here, glassy eyed, like a doll? She smoothed her skirts and straightened her back.

But it was not Mary standing in the doorway. It was *she*, Jacob's newest girl. *She*, the brave girl who had given the outlaw water in front of the Sheriff and his deputy, in front of the mob. *She* who had suffered a stinging slap from Loeb, the loathsome coward. *She*, another wayward girl like Hattie.

As if startled, Annabel stood and hastened to the girl. She had not witnessed the fiasco herself—she did have a post office to run after all—but she had heard the story from a half-dozen townfolk already.

Up close the girl even looked like Hattie. They could have been sisters. Annabel felt a lump rise in her throat. "That was a kind thing you did today for that man," she said when the girl had come inside, blonde curls glowing gold in the lamplight.

"It was nothing."

Annabel could see the redness of Loeb's hand still upon her pale check. "I'm afraid I don't know your name."

"Kat."

"Pleased to meet you, Kat. I'm Annabel, but I guess you knew that."

"Yes. I learned it from Minnie, who said you might help me."

"Did you want to learn to read?"

Kat shook her head. "I know how to read. I came for Sal."

Annabel sighed. *Yes, the girl is just like Hattie.*

"I didn't know where else to go," Kat admitted. She looked around the room as if for comfort or a sign.

Annabel felt the familiar swell of sympathy in her breast—the one that rose every time she met a needful girl.

"Sal is locked up. He is hurt. And you must have heard the Sheriff is going to have him hanged the day after tomorrow." Kat's manner was firm, resolute, implacable.

Annabel had heard tell of his fate, too. She lamented it, the injustice of it—a bare rope and a sheriff's will. But she also knew that Sal would be a distraction. Jacob's supporters, few as they might seem, were united against the closing of the saloon, not the hanging of the outlaw. Many of them would want to see the boy die for his part in Chasby's death.

And yet, she reflected, *the hanging is a powerful symbol for John, a last, violent gasp of strength.*

Suddenly Annabel saw herself as the departed Pastor Bonham would have seen her and was aghast. She had not given a single compassionate thought to the boy but to wonder how he would play like a card in a game of stud. And for all she knew, she had hastened his capture, however unwillingly, by trading his letter for her station, for giving in to John's demand the same way Lem had done.

Annabel beckoned the girl behind the counter where stools were still set side by side for Mary's lesson. "How do you think I can help?" she asked, taking a seat herself.

"I've heard the girls talk about you. I know you're close with Jacob and with the Sheriff." Kat's composure began to crack. She blinked back tears, and the words began to spill from her. "There must be something you can do. The whole town has agreed to hang him. And for what? There were four men who fired guns in that barroom, and only one is guilty? Is it just that he was the only one caught? What about the others who fled? What has Jacob said?"

"Only that it was not his gun that did the killing." It sounded cynical, disinterested when she said it. She wished she had asked him more, but at the time it had seemed enough to know her candidate—her friend—was not guilty. "And that he believes Donovan hired Sal to start trouble in the saloon, to give him a reason to close it."

"A lie!" Kat cried, shaken. "He never knew the man!"

"I know," Annabel assured her. "John imputes the same crime to Jacob. But the fact remains, whatever his motive, he was there, a stranger, and the Reverend's boy was killed."

"Do you want him to hang too, then, like the rest?"

"Of course not!" In her heart Annabel wanted to see no man hanged. "It's why Jacob is running—to uphold the rule of law." Annabel wrestled against her nature. She could not be a mother to everyone, and yet without her conscience as a guide, what would keep her from wearing the mantle of power as John had done—John, who had once been the servant of a nuanced justice, powerful, yet . . .

"The boy," Annabel said. "Sal—you're sure he's innocent?"

Kat brought her hand to her neck, and for a moment she was quiet, her mind elsewhere. Then, coming to, she shrugged, but there was no ambivalence in the gesture, only a kind of defiance. "Maybe it was his bullet that killed the preacher's boy. Then maybe it wasn't. But I know it was the others who started it—the ones who cheated him at cards. I heard them myself, from upstairs. I heard them arguing."

Annabel nodded, knowing the reputations of Rod and Ike already. It was no surprise Chasby found his way into their company. She was lucky Hattie had not followed.

"It will not be easy to convince the town to stop the hanging," Annabel said. "To have blood spilled that way without reprisal—it would be a dishonor. They will demand someone pay for Chasby's death."

"On that Sheriff's word alone?"

"In the old days, yes. Today? I don't know."

"What about a trial?" Kat asked. Her lip was trembling pitifully. How young she looked then!

Annabel chewed her own lip as if to steady it. "We do have a circuit." She stood and rummaged around beneath the counter for her date book. She found the entry. "They're due in three weeks' time."

"Then we *could* ask for a trial?"

"It won't be an easy argument. Lawmen and townfolk don't like leaving high crimes to the uncertainty of judges." Annabel breathed deeply, wondering whether she could take this mission, too, whether the *town* could take it along with the rest—temperance, drought, religion.

But what choice did she have? She thought of the Reverend's service, of the men and women—*and the children!*—sitting rapt before him, that charmer of snakes. The hanging would not be justice, even if Sal had killed Chasby. It was blood sacrifice.

"You've already given him humanity," Annabel said at length. "In the street. You've done well."

Kat blushed, the color camouflaging Loeb's mark.

"We'd have to make the townfolk doubt," Annabel said. She sighed. "I'll talk to Jacob and the others. But the boy will have to make his own case before the town, and I fear his only chance will come upon the scaffold. It will be a final plea."

CHAPTER 38

Kat

Kat woke in the morning to the sounds of horses and men and the scrape and clatter of wagons.

She walked to the window in her white nightdress and parted the curtains. Three men were unloading lumber from a wagon in the center of the street. A chill ran through her when she realized its purpose.

They unloaded boards and tools, which they dropped in the dust beside a patch of square-staked ground—mallets and saws arrayed like instruments of torture. Then one of the men—they all looked alike, the Brandywines—took the wagon and team back for another load, and the process started over again, the boards stacked higher, the tools multiplied.

Kat marveled to think of a seed carried in the wind, grown a generation in some faraway land, destined to be felled and floated down a river and milled and shipped and hewn into the board beneath the executioner's boot or the frame of the gibbet itself from which Sal would hang.

As improbable as a girl born in Russia, raised in San Francisco, come to Texas.

She watched the carpenters' steady progress with a lump in her throat, her fingernails digging into her palms, leaving half-moon blood blisters like smiling eyes. She pulled on her gloves.

When Annabel came to call, the men had already sunk posts in the ground and begun the task of measuring and sawing and planing their lumber.

Annabel gave Kat a doleful, dark-eyed look as if the burden were hers to share.

Kat resented her for it, even though Annabel was going out of her way to help. It was another debt to owe.

They spoke in the alley between the saloon and the general store. It looked shabby in daylight—not like before, when she had followed Sal at night, running breathless to his room.

"I don't know how long you'll have," Annabel said. "Or whether we'll really be able to get you alone. You'll have to be quick."

Kat nodded, but her thoughts were on Sal, who was hurt and alone in the jailhouse, waking to the sounds of men at work on his gallows.

She had heard of lynchings—had even seen men leave on a lynching party—but they were hasty affairs with ropes and trees, done quickly before men's blood could cool, before reason—*compassion?*—could reassert its temper.

This was something else entirely, a conspiracy, deliberate and planned.

The deputy sat on the jailhouse porch, his legs crossed and propped against a column.

He did not look up until he heard the clack of their shoes on the wooden walk. He was chewing tobacco and whittling a stick into what looked like a spoon.

When he saw them, he stopped whittling and folded his arms across his lap, letting the knife hang loose in his right hand where they could see it. He leered beneath the brim of a hat pulled low over his sleepy brow.

"Morning, ladies," he said, touching his brim with the end of the nascent spoon. "You come to visit me?"

"Sure did, Mance," Annabel said, smiling and bending her knees to give the briefest impression of a curtsy.

Mance seemed surprised to hear it. He straightened up and set his boots on the ground. Boot, anyway. His peg was uncovered today, worn smooth like the butt of an old rifle.

He looked from Annabel to Kat, where his eyes settled.

Kat met his gaze only briefly. She could not help glancing at the door to the jailhouse. It was cracked half open, as if to admit the sound of hammering.

"Whaddya want to see me about?" Mance asked, suspicious. No doubt the women of the town did not call on him often.

"Kat here would like to see Sal," Annabel said, stopping on the boardwalk at the edge of the jailhouse porch. Since Mance was seated, their eyes were nearly level.

Mance leaned forward and said, "Who's Sal?"

"Your prisoner. The boy."

"The murderer?" Mance asked, frowning and sucking his teeth.

"He's no murderer," Kat put in, feeling the bite of her nails on her palms again. She tried to repress her loathing, which was mixed up in a pity for Minnie, now tied to this man by blood.

"He's a murderer sure enough," Mance said, evidently savoring Kat's displeasure. "Unless you find the preacher's boy has got himself up after three days on ice."

"Even so," Annabel said, cutting in before Kat had a chance to argue, "he deserves to be looked after. He was ill when you brought him in. Has he seen a doctor? We just want to make sure he's okay."

Mance leaned back in his chair, bored of the exchange. "Doc Marshall had a look, and he's alright. He'd seen a doctor before that, too, in another town. Two doctors in a week." Mance whistled. "More'n I seen in a lifetime. So you women can rest easy."

The deputy began to pick at his nails with the knife. But it did not take long for his lewd eyes to wander back to Kat.

She felt them searching—down her bodice and beneath her skirts— as if she had hidden something that was his.

"What's he to you anyway?" Mance asked, addressing Kat over knife and nails.

"He's a friend," she said. "In a strange country, a friend is a valuable thing."

"I saw you in the street. Looked like more than friends to me."

Kat blushed but kept silent. She was beginning to worry that the plan might not work, that Minnie would not come.

"Is this the way you speak to all townfolk who need your help?" Annabel demanded. Her voice was calm but with an edge now that Kat had not heard in it before.

The deputy turned sullen. "Sheriff said the boy, err, outlaw, can't talk to nobody."

"And where's John now?" Annabel asked, knowing full well he had gone to meet with the Reverend. She and Kat had watched him all the way to the church, just after they left Minnie.

The deputy shrugged. "In a meeting. Or sleeping, maybe. Ain't much sleep on a chase like we had, you know."

"I'm sure!" Annabel said, her tone suddenly admiring. "You must be tired, too! We don't mean to bother, see. We only want to lay eyes on the boy and let him know he's not alone in there."

Mance grunted, but Annabel's praise seemed to have softened him.

"How much trouble could we really be, a widow and a whore?"

The word struck Kat unawares as had Loeb's hand. She flinched to hear it, even though she knew it was intended for effect. It was as if it had come from the fleshless lips of her mother's ghost, an accusation.

Mance regarded his nails thoughtfully.

"I reckon it cain't hurt," he said after a minute. He rose from his chair and walked to the jailhouse door. "But I'll be standing right behind—so nothing funny or the boy will pay, understand?"

Kat nodded, and her heart began to beat fast. She climbed the stairs behind Annabel on shaking knees.

What will I say to him? All the words she had practiced seemed wrong in the moment. Her throat felt dry.

"Go ahead, Kat," Annabel said kindly, motioning for her to go first.

Mance stood holding the door open, his peg leg over the threshold, his body turned sideways in the doorway.

Kat could not enter without brushing against him, and the deputy took the opportunity to put his hands on her.

"Deputy!" Annabel shouted.

Mance only laughed. "I got to be sure she ain't carrying a weapon!"

Kat surged with anger but did not stop, afraid of being turned from her purpose.

It took a second for her eyes to adjust to the dimness. Then she saw Sal sitting in the corner, wrapped in a gray woolen blanket. His eyes were closed, and for a moment she wondered if she should let him sleep.

"Mance!" A woman's voice came through the door. It was Minnie, come as if by accident just as planned. Kat let out a small sigh of relief. She had feared the woman might balk.

Kat watched Mance step back onto the porch. Then Annabel discretely closed the door behind him, leaving Kat alone with Sal for the first time in what felt like ages.

"Sal!" she whispered. "It's me!"

Sal stirred, his shaggy dark hair flopping as he shook himself awake.

"Kat?" he asked with the uncertainty of someone accustomed to delirium. "How—?"

Kat rushed and knelt beside the cell, her knees slotting between the bars, her feet folded beneath her. "We don't have long," she said hurriedly.

Suddenly Sal came to himself. He threw off the blankets and rose to meet Kat, kneeling and putting his left hand on her leg as if to anchor her there. His right arm was immobilized in a sling.

"Kat!" he said again as if he could not believe it. "Kat, I'm sorry!"

"Are you alright?" she asked, laying her gloved hands against his chest, his face, his hair.

"Yes," he said, looking at the sling as if only just remembering. "Yes, I'm fine. I thought—" He stopped and swallowed, looking her in the eye, searching. "I thought I was going to die on the back of that horse. Maybe I nearly did." Then he added, "But the worst part was I thought I'd die without seeing you again, without explaining."

Kat smiled. Her lip trembled. She put her face to the bars, and Sal kissed her. Even confined to the cell he radiated the scent of sunshine, of freedom.

"Sal," she said, pulling back. "They're going to hang you tomorrow! You have to defend yourself!"

"I haven't got a weapon—"

"Not with a gun. You've got to explain yourself. When they bring you onto the scaffold. You've got to make your case to the town and ask for a trial."

"A trial?" Sal repeated dumbly.

She watched him coming back to her slowly like a man waking up from a blow to the head.

"Yes," she said earnestly. "Annabel said—"

"Annabel?"

"The postmaster—a friend. It doesn't matter. She said the circuit's coming to town in three weeks' time. The Sheriff—he wants you hanged to make a show of you, to prove something to the town. There's an election, see?" She knew she was rambling.

But there is so much to say! And who knows how long to say it!

She could hear Minnie's voice through the door like a melody, accompanied by Mance's rumbling bass and the staccato beat of his artificial leg.

"He and the mayor—they want you hanged, and the people do, too," Kat continued. "Some of them anyway. Do you remember? Yesterday? You were there. You have to ask for a trial! Do you understand?" She was gripping Sal's hand so the bone of her knuckles showed white through the skin.

"Yesterday?" he asked, screwing his eyes together. "It's a blur I don't know. I don't know what I dreamed, but I remember you. You brought me water. Was that real?"

She smiled, and she felt tears squeezing out of her eyes, and in that moment she was appalled. *How did I let this happen? To fall for another man—any man—after Vern?* Even the hammer blows in the street could not beat sense into her.

"Yes," she said. "That was real."

He smiled at her like knowing was all that mattered.

"You'll ask for a trial?" she repeated, wiping her eyes.

"It won't do any good," Sal said, his smile fading. "The Sheriff—he had my letter. He burned it. It's no good. He said he'd kill me, and by God—a man like that?—he means it."

"Letter?"

Sal chewed his lip a while. Too long. They did not have much time. "There's something you've got to know," he said finally, putting his hand on the curve of her cheek.

Kat looked at him, aware that she had stopped breathing, feeling like she was teetering on the edge of one of the great precipices of life.

"I'm an outlaw," he said, the words coming in a rush all of a sudden. "I've got a gang and a fortune in loot buried outside town—did you hear about the *Oregon*? It's enough to make a new life and live rich for the rest of our days! We can go to California like you want. No more waiting."

"California?" she asked, her mind reeling. For a moment she was transported to the bluffs overlooking the bay. "No more waiting?"

"No," Sal said.

"A house on the bay? Do you swear?"

"Sure." He said it like it was the easiest thing in the world for a man in jail and condemned to die. "And the trial—I'll ask for it if it comes to that, but we can't rely on them to spare me. We've got to take it into our own hands."

"How?" Kat asked, ears pricking, her fear suddenly erased by the unwavering confidence of the pale-eyed boy.

As Sal whispered to her through the bars of love and plots and fairytale things, Kat heard Mance—that new father—begin to curse as Minnie gave him the news.

CHAPTER 39

Donovan

THE REVEREND SAT BEHIND HIS PLAIN WOODEN DESK, HIS FACE ILLUMI-nated by candlelight. Black curtains were pulled tight across the only window, blocking every last ray of afternoon sun, casting the fulsome shadow of night across the office.

The Reverend was dressed head to toe in black with a black riding cape to match, but all of it was dull matte compared to the living blackness of his hair and eyes.

On his way through the church, Donovan had seen Chasby's corpse. It was pallid and waxy where the skin showed outside his suit, and it was packed with ice—an expensive means of preservation—as if science would do what goodliness could not.

The lid of the casket was turned open as if the boy was lying in state. The casket was plain pine, but it was upholstered in silk and velvet.

Donovan had not been able to look for long. In fact he had barely broken stride. For all the death he had seen, the boy was too pitiable for Donovan to look at, his weakness disgusting even in death.

Donovan fancied that he could still detect the faint aroma of alcohol surrounding the corpse like a perfume. It was an honest eulogy.

"Reverend," Donovan said, belatedly combing his fingers through his greasy hair and taking a seat before the desk.

"John," Aaron replied. He gave no inclination of welcome. His face was pinched in pain or maybe disgust.

"I tried to come yesterday," Donovan said. "But your men wouldn't let me." He left out that it was Loeb who had denied him, that he had come close to throttling the man.

"Yesterday was a day given to grief," Aaron replied.

Donovan heard the hiss of a snake and instinctively looked to his boots. But even the conniving serpent could not dampen his spirits. Two nights straight, Donovan had retired early and slept some sixteen hours. It was the best sleep of his life, and he awoke feeling like he had shed his ailing body in the night and taken another form. A certain mania had crept over him.

"Things are looking up, Reverend," Donovan began, diving into the stream of his consciousness. "The outlaw is behind bars where he belongs."

When the Reverend said nothing, Donovan added, "Your boy, Chasby, will be avenged tomorrow."

Still the Reverend made no comment, betrayed no emotion.

"It's God's will, see?" Donovan was eager to show the Reverend the inevitability of his logic. These thoughts had been turning over in his head some time like river rock. They were smooth and polished as he lay them before this, his spiritual guide.

"The outlaw came to us, to Mance and I, on the plain in gift wrap. He was *handed* to us. We showed our faith on that ride, Reverend, because I was sick—too sick to stand, much less ride a horse—and yet I trusted in your wisdom, in God's wisdom, and I went forth, and we were rewarded for our faith with a gift: the outlaw bound and gagged—the sacrificial lamb!"

With a sudden movement the ethereal Reverend swept a vase off his desk. It crashed to the floor with a spray of water and wildflowers. "Chasby is the lamb!" he cried. "Chasby is the lamb!" He rose partway in his seat before subsiding.

"Yes," Donovan stammered, completely derailed.

He saw in the Reverend's black eyes and dress, in the shadows that clung to him, in the dark room where he had shut himself with the meager light of a flickering candle, a physical power that he had not recognized before, and the man's mourning garb suddenly seemed less overwrought, more sinister.

"Surely Chasby was the lamb, but all the same, the outlaw—he was a sign from God, too, when we found him bound and gagged. And I know this because of the show of faith it took to apprehend him, and I know it because the cancer—" Donovan pointed at his gut and followed the finger with his own eyes, as if to peer inward at the throbbing tumor "—it's already starting to disappear!"

The Reverend looked at Donovan a long while then nodded. "Yes," he said. "I see your point about the outlaw."

Donovan sat back and felt a flood of joy and relief at having received even this reluctant benediction. A man himself might doubt a thing for a sign. He might wonder if he has played a trick on himself by interpreting something as such. But for another man, a holy man, to see the same sign and understand its significance, that was something too remarkable to doubt.

"For the first time in a long time, Reverend—and thanks to you—I feel like I can attend the business I was meant to attend, the business I have neglected."

"Yes," the Reverend mused. "Neglected, indeed. You must know Jacob is entertaining in the saloon again. Or perhaps you did not know, as you have been early to bed of late."

Donovan did not care to wonder how the Reverend knew his habits. "I know it well, and I know the mayor's error, to have exposed us as he did."

"Bah," the Reverend waved his hand. He leaned forward, overtaken by one of his sudden bouts of loquaciousness, his pale fingers stretched on the tabletop like the legs of a spider. "Righteousness should not be hidden, John. We must show God and the flock once more that our faith is unshaken, that our purpose has mettle. Only then can we rest assured we have His blessing in the election. We will not let this challenge to our power go unanswered.

"You must close the saloon this very day! And for good!" the Reverend sneered, his teeth gleaming and his mouth wide so that Donovan could see the blackness of the chasm beyond. "Then the election will be a referendum on our transformative action, and our victory will be a mandate to go yet further, to consolidate our power."

Suddenly the room seemed oppressively hot. Donovan felt a stab of pain in his back and understood that it was God prodding him forward as a farmer prods his mule. He absentmindedly patted the pocket where he stored the opiate elixir.

"Don't worry about the townspeople," the Reverend continued. "Worry about God. God will move the hearts of the people. It is true: We have seen the signs. Chasby's death was a sign, and so was the outlaw's capture, and so is the town's willingness to hang him. All these point to one thing: The flock is ready, and we must complete the act of salvation!"

"How?"

"What has been closed once can be closed again." The Reverend's jaw was set. He was implacable. "Tell me, do you think in that short time Jacob could scrub my boy's blood from his floor? The stain of the crime is still there—a sign for all to see. I'm sure of this. Go to the saloon and uncover the stain and close it, and when the thing is done, then tell them—the town—that it is done for all time. Tell them at the hanging."

Donovan looked down at his hands, and this was to be taken as a show of acquiescence. He listened to the spit of the candle, scented the melting tallow.

"Do you think Chasby is with God?" the Reverend asked after a while.

Donovan was taken aback. "Of course," he stammered. "You said it yourself—he was a sacrifice."

"Does a sacrifice always find his way to God?"

Donovan did not know what to say, so he kept quiet. He had trouble meeting the Reverend's eye.

"Even Jesus Christ did not rise until the third day," the Reverend mused. "Where was he in that time?" This time he did not give Donovan a chance to answer. "I have told you before that Heaven and Hell are one place.

"When Chasby was a boy, he would not mind my commandments, and I would whip him for it, and I would damn him for it, and still he would not mind—his blood father was an atheist you know, an *intellectual*. When Chasby grew older, he would defy me, although I saw it was hard for him, and I knew in his heart he wanted to obey, but the meat of his flesh could not.

"As a younger man, I believed that free will meant choice—the choice to do right or wrong—and that good men chose right and bad men chose wrong. Good *souls* chose right and bad souls wrong. But watching Chasby struggle, I saw in him a good soul that chose wrong, like he was born into the wrong body.

"Of course this is impossible. God, who makes us whole, could not make such a mistake. The error is with me, that I could not understand the mind of God, and with me further that I would even *try*.

"Yet now I see a logic in it—too late of course—that is the way of these things. Chasby was a sacrifice—the lamb as we have said—who could not have played his part if his good soul had always chosen right. His was a good soul that chose wrong *at God's behest*. Do you see?

"And all that time I tried to render the wrong from him, to boil it off. I tortured him. Am I a good soul? Am I a good soul who chooses wrong at God's behest? How else could I have behaved? Confronted with a boy who would not obey his master?" The Reverend shook his head, but it was a gesture of awe. He was marveling at the complexity of the universe and of God, which Donovan understood must be the same as lamenting one's own limitations.

"Three days Christ himself was subjected to Hell," Aaron continued. "Though he was the son of God, his form was human, and that human weakness—the weakness that is inseparable from the flesh even with his distilled spirit—it had to be purged.

"And now I think Chasby lived nineteen years in hell under my roof, where I was the tormenter, the good soul doing wrong for the right reason."

The Reverend hung his head, and Donovan thought it was to hide his emotion. When he raised it, the shadows were too deep to see his eyes but for the reflection of that candle flame.

"So yes, John, I believe Chasby is with God. His was a good soul that chose bad, and he was rewarded—just as you shall be."

Donovan only hoped his reward would be better than Chasby's had been.

CHAPTER 40

Haddock

Dear Jacob,

I'm anxious that this letter finds you soon. I can picture you looking out the windows with that far-off look you get, waiting to glimpse a smudge on the horizon that might be me, coming from St. Aleta or Austin or some such. I hope this letter finds you, because there won't be a smudge, or a stroll down Front. I've made up my mind to leave Three Chop for good and have already left it.

We talked about it a hundred times, so I won't bring it out again to be worried over like mother's Bible. I'll only say that civilization found us faster than we thought. I remember thinking Three Chop was the end of the Earth, that we'd—I'd—be safe there long as I lived, long as it took for the dust of war to settle and the new law to take effect.

God, but weren't we fooled? Maybe it was when the cowpunchers first started flooding in. Maybe seeing half a hundred Negro cowboys and not a one make trail hand. Maybe it was when the railroad came, and men and women from all around arrived to gawk and grumble at the Lady May's Negro piano man.

Or maybe it was that dark-haired Reverend. When I caught his eyes the first time, I saw the hate.

The black folk have stopped coming to town. Have you noticed it?

But if Aaron was the reason I left, he was not the only one. I thought you looked a little surprised when I agreed to go so easily after the Reverend's boy was killed. You thought I would demand to stay by you. And you thought you would agree, because you would believe you could protect me.

Maybe you could.

But I agreed to go, because the time was long passed. I agreed to go the same way I agreed to follow you off your daddy's riverboat, sneaking away under cover of night, two men made fugitives by the simple act of walking away. I agreed to go the same way I agreed to settle down in a town that was little more than ink on a map and not yet dry at that, settled down in a town situated in Texas, no less.

How I wish we had gone to Montana, to a place where no man passed within a hundred miles. That's where I should have gone. And it would have been only you and me. And our company would be the work it took to wrest a living from that far-off land. And we could have invited folk, but they would have been our folk, and we could have started a new kind of town.

Yes, a new kind of town!

When I told you to run for mayor, that's what I said, "We could start a new kind of town." I know you wanted it. I know you'd work at it. And so we agreed like we always do. But in my heart I knew the town would not change, men's hearts would not change. Might as well change the turning of the Earth by setting your shoulder against the mountain.

So why I left was not just the Reverend, though he was part of it. I agreed to go because I'm done agreeing. Twenty years we did it your way. Twenty years I kept my tongue. I bent my back. Now I will bend it another way, bend it in a new place to new ends.

I grow upset even as I dictate these letters. But they don't spell regrets. Nor complaints. They spell truths. Some are happy truths. I have always been happy with you, even when I was uncertain or scared. I tell them to you so you understand. I tell them to you so you'll see that I must go a different way, and I beg you to join me.

I am writing from Denver. It's farther than you were expecting, I know. I rode most of the way until I could hop a coach. And my, the mountains! I have never pictured the like, would not have believed it until I saw them, those giants capped in white. Our track looked but a thread fallen at their feet. I never thought the engine would survive the climb, and I thought of all those folks in tales who get stranded up here and turn to eating one another. Yet here I am, alive and well.

I found a friendly newspaperman by the name of Herbert Gailsbraith, who is helping me write this letter. He is a fellow like us, his own kind of man.

He's a newspaperman. Says he knows Rascal from the wires, and he has proven himself helpful and reliable.

Mr. Gailsbraith says you can send return letters to him at the Denver Star Courier, *and he'll make sure I get them. And if you don't send them in time and I'm already gone, I'll leave word for you with him.*

Two weeks, Jacob. I leave in two weeks. Agree to come with me this time?

Yours,
Haddock Beauvoir

CHAPTER 41

Pete

"WON'T BE FAR NOW," PETE SAID, GRINDING HIS TEETH. HIS MOOD WAS foul. He was exhausted from lack of sleep and food, and he was broiling beneath the eye of the prairie sun. He vowed that his first stop in Three Chop would be the saloon. *Wonder if it's still the same old Lady May?* He imagined the taste of beer and sausage and a plate of beans and licked his lips.

"Ungh," Bill grunted, spitting into the dirt.

Bill had been in a black mood since Pete had killed Tim.

Tim had pleaded for his life, even though he must have known his wounded leg would kill him before long—and painfully so.

The smell alone should have been enough to convince anyone of the necessity, never mind the color—black and green and yellow and red, every color but the natural tone of flesh—but apparently it was not enough to convince Tim, nor Bill for that matter.

"Ain't right," Bill had grumbled after Pete sent two bullets through the wounded man's skull, smoke still issuing from the end of his gun. "He brought us this far."

"He's a double-crosser," Pete had replied, jamming the hot barrel in his holster.

"Aren't we all?" Bill had said sourly, and he had brooded ever since.

For his part Owl had been unflappable. As ever, he seemed more interested in something far off than the goings on around him.

Pete wondered why Bill had been so partial to Tim. Sometimes an old man just picked out a younger to mentor for no other reason than an urge to leave something behind when he was gone. Bill had no kids that

239

he knew of. Is that how Bill had seen Tim? Or had there been something more to it?

Pete put Bill's insubordination out of mind. Tim had been a double-crosser, and he had slowed them down besides, and if Jack was not going to do the work himself on account of some weak excuse of a debt, Pete would do what had to be done the way he always had. His only regret was knowing Jack had probably planned it this way to divide him and Bill.

Pete's thoughts turned to the job ahead. He had not been to Three Chop since that fateful day when Nash Warrick had been killed. He still had frequent dreams about it—the noonday sun shining bright—the lone man standing before them, a green man, a weak man, as determined as he was foolish.

The damnable Sheriff.

"Be there by sundown I reckon," Owl said with the far-off look in his eye.

Pete had known many men who thought that look made Owl wise, but he suspected there was nothing behind it except a keen sense of hearing.

Even as he thought these things, Pete saw Owl cock his head.

"Hear somethin'?" he asked, watching the man's eyes, now squinted and searching.

"Not with you talking like that," Owl said. He said it in his own way. It was not an insult but a fact.

Still, Bill grinned, and Pete shot him an angry look.

"Maybe," Owl said after a minute. "Hard to say—could be cow or deer or maybe horse."

"Horse and riders?" Pete asked. The fingers of his gun hand itched ominously.

"Hard to say," Owl repeated.

But Pete could tell he was listening still. He thought about dismounting to skylight, but his knees were sore, and he was not sure he would be able to mount his horse again.

Then again it was that kind of laziness that might get a man killed.

A few minutes later a gunshot sounded. Pete did not need Owl to hear it. The sound rolled across the plains like thunder on the wind.

The three men drew rein immediately and circled, scanning the horizon in three directions at once.

Seeing no immediate danger, Bill hopped off his horse and squatted, looking for shapes moving against the backdrop of blue sky.

"Ahead," he said, pointing roughly in the direction they had been riding.

Pete squinted beneath the brim of his hat but saw only the shimmer of heat and reflected scrub grass.

"Maybe hunters?" Bill asked, peering up at Owl.

"Weren't no rifle shot," Owl said, and his pronouncements on these things were as good as settled. He took his own rifle from his saddlebag and laid it across his lap.

"How many?" Pete asked. The grass swam before his eye.

"Couldn't say," Bill said thoughtfully as he pressed his ear to the ground.

Pete held his breath as if it might disturb the man's concentration.

"No," Bill said, standing up and brushing off his trousers. He hoisted himself into his stirrup. "I cain't hear 'em. Don't know how many, but it ain't the cavalry at least."

Pete nodded, and Owl listened.

"Well I ain't knowed a man to fear on these plains since Nash Warrick," Pete said after a while. He spit, trying for the thousandth time to clear the dirt from his mouth. "Let's see what these sons of bitches have to say for themselves."

"Gentlemen," said the stranger on the left, nodding his head. The brim of the man's hat cast a thin band of shadow across his eyes, but otherwise he was practically staring into the sun.

Pete felt almost sorry for him.

There were two men—one with dark features and a salt-and-pepper beard, the other a thin wisp of a man with a cruel and stupid look about him. They looked desperate—thin, wan, and stained with old blood. They were fleeing something, alright. Maybe they had not eaten in days. And they had a single, exhausted horse between them—that could mean death in this expanse. They looked like men who had cornered a bear and did not know what to do with it.

"Where ya headed?" the bearded man asked.

Bill growled.

Pete only looked at the men, his head cocked sideways, considering. He saw the bearded man had his hand on his pistol. The reedy man did, too, and he looked nervous.

"It ain't polite to fire your gun at folks," Pete said after a minute. "You want to talk to us, you could wave us down. Sure don't need to fire your gun."

The bearded man smiled in a way that made Pete think he did not really understand what the expression was for.

"Didn't mean no harm," he said, biting his lower lip. "Thing is," he started almost as an afterthought. "Thing is, we're the law around here, and the law does as it likes."

The thin man smirked, but there was no joy in it.

"The law?" Bill scoffed. "I don't see no badges."

The bearded man laughed and gestured to his companion. "He says he don't see no badges, Ike." He laughed again, shaking his head. Turning back to Pete, he said, "You sure you could see 'em if we had 'em?" The man tapped his eye. "You know if that good one goes bad . . ."

Pete spit in the dirt. "I figure I can see well enough to shoot," he said, raising his hand to the man, making a gun with his thumb and forefinger. He winked with his good eye as he dropped the hammer. "What do you want with us anyway, lawmen? To give us an eye exam? Or maybe to borrow our horses?"

Pete patted his horse's neck affectionately.

"You boys had any trouble on these plains?" the bearded man asked obliquely. He kept his hand on his gun.

"Not 'til now!" Bill said angrily.

"Well I reckon that's on account of us. Like I said, we're the law around these parts, and we keep these here plains safe from outlaws and bandits of the kind that might harass travelers like yerselves."

Pete looked around and spit. "You get a lot of outlaws in these parts?"

"Oh, sure," the bearded man replied. "All kinds. Not as many as we used to, mind you. Because we're good lawmen, see?"

Pete shrugged, indicating he did not.

"Thing is," the man continued, "it ain't a service we can provide for free."

Pete smiled, for he had his part to play and knew it well, and in his gut he felt joyful. He knew what was coming next. He had an appetite to whet after all.

"See," the man said, "there's a tax through these parts we got to collect to keep on keepin' folks safe."

"What kind of tax?" Pete asked, savoring that slow, inexorable slide into violence.

"Them horses, for starters," the bearded man said.

In a flash the man drew his pistol, and the reedy man leveled his own, but neither stood one chance in twenty of getting off a shot.

Desperate fools.

Pete squeezed off three rounds, firing from his hip. The first hit the bearded man in the arm. The second missed wide, but the third got him in the face, tearing through the man's teeth and lodging somewhere in the flesh at the back of his throat.

The man's head flew back, spraying a liquid arc of blood in the air. He grabbed at his face. His jaw hung unnaturally loose, and blood ran through his beard and down the front of his shirt.

Pete marveled as he always did at that irrevocable instant in which a perfectly whole man is mangled unalterably. *How he must wish to have that moment back!*

A fourth shot—this one well aimed—ended the man's anguish along with whatever regret he may have felt for initiating the conflict.

A mercy, Pete thought. *Just like I did for Tim.*

Meanwhile, Bill had shot the reedy man in the belly and Owl had blown his shoulder apart.

Another well-aimed shot from Pete finished him, too.

Then Pete saw it—the barrel of Bill's own gun, turning, glinting in the sun as it escaped his shadow. Pete swung his own arm, but as slow as the barrel of Bill's gun turned, Pete's arm rose slower.

He had one bullet left, but he knew he would not get the chance to use it.

Why, Bill? he wondered. *For Tim?*

But just as Pete was steeling himself for the searing pain of hot lead, he saw the turning gun barrel falter and begin to dip.

A shot had rung out in that moment, surprising Pete, who had not pulled his trigger.

Owl?

Pete watched Bill, a look of confusion overcoming the man's face. It froze there. It was his last expression. He slumped forward and slid off his horse, his foot still tangled in the stirrup.

The mount, smelling blood—increasingly covered in it—whickered and took off.

The motion shook Bill free of the stirrup. He lay face down in the dirt a few yards away, sprawled beside the bearded man and reedy man, his long brown beard matted with blood like the other.

Owl shook his head. "Sorry, Pete. I thought we could trust him."

"Shit, Owl. You did good!" Pete said, and he laughed. It was an honest laugh—as honest as he had made in a long while.

Owl smiled. "I always knew you was the right man to follow, Pete."

Pete nodded, thinking that Owl might have more sense than he had ever given him credit for. He certainly had more sense than Jack did, sending them ahead. More than Bill, too, obviously.

"Say, Owl. You understand we had to get rid of Tim, don't ya?"

"Sure," Owl said, shrugging, his stare returning to the horizon. "He'd've slowed us down."

"Damn right," Pete agreed, truly impressed.

Pete urged his horse through the mayhem, guiding the stallion around Bill's corpse, though he would have rather trod upon it.

It did not bother Pete that he had almost died—he had *almost* died countless times. It was his specialty, the almost. It was what separated him from most of the men he had known in his life—even the great men, the men he admired, like Nash Warrick.

They rode the afternoon in silence, Pete falling in and out of sleep the way a man could when he had spent his life on horseback. He lost himself in reminiscence, which likewise spanned his thoughts and dreams.

The sun dipped below the horizon and Pete's shadow stretched to meet the infinite darkness. He wondered what Nash would say if he could see him now.

A while after sunset, the lights of the town came into view—Three Chop at last, a homecoming of sorts.

Part IV:
...To a Woman with a Gun

CHAPTER 42

Jacob

JACOB SAT AT HIS BAR, A GLASS OF WHISKEY SET BEFORE HIM.

In the night he had dreamed of Haddock on the plain, alone, chased by hounds, much as they had been the night they fled the old riverboat, the night they forged their bond. To be overcome by a dream was foolish. Haddock would have told him as much. And yet Jacob could not forget the image of that brave man, silhouetted in the moonlight, terrified and hunted.

He tried to find some feeling for the boy, too, who had died before his very eyes, died in a pool of blood, his green eyes wide in disbelief. *And something else? Relief?*

But he felt nothing. If there was any sympathy in him for Chasby, it was wrapped up in his fear for Haddock, and now, after Haddock's letter, in grief.

Through the window, Jacob watched the sun begin to set. Drinking hours, and yet he was alone. He did not bother to light the lamps inside. Most of his regular patrons had worn themselves out opening the saloon and keeping it open the last few nights.

This day only Madame Fuselli's footsteps sounded from upstairs, padding softly like a cat. The girls were either out or in bed. Occasionally he heard snatches of ghostly laughter.

Jacob brooded over Haddock, over the choice he had been given—to let go his heart or the life he had built for twenty years.

If he chose to stay, what life would be left to him? What chance had he to win the election, to fend off the rabid drys? Even the groundswell of support the town had shown these last two days could not lift his spirits, for as numerous as those supporters might be, he would need many more to win.

Jacob was not surprised when Donovan entered. He had pictured this meeting a hundred times since he had announced his candidacy.

The Sheriff arrived with the squeak of the back-door hinge. He stood a long moment in the doorway, contemplating the empty barroom, silhouetted—a dark sigil upon a field of yellow orange, the color of sunset.

What did surprise Jacob were Donovan's companions. His deputy filed in behind him, and there were others, too, including the stoop-shouldered Loeb, whose craggy face practically glowed with unadulterated pleasure.

The Lord's men, Jacob realized. He held the picture of them in his mind even as he turned back to his drink. He would not gape. There were seven men in all.

A sheriff, his deputy, and five . . . farmers? Acolytes? Soldiers?

He strove to appear unafraid. He clung to his dignity. The anger helped. Yes, anger was far more useful than shame.

"Afternoon, Sheriff," Jacob said into his cup. He took another swill. The glass was nearly empty.

"Jacob," Donovan said coolly.

Donovan must have made some signal, because the acolytes fanned out as one and began to collect bottles. They worked silently, but triumph was written on their faces as plain as the guns on their hips.

Soldiers.

"Is this about the billiards table?" Jacob asked after a long silence. He sipped his drink.

"What?"

"The billiards table—don't you remember? In the early days when I was still deciding what kind of place this would be, you told me, 'Jake, you need a billiards table. Folks like to play billiards.'

"But it was years before I got one—didn't have the money then, and I figured since mine was the only saloon in town it'd do a decent business. I always thought maybe you held that against me."

Donovan grunted. "You oughtta look a man in the eye when you talk to him."

Jacob grinned to himself, to his drink. "A man, sure. But a thief? What does he deserve?"

The acolytes stopped, their bottles rattling, scowling at the accusation.

Through the back door, which Mance had propped open, Jacob could see there were more of them—many more, women mostly—standing quietly outside in a half circle almost like a group of carolers come to call.

Apparently not all the women of the county would be voting for him despite Annabel's best efforts.

Jacob glanced at Donovan.

"Thief?" Donovan asked, his face coloring.

"What would you call a man who comes into another man's house and takes his property?"

Donovan strode to Jacob, put his hand on his shoulder, forced him to meet his eye. "The law follows the law."

Jacob returned Donovan's stare, and though his heart was beating fast now, he knew his countenance was cold and unyielding as a block of ice. "Guess that means you can't be a murderer either? Even as you hang a boy without trial?"

"Watch your mouth, Jake," Donovan said, his hooded eyes flashing danger.

Jacob recognized that look. It betrayed something like his own seething hatred.

"I'm closing you down, because this is a crime scene, because I already closed it down once, and you reopened it against my command."

Donovan went to the corner of the rug that Jacob had brought downstairs to cover the stain of Chasby's blood. Wordless, he peeled it back, kicking over furniture until the thing was revealed.

Loeb gasped when he saw it, quaking.

Donovan stood, letting the spot speak on his behalf.

"What'll you do with it?" Jacob asked, uninterested in Donovan's theatrics. He nodded to the liquor being borne away in procession as if by ants.

"To the church!" Loeb screeched. "Where it cannot be used again for evil!"

Jacob almost laughed at that final irony.

"Tell me, John. Do you really think it was liquor that killed Chasby?"

"Can you doubt it?" Loeb asked, his jaw slack with childlike incredulity. Donovan remained impassive.

"Because, if liquor it was," Jacob continued, letting Loeb's words speak for Donovan, "why then do you hang the boy?"

Donovan kicked over another chair, and it splintered. He crossed the room to Jacob, sticking a finger in his face.

"The Reverend's boy died in this place because of you," he growled. "And if that outlaw is anyone's man, he's yours."

"The Reverend killed him," Jacob said evenly. "His black heart will kill any man who comes too close. The whole town, even." Jacob looked hard at Donovan, into Donovan, and he saw that Donovan knew this truth already, but that his pride would not admit it, that his pride whispered in his ear, telling him the man who killed Nash Warrick could not be thwarted by some insubstantial demagogue.

Loeb did not take Jacob's accusation well. He screeched unintelligibly then grabbed a bottle of liquor and hurled it at Jacob. It sailed well wide, but it crashed into the mirror on the wall behind the bar, bottle and mirror alike shattering in an explosion of glass.

Donovan turned to Loeb, bore down upon him, grabbing him by the neck. Donovan lifted him bodily into the air, threw him out of doors, into the street. "Get back to the Reverend, you dog," he bellowed. "If I catch sight of you again tonight, I'll hang you beside the outlaw."

The triumphant serenity of the women drys broke into screams and shrinking confusion.

For his part, Jacob laughed. Surely Donovan must know what a fool he had made of himself, cleaving to this rabble.

"And here I thought you'd found religion!" Jacob said, wiping his mouth.

Donovan turned, glowered. "Loeb is scum," he said, wiping his brow with his shirtsleeve. "But out there are a hundred good folk—mothers and grandmothers, hardworking men—industrious people standing for their way of life. Good people united in a hatred of violence and a thirst for order.

"A hundred people came to stand against you, a fraction of those who will watch the outlaw hang, a fraction of those who will vote against you in the election. You are finished."

Jacob knew Donovan was right, knew it by the departure of those clinking bottles.

He picked up his personal bottle and poured himself another finger of whiskey. If he was going to do it, he might as well do it with a warmth in his belly.

"You don't know what's real anymore, do you, John? You've lied to yourself—to the town—so long, you've forgotten the truth."

"I've heard of it before, of men losing themselves in their own myth. But you—your entire *life*, your reputation, is built on a lie."

"What are you getting at, Jacob?" Donovan seemed to be somewhere else, his mind turned to the next task, Jacob something foul but harmless like shit left in the street after a cattle drive.

The Reverend's men had finished with the last of the liquor, had even taken the big casks of beer. The shelves behind the bar stood bare, the bareness doubled in fragments of the mirror behind them. Those shelves that had sagged beneath so much accumulated inventory now ran straight and true, a great weight removed from them—the weight of Jacob's livelihood.

The men shuffled through the door, leaving Jacob and Donovan alone.

Jacob could hear a celebration beginning outside, voices of praise calling to the twilit sky.

"Drink?" Jacob offered.

"Speak your piece, Jacob."

Jacob savored the moment of this small triumph, knowing it might be his last.

"The great Sheriff, John Donovan, the man who killed Nash Warrick," he began, his mouth twisting into a sneer. "What do you think people would say if I told them the truth?"

Donovan only looked impatient. "Quit riddling," he growled.

"It was *me*, John. *I* killed Nash Warrick. I, who cannot be trusted to aim a gun. From the roof of this very saloon—it was one story then, remember? I watched him count his steps, I saw him turn, and I shot him through the heart, shot him just as he was about to kill you—saved your life."

Jacob laid his secret bare between them, like a body disinterred and resurrected. All this time he thought Donovan had known. Maybe Donovan had always deluded himself, had never let the truth enter his memory.

Donovan did not speak. His face was unreadable.

Jacob shook his head, grinning, awed by the great remembrance. It was the first—the only—man he had ever killed, as far as he knew.

"Lies," Donovan said finally, as if history was a question of making up one's mind. "You fled with the rest. I stood alone. I prevailed *alone*."

"I shot Nash Warrick through the chest," Jacob whispered. He could not stop himself from grinning. "Think back on it, count the gunshots."

Jacob watched the smolder in Donovan's eyes. His own hate had given him the strength to wrest Donovan's legacy from him. Now it would give him the strength to endure. He raised the glass to his lips for a triumphal drink.

Donovan swung his fist then, balled like a rock, punching the glass into Jacob's mouth. It broke his front teeth and sliced through his lip as it shattered.

Jacob felt warm blood running down his chin, staining his shirt. But he did not reach for his kerchief. He did not cry out. He only grinned wider, probing the roots of his missing teeth with his tongue.

"You're a goddamn liar!" Donovan screamed, screamed it so loud its resonance rang the brass of the unlit lamps. "And no one will believe you! You're a town man—rich and soft and half a woman. They'll know the truth with their eyes when they see me hang that outlaw! Which of us is strong enough to have killed Nash Warrick!"

Jacob spat a fragment of tooth to the floor. Vaguely he heard the sound of footsteps on the stair.

He is not the man I knew.

"Your first bullet sprayed wide. Your second hit Pete. You never hit Nash." Without his teeth, Jacob lisped like a snake.

Donovan grabbed Jacob by the neck and lifted him partway out of his chair, much as he had done to Loeb.

Jacob clung to his dignity, that most private possession, even in the face of this brutality. His neck was soft, pressed beneath Donovan's fingers, and yet he did not flinch.

"Times are changing, and you're on the wrong side of history," Donovan raged, his voice a guttural whisper filtered through the vice-clamp of his still whole teeth. He hissed into Jacob's ear so he could feel the moistened heat of his breath. "Don't make this harder on yourself than it has to be."

"Unhand him," came the voice of the madam, controlled even as she burst into the room.

Jacob did not need to look to know she held her revolver.

Donovan let go, and Jacob slumped heavily onto his stool, dimly aware he was gasping. He felt the tenderness in his neck with his hands, scrubbing at it like it was some stain of defilement.

For a moment Jacob thought Donovan might kill him anyway, but instead the Sheriff turned and stalked to the door, his shoulders pinched tight in unrelinquished anger.

Jacob looked to the madam.

Her hand was steady.

He blinked his thanks.

Donovan opened the door but paused on the threshold the same way he had when he entered—his silhouette no different going than coming—as if to take one last look at his vanquished foe.

Except this time, after a moment, he swayed, and—like a jar on the verge of tipping, balanced on that uncertain point—the outcome was a roll of dice or a shuffling of cards.

Just like Chasby in that chair—tipping, tipping, falling, falling. Falling into the stain. Had it always been there?

Then the silhouette crumpled into a heap—legs within the saloon, torso and head without—the equator of the belly aligned perfectly with the threshold.

The madam cursed.

Jacob found himself standing, running.

Why?

His neck still throbbed, his teeth roots still bled in profusion, and yet he was running to this man, kneeling now beside him.

Why?

He pressed his fingers into the Sheriff's neck, feeling for the universal rhythm, his mouth dripping blood onto the man's uniform.

Why?

Because a town that would not scruple to let a man die this way would not scruple to save a boy's life, or a slave's.

CHAPTER 43

Pete

PETE'S STOMACH BEGAN CHURNING THE MOMENT HE SAW THREE CHOP in the distance, its lights now shining like stars reflected off a sea.

He had not been to this place in twenty years—not since the day Nash Warrick died. He did not dwell on the reasons why. It had not been conscious.

He felt lightheaded, manic, his belly a vat of acid. It was the same feeling he got after too many cups of campfire coffee on an empty stomach.

Must be hungry is all, he told himself.

But there was dread in the feeling, and Pete wondered too if he was afraid.

Pete was a man to fight fire with fire, and he decided a shot of whiskey was the thing to settle his nerves and settle the roiling of his stomach. He wished he'd hung around Graves Point long enough to collect on that bottle of mezcal promised by the sheriff.

"Let's start at the saloon," Pete said to Owl, who rode a few yards behind.

"Did Jack tell you what we're to do?" Owl asked, looking over his shoulder.

Pete spat. "He's playing us, Owl. I don't know how yet, but he's sent us ahead, all of us who can see his weakness, sent us off together. Now Bill's dead, and it's just you and me. And I cain't figure exactly what his aim is, but somehow I expect he means to see us killed before this ends."

Owl chewed on that a bit, then said, "I reckon you might be right, Pete, although I never knowed Jack to be so false."

"He left us to kill Tim, didn't he?" Pete asked. "And Bill, too, in a way. Maybe he expects you and I'll kill each other. That'd take more than a few problems off his hands.

"No," Pete continued. "As far as I can tell, our best bet is to look after ourselves now, and I cain't think of a better way to start than by finding Sal."

"Jack'll hound us forever—to hell if it comes to't," Owl said cautiously.

"Here's where you got to trust me, Owl, same way I trust you."

"Alright, Pete. You know we got trust."

They slowed their mounts when they reached the outskirts of town. Like a cancer, the town had grown far beyond the bounds Pete remembered. When he imagined Three Chop, he imagined it as it was twenty years past—a clump of ramshackle A-frames sprung up like mushrooms, its only distinguishing feature a claptrap paper printed on an outdoor press.

When he had last seen it, it was empty but for tumbleweeds and for that lone man marking the time with his shadow, standing in the middle of a street too disused even to show the ruts of wagon tracks.

After Nash died, Pete had roamed as far as California and Oregon, then on to the Dakotas—that was where he had hooked up with Jack. All that wandering seemed to him now like a great ribbon snaking across the map, a single track for all its winding, an odyssey, its object to return him here to this same point in space at a different point in time, a different man, ready to meet his destiny.

To avenge the man.

The clarity of this vision nearly bowled Pete from his saddle. It was a chance to right a wrong, to pull up the old city slicker by the root and cast him back east. And what would be his reward for the effort, besides the symbolism, the karma, the justice?

Ain't that enough?

Pete licked his lips. Revenge and a half-million dollars. That was justice.

As much as he hated the town, Pete could not help but marvel at its vastness. It took ten minutes' riding along Front Street to spot the saloon.

Like the rest of the town, it was bigger than Pete remembered, rambling, grown up.

Layers on layers. Mushrooms.

The mushrooms must have fed off Warrick's blood like a fertilizer.

But there was something else there, too, looming out of the darkness. They came upon it cautiously, reverently, even, until it resolved itself—a great scaffold in the center of the street where once he had stood.

"Might be they've already hung him," Owl said under his breath.

"Huh," Pete grunted, eyeing the gibbet, thinking of himself, of the Creole woman.

Pete was not afraid to hang. It was an easy death, so long as you relaxed and let your neck snap. It was better than being shot as Nash had proved as he drowned in the middle of the plain in the only ready source of water that was his own life's blood. Tim proved it further still with his festering knee. If brutal, hanging was a mercy—like killing cattle with a hammer—so long as it was done right.

"Maybe we're here just in time," Owl said hopefully.

"Or just too late," Pete replied, stepping from his stirrups.

They hitched their mounts to the tie rail before the saloon and stepped onto the boardwalk, knocking the mud from their boots on the way.

Only then did Pete notice the saloon was boarded up. He cursed.

"There's a piano going," Owl said. "Hear it?"

Pete nodded. "Somebody's home all right." He pounded on the door, rattling the glass panes in the windows.

The piano kept on.

Pete cursed and circled the building. The back door was unboarded and unlocked.

It was a short, balding man seated at the piano bench. He was dressed as if for the opera or a funeral, all done up in black and with a silk bow tie to match, though he did not appear to be expecting visitors.

"Is this a saloon or ain't it?" Pete called out gruffly, surveying the rows of empty shelves.

The man at the piano started, turned.

Pete was surprised to find he recognized the man. He had aged, grown a curling moustache, but he was one of the old faces, the fled faces, the first transgressors.

"It was," the barman said with a strange lisp, seeming put out. His eyes narrowed.

"Well, you got food and drink, or don't you?" Pete demanded.

"We need to water them horses, too," Owl added, motioning to the front door.

"You can water your own horses from the trough," the man said. "As for food and drink—we're closed."

The barman stood then, moving to reintroduce them to the door by which they had just entered.

As he came close, Pete saw a fresh wound on the man's face, noted his broken teeth.

"Hey now," Pete said, flashing a dangerous smile. "That ain't no way to treat a guest. Looks like maybe someone already tried to learn you that lesson tonight."

"Feel free to help yourselves to whatever I got," the barman said, throwing up his hands. He seemed like a man past caring. There was opportunity in a man like that—and danger.

"What happened to yer liquor?" Pete asked, surveying the empty room.

"The Sheriff happened," the barman said bitterly.

Pete got the sense he had interposed himself in some previous, ongoing argument. Was it the Sheriff who had broken this man's teeth?

"Donovan?" Pete asked like they were old friends. "I never had him pegged for a dry."

The barman blinked then looked at him again, eyes narrowing. "Do I know you?" he asked.

"Doubt it," Pete said. "I ain't been here in quite some time."

"An old friend of Donovan's?"

"Sure," Pete said, grinning. "The two of us go way back." He tapped the side of his head knowingly.

"He took your eye?"

"No," Pete said. "That's another story entire. But he did take something of mine—a friend, an old friend—by the name of Nash Warrick."

A queer look passed over the barman's face. He walked stiffly to the bar, where he reached below the counter and brought out a bottle of whiskey two-thirds drunk.

"This is all I got left in the place," the barman murmured almost as if to himself. "The Sheriff was kind enough to leave me a bottle for personal use."

He set three glasses on the counter and divided the remaining liquid evenly among them, his hand trembling slightly as he poured. "To old friends," he said when he had finished. He raised his glass.

"Old friends," Pete said, raising his own alongside Owl.

Pete saw with his one good eye that the barman's appraising stare never left him, even as he knocked back a mouthful of whiskey, and he had begun to sweat.

"Who's the poor bastard with the honor?" Pete asked, jerking his thumb toward the gallows outside.

"An outlaw—a boy," the barman answered.

"Rustler?"

The barman shook his head. "We ain't had rustlers to speak of in fifteen years. Murder. He killed a preacher's boy over a card game."

Pete scoffed. What had Jack expected? At least it sounded like Sal had kept his mouth shut. The gap-toothed barman made no mention of treasure or the *Oregon*.

Pete nodded and sipped his whiskey in solidarity. "Shame," he said, fogging the glass with his breath. "Did he hang well?"

"We'll find out tomorrow, I guess," the barman said.

Pete nodded again, trying not to betray his relief that the deed had not yet been done. "I always did enjoy a good hangin'. Some people say it ain't the kind of thing to be enjoyed, but I figure if yer hangin' a man, you must be pretty well sure he deserves it, and there shouldn't be nothing unpalatable about seeing it done."

The barman grunted.

Pete swirled his whiskey a while then said, "And where's the Sheriff now?"

It was the barman's turn to consider. Pete watched the man, and the man watched him. He saw the scales behind the man's eyes, weighing, calibrating, and weighing once more. There was something more to know here—an undercurrent to discover. But time was short. *Who knows how long before Jack arrives? Two days? One?* And who knew his aim? Pete would not put it past Jack to shoot him in the back the first chance he got.

Finally, the barman made up his mind, although he looked a little sick over it. "He isn't well, actually."

The barman would not meet his eye now. He began wiping the counter with a towel, though he had not spilled a drop with his pour.

"Oh?" Pete asked, pausing with his glass halfway to his lips.

"He's with the doctor."

Pete nodded and knocked back the rest of his drink.

"And where's the doc?"

"That-a-way," the barman said, pointing, though he did not follow the direction of his finger with his eyes. "Across the street, a few houses back. It's big and brick with a white column porch. You can't miss it."

"Alright," Pete said, finishing his drink in one great gulp. He looked at Owl, who understood and did likewise, setting the glass on the counter with a crack that made the barman jump.

Pete put a dollar on the counter and turned to the door.

"You been a fine host," he called over his shoulder. Then he took his leave, Owl following him outside. A gravity had begun to build. Pete had the sense that events were picking up speed, that he was on the path of destiny. Still, he could not shake the nagging feeling that he had merely stumbled into something, that maybe he was about the barman's business now, that maybe his whole life had been like this—spent running errands for weaker men, the joke of a cruel God.

CHAPTER 44

Annabel

ANNABEL LEFT TO SEE JACOB LONG AFTER THE SUN HAD SET. SHE HAD already spoken with him once that day, yet she was possessed of a restless energy. She had spent the remainder of her day speaking with the women of the town, and she had a growing sense that there was real unity there, real power to be channeled on election day.

As she walked through the darkened streets, a stone skipping from one puddle of light to another, an irrational fear grew in her. She felt danger around every corner—men who would hurl stones as they had done to Haddock, or step menacingly from the shadows to surround her—acolytes, outlaws.

On her way to the saloon, she paused by the gallows, touching its solid frame with her hand, a monster of the imagination come to life. She wondered if the Brandywines felt complicit or if it was to them a job like any other.

She started to cut down the alley to the rear of the saloon when she saw that the boards shuttering the front door had been taken down. She changed course and went to the porch. A dozen wood planks were heaped against the railing, iron nails protruding spinelike in the weak light. *It's too soon*, she worried. Too soon to defy John so brazenly—what was Jacob thinking?

Compulsively, she reached a hand out to touch one of those spent nails. It bit sharp into her finger, rough, barbed as a scorpion's tail. She shuddered.

Just then a mournful piano sounded its first notes from inside, startling her. Wiping her finger on her skirt, Annabel tried first to peer through the window, but the curtains were drawn. She pushed through the front door.

Annabel found Jacob at the piano, dressed in black, playing a haunting and overindulgent rendition of the *Moonlight Sonata* in the near dark.

She bit her lip and schooled herself in patience.

Excepting the music, the saloon was eerily quiet. Annabel could not remember the last time she had gone out so late. Even the girls upstairs must have been asleep.

The solitary waking soul seemed to be the madam's white cat, Abella, which sat atop the piano as if to appreciate the music.

"Jacob, the door," Annabel began, "it's too soon—" She stopped short, noticing for the first time the emptiness of the shelves behind the bar. Her face went slack.

"Just let me finish," Jacob said without looking up from those yellowed keys. He held the final notes until they lapsed into the silence.

"It won't matter," he finally said, turning around on the bench so he faced her, the emptiness behind her. "The boards. John won't . . . he won't mind. He's taken everything anyway."

"Your mouth!" Annabel cried, seeing the thin, jagged gash that cut from philtrum to chin, the blood crusted in his grand moustache.

Jacob grunted, baring his teeth, and Annabel saw that those were broken, too.

She went to him, sat beside him on the bench, grasped his hands in her own. She had not realized how cold her hands were until she felt his warmth.

"He came near sunset," Jacob said. "He brought his deputy and some of the Reverend's men, Loeb among them. I was to blame in part. I goaded him. He's unstable, you know. And sick."

"He's dying," Annabel said, and in saying it she realized it was true. How long had she suspected? It was the only explanation for the change in him, his tiredness, his heavy-handedness, his haste. He seemed to know he did not have much time left.

Jacob only nodded as if that made sense, or as if he had already known it. A strange look came upon him, though, like he might be sick. Finally, he said, "He is already dead."

"Who?" Annabel asked stupidly.

"Him, Donovan."

"Dead?" she whispered. The room receded. Jacob was a man far off, a disembodied voice, all the light in the room a glimmer in his eye.

"There—in the doorway—he collapsed." Jacob pointed to the back door. "Slumped over."

Annabel raised a trembling hand to her mouth. "And he died there? In the doorway?" she asked, horrified. Should she not have felt something when he passed? A shiver in her soul as she came upon his deathbed?

"No," Jacob said, eyes unfocused. "No, he didn't die then. I went to him. Even bloodied, I went to him."

Then, forcefully, he added, "I saved him *first!*"

"What do you mean, first?" Annabel asked, her hand still covering her mouth.

"I saved him there!" He pointed again to the back doorway. "Sent him to Doc Marshall's even as he stole my livelihood! Even as he betrayed me and the town! Even as he drove Haddock off!"

Annabel did not understand.

"Only after did I send the other men . . . to do the hard work for us." He sighed deeply then, a hitched sigh, gravid with emotion.

"The hard work?" Annabel's stomach lurched sickeningly.

"To do the work we could not do. It's what my father would have done."

"Sent who?" Annabel demanded. The room twisted and shimmered before her like an image seen through the flame of a candle. She could not tell if she breathed, if she would ever breathe again.

"The one-eyed assassin," Jacob said, leaning back against the piano.

"What assassin?" she demanded, rising.

"The one-eyed man," Jacob said. "You know him as well as I do. He's older now."

A one-eyed outlaw.

She knew the man, knew how he looked and how he sounded though she had never met him—knew him by the stories and by the fear. And standing astride those memories like a colossus was John—the young Sheriff, the handsome Easterner, the savior of this onetime shantytown and her onetime betrothed.

"Pete," she said, the word a curse. It was an old word, a lost language, an old fear.

"Pete," Jacob replied, dispassionate, resigned, the name sounding oddly from his wounded mouth.

"You really did call them, then? The outlaws? Sal and the rest?" Annabel asked, swallowing bile.

"No!" Jacob cried, stung by the accusation, as if it made a difference. "They came here, tonight. For all I know John wanted them, called them himself! Yes, that's it! He called them himself!"

Annabel turned to go.

"Wait!" Jacob cried, coming to himself. "You can't go alone!"

"There's no time."

She ran to the door, skirts billowing behind her.

She ran through the street and past the gallows.

She ran to the doctor's house, the bulk of Lem's revolver lending a hitch to her stride.

She ran to save John.

She ran to meet death.

CHAPTER 45

Donovan

DONOVAN WOKE BLEARY-EYED IN A ROOM THAT HAD NOT CHANGED IN twenty years. The crown molding, the plants on the windowsill, the bed sheets, even the vase of flowers on the side table—they were all the same.

He wondered if he had awoken inside a memory.

Or am I dead?

Bathed in candlelight, the room was soft and yellow as butter, though he knew the walls were bleach white.

He remembered falling in the saloon, and shame came hot to his cheeks.

Better if I'm dead, maybe.

But he knew he was not. The detail of the room was too much for a dream, and what is a dream but a glimpse of death? He felt the threading of embroidered sheets beneath his fingertips.

No, this is not a dream. It is not death.

And if the detail of it was not enough, there was the voice to tell him—gruff and triumphant.

"Evenin', Sheriff," said the voice, a man's voice.

Because he was still sorting dreams from memories from reality, he was not startled by the voice at first. It fit the narrative as well as any of it. *The falling—but I was feeling better! The sick room—how did I come here?*

But the voice—or the memory of it—grew uneasy with him, and it propelled him through the mist of unreality and into the room, which smelled of vanilla just as it always had. He blinked.

How long have I been out?

266

It could have been hours or years. Or maybe his life had been a fitful fever dream—his wife, his boys, Three Chop, his cancer, the saloon, the Reverend—and he was waking up twenty years past.

He half expected Missy to appear then. He felt his gut, but there were no bandages, no bullet hole, no pain.

Something scrabbled at his consciousness, trying to force its way in like the prying at a door. Donovan did not know what it was, but he knew he should fear it. It was something hateful.

And the voice again.

"You were out pretty good. I tried to wake you."

Donovan heard the creaking of wooden joints as the speaker repositioned himself in a chair, heard the squeak of leather.

He turned his head, suddenly filled with foreboding.

Like everything else, the chair was the same—slat-backed with a leather cushion—but the body was different. It was a man—older much like himself—but unmistakable. A grizzled cyclops.

He remembered it then, the hateful thing that gnawed at him. He remembered Jacob's words as if he had always known them, "It was *me*, John. *I* killed Nash Warrick. I, who cannot be trusted to aim a gun. From the roof of this very saloon." And with remembrance came a certainty that he would die in this room, the same one in which he had been saved so long ago, because the truth was that he had never killed Nash Warrick, that he had barely wounded One-Eyed Pete, that he had been no one except the man *Jacob* had made him.

"Comin' round?" Pete asked, pulling his chair from the wall to face the bed.

Donovan struggled to sit up, floundering in the sheets. He managed to prop himself against the headboard, breathing heavily. He felt a stiffness in his back that he knew should be excruciating and deduced that he had been dosed heavily with laudanum.

"Yes," Pete said, grinning. "I see that you recognize me."

Donovan tried to call out, but the wind stuck in his throat, and he could only heave a shaking sigh.

"Easy," Pete hushed. He set a revolver on the bedside table. "Mind that I got all the cards here. My men got yer doctor tied up downstairs.

Nice fella. One of the old boys, eh? I guess I hadn't realized how many of you there were even then. Only you stayed, though. I remember that."

But Donovan knew now he had not been the only one. That had been a lie. He was an old man—sick and cornered and beaten—now at the mercy of an old foe, a relic of the old memories, false as they may be.

"It's okay, I just want to talk," Pete said. He leaned forward, studying Donovan's face, casting his eye over his decrepit frame. "Hard to believe," he said after a while, shaking his head. "Hard to believe this is the man who killed Nash Warrick." He spit on the floor like the words still pained him.

Donovan almost told him then. Why? To confess? Or was it cowardice, hope that Pete would leave him be and turn his vengeance on Jacob? He almost said the words, but at the last moment he bit them back. Only he and Jacob knew the truth. He and Jacob and God. And that meant that, for all his weakness, for all the man's disdain, Pete might yet fear him.

"How do you like Three Chop?" Donovan asked, finding his voice for the first time since the fall.

Pete sat back. "Fine enough town I guess," he allowed, looking around the room like the walls had fallen away and he was surveying the place itself. "I've seen worse, and I've seen better."

"It wouldn't be here if your friend Warrick had his way," Donovan said. "All these people, their farms and shops—they'd be somewhere else if I hadn't killed him. Or maybe they wouldn't exist at all."

"I wonder what lives died with Nash," Pete mused.

"None, I'm sure. Nash never built a thing in his life. He only tore down what other men had made for themselves."

Pete listened quietly, and by the look on his face, Donovan could tell he was savoring this, storing up every blasphemy to stoke his revenge.

"You think this place is better fer the town?" Pete demanded. "All you did is move some buildings and whores from one place on the map to another. You don't think there're hundreds of Three Chops? Thousands? Why do men like you insist on bringing them west and calling it progress?

"The West used to *be* something, something set apart, a wilderness where wild souls could take their comfort, a place where poor men could come to make their fortunes. Men like you don't care about building things. You want to put people in a *box*, just like you done with Sal. And over what? A game of *cards*?" Pete shook his head. "You think if you put enough pins in the map and connect 'em with railroad tracks, you can pen us in like cattle, brand us, take us to market.

"But every sheriff killed, every tie torn out, every train robbed, every longhorn rustled is a broken fence rail you got to mend. And when you've mended that fence a thousand times, maybe you'll finally realize the truth—the fence ain't worth the trouble. You cain't tame the West. This land ain't to be owned and allotted to rich men with pocket watches and Pullman cars. Even the Injuns knew that."

Pete paused, breathing heavily. *How long had he been waiting to say these things?* Donovan wondered. He reminded Donovan of the Reverend ensconced in his pulpit. He had the same wild gleam in his eye like his own truth was a virus that wanted spreading.

"That's what Noah Warrick believed," Pete said, quietly now, gritting his teeth. "That's what he died for."

"So you've come for the boy," Donovan said, understanding now the impetus for this improbable reunion. "You're a part of his gang." Perhaps the letter could not be dismissed as a young man's aggrandizement after all.

"Ha!" Pete scoffed. "Ain't that a load of shit. *His* gang?" He spat. "I got my own goddamn gang, Sheriff. But yer right that I come for him. He's got something of mine, and I aim to get it back."

But I burned the letter! I saw the look on the boy's face!

"What's a boy got on an old hand like you, Pete?" Donovan asked. He knew he had leverage now, if only a little, and he intended to push the man as far as he could. Pete never had a reputation for being smart, but any old badger that lived this long must be possessed of a certain low cunning.

"Ain't my doing, Sheriff," Pete said. "He'd be dead already if I had my way."

"I thought you had your own gang? Who's to stop you having your way?"

That must have struck a nerve, for Pete stood suddenly and grabbed the pistol off the table, whipping Donovan across the face with the gleaming butt.

Donovan felt the crack of a tooth and the seep of bruise-blood in his cheek, but he had narcotics in his system, too, and to him the blow was mechanical, painless. It turned his neck. *Then again maybe I turned it myself.*

He grinned. "You think the man who killed Nash Warrick is gonna cry over a crack on the chin?" he asked. Blood ran hot from the corner of his mouth and blotted the sheets scarlet.

For a moment after the blow, Pete looked uncertain.

Afraid!

Donovan laughed again, louder.

Pete pulled back the hammer on his pistol and aimed it at Donovan's face.

Every second stretched to eternity then. *How many times will I die today?* Donovan wondered. But he did not fear. Better to die like this than collapsed in a doorway, and with such poesy! Yes, this was dying!

But Pete thought better and moved the gun to Donovan's knee.

"I'll kill you, but I'm gonna make it hurt first—for Nash and for the West."

Donovan's knee throbbed with anticipation. He heard a click.

He grunted, thinking it the grate of the trigger or the falling of the hammer, but it was not. His knee remained whole.

A frown crossed Pete's face, and he turned his head as Donovan did—toward the door—his gun still trained on Donovan's knee.

The door swung slowly open. It seemed endless in those overwrought seconds.

The click had been the sound of a spring latch withdrawn by the brass knob, turned by a delicate hand.

Annabel!

She held a revolver at eye level, trained on the rounded form of Pete's back.

Pete looked more confused than afraid.

"Put it down," Annabel said. Her voice shook, but her hands did not.

Donovan could see Pete calculating. He began to turn slowly, bringing the gun toward her, testing her mettle.

"Don't move, or I'll—" Annabel interrupted her own warning with the bark of the gun. It jumped in her arms, but she held firm.

The bullet tore into Pete's flank. He took the blow with a grunt, stepping back to maintain his balance.

"Alright, alright, missus!" he said, dropping his weapon. It spun on the floor like a die.

He clutched his side and brought his hand away slick with blood.

Donovan swung his legs over the edge of the bed. He started to stand, to come to her, but Annabel turned the barrel of the gun on him.

"Stop," she commanded.

"Annabel!" Donovan began, but she cut him off with a brief shake of her head. He saw Pete's eyes looking between Annabel and his own gun where it still lay on the floor.

Annabel must have seen, too, for she trained the barrel on Pete again, holding them both at bay with her swiveling shoulders, her unshaking arms. "Sit on the bed," she told Pete.

The outlaw moved slowly, but he sat beside Donovan, his weight bending the mattress with a groan.

Annabel stared at Pete, breathing heavily, until she was sure he wouldn't move. Then she swiveled to Donovan, her eyes still darting between the men. "Before I let you up, John, you must make me a promise. It's a promise I didn't expect to have to get from you, but things as they are, I'll have it. The boy, Sal—you must promise you won't hang him tomorrow. Promise you'll wait for the circuit. Promise you'll give him a fair trial."

Donovan almost laughed, it was so like Annabel. Standing before him, gun raised, threatening to leave him at Pete's mercy, she could have asked for anything, asked him to reopen the saloon, asked him to crown *her* mayor of Three Chop. But she asked only for help with another in her menagerie of lost souls. And did he not owe her that much? After he had jilted her, had thrown a stone through her window? After he threatened to remove her from her office?

"I promise," he said, holding Annabel's eyes, giving his word—the word of a lawman, the word of the Sheriff of Three Chop.

"And him," Annabel said, waving her gun at Pete. "Promise you won't hang him, either, until the circuit rides."

Donovan frowned. But he supposed justice had waited so long for Pete it could wait a little longer. "Fine," he said. "I swear."

Annabel nodded, letting the tension leave her body in a visible rush, turning her gun on Pete with finality.

Donovan stood, a little chagrined to be dressed only in his long johns. He stooped to retrieve Pete's gun then walked to Annabel's side. He looked down at her and she, briefly, at him. It was an unfathomable exchange, but Donovan could tell she knew—knew about the saloon, about the cancer—and understood in her own way. She had always understood.

Feeling overcame him. It was shame, in part, and sadness, but without object—a lamentation and a resolution. *Of what? Of life?*

He saw she was breathing heavily, and he realized how foreign and terrifying this night must be for her. Then his mind sprung into the familiar calculi of life and death.

"On your belly, Pete," Donovan commanded, sounding stronger than he felt.

The man did as he was bade.

"Were there any more?" Donovan asked Annabel.

"One—I left him with Doc Marshall. He had the doctor tied up, and—" Annabel stopped, evidently controlling the nerves that had not shown until now. "Just the one. He wasn't too happy to see me—wasn't too happy to see Lem's gun anyway. Now the doctor has him tied up."

Donovan marveled at Annabel's easy courage. She had subdued two hardened outlaws, shot one. *She saved me.* Not for the first time he wondered what it would have been like to go through life with this woman at his side. He turned to Pete, gritting his teeth in a wash of guilt.

"Is that right, Pete?" Donovan asked the old outlaw. "Only one other?" Pete was bleeding through his shirt, but Donovan could already tell it was not a mortal wound by the slowness of the seep. "Your gang is two men? Sal making three?"

"Yeah," Pete grunted into the floorboards. "That's right."

Donovan walked to the window, peering through the curtain to the street below as if he might see an army waiting there. He saw nothing. He heard nothing.

Perhaps Pete had lied. Perhaps he had not.

It took ten minutes to get changed and to cuff Pete and to make sure the other man, who called himself Owl, was cuffed, too. Donovan put them in separate rooms so he could corroborate their stories. Pete sat in the same sick room and in the same wooden chair he had occupied when he first woke Donovan, thinking to kill him. But the intervening minutes had changed his fortune completely. Now Pete was captive, his hands bound behind him, facing Donovan and Annabel, who sat regarding him from chairs brought up from the kitchen.

Ordinarily Donovan would have made Annabel go home or at least wait downstairs, but given the circumstances . . .

He had tried to send her to fetch Mance from the jailhouse instead. When she refused, he sent Doc Marshall.

"What do you want with the boy?" Donovan asked, resting one foot atop the other.

"He owes me a debt," Pete said disinterestedly. He wore a clean shirt—one of Doc Marshall's, which the man had provided after bandaging his side. There was no bullet in him. It had torn through his side and lodged in a dresser behind, leaving a clean wound that oozed blood like a sap spout.

"So you want him dead?" Donovan asked.

"Dead man cain't pay debts," Pete replied. "I just want to talk to him."

"You're a wanted man, Pete. Been wanted for years. It's quite a risk you took, coming here. Must be something important afoot."

"Somethin' of a very personal nature," Pete said, meeting his eyes.

"Something worth hanging over?"

Pete shrugged. "Don't sound like I'll risk hanging after all."

Donovan clenched his fist. "Not tomorrow, no. But you'll hang sure as justice."

Annabel touched his arm then, encouraging him. He felt a shock of pleasure and wondered when last he had felt her touch, or the touch of any woman for that matter. Had it been as long as Missy? The warmth stayed a while even after she moved her hand.

Pete's look curdled. He sucked his teeth, considering, then said, "Mayhaps I got somethin' worth a bargain."

"A bargain?" Donovan asked, leaning forward in his chair. "For what?"

"My freedom. My life."

Donovan snorted. "What could you possibly have to trade?"

"A warning."

The candor in Pete's voice sent a shiver down Donovan's spine, even in the warmth of that laudanum cocoon. He wondered where Mance and the doctor were. They should have returned by now.

"Say your piece," commanded Donovan.

"First yer promise, like you gave the woman."

"Annabel," Annabel corrected.

Pete winked.

"I already promised not to hang you right away. Now I'll hear you out."

Pete regarded Donovan some time. Then, with the look of an inveterate gambler about to wager his last dollar, he said, "It ain't my gang. And it ain't just three of us. It's closer to a dozen. And the gang is Jack Holloway's."

Annabel gasped.

Donovan clenched and flexed his hand then stood and strode to the window, peering again through the curtain and into the street. Nothing moved. Nothing sounded. There was no sign of outlaws, but there was no sign of allies, either.

"How do I know you're telling the truth?" Donovan asked, a kind of nervous excitement rising within him. He realized he *wanted* it to be true. He *wanted* another chance to prove himself, to redeem himself by killing a famed outlaw, this time by his own hand.

"You cain't," Pete said. "You can ask Owl. He'll tell you the truth if you tell him I said to. Sal won't tell. He'll stay loyal, I think. But Owl will tell you. Besides," Pete shrugged, "you cain't afford not to believe me.

"All I ask is to go free before he gets here. Then Jack Holloway is yours, and so's the loot if you like, or at least the reward."

Donovan swallowed. *Surely this is another sign!*

"When do you expect them?" he asked, trying to hide his excitement.

"Don't know," Pete said. "A day or two most likely."

Then Donovan heard a noise in the street, a bootfall on the boardwalk.

He turned his head to the window in time to glimpse the doctor step from the boardwalk to the porch. It was a harried gait for a snow-haired man like the doctor, urgent, even.

And he was alone.

If not for Pete, Donovan would have cursed.

"Keep an eye on him, Annabel," Donovan said.

She nodded, grasping her gun, which she had been cradling in her lap.

Donovan moved to the hall, shutting the door behind him. He met the doctor coming up the stair, using the newel post like a cane.

Doc Marshall breathed heavily.

"Speak soft," Donovan whispered, holding a finger to his lips. "Where's Mance?"

The doctor shook his head. "I don't know," he said, wheezing. "I looked everywhere. Nobody's seen him. Not Minnie, not anybody."

Donovan's stomach lurched somewhere in the numbness of his torso. "The jailhouse?" Donovan asked, fear sounding in his voice. *Could the outlaws be here already?*

The doctor hesitated. "It was the first place I checked," he said, wiping sweat from his forehead. He must have run hard, for the night was cool, almost cold. "It was dark. But I could still see the boy in there—in his cell."

Donovan breathed a sigh of relief. The boy was the key to all this, somehow. He had to be watched.

"Damned deputy has a poor sense of timing," Donovan muttered. "Still, I'll need to check on things myself. Grab Owl. I'll get Pete. We'll bring them to the jail. They'll be happy to go. I suspect they want a rendezvous with the Salamander anyway."

The walk to the jailhouse felt interminable.

Donovan half expected a gang of outlaws to attack him from every alley. He would have run if Pete was not there to hinder him—an old man with bound hands.

Besides, the doctor was still wheezing.

Donovan's mind raced. He still felt dread kicking there in the numbness of his belly. Yes, this was something monumental—something grand, even—and if it was a test, it would not be easy, but the difficulty would surely be in proportion to the reward. He would meet it as he always had.

He paused at intervals to peer around corners into alleys and cross streets, his gun drawn and gleaming in the moonlight.

Annabel held Lem's gun close, too, straining her eyes against the darkness.

When they finally came upon it, the jailhouse was darker still—dark and silent as a tomb.

Donovan mounted the porch quiet as breath, motioning for the others to follow carefully.

Inside, he saw the familiar lump of the outlaw on the floor, lying on his side, his back to the door. Donovan sighed again, releasing some of his tension, standing from his half crouch.

It was as the doctor had described.

He started to light a lamp, but the thud of his boot woke the sleeping outlaw. He wriggled like a worm, its groans muffled and pitiful.

Yet something was not right. The form kept wriggling—violently now, panicked, as if it was seizing.

Donovan's chest locked so he could not breathe, so his heart barely had room to beat.

He fumbled with a match. When it caught, he held it before him, ignoring the lamp, too excited to waste a moment.

The flame burned rapidly down to his fingers. He dropped the match and lit another, walking toward the cell, kneeling.

The muffled sounds were cries filtered through the coarse fabric of a gag—the hands and feet tied like a hog.

Donovan kept lighting matches, kneeling.

A face stared back at him, but it was not the Salamander's visage. No, it was Mance's.

Donovan dropped the matches and began to fumble with his keys.

By the time he opened the door to the cell, Annabel had lit the lamp.

The deputy lay helpless on the floor, his pants pulled down around his knees, his face and neck flushed red with shame and anger, those twin pillars of man's conceit.

Donovan pulled the gag from the deputy's mouth.

Mance coughed, sputtered, and retched on the ground. His eyes ran with tears from the exertion. "The whore!" he cried. "The new girl—it was her! Jacob's!" He retched again.

Donovan turned to look at Annabel. She was frozen in shock—they all were. The only movement in the room was the flicker of their shadows.

And Pete. His face was half a grin, half a curse.

"You!" Donovan cried, shining the spotlight of his rage upon Pete. "What have you done!"

Without waiting for a reply, Donovan strode to Pete, punching him full force in the gut, doubling the man over.

"John!" Annabel yelled.

When Pete righted himself, Donovan hit him again. "You're a god-damn liar!"

"It was the whore!" Mance repeated, but Donovan barely heard him.

"John!" Annabel's hands were on him now. He wanted to shove her—to push her away—the embodiment of all the forces that restrained him—the laws of man and God that said he could not love two women, the laws of time and the corporeal that ravaged his once strong body and took his boys, the laws of representative government and of the people that kept him from shooting Jacob in the head and turning to the town and telling them how it must be. But he could not do it, would not hurt the object that had harbored his affection all these years, if only out of respect for the memory of the man he had been.

He turned to her, sweat streaming down his face, breath coming in short bursts. He felt lightheaded, like he might faint again, but he did not.

"It was the girl, John," Annabel said, pleading almost. "She came to me—asked me to help her, to convince you not to hang the boy. She must have had something planned. I didn't know, I—"

Donovan cut her off with a nod, sweat still pooling at his boots. It was a promise not to injure Pete further for the crime of another. "Leave us," he said, motioning to Annabel and Doc Marshall.

Annabel gave him a last, lingering look as she went, an exhortation.

Donovan knelt to untie his deputy.

Someone would have to pay for this injustice after all.

CHAPTER 46

Annabel

ANNABEL PERCHED IMMOBILE AS A GARGOYLE ON THE STEPS OF THE saloon, watching dawn come gray then yellow over the town. The gallows cast a long shadow down Front, a walkway that would be trod by hundreds of expectant feet.

They came shortly after daybreak and continued in a long procession, like clergy walking the aisle of a great funeral—the aisle the street, the vault the vastness of God's own great sky.

The women came with picnic lunches. The men came with guns. Where a family had more than one shotgun or rifle, the mother carried another or even an eldest child.

John must have gotten word out there might be trouble, though he had not yet broken the news about Sal or the postponement of the hanging. She wondered why he waited and decided he must mean to turn the bloodthirsty crowd, a waiting army, to the defense of the town.

A part of her really did wonder if John had staged the whole thing—Sal, Pete, the outlaw gang—to give himself another excuse to tighten his grip, another existential threat to overcome.

The Reverend appeared wearing a rich, black riding cape to show the color of his mourning. The cape was a necessary addition, since he always wore black. His face was serene, yet his eyes shone with the afterglow of a crucible. He wore a cross about his neck and carried a Bible in his hand, a small, forlorn pocket Bible.

The mood of the congregation was a strange mix of vengeance and the self-possessed humility of despair—respect for the dead and revilement for the dying.

Annabel closed her eyes. She had not stayed up all night since Hattie was a babe, and her limbs still trembled from the excitement of her encounter with Pete.

It was hardly possible to believe she had shot a man. If she had slept, she would have thought it was a dream. She had been relieved beyond measure when Doc Marshall informed her the wound was not fatal.

The Reverend's congregation continued to grow. Annabel thought there must have been a hundred people in the street already, and more kept coming, more processing down that dusty aisle.

Today they rallied for a hanging. Soon they would rally for an election.

How will they react when John tells them the boy is fled? When he tells them Pete will wait to stand trial? What will they do when they realize there will be no hanging?

By nine o'clock the townfolk had added their full numbers to the crowd, though they did not mix easily with the farmers and other supplicants. It was a volatile gathering, and the borders of the factions were tense and unbridgeable as a swollen river dividing armies. The townfolk had brought their guns, too.

Gooseflesh raised along her arms and neck. She felt like a soldier anticipating battle, overcome by nerves.

She glanced at the jailhouse. *John must come soon!*

She rose then and entered the saloon. The time had come to wake Jacob.

He was asleep on a stool, his head resting on his own bar top.

She shook him gently.

He woke uncomprehending, his forehead marked by a deep red bruise that showed the mold of the wood grain.

"There's a crowd already gathered," she said. "They're armed."

"Donovan's men?" Jacob asked, rubbing his eyes, his words lisped through broken teeth.

"Yes, with their women and children. Townfolk, too, in near equal measure now."

Jacob nodded, moving to the window to see for himself.

"Look," Jacob said, tapping his finger against the pane as Sallie Winthrop, Doc Marshall, and Todd Waiverly came down the boardwalk. "At least we have a few allies left."

Wordlessly, they joined their friends on the porch.

The party stood in silence for some time, entranced by the crowd as it shifted and surged, unable to express their apprehension as if saying the thing might make it come true. They stood like sentries until they saw movement in the jailhouse, until the door opened, until a figure emerged—the Sheriff in his black hat.

John left the jailhouse alone, casting an acute shadow that appeared to cut him in half.

He disappeared into the crowd, which swallowed him then parted, a ripple of quiet spreading out until the sound of his boots on the stairs of the gallows could be heard from the saloon porch.

"Mornin', folks!" he cried. His voice was strong. He did not need to yell. He orated.

Annabel saw in him the John of old—his movements deft, his bearing strong and confident. And yet she had seen him only hours before, pronate upon his sickbed, prepared to meet death at the hand of an old enemy, too weak to offer resistance. His was a flickering reality.

"It's a fine sight to behold so many here in the interest of the town, here to see justice served!" John said, smiling broadly.

The crowd cheered. Men held their guns in the air, and women fluttered their kerchiefs or held their children up to wave.

"Reverend, Mr. Mayor, please, join me," Donovan exhorted, beckoning with his hand.

The Reverend glided onto the platform.

Donovan grasped the man's hand, looked him in the eye, and offered what appeared to be a heartfelt condolence. Then he leaned forward and whispered something in his ear.

The Reverend paused briefly, as if arrested by some shock, then took his place behind the Sheriff, turning his dark and scowling visage to the crowd.

A few moments later, Mayor Cordell ascended the stair to join them, the tails of his coat fluttering in the breeze, exposing the tentlike expanse of his suit pants to the pleasure of the crowd.

"Let's hear it for our Sheriff!" Cordell said as he shook John's hand.

The crowd erupted in a roar, led by the mayor himself in a round of applause that lasted some minutes.

John nodded graciously, smiling upon the restive crowd.

"Thank you, truly," he said when the applause had died and the mayor had surrendered the spotlight. He paused, head bowed, letting the moment linger and turn serious. "For twenty years I've done whatever it took to keep this town safe," he said, lifting his face.

"And you done good, Sheriff!" a man shouted, setting off another round of applause.

"Thank you," John said, nodding and giving a small bow.

Beside Annabel, Jacob scoffed and Sallie muttered.

"Doing those things—the things that kept the town safe—they weren't always easy, and I don't just mean the posses and the pursuits."

More applause.

"There were *hard* decisions to be made. Like the decision to close the saloon for good." Here John raised his hand and turned toward the *Lady May*, thrusting Annabel and Jacob and the rest suddenly before the collective eye of the crowd.

Annabel felt herself blush. Or maybe it was the radiated heat of Jacob's anger.

The crowd was conflicted. The Reverend's congregants hooted and whistled and jeered, while the rest of the town and many of the farmers—some of them hearing of the closure for the first time—shook their heads and scratched their chins. A few even booed.

"It was a hard decision," John said, lowering his arm and bringing the attention back to himself. "But it had to be made, because—as our mayor said before—the saloon was the root of the crime, the instigator of a sequence of events connected like a chain, ending in death, in murder!

"And the outlaw, Sal—"

Here John was interrupted by a great hiss that rose and spread, ringing off the buildings that lined the street, each note quiet yet bound together in a deafening chord, an avalanche of sinister white noise.

"He was one of those links, and for that he deserves whatever punishment we give him!"

The crowd cheered again.

"But the chain goes on! It goes further than the saloon! It goes back to a time before Three Chop, when the West was yet wild, when it was ruled by men wilder still!

"The chain is anchored there—in the murky mist of time—to that most ancestral evil—human nature itself!"

Townfolk and parishioners alike paused in their fury, scratched their heads, shifted their hats, turned to their neighbors, the jeers and cries silent on their lips. The crowd rippled as dozens of shoulders shrugged and twisted, as heads craned to hear better, as if that might help them understand this unexpected departure into metaphysics.

"Human nature, unfettered, was the way of the West before towns like Three Chop civilized it," John spoke into the newfound silence, undeterred. "And the men that ran it then and their spirits begot the unruly saloon and the boy outlaw who raised his gun against our dear Chasby. They were the links *before* the saloon, *before* the murder.

"And last night, one of those ancestral spirits visited me in my room— a man from my past, a man you've maybe heard me name. The man was One-Eyed Pete, Nash Warrick's right-hand gun!"

An excited murmur swept the crowd, buoyed its spirits. The spectators had endured the poetry and began to see now the object of John's declamation. They had been told there were outlaws afoot. Now they understood.

The town's collective attention turned to the jailhouse, where on cue Mance had pushed a grizzled man outside and was prodding him toward the stage with the barrel of a rifle. The man's hands were bound behind his back.

Pandemonium broke out. Even the townfolk were smiling and exclaiming and shaking their heads in wonderment at this new conquest.

"Donovan!" a voice cheered.

"Two outlaws in a week?" came another.

"Is it really him? One-Eyed Pete?"

The crowd parted before this relic like it had for Donovan, and Pete and Mance emerged to climb the stair and take their places on stage behind John with the rest of the pageant cast.

Mayor Cordell smiled nervously and stepped backward to put more distance between himself and the historic captive.

Aaron seemed undisturbed, except that his eyes had narrowed in suspicion.

Jacob gave Annabel an almost apologetic look, which at first she did not understand.

"Parading him before the town—" she started to say—*a cheap ploy*— but she stopped as Donovan spoke again.

"Today he stands before you to answer for his crimes!"

"No!" Annabel breathed, her eyes going wide with incomprehension. *He gave his word!*

John grabbed Pete by the collar and walked him up and down the dais like a magician showing the crowd the integrity of the object he was about to disappear.

"Justice for the boy can wait," John said finally. "We've got ourselves a man!"

Those nearest the gallows began to chant, "Hang him! Hang him! Hang him!" as if they had forgotten Chasby ever existed. Soon the street reverberated with the chant—all those voices joined in the unholy exhortation.

Only the Reverend looked as grim as Annabel.

Donovan spread his arms, palms down, and waved them slowly, signaling for the crowd to calm itself.

It took some time, but they did his bidding.

"There's more," he said, grinning again like a politician or a salesman. "There are other links in the chain—more outlaws, a whole gang of them.

"A gang led by a man named Jack Holloway."

John's words had a strange effect on the crowd. Some cheered—young men mostly. But others—women, fathers, older men who had known what it was to war—grew solemn in the reality of this new danger, now given a name.

"So I'm glad to see you've brought your guns," John continued, knowing he had enraptured his people—enough of them at least—*his* people. "Because as soon as One-Eyed Pete is hanged, we ride south after the Holloway gang!" He yelled the last of this utterance so it became a battle cry, taken up now by the men of the crowd, all of them, for even the reluctant must be swept along by that martial tide. These, her neighbors, and among them, surely, a man, a faceless soldier, who had thrown a rock through her window.

The chanting grew, unintelligible. The crowd was a tumult, white-capped as a wind-whipped sea.

And yet none of it registered for Annabel, who was still consumed by John's betrayal, by the final proof of his change of character, of his rebirth.

She cursed her weakness, her credulity, and the guilt she felt for shooting Pete multiplied tenfold.

Shot him to save another, another not worth saving! It was the farmers' petition all over again, her will asserted to help John only to realize the consequences too late. She felt the kick of the gun, a phantom in her hands, and remembered the sound of the bullet striking flesh.

She was roused from her reflection by the noise of the boisterous crowd, a single interconnected entity undulating like a sheet on the line in high wind.

Cries of "Hang him! Hang him! Hang him!" started again with renewed vigor. The air vibrated with the force of so many unified lungs.

Annabel watched as if through someone else's eyes as Mance produced a rope and threw it over the beam.

John grabbed Pete—not ungently this time—by the arm for another round of parading before he positioned him carefully over the trap door like a stage director, talking to him all the time as if he were livestock being coerced into the chute.

Oddly, the imperturbable grin Annabel had seen on Pete's face the night before had returned. He seemed unmoved, and she understood that he had known, too—had probably known since they entered the jailhouse to find Sal gone. Of what could he possibly be thinking to make him smile at such a time?

Donovan tried to quiet the crowd so the Reverend could say a prayer for the condemned man, but they were wound too tight now to quiet, and Pete appeared to dismiss the attempt anyway.

Donovan stood back, yelling, trying to make himself heard above the din. He said something Annabel could not quite make out.

For Three Chop? For Chasby?

They've forgotten all about Sal! she realized. All except the Reverend, who watched the theater before him with cold disdain.

John checked that the noose was secure around Pete's neck one last time, and he checked that Mance had tied the other end properly to the platform.

Satisfied, he put his hand on the lever that would do the trick, and then, after the briefest hesitation, he threw it, shouting another unintelligible phrase.

Another battle cry. She thought it might as well have been her hand to throw the lever.

It was as if no one had truly believed the thing would happen. The crowd suddenly hushed, overcome by the indifference of that lever, of the sight of the falling man—so clearly unafraid—through the floor of the dais to hang by the neck.

And it was in that hush that the shot rang out, a single shot that sounded like many as it echoed down the street, cleaving the rope of the noose in two in the last moment before it stretched taut.

CHAPTER 47

All Together Now

DONOVAN

At first Donovan thought the gunshot was the work of an over-exuberant spectator, one among the forest of guns before him accidentally discharged. But in the seconds that followed, the calculation of a trained ear told him the sound had come from too far off.

I thought we had more time! So much for riding south at the head of a citizen army.

His first reaction should have been to take cover.

Aaron, Cordell, and Mance had each fallen immediately to the floor of the gallows, and the mayor had taken the extra precaution of rolling himself clean off the platform. Instead, Donovan leaned over the open trap door, like looking down a well, where he saw Pete hit the ground in a crouch and roll away beneath the scaffolding, his hands still bound behind him.

Donovan stared into the shadows, the afterimage of his rival still before him in that patch of sunlight, until the sound of a second shot awakened him from his trance.

He looked around, the cries of the panicked crowd reaching his ears for the first time.

The crowd thrashed and churned, tearing apart in a mad scramble for cover.

He saw some of the quick-witted men and women run for the alleys, but in no particular direction. No one seemed to know where the shot had come from.

He searched the memory of it, but all he found was a booming that buffeted him from all sides, and the sight of Pete rolling blithely away.

As he considered, another shot echoed. He held onto the sound, whirling. He thought it came from the west. *From a height?*

But even as he thought these things, a fourth came from the south.

This time he saw a man fall with the shot, spilling his own shotgun as he skidded, limp, into the dust.

A circle cleared instantly around the man the way a drop of water makes a crater in the dirt.

A fifth shot and sixth rang out in succession, each from a different position, but each from a height, he was sure now.

Instinctively, Donovan dropped into a crouch. He felt a murky, dislocated pain then—his cancer protesting the acrobatics from the depths of an opium lake.

The crowd had scattered. The street was clear except for several bodies—mostly dead—maimed by bullets or trampling or both.

A shock of fear lanced down his back to his groin. *Jack Holloway.*

Perhaps he had not truly believed it when Pete had told him of the gang. He did now.

Suddenly Donovan realized he was alone, standing atop the gallows like a castaway on some far-off island.

Even the dogs had run off.

JACK

"Nice shot, Monty," Jack breathed as he watched the rope of Pete's noose split in two.

Eagle-Eye Monty opened his left eye and raised his head, exhaling. "Might be the best I ever made," he acknowledged flatly.

Jack removed the spyglass from his eye to take in the fullness of the scene. They had found the spyglass on their way into town on one of the corpses beside Bill. Unlike Tim's body, Bill's had been unexpected. But who could know the mind of a man like Pete?

Jack watched the men on the gallows platform scatter. The fat one even rolled himself off, falling four feet onto the hard ground, which had just been vacated by panicked bystanders.

Jack shook his head, shielding his eyes against the sun.

He waited a few beats to see if anyone had located the sound of the shot, then raised his arm.

Another shot followed the signal, then another.

Jack watched with satisfaction as the crowd devolved further into chaos.

"Like a stampede of spooked cattle."

He had not ordered his men to kill anyone in particular, except that they should aim for anyone carrying a weapon, which seemed to be everyone.

The small of Jack's back ached from lying on his stomach so long. He had been atop a water tower with Monty since before dawn, waiting for the show to begin, hoping they were not too late for whatever was planned. They had not actually pitched camp when Pete left them at the Caprocks. They had only waited and followed. Jack was a little surprised Pete had been fooled so easily. It was almost disappointing.

Jack lifted the spyglass again and trained it on the one man who remained atop the gallows.

"I think that's our man," he said. "John Donovan, the giant slayer. Must've rankled Pete mighty good to be hanged by the same man who killed Nash." He smiled at the thought. *Then to be saved by me* . . .

He trained the spyglass on the scaffolding below the gallows. "You seen Pete come out?"

"No," Sam answered.

"What about Sal? You seen him?"

"Not him, neither."

Jack cursed. "We got to make sure we keep them alive. Hopefully the rest have enough sense not to shoot Pete in case he knows something."

"They'll figure," Monty said absentmindedly as he scanned the street.

"Who's that?" Jack asked, pointing to a tall man loping to the jailhouse, his gait hitched by a peg leg. He held a rifle in hand like a man who knew how to use it.

"Deputy?" Monty guessed.

"See if you can get him."

Monty lowered his head, squinting his left eye. He breathed deeply and held his air, the prelude to the shot. When it came, it echoed off the buildings like a gunshot in a canyon.

Jack watched the man fold up and skid across the dirt like a running buck.

"Hm," Jack grunted. "You're hot today."

Monty raised his head and reloaded.

"We oughtta move quick before they regroup," Jack said, raising himself into a sitting position. "There are a lot of goddamn guns down there, and we need to find out about Sal."

"Jailhouse?" Monty asked.

"I reckon."

Jack looked to the rooftops where the rest of the gang was firing. "I hope they start setting them fires soon."

JACOB

Jacob parted the curtain with a trembling hand and peered into the street. He saw nothing except the chaos of frightened townspeople and farmers in the alleys.

He recalled the moments since the gunshot with a certain detachment, as if he had borrowed someone else's courage, and yet as he turned to survey the room he could not help but feel an inkling of pride at his wherewithal.

He had ordered the piano overturned and set in front of the door to barricade it, wishing belatedly he had left the boards up after all. He wondered what Haddock would say to see his instrument mistreated so, and he vowed to buy the man a grand piano if he ever saw him again.

Annabel and the rest had ducked inside by the time the second shot came. A dozen or so other fast thinkers had followed before Jacob got the door shut. There were five additional townspeople in all—Evelyn Barry and her young girls made a useless, unarmed threesome huddled in the corner, but Bob Coruthers and Kevin Moore had come, too. They were older men—widowers—but they had guns with them, and they were veterans of the war.

The rest were a mix of men and women from outside town—Aaron's folks—standing uncertain in a ring in the back of the room as if only just awaking to find themselves in the lion's den. There were four guns among them.

Jacob moved behind the bar and set his shotgun on the counter along with three revolvers and a dozen boxes of ammunition. He beckoned Todd Waiverly and Doc Marshall both to take revolvers, which they did without hesitation, loading them and spinning the chambers expertly and filling their pockets with bullets.

"Annabel? Sallie?" he asked, holding up the third. "Which one of you wants it?"

"I'll take it," Sallie said. "Annabel's already got one—and she's used it."

Jacob turned his attention to Bob and Kevin then. "Barricade the back door," he said, pointing. "And watch it for all you're worth. Don't let anyone in, not even if it's your own goddamn mother."

PETE

"Relax and it'll end clean. It's the ones who fight it that die hardest."

Those were the words Donovan had spoken in Pete's ear before he threw the lever. They were not kind words but not unhelpful, either. Of course, Pete already knew them to be true, knew them from the experience of watching other men. He had paid attention, because he had known a long time that he would die by the noose.

He had been surprised how long he fell.

When the gunshot came, he first thought it was the sound of his own neck snapping. By the time he hit the ground, he understood the sound was not his neck but something else—something had severed the rope.

The will of an old bull?

Instinctively, he met the ground with crouched legs, turning the fall into a kind of somersault. He came up squatting among the joists undergirding the gallows. He inspected the loose end of the rope that hung about his neck. It was torn clean through.

There was only one man who could pull off a shot like that.

Monty. At Jack's direction, of course. Why not let him hang? What was the man after?

Pete shrugged out of the noose.

He heard the spit of gunfire overhead. One shot then two then three. He heard the screams of a hundred throats but could see only legs and feet milling, stamping, fleeing on four sides. He heard the sound of footsteps and the thud of bodies above him, too.

Men fell and clambered down from the platform—three of them where there had been four. He never saw the boots of the Sheriff, but then he could not watch in four directions at once.

Even with the crowd panicked, the townfolk on their heels—a perfect cover—Pete did not venture out from under the gallows. He had come too near death to risk it again so soon. It would only take one man to recognize him and shoot him dead. And there was something else, too, besides his hesitation. Pete could feel that this was not a time to run. A reckoning was at hand just as it had been so long ago in this selfsame spot, and whether it was with a rope or not, he would be here to meet it.

He looked for something to sever the cord that bound his hands. A little searching revealed the sharp point of an iron nail driven through the floorboards above, a nail that had missed its joist. Pete stood in a half crouch, fumbling until he felt the nail scrape at his bonds. Grunting, he began to rock back and forth, stabbing his wrists as often as the cord.

It would take time, but he had nowhere to go, and every breath was a reprieve.

DONOVAN

It could not have been more than a minute or two since the anonymous gunfire had cleared the street, but Donovan knew he would have been dead already—still standing atop the gallows—if they wanted him dead.

I have something they need. Do they think I have Sal? Or Pete? Or that I know whatever it is they're after?

Whatever the reason, Donovan found himself indispensable, which meant he still had a chance. The job now was to avoid being caught.

God knows what those bastards would do to me.

He had seen the remnants of outlaw interrogations a few times in his life. He promised to pull the trigger himself before he let them take him.

He looked up and down the street. There was no one after him, yet. But every second mattered.

Why he started toward the saloon he could not say.

And when the bullets started kicking up dirt around his feet, following him as he ran, he could not say who was firing them or whether they were intended to hit or miss.

ANNABEL

"You have to let him in!"

Jacob's face screwed into a disgusted grimace. "You think he'd do the same for us?"

The door sounded alternately with hammering and with the frantic trying of the handle.

"Open up for Christ sake!" John called.

"Yes!" Annabel cried. *He would for me at least.* Even after all that had transpired between them in the last week, she knew this to be true.

Jacob gave her a weary look. "Todd, help me with the piano," he said, setting his shotgun on the windowsill. "Annabel, if we're gonna do this, you better make sure Donovan's the only man comes in!"

Annabel nodded, running to the window and opening it enough for a clear shot at the porch.

"Coming, John," she said, her frantic reassurance poisoned by the venom of her disappointment, her betrayal.

She heard the scrape of the old piano and the turn of the lock, then John was inside, gasping for breath, leaning against the wall with his hands on his knees.

She took a last look at the street and saw faces for the first time—hard faces—peering over the facade of the jailhouse.

"Look!" she cried, pointing.

Jacob ran to the opposite window, followed closely by the lumbering, wheezing John.

Together they shouldered a table aside and watched in astonishment as a man swung down from the jailhouse roof onto the porch below, landing light as a cat after an eight-foot fall.

He disappeared inside.

A moment later, Stuart Lassiter and his companion Marvin Step-shaw burst onto the porch, fleeing as if for their lives, which very probably they were. Annabel had never seen Stuart move so fast—legs pumping furiously, hands thrown over his head to anchor his hat. They tore down Front in the general direction of the bank, kicking up a cloud of dust behind them.

JACOB

"How many are there?" Jacob asked.

"I don't know for sure," Donovan panted. He would not meet Jacob's eye. "Pete said there were fifteen of 'em. But I don't know. How many have we got here?"

"Twelve with guns who can use 'em. Plus you makes thirteen," Jacob said, returning to the window.

"We need more."

"We got more men than we got windows and doors—surely we can hold 'em off."

And since it's you they want, we could always put you out, Jacob thought, though he kept it to himself.

If Donovan suspected his intent, he gave no indication. "The outlaws will be better shots than our folks. Not to mention we're holed up here like rats. Wouldn't take but a little fire to smoke us out. Do you have windows with a view of the whole perimeter?"

Jacob winced. "I guess we haven't."

"And the madam said there were outlaws on the roof," Annabel added.

"We need more men," Donovan repeated, drumming his fingers on the bar top. "See anything in the jailhouse?"

Jacob had been watching the jailhouse intently, half expecting a gang of gunslingers to burst out and rush the saloon. But he could only see the occasional shadow cross the window.

"Nothing far as I can tell," he said. "Someone's definitely in there though."

"Okay," Donovan said, making up his mind on something. He stood up. "I'll find reinforcements."

Jacob had to admire the Sheriff's courage, even if he had brought this cataclysm on himself—on all of them.

JACK

Jack had never seen a man look so happy as Owl to be on the wrong side of a jail cell.

"You ever think you'd see me again?" Jack asked, absentmindedly checking that his revolvers were loaded. He spun the chambers and re-holstered them.

Owl shrugged. "I reckon I knew there was a chance."

"And you must've known if you did that I'd kill you."

"I reckon I knew there was a chance of that, too."

"You thought you and Pete could hold us off? Take all that loot for yourselves?"

Owl's face showed desperation. "No, Jack. We was waiting for you. We was following the plan."

"I guess that's why you killed Bill," Jack said. "Split the loot two ways instead of three." He saw Owl was afraid, but he was not terrified the way Jack had seen some men before death. *Too dumb to know terror, to contemplate the emptiness of it.*

"No, Jack," Owl pleaded.

"What were they hanging Pete for anyway? He kill someone when you got in?"

"Nah. For old times' sake I think."

"Where's Sal?" Jack asked, changing tack.

"Gone. Don't know where. He was gone when we got here."

"Sheriff know where?"

"Don't think so. He seemed as surprised as any of 'em. The deputy said he ran off with a whore."

"Did Sal give us up?"

Owl shook his head. "Not that I know of anyway."

Jack saw the man begin to close up.

"Did you?" he asked, though he knew the answer, knew it by the fact that an army had shown up for the hanging.

"No," Owl muttered. He looked at the floor.

"Pete?" Jack pressed. "Did Pete tell that Sheriff about us?"

Owl looked at him then back at the floor, stubbing at the boards with the toe of his boot. "I reckon I stuck with Pete this far," he said, then turned and sat on the bench at the back of the cell with his back to Jack.

Jack understood. He was impressed with Owl.

Just picked the wrong man to follow.

Jack struck a match and lit the oil lamp on the Sheriff's desk. He let the nascent flame mature, then he dashed the lamp on the floor, instantly producing a scar of flame three feet long.

Owl looked over his shoulder at the sound. His eyes grew wide.

"Jack!" he pleaded. "He told, okay? He told 'em you was comin'. I had nothin' to do with it!"

"It was the only way you two could've hoped to get away—having that old Sheriff kill us," Jack said. He could tell Owl had not thought of this. Pete would have, though.

Owl was quiet, staring at Jack with those wide eyes. Then he turned his back to Jack again. The flames were growing, the jailhouse beginning to fill with black smoke. "I hope they kill you, Jack Holloway," he said to the wall, to himself.

"I reckon there's a chance," Jack allowed.

ANNABEL

At first Annabel thought it was gun smoke.

She was kneeling next to the madam by an upstairs window.

The madam had just shot and killed an outlaw—the only enemy casualty as far as anyone could tell.

But when that blue brimstone cloud had dissipated, it was still there, unmistakable—the smell of smoke.

She listened for footsteps on the roof.

Instead she heard shouting in the street.

Half a dozen men below held pitched torches. But they were no outlaws. They were the Reverend's men.

Annabel watched in horror as they heaved their torches onto the saloon porch in unison as if performing a rite.

"Bastards!" the madam cursed. She emptied her revolver into the street without taking the time to aim. One of the fleeing men stumbled, his gate hitching. He hopped ungainly into the safety of an alley.

Smoke began to rise in earnest then.

Aaron's men were burning down their own town.

Annabel took one last look out the window then joined the exodus in the hall. Jacob's girls had grabbed their things and were running down the narrow stair, a crimson rush like an evacuating artery. She was swept along in the current. All the while she could hear the madam hurrying the girls like a ship's captain loading the lifeboats.

PETE

Pete watched black boots in the alley.

He had seen the fires sprout, and they were accomplishing what he had not been able to in so many years, nor Noah Warrick for that matter.

Got to hand it to Jack, even if I cain't stomach him.

He squared his shoulders and waited patiently for the black boots to come to him.

DONOVAN

Donovan saw black smoke rising into the air, the exhaust of many fires mingled in one great pillar above his beloved town, a mark of destruction to be seen for miles.

He redoubled his efforts, knocking on doors, cajoling men outside to join the growing horde. Just as often the women volunteered alongside the men.

When a posse grew large enough, he would send all but a handful of them back in the direction of the saloon with orders to follow Jacob's lead. The remainder he would keep to seed the next group. He found the example made it easier to coax the reluctant men out of their homes.

They'd need many more to fight those fires.

And where was Mance?

PETE

"Pete," Jack said, kneeling below the scaffold.

Pete grunted. Frayed knots of rope still hung from his wrists where he had severed his bonds.

Boots stood around Jack—four pairs in all.

Pete heard the guns of other boots firing from roofs and alleys. *They must be making short work.* Those few outlaws made a racket like fifty.

"Ain't got long," Jack said.

The boots turned circles in place, watching in every direction.

"Out of the frying pan and into the fire," Pete said.

Jack smiled. "Where's Sal?"

"Gone."

Jack nodded. "That's what Owl said."

"Where's Owl?" Pete asked.

Jack was silent, and Pete understood.

"Gone where?" Jack asked.

"You gonna kill me?"

"Depends."

It was Pete's turn to nod.

"What was it made you so loyal to Nash, where you'd go and betray me?" Jack asked.

"I didn't betray you."

"Don't lie to me. Not now. You even betrayed your own. Bill?"

"Nash was a man," Pete said, ignoring Jack's accusation.

Jack was thoughtful. "You know where Sal's gone? Or anything about the loot?"

Pete grinned. "I reckon I know a little something," he lied.

"Go on," Jack said.

Pete shook his head. "Enough to keep me alive. Maybe even get me a share yet."

Jack fixed him with a blank stare.

"You take me with you," Pete said. "I'll show you—"

Before he could finish, Jack drew his gun.

"You always were a lyin' son of a bitch, Pete."

Pete shut his mouth stubbornly.

"Give my regards to Nash," Jack added, pointing the barrel at Pete's belly.

Pete shook his head, showing the wry grin that irked Jack so. "Should've known you'd do me this way."

Jack scoffed. "What? Give you a long life full of comfort?"

"Kill me unarmed like a coward. Only I had thought maybe it'd be in my sleep or in my back." He looked down the open end of the revolver. "I guess it's in the stomach, just like Arch."

Jack studied Pete a moment, then spun the revolver around, catching it by the barrel and handing it to one of the booted men. "Come out of your hole then," he said, standing.

Pete crawled out from under the platform, shading his eyes while they adjusted to the light of the street.

Jack's men spread out, marking the four corners of a square like a boxing ring.

Pete looked from one familiar face to another, faces he had ridden with and bivouacked with, but they were closed to him now.

Jack took off his hat and tossed it to one of the ring posts. He smiled. It was the most emotion Pete had seen on the man, ever. Then in a flash he lunged at Pete.

Pete dodged, his boots digging lines in the dirt.

Jack feinted right, and, turning to meet him, Pete lost his balance.

He's a fast son of a bitch. But Pete knew he only needed to land one punch.

Pete staggered, catching himself, but by then Jack had him around the leg.

Jack stood, pulling Pete's leg from under him.

After an awkward hop, Pete fell twisting into the dirt. He managed to turn himself on his back and to grab Jack by the throat as Jack fell on top of him.

But Jack was too fast. He brought his knee into Pete's groin then jabbed his one good eye with a thumb.

Pete felt a fingernail tear a gash in it. The sting of it blurred his vision, and he saw clouds of blue and purple. He was blind except for the awareness of sky around the edges. *How did it happen so fast?* Only a moment ago he had been standing on his feet, ready to break Jack's jaw.

This goddamn town.

JACK

A lifetime of frustration burned in his hands.

He felt the tough old cords of Pete's neck through a facade of sagging flesh.

He looked him in the eye, bloodied though it was, and he saw shock and regret and still somehow the wryness of the smile he always showed Jack—the smile Jack knew he had never shown Nash, even though Nash had been a two-bit bully motivated by meanness and stupidity.

There were other necks there, too. Jack's father's, maybe. Even his brother's, though he loved him.

Jack tightened his grip even further. He felt his knuckles pop under the strain.

Pete's face was purple. He quaked, a slow seizure.

"You know what I told Arch in those last moments?" Jack asked, whispering in the man's ear. "When he was laying there on the ground, bleeding out?

"You know what I told him?" Jack repeated, feeling the crunch of cartilage in Pete's neck. "I told him for all his strength, it was little Jackie who killed him in the end."

Pete affected a final, knowing grin, then his eye rolled back in his head, and a moment later he was still.

Jack sat up, still straddling the man. He wiped his brow then rested his hands on his knees to catch his breath.

In death, Pete's smile was finally gone.

Jack removed Pete's eyepatch before he left, so the world could see him as he truly was.

DONOVAN

Through his journey of conscription, Donovan found he had made a wide arc of sorts that brought him to the back of the Reverend's Church of the Holy Light. He grinned when he saw it. There must have been fifty armed men ringing the building—an army standing shoulder to shoulder, held in reserve. And it might take fifty men to fight off this group of hard-bitten outlaws, to fight those fires.

He turned to the group stalking behind him. They walked two abreast, guns drawn, looking up, down, and every direction in between like explorers on a jungle path. He counted eleven.

"Alright folks," he said, touching the brim of his Stetson. "I reckon we've got enough for you to make it to the saloon like the rest and do what Jacob tells you."

They hesitated, preferring to join the safety of the men around the church. The question hung on their lips, unasked.

"You ain't comin', Sheriff?" asked one farmer—a lantern-jawed man with narrow-set eyes.

"No, I got business to attend. Stick to the alleys and don't linger on Front. I reckon you'll be fine. Haven't heard a gunshot for a while yet. More to fear in the fire than the firing."

The group hesitated a moment, then started forward, fear quickening their gaits.

Donovan went around the church, smiling all the way.

He found the men arrayed two-deep before the entrance.

"Reverend inside?" he asked.

His question was met stone faced and silent. This was the first indication of trouble.

"Where's the Reverend, I said," he repeated. "You know there's a battle on, don't you?"

The men looked at him now, then at one another, then a short, sunburnt man broke rank and climbed the porch to rap on a window with one knuckle.

Donovan saw the window was open a few inches. He watched as a curtain was pulled aside and strained his ears to overhear the ensuing conversation. He glanced around nervously at the rooftops, wondering how much longer he could stand in the street, even if a lull had overcome the gunfighting.

"Com'ere," the short man grunted, rising from the sill, beckoning Donovan with a wave of his hand.

Donovan bottled up his frustration.

Stooping hurt his back, so he knelt on one knee, resting his forearms across the thigh of the other to speak through the cracked window.

"Reverend?"

"The Reverend's in his office," a voice responded. It had a grating quality, and a moment later Donovan saw the creased face of Loeb appear, distorted through a pane of leaded glass. "What do you want?"

Donovan bit his tongue. "I want to get these men after the outlaws, to get them to work putting out the fires."

"They're protecting the church."

"Get the Reverend, Loeb. I haven't got time for this. Forget the church—there won't be a town left if you don't hurry."

"The Reverend said not to disturb him."

Donovan could not believe what he was hearing. "Loeb, I'll have your hide after this." He left the window, standing and turning to address the backs of the soldiers.

"Men!" he cried. "I've got forty others already rallied at the saloon. Leave ten of your best to guard the church, and the rest of you come with me! We've got to root out these outlaws before the town burns!"

A few of the men turned to look at him, but none moved. None smiled nor even acknowledged him otherwise. And when he had finished speaking, they shook their heads and turned away.

"We stay with the church," a voice called.

"Our kin are in there," said another.

"Reverend's orders."

Donovan strode to the nearest man and grabbed him by the collar, wrenching him around.

"Man!" he cried, looking down the man's eyes and into his heart. "What kind of coward are you? Get these moving—"

Donovan was interrupted by a screech from the window—Loeb. "Stop it, you fool!" he cried. "You'll draw them here! Begone!"

Donovan strode back to the window and punched his fist through the glass, shattering it and striking Loeb's face in a single swing. He felt the crunch of teeth. He was starting to make a habit of that.

Loeb cried out, clutching his mouth. When he staggered back, the curtain fell in place, blocking Donovan's view.

Loeb's whimpers gave him some slight satisfaction.

As he started to turn, hands grabbed his shoulders. He felt the scrape of his gun as it was removed from its holster.

"I'm the goddamn Sheriff!" he protested.

The sunburnt man rapped thrice on the door. There was a scraping and a moment later it opened, and Donovan was propelled inside by a bevy of angry hands.

After all I've done for these people! The cowards!

ANNABEL

"There!" Annabel yelled, pointing to an orange ember that had settled squat and angry on the porch of Sallie's general store.

Following her arm, a man ran to smother the coal with a wet blanket.

The saloon was too far gone to save.

She eyed the structure nervously. Flames now raged through the windows on the third floor, gasping for air with a sickening roar.

We'll have to fall back soon, before it collapses.

At first Jacob had stood dumbly in the street, watching his saloon burn like the last vestiges of himself were lost within it. But the arrival of nervous men with guns had given him purpose. He had directed them to Bob and Kevin, the old soldiers, who organized the men with reflexive discipline and sent them through the streets in search of outlaws and arsonists.

A steady flow of men came, all of them sent by Donovan.

She wondered what it would mean if that stream ever stopped.

She shut her eyes to the sting of smoke and wiped her brow. The immediacy of her work had pushed all instinct for self-reproach aside. She breathed heavily, and in a strange way her body felt good, strong.

Jacob had started to siphon every third man to help fight the fire, directing them to Annabel. Now there were fifteen rushing around her—men with wet blankets smothering embers, men with buckets in a chain emptying every trough on Front Street, every fire barrel in the alleys, to wet the walls of nearby buildings, men covering their faces and running through alleys to clear flammable debris. They followed her pointing finger and heeded her shouts.

Women had joined, too—those who could not stand to sit idly while their men fought outlaws and their town burned around them—Jacob's girls, farmers, townfolk alike. Minnie did the work of two men as part of the bucket line.

There were fires all over now—probably a dozen. Annabel had sent as many bodies as she could spare to fight those, too, before they grew as large as the one consuming the saloon.

She wondered if the saloon was the only building the Reverend's men had burned. She thought of the stone thrown through her window and wondered whether they would burn her house down, too.

DONOVAN

Inside the church, Donovan saw the women and children of fifty families seated in the pews. They did not seem afraid. They looked at him with hard, cold eyes. Crates of liquor and barrels of beer lined the walls and crowded the aisles as if the congregation was preparing for some great celebration.

Donovan felt a moment's remorse before he was roughly shoved from behind. He stumbled, fell, was righted by the same restraining hands.

Loeb led his prisoner to the Reverend's office. He knocked hesitantly on the door.

"The Sheriff is here," Loeb said, his hand pressed against the door in reverence.

At first the announcement was met with silence.

"Coming," Aaron finally called. A moment later the lock turned, and the door opened inward, revealing the black-clad Reverend.

"What's this about?" he asked, seeing Donovan captive.

"He came to cause trouble," Loeb began, his mouth still full of blood. "He struck me—"

The Reverend waved him off with the flick of his wrist.

"Let him come, and leave us," the Reverend said, turning.

Loeb bowed and stepped away, casting down his eyes but not before flashing Donovan a glare of murderous promise. He practically trembled with hate.

The men turned their Sheriff loose, pushing him through the door, which closed behind him.

"Turn the key, would you?" the Reverend asked, taking a seat at his desk, which had been pulled into the corner of the room away from the window.

Donovan obliged, re-locking the door to the Reverend's personal sanctuary. The ever-present candle flame sputtered as he approached the Reverend's desk. Gunfire sounded muted through the walls, rattling the windowpanes, but leaving them otherwise undisturbed.

"I'll have that man whipped through the street!" Donovan said, clenching his fist.

"Who? Loeb?" the Reverend asked absentmindedly.

"I need some of your men," Donovan said, unwilling to waste another minute. "We've got to round up those outlaws before they destroy any more of the town. They're setting fires now!"

The Reverend's face was a pale orb in the shadow of the half-lit room. "My men are protecting the church."

Donovan's mouth hung open. He had thought the Reverend at least would listen to sense. "The church is one building! It's nothing without the town. We need those men! They won't be able to stop the fires if they reach this far!"

The Reverend shook his head regretfully. "I can't in good conscience." He pointed in the direction of the sanctuary. "I'm responsible for those people."

"Your people are dying!" Donovan bellowed. He was suddenly a reservoir of rage. "Your town is burning! And you sit with the door barred and do nothing? Jacob is out there with an army! Fighting!"

"*My* people?" the Reverend said, calmly. "My people are safe in the sanctuary."

Donovan clenched his fists, incredulous. He beat upon the desk. "I've seen *your* people dead in the street! I've seen them huddled in houses with their neighbors—neighbors who opened their doors!"

The Reverend remained unmoved. He shook his head slowly. "John," he said after a while. "What have you done?"

Donovan was taken aback. "What have I done?" he asked dumbly. "I've done what you asked! I've done everything you asked! I captured the outlaw. I closed the saloon. I've done your will. I've done God's will!"

"No, no," the Reverend said, rising from his chair. He clasped his hands behind his back and began to pace behind the desk, careful never to pass too near the curtained window. "There's too much blood for this to be God's will. Closing the saloon, yes. But burning it down? And this business with the one-eyed man? And the war on the outlaws? And giving women the vote? Who told you to do these things? Not I." The Reverend wrung his hands. "Surely not God."

Donovan erupted in a splutter of inarticulate confusion. "It's destiny!" he cried. "Can't you see?" Then, when he had time to fully digest the Reverend's words, he asked, "Burn the saloon? I never—"

"Men dead in the street," the Reverend interrupted, clucking. "You—you *fucked* this thing!" He said it in a flash of anger. He was unaccustomed to cursing, and it showed on his face. He pronounced the word with disgust, an unavoidable sin. "Imagine my surprise when you brought that old man out to be hanged instead of the one who murdered my boy!"

"I did what I had to do for Chasby and for you," Donovan said, his color rising. "I didn't invite those goddamn outlaws here. They came for the Salamander. And once they came—once Pete came—what would you have me do?"

"I'm not the Sheriff of Three Chop," the Reverend sneered. "It's not my place to know what to do with outlaws. But I'm quite sure whatever it is—this isn't it! Now what of the outlaw who killed my boy? Where is Chasby's justice?"

Donovan fell silent. He could hear shouting in the streets and renewed gunfire.

"You've lost him, haven't you?" the Reverend said, studying him. He looked away in disgust, his jaw jutting forward like he might unhinge it to swallow Donovan whole. "I knew it. Somehow, I knew it," he said almost to himself. "I should have had him killed immediately, him and that crippled Negro."

"I'm only one man!" Donovan protested, clenching his fists. "Everything I did, I did for God as you bade me! Close down the saloon?"

Donovan hammered his fist on the desk. "If it's burned then it's goddamn well closed, isn't it? I brought the Salamander in once—I'll bring him in again! This isn't the end. But by God you've got to fight! You've got to make them fight!"

The Reverend shook his head. "What you did you did to save yourself, John, and only to save yourself. Maybe God will forgive that weakness. Men are his instruments, and even in following his will they follow out of fear and out of self-preservation, because they know he is their master, and he can damn them to Hell."

"How can you preach at a time like this?"

"If ever there were a time!" the Reverend roared. "It's one thing to do his will and another to commit evil by doing it! That evil does not come from God, even if it's motivated by a sense of duty and self-preservation. That evil comes from the Devil, from Beelzebub, and it takes a godly man to tell the difference."

The Reverend had stopped pacing now, and Donovan shuddered to see the heat of the fire he had so often seen in the man's eyes directed now toward him like some premonition of hellfire.

Donovan stared him down, vacillating internally between fear, shame, and anger before settling stubbornly on the latter. The Reverend had driven him to this end, had promised him salvation in this life and in the next, and now, seeing the effect of his machinations, he had deserted him before the town as he would surely desert him before God.

Donovan opened his mouth to speak some rejoinder, but he stopped, transfixed by the look of confusion that had overcome the Reverend's face.

The Reverend sniffed the air like a dog finding a scent in the wind, his nose wrinkling, his black eyes searching. Then his eyes grew wide with fear.

"The church is on fire!" he exclaimed, his terror sounding primeval. "But how?"

Donovan smelled the smoke himself, but anger overwhelmed whatever fear he may have otherwise felt.

The Reverend made a move to the door, but Donovan stepped in front, roiling a thin layer of near-translucent smoke now gathering below the ceiling. It swirled and billowed like a storm cloud.

"What are you doing?" the Reverend cried, reaching toward the door handle.

Donovan shoved him to the floor.

ANNABEL

He stepped through the shimmering air like a spirit, resolving from several wavering points into a man—slight, tawny, lithe, *dangerous*. She knew this innately. Even if she had not, the gun in his hand would have told her.

Annabel stood at one corner of Lassiter's Bank and Trust, having hurried a handful of new women recruits around the front of the building to join the bucket lines and the smothering teams. Lassiter had fled inside the bank to the vault, where he was filling great, wetted sacks with coin, currency, and bullion.

The gathered farmfolk wore strange expressions, eyeing the burning bank with a predatory longing even as they worked to put out the fires that licked at its sides. Jacob's exhortations kept them laboring diligently. He was stripped near to the waist, the silver hair of his chest matted against his flushed skin, his moustache slicked back with sweat instead of wax.

Annabel did not want to see what chaos would follow if the firefighters failed and Stuart had to carry those sacks outside the bank. She was not sure the 11th Cavalry could stop the farmfolk from rioting, from burning their deeds, from freeing themselves.

But that was a problem for someone else, someone who was not rooted to the earth, transfixed.

She stood somehow alone amid the chaos, knowing if she cried out none might hear her save the one approaching, the mirage.

He held a cigarette between his lips, unlit, this thing made to burn, even though he had emerged from the flame, as if his aura protected it, kept it from igniting. And the jaunty angle it cut—it made him seem so easy, so unconcerned even in the maw of hell.

She recognized him as the man who had swung down from the roof of the jailhouse when the fires first began. She recognized him as if she had known him all her life, though she saw, too, that he was unknowable.

He was an outlaw—*the* outlaw. He was Jack Holloway.

He stopped not three yards from her, standing between two burning buildings, and he watched her, unmoving, the two of them alone.

"What do you want?" she heard herself say. The words had come of their own volition. She had no chance to stifle them.

Jack cocked his head, puzzling.

"What are you after?" Annabel repeated. Again the words were subconscious, traitorous to her very existence.

He held the cigarette to the stave of a barrel burning hot as coals. When it lit, he put it to his lips, becoming a part of the fire himself.

She saw sweat glistening on his face and neck. At least it was some meager proof that he was human.

"The boy," Jack said at last.

Another form resolved behind him then, tall and lanky with a strange, paper-colored skin and with wiry, orange hair. The newcomer took his place at Jack's side.

Jack seemed to sense him there, to have expected him. Neither moved to raise his gun.

"Boy?" Annabel asked. "Sal?"

Jack nodded.

"He's gone," she said, speaking simply so there could be no misunderstanding. She looked west, though she did not know why. Another feeling. "Escaped, fled."

Jack seemed to consider this. "How?" he asked finally.

"He had help—a girl. They are in love."

Jack nodded sagely. "Young men." His eyes quirked the way a man's might if he had smiled.

Annabel could hear the shouts of her companions, dozens of them, as they battled flames just one alley down, yet she was still alone, still exposed. How long before someone came to her?

"He's gone," Annabel repeated. "I tried to save him—to keep his neck from the rope until he had a trial at least. But he saved himself. Now what do you *want* that you are burning our town to the ground?" More anger than fear sounded in her voice.

This seemed to amuse the man.

"What you just told me," Jack said.

"You should have just asked."

Jack's eyes smiled fully then.

Annabel shifted nervously, wondering if the man realized this was the bank that was on fire, realized he could walk around front and grab a gunnysack full of cash as easy as he liked.

"Leave us, then," she said to Jack, heard herself say, more like. "You learned what we know. You see he's not here. No one will follow." She motioned to the town that burned around her. "We're occupied."

"And the Sheriff?" Jack asked. "The one who killed Nash Warrick?" There was a wryness to him now, though Annabel could not say for certain that his face had changed at all.

"He is a sick man and nearly dead," Annabel said.

Again Jack studied her. Again he seemed to believe. He shrugged. "Monty," he said without looking at the red-haired man. "Tell the men to withdraw. We'll ride west. Sal can't be far."

Monty nodded and disappeared into the alley as he had come, shying from the flames in a way Jack had not.

Another look, another smile in his eyes, and Jack melted, too, dissolving into those shimmering points, disappearing.

There was a shout from behind the bank. The firefighters must have turned the corner and seen Jack, but Annabel knew he would have already vanished like a puff of smoke.

Sallie came around the corner then, Jacob's shotgun in her hands. "Annabel?" she asked. "Are you alright?"

"Fine," Annabel said. "I'm fine."

"The Loan and Trust is saved," Sallie said. "We're headed to the church."

DONOVAN

"You betrayed me, Reverend," Donovan said. He clenched and flexed his fist and savored the metallic taste of vengeance in his mouth—pure and powerful as any tincture.

The Reverend scrambled to his feet, and Donovan shoved him to the ground again.

"You'll kill us both, you idiot!" the Reverend cried. But his panic only satisfied the growing urge in Donovan to inflict pain.

"Reverend!" a frantic voice came from outside the door. It was Loeb. "The church is on fire!"

A man possessed, Donovan gripped the door handle and broke it cleanly from the fixture, jamming the latch. He marveled at his own strength. He could feel the heat through the door, already hot as any furnace.

Loeb continued to scream, scrabbling at the door. *How can he stand it?* Donovan wondered.

When he turned back to the Reverend, he caught sight of something gleaming in the man's hand.

In a flash the Reverend swung one of Jacob's confiscated whiskey bottles at Donovan's head.

Donovan reacted too slowly to stop the blow, but he deflected it enough that the bottle did not connect squarely. Still it shattered and cut his forehead so blood began to drip into his eyes.

Blinking through the redness—*blood or anger?*—Donovan fell upon the Reverend, smothering the flailing man with his frame.

"Reverend!" came the voice from outside the door, weak, almost gasping. "Reverend! What's happening?"

But if slight, the Reverend was a wiry man. He managed to reach his arms around Donovan's waist and lock his hands. He began to squeeze.

At first Donovan kept smothering the man, but as the tension of the Reverend's arms mounted, he found he could not resist, and his back arched painfully. Now it was Donovan who struggled to free himself as the Reverend's arms continued tightening like the muscular coils of a boa constrictor.

The hammering at the door came like a drumbeat. Then suddenly it subsided in a withering scream. *Loeb. Fled or melted?*

The vice grip of the Reverend grew tighter still.

Then to the surprise of both men, Donovan's back broke in half. It was instantaneous, so much had the cancer weakened his bones, more of a crumbling than a snap, like his vertebrae were lumps of chalk.

Donovan let out a scream. The pain blinded him. He continued to yell and flail his arms as the Reverend rolled his bulk to the side. Donovan struggled on his back, but his hips and legs were strangely lifeless. He managed to prop himself against the desk in a half-sitting position. He reached for his revolver then remembered it was gone.

The Reverend stood a moment, staring at Donovan as he caught his breath. There was no emotion in his face now—no fire in his eyes—only a kind of curiosity at the anatomical anomaly before him.

"Does it hurt?" he asked, a keenness in his expression, like he had always wondered.

When Donovan did not answer, the Reverend pursed his lips and resumed his flight.

He ran to the door, but when he tried what remained of the handle, it seared the flesh of his palm and fingers. He cursed and tried it again with the hem of his shirt, but there was no knob to turn. The useless key, still in the lock, glowed orange. Smoke poured in steadily around the door.

Coughing, sputtering, the Reverend strode to his desk, where he grabbed a paperweight. He threw it through the window, curtains and all. The glass shattered, leaving a ring of jagged edges around the frame like teeth. He picked up his plain wooden office chair and swung it madly, knocking shards from the window frame until he could safely climb through.

"Wait!" Donovan rasped. Suddenly the fear of death overwhelmed him. "Don't leave me like this, Aaron!"

The Reverend turned to look at Donovan.

The Sheriff of Three Chop was dragging himself pitifully toward the window.

There was an explosion in the sanctuary that startled both men. The door burst open, jetting a column of flame.

Donovan realized the fire must have reached the liquor. He thought of all those women and children and prayed none had been caught in the conflagration.

The Reverend stole a final glance at Donovan then hoisted himself onto the windowsill and tumbled into the daylight.

Donovan watched the window, remembering the way Pete had fallen through the gallows, leaving him to stare at the empty patch of light.

The smoke had nearly reached the level of his head now. The window looked so tantalizingly close, yet he knew he would never be able to pull himself through it.

He listened to the sounds of the street. He heard the beating of horse hooves and the rumble and crack of gunfire above the roar of the flames around him.

He thought of Missy and of his boys and of Annabel and of the town when it was young and how it would be a thousand years from now, a bulwark on that endless plain. He understood in a flash of revelation that whatever terror had visited Three Chop this day, the town would not succumb. It was a thing bigger than himself, bigger than Jacob, Annabel, Nash Warrick, Pete, or Jack Holloway.

With this new insight, the fear fled him. Donovan was ready to go to God, proud of all he had done.

Then he felt something cold and wet slither across his leg, and the fear boiled up in him again like it had never left.

Epilogue

Kat

They rode hard until the horses were stumbling.

It was early afternoon when they came to the arroyo. They stopped, dismounted, looking for a puddle to water the horses.

This was the first time Kat dared look back. She expected to see a trail of dust, a sign of pursuit.

Sal had buried the loot in sight of the town. But it had taken them all night and most of the morning to find and unearth it with his arm still in a sling, digging with their bare hands, and they had only put an hour's ride between them and Three Chop. She had the terrible feeling that deliverance would be snatched from her in the last moment—just as she started to believe in it.

But there was no trail of pursuing dust—only a column of black smoke rising where Three Chop stood some twenty miles distant.

"Sal," she called. "What's going on?"

Sal was busy rifling one-armed through those ponderous saddle bags. He was checking again—*for the fourth time? fifth?*—that all the treasure was there. She would never forget the yellow glow that had shone on Sal's face when he opened the first bag—never in her life.

Sal had stared for a long time, then broke into a grin.

He had that same grin now.

"It's Jack!" he said excitedly, pushing his hat back to reveal dark, sweaty hair. "I don't know how, but it's got to be! He's tearing that goddamn town apart looking for me! That's why no one's come after us!"

Sal dropped to his knees in thanks.

Kat thought he would weep.

"We should move on," she said hesitantly. She had told him the same thing when they first escaped the jail. The treasure was not worth the risk; they could earn money another way. They should be off as fast as the horses would carry them. But Sal had refused, and she had followed,

315

fretting all the while. Now she felt it happening again, his dismissal. *The minute I started to believe . . .*

"Move on?" Sal exclaimed, looking at her like she had lost her mind. "What for? He's found us!" He stood up and began cinching the saddle bags, preparing to ride.

Where? But Kat knew.

"Sal—" she started, but she did not know how to finish.

"Huh?" he said, absentmindedly.

"You don't know it's him. It could be anyone. It could be a trick."

Sal looked again at the horizon. He shook his head. "It ain't a trick to burn your own town. That's Jack—I'm sure of it."

"But you promised!" Kat pleaded. She touched her dress reflexively where she had folded the drawing he had made her, as if to remind herself what she meant to him.

"That was before," Sal said. He was walking the horses toward her. "But now that Jack's here—we can split the loot with him, and by God there's more where that came from!"

"But you promised." Her protest was feeble.

How many times will I hang my hopes on a man's promise?

"We'll go yet!" Sal said. He was in front of her now, his handsome face showing with a light of its own. "We'll go there with the whole goddamn gang. We'll make ourselves richer the whole way!"

Kat twisted her mouth to keep from crying. Once more she repeated herself. "Sal—you said—"

But he was not even looking at her now. His eyes were fixated on that black column, mesmerized.

I had to try, she told herself.

While his eyes were still on the horizon, she pulled the heavy gun from her belt. It was the deputy's gun, taken from the man at the very moment he expected to receive his pleasure. The look on his face when she had stood up with the gun instead she would never forget. "Dewlap," he had called it.

Sal started to turn.

She fired quickly, a single shot. She wanted it over before he saw, like shooting a horse before the innocent thing could comprehend the betrayal.

He had lied of course, had made his own kind of betrayal.

But that is the nature of men.

She thought about turning him over to take one last look at the beautiful face with the wide mouth and the pale eyes, but she decided it might ruin her memory of him. She did not have the stomach for what she might find, so she left him face down on the plain.

She tied Sal's horse to her own and set off again, spurring the tired beasts to a trot to ease her nerves.

Some ways off, as dusk began to settle, she came upon a stream. Feeling better, she dismounted and let the horses drink.

The smoke of Three Chop had disappeared behind her.

BIBLIOGRAPHY

Brands, H. W. *The Age of Gold: The California Gold Rush and the New American Dream.* New York: First Anchor Books, 2003.

Flexner, Eleanor. *Century of Struggle: The Woman's Rights Movement in the United States.* New York: Atheneum, 1974.

Gwynne, S. C. *Empire of the Summer Moon: Quanah Parker and the Rise and Fall of the Comanches, the Most Powerful Indian Tribe in American History.* New York: Scribner, 2011.

Hofstadter, Richard. *The Age of Reform.* New York: Vintage Books, 1955.

Library of Congress. "Fort Worth Gazette (Fort Worth, Texas)," January 12, 1895. *Chronicling America: Historic American Newspapers.* https://chroniclingamerica.loc.gov/lccn/sn86071158/1895-01-12/ed-1/seq-1/.

Marrin, Albert. *Cowboys, Indians, and Gunfighters.* New York: Atheneum, 1993.

McPherson, James. *Battle Cry of Freedom.* New York: Oxford University Press, 1988.

Meltzer, Milton, ed. *In Their Own Words: A History of the American Negro.* New York: Thomas Y. Crowell Company, 1965.

Pace, Robert, and Frazier, Donald. *Frontier Texas: History of a Borderland to 1880.* Abilene: State House Press, 2004.

Rose, Francis, and Strandtmann, Russell. *Wildflowers of the Llano Estacado.* Dallas: Taylor Publishing Company, 1986.

Seagraves, Anne. *Soiled Doves: Prostitution in the Early West.* Hayden: Wesanne Publications, 1994.

Stewart, Elinore Pruitt. *Letters of a Woman Homesteader.* Boston: Houghton Mifflin Company, 1982.

Thomas, Dianne, ed. *Time Life Books: The Old West.* New York: Prentice Hall Press, 1990.

Van Orman, Richard. *A Room for the Night: Hotels of the Old West.* New York: Bonanza Books, 1966.

Acknowledgments

We began this book in 2013 out of a desire to pay homage to, but also modernize, the classic Western movies we grew up watching with our dads. Bill and Randy, you are the examples we strive to live up to.

Thank you to our moms, Elizabeth and Leslie, for your unconditional love and encouragement. You are the reason we were determined to give this book a strong maternal presence in Annabel.

Hannah and Leanne, we are proud to be your husbands. The support you gave this project long before it looked anything like a book was indispensable and selfless.

Emmett and Avery, you are a beacon of hope in a precarious world.

To our siblings—Dave, Will, Ty, Jacquelyn, and Courtney—you've filled our lives with joy and laughter from the beginning.

Austin would like to thank his grandparents Dandy and DeeDee, who were extremely special to him and important to his development as a writer. Dandy was the subject of Austin's first (unpublished) book.

To our wives' families, you have welcomed us and provided strength and support in every aspect of our lives. Thank you to Dave and Shelli; Heather and Nate; Nancy and Ben; Elizabeth, Marissa, and Winnie.

We would like to give a special thanks to Bob Shuman of the Marit Literary Agency. We sent our manuscript to dozens of agents, many of whom responded with some version of: You can't sell a Western in today's market. Bob could, and did. He believed in our novel and got it in front of the right people. Along the way, he provided expert editorial guidance, pushing us to make it "sparer, tighter, and tougher."

Thank you to our wonderful editor, Erin Turner, production editor Lynn Zelem, and the entire team at TwoDot and Rowman & Littlefield.

Thank you to Jeff Guinn for your willingness to read and provide a blurb for a manuscript by two completely unknown authors. We continue to be amazed by your graciousness.

Thank you to Bob Hillman, who was a mentor to Austin at *Politico* and provided much-needed assistance during our journey to publication.

We would like to thank our beta readers, who slogged through early drafts to help make *The Sheriff* what it is—Hannah, Leanne, Bill, Elizabeth, Dave, Randy, Leslie, Calvin, PJ, Elizabeth T., and Nancy.

Finally, we would like to thank the unsung heroes of our lives, the many teachers, coaches, and professors who inspired us during our formative years. We would especially like to thank the staff of Douglas S. Freeman High School—in particular Mr. Peck, Mr. Dozier, Ms. Baylor, Coach Bright, and Coach Butcher.

It was at Freeman that the two of us met and began writing fiction together. Two decades later, we have published our first novel—a testament to the power of friendship and perseverance.

ABOUT THE AUTHORS

Robert Dwyer is a history buff with an abiding interest in the West, which looms large in the American psyche—a canvas for big stories and big ideas. He lives with his wife and dog in Alexandria, Virginia.

Austin Wright started watching John Wayne movies with his dad before he was old enough to talk—and he's been hooked on Westerns ever since. He lives with his wife, son, and daughter in Annandale, Virginia.